GETTING SOME
OF HER OWN

Gwynne Forster

GETTING SOME
OF HER OWN

KENSINGTON PUBLISHING CORP.
http://www.kensingtonbooks.com

ACKNOWLEDGMENTS

My thanks to my stepson, Peter, the most precious gift I have ever received; to my husband who is always there for me, as faithful as daybreak; and to my Heavenly Father for the talent he has given me and the opportunity to use it.

Chapter One

"I've never done one wild thing in my entire life," Susan Pettiford said aloud to herself as she left the doctor's office that early October morning, shading her eyes from the bright sun, "but there's a first time for everything. I'm going to know what it's really like, if it's the last thing I do."

As cold as it was that mid-October morning, perspiration streamed from her scalp to her chin, and she rolled down the window of her bright-red Taurus, eased away from the curb and headed for the apartment she'd sublet a few days earlier. What a blow! She'd come back to Woodmore, North Carolina, after an absence of sixteen years because her late father's only sister had died and left her heir to all that she had, including a house. Settling in a town of thirty-five or forty-thousand inhabitants wasn't her idea of a life, but fate seemed to be making decisions for her.

Pains shot through her middle, and she tried to ignore it as, for months, she'd tried to overlook her other symptoms. She thought of going back to New York and seeing a doctor there, but she knew the diagnosis was correct, knew it before she went to the specialist. Driving fast, as usual, she put the thirty-five miles that separated Winston-Salem from Woodmore, North Carolina, quickly behind her. Inside her rented apartment, she dropped herself on the oversize leather sofa.

Susan leaned forward, braced her elbows on her thighs and

cupped her chin with her palms. Her life, all that she'd hoped for and dreamed of right down the drain. Had a sigh ever seemed so ominous? The breath that seeped out of her had the sound of agony, and of hopelessness, too.

She got up, opened a crate and let its contents spill out on the bedroom floor. Then, she wrapped her hands around the purple-velvet box that she bought with her babysitting money when she was thirteen. She opened the box and looked at the four little dolls, two female and two male—symbols of the children she hoped one day to have—and went into the kitchen and tossed the box into the trash bag.

Seemingly drawn to the floor-length mirror in the narrow hall, she stopped and stared at herself. She looked the same. She felt the same. But she wasn't the same. In two weeks, she'd be half a woman. Thirty-four years old and unable to bear children.

"Count your blessings," the doctor had said. "I just told a thirty-year-old woman that she has breast cancer."

I hope you announced that to her with more compassion than you just showed me, she thought, but didn't say.

Susan gathered her resolve, strode to the telephone and dialed the doctor. "This is Susan Pettiford. Is there anything you haven't told me?" she asked when he took the phone. "I want to know everything right now."

"Well, you'll have hot flashes, but we can give you something for that. Some women have difficulty with sex, but that's partly a matter of attitude. Of course—"

She interrupted him. "And partly a matter of what else?"

"Oh, it may not happen in your case. We'll cross that bridge when we get to it."

She hung up, dissatisfied, hurt and angry. It wasn't his body. She wished she knew someone who'd had a hysterectomy and with whom she could discuss it.

While eating her lunch of milk and a peanut butter and raspberry sandwich, she remembered that the lawyer for her aunt's estate had invited her to his wife's birthday party that night. *At least it'll take my mind off that operation.* She wanted to wear red to the party, but decided that flamboyance wasn't in order, and chose a short, pale-green chiffon evening dress. And silver accessories. Since she didn't know how the local women dressed, she decided not to wear her mink coat—a mark of distinction in New York—and put on her beige cashmere coat instead.

Susan hadn't previously been in the Woodmore Hotel, and its elegance surprised her. Crystal chandeliers sparkled in each of the public rooms and gave the suite housing the party a grandeur that offset the chic appearances of those present. The bartenders wore tuxedos and served the latest alcoholic concoctions in long-stem crystal glasses. The drapes were made of royal blue silk, which covered the walls as well as the chairs and sofas, and the women must have known that, for only she wore a gown the color of which clashed with the room's furnishings. Glitter was the last thing she had expected to find in Woodmore, but Mark Harris' friends had it in abundance.

She saw him the minute she entered the room. She couldn't have missed him, for he towered over everyone there and his persona commanded attention. And when he looked at her, she was glad she'd left that red dress home. Almost immediately, the man headed toward her with their host, Mark Harris, at his elbow.

"I'm so glad you could come, Susan," Mark said. "This is Lucas Hamilton, a close friend and former classmate. Lucas, Susan Pettiford is an interior decorator, so I expect the two of you will find that you have much in common."

The bulk of Lucas Hamilton blotted out all else from her vision—she could not pull her gaze away from the eyes of one of the most handsome men she'd ever met.

"Mark said you're new in town. Would you have dinner with me tomorrow, Sunday? I'd like to get to know you."

She looked around for Mark and saw that he was on the other side of the room. "Why does he think we have so much in common?"

"I suppose because I'm an architect. You didn't say whether you would or wouldn't have dinner with me Sunday evening."

A week earlier, she would have glowed with delight, but now she couldn't encourage a man's attention. She had no right.

She laid back her shoulders and got a firm grip on her resolve. "That's right. I didn't. I'm sure we'll have other opportunities to see each other. This is, after all, a small town."

Both of his eyebrows shot up, and she'd have sworn that his chin jutted out. "As you wish," he said. "It's been interesting." She watched him walk away, and it struck her that Lucas Hamilton was unaccustomed to rejection for any reason or by anyone. *Oh, well. He can't possibly be as disappointed as I am. The kind of man I've always wanted in my life, and I have to let him go.*

She spent a few minutes talking with a local minister, who introduced himself as the Reverend Gilford Ripple, and with Sharon Hairston-McCall, publisher of *The Woodmore Times*. An interesting woman. The idea dawned that life in Woodmore might be more rewarding than she'd imagined, and she began to mingle with the guests, hoping to find among them a future friend.

Sitting in the comfort of his cathedral-ceiling living room later that night, Lucas Hamilton reflected that he'd just had his first dusting off by a female, a woman who interested him as much as any woman he'd ever met. She didn't even try to make it palatable, didn't offer an excuse. He'd been thirteen years old when he asked his mother's best friend what was so great about sex—and he'd asked her because he'd caught her staring at his crotch on more than one occasion. She'd asked if he really wanted to know, and when he said yes, she opened her arms, spread her legs and gave him what he now regarded as a degree in the techniques of lovemaking. And she eagerly polished his skill at it whenever he thought he needed it. To her credit, the first time she saw him with a girl, she smiled, waved and never made another move toward him. He'd often wondered why he hadn't become attached to her. His approach to her was the first he'd made to a female and, in twenty-two years, he hadn't had a single refusal—until tonight. Susan Pettiford intrigued him, but not sufficiently to cause him to chase her. He had more important things to do with his time.

Lucas leaned back in the recliner and let his gaze roam over the house he had designed to his own taste and for his own comfort. He had done well as an architect, had carved a name for himself in Woodmore and as far away as Nashville. But he knew he wouldn't be satisfied until he wielded more influence and his name carried more prestige than that of Calvin Jackson, the man who sired him. He wasn't after the man's blood. His mother chose to have a four-year affair with a married man, but she had no right to deny that man access to his son and to withhold from her son a father's care and nurturing. But that did not absolve Calvin Jackson; in thirty-five years, the man hadn't once reached out to him. The short distance of twenty miles separating Danvers, where Calvin lived, and Woodmore made that seem ridiculous. He'd never spoken with his father, and if he ever did, he wouldn't be the one to initiate the conversation.

He got up and tuned the radio to the station that played golden oldies. His eyes widened when he heard "If you knew Susie, like I know Susie." Laughter poured out of him. "Well, I'll be damned. That gal must be a little witch," he said aloud and turned off the radio.

If Susan had been a witch, she would have ordered her life differently. The morning after meeting Lucas, she set about trying to make a liar out of the doctor who gave her that heart-rending diagnosis. "I'm not taking this lying down," she said to herself and dialed the office of a famous endocrinologist.

"What will this do to my hormones?" she asked him. "Will I grow facial hair, and what about sex?"

"Of course, it will affect your hormones, and how it affects sex varies. I doubt you'll grow any facial hair. If you have problems, make an appointment to come in and see me."

Thanks for nothing, she thought after ending the call. Before she could ponder more, the phone rang. It was Mark Harris, the lawyer for her aunt's estate. "If you want to sell your aunt's house, I have a prospective buyer. I ought to tell you that your aunt enjoyed a bit of notoriety. At forty-eight, she was one of the best-looking women in town, and the local men paid due homage. I suspect more than one person will want that house, so you may wish to take your time about selling it."

She thanked him and hung up. She'd always known of her aunt's beauty, and now, she suspected that her unmarried relative enjoyed a full and fulfilling sex life, something that wasn't guaranteed her. Indeed, it would probably be her fate that the operation would leave her asexual. Frigid.

She was not a virgin, but the earth had never moved for her, although she'd given more than one man an opportunity to create an eruption. The most she'd experienced was a few tremors, and she was damned if she'd settle for that.

I'm not undergoing that operation until I have myself one mind-blowing affair with a man I can dream about for the rest of my life. But how was she going to manage that in a place where she knew exactly six people, including two men, one of whom was married.

I shouldn't have been so quick to brush off Lucas Hamilton. He's not self-assured for nothing. The man wears his success with women the way a peacock wears his feathers. And Lord, you could drown in his eyes.

A week later, still in a quandary, Susan lifted the telephone receiver from its cradle and dialed information. "Could you please give me the number for Lucas Hamilton, the architect?" Her fingers shook as she jotted down the number. She didn't think he would turn her down, because his curiosity wouldn't let him. She dialed the number, and as she waited, she could neither breathe nor swallow.

"Lucas Hamilton's office," a clipped-female voice answered.

"I'm Susan Pettiford. May I please speak with Mr. Hamilton?" She thought her teeth chattered, but she wasn't sure. At the moment, nothing seemed real.

After a brief pause, she heard, "This is Hamilton." She nearly dropped the phone. What would she say to him? Gathering her courage, she let out a long breath and began. "Mr. Hamilton, I hope you remember me, I'm—"

He interrupted her. "I certainly do, Miss Pettiford, and considering the reception I received when we met last week, I'm surprised to hear from you."

So far, not good. Best to brazen it out. "I can imagine, but I've spent an entire week without speaking to anybody except sales-people and, well, I've been led to believe that small-town people are friendly, and I—"

"A city of forty thousand isn't exactly a hamlet, Miss Pettiford."

May as well cut to the chase. "Look . . . will you forgive me for being foolish and have dinner with me Saturday evening? It's rumored that I'm a great cook."

"Will I . . . *what*?"

"Have dinner with me. I promise to pull out the stops."

In the lengthy silence, perspiration dampened her from her scalp to her waist. As she prepared herself to find a gracious way out of it, he said, "My curiosity won't let me decline. I'll be de-lighted. Where do you live?"

She gave him her address. "Seven-thirty?"

"I'll be there. Thank you."

"Till then," she said and barely managed to hang up without dropping the receiver. As she had suspected, Lucas Hamilton had the manners of a polished gentleman, but beneath it she de-tected a core of steel. She'd better be careful.

In the three days that followed, Susan did her best to make the furnished apartment that she sublet more like her own envi-ronment. Being an interior decorator, there wasn't much about that furnished apartment that she liked. She softened the mascu-line appearance of the living room with an antique gold and brown African print that she threw across the sofa, then added burnt-orange colored velvet cushions, a large ficus plant, and placed a crystal vase of tea roses on the glass coffee table.

Saturday finally arrived, and after preparing a seven-course meal worthy of Buckingham Palace, Susan set a table equal to the standard of the meal, pampered her body, and dressed in a deceptively simple sheath. The long-sleeved, high neck, burnt-orange jersey dress would have seemed prim, but for its color and a right side seam that was slit from ankle to mid-thigh. With nothing beneath the dress but bikini panties and a demi bra of matching color, she figured that she was displaying her assets to their best advantage. Gold hoops in her earlobes softened her pixie haircut.

At ten minutes before the appointed time, she stopped pacing the floor, remembered to dab perfume behind her ears, to lower the living room lights, put some soft music on the CD player and take ice cubes out of the refrigerator. What else had she forgotten? Too late for that. The door bell rang, and as if she'd been soldered to the floor, she couldn't move her feet. The bell rang again, this time with greater urgency, or at least so it seemed to her, and chills plowed through her body. Could she go through with it? What if he didn't fall for it?

The bell rang again, and to her it sounded like a warning. Maybe he would leave. She shook herself out of her trance, rushed to the door and opened it.

"Hi."

His eyebrows shot up, and she knew that the apparent primness of her dress had registered with him. "Hi. I thought for a while there that you had changed your mind and hadn't bothered to tell me."

She forced a smile. Forced it because the man's commanding presence unnerved her; not because she lacked confidence, but because she disdained trickery, was about to engage in it, and his bearing said he wouldn't tolerate it.

"I was raised better than that," she told him. "Come on in."

When he handed her a large bouquet of yellow roses and a bottle of Moët and Chandon champagne, it was her turn to raise an eyebrow. "Thank you, Lucas," she said, trying out his first name. "Yellow roses are my favorite flower, and I love champagne. We'll have it for dessert."

"I'm afraid it isn't chilled."

She smiled to put him at ease, but if truth be told, he seemed at home. It was she who needed bolstering. "By the time we get around to dessert, it will be good and cold," she assured him. "Have a seat." She led him to the living room, then went into the kitchen to refrigerate the champagne. When she returned, he stood where she'd left him.

His words were the only evidence that he'd watched her walk away from him, but those words were revealing indeed. "I hope you don't mind my telling you that your dress had me fooled. I thought you'd shrouded yourself for protection."

Protection, eh? She sat on the sofa and motioned for him to sit in the chair opposite her. And in spite of her effort to appear dignified, laughter took possession of her until she bordered on hysterics. After trying unsuccessfully to pry from her the reason for her amusement, Lucas went into the kitchen, got a glass of water and brought it to her.

"Drink this." She took a few swallows, and he repeated the question. "Now, what was so funny?"

That was the opening line she needed. "I guess it was the idea that I needed to protect myself from you. To tell you the truth, the suggestion seemed ludicrous."

His face darkened into a frown. "So I'm harmless? I'd like to know your other thoughts about me."

She ignored the remark. "I seem to have forgotten my manners. What would you like to drink?"

She knew she hadn't fooled him when a half smile eased across his face. "Usually bourbon and water, but—"

"Bourbon and water it will be."

They had already begun to fence with each other, and she didn't think that was the route to her goal. She'd have to change the mood. Susan put a dish of hot canapés on a tray along with the drinks—bourbon for Lucas and white wine for her—and went back to him.

"I hope you like these. In fact, I'm hoping you will like everything I cooked for you and that you're hungry."

He smiled again, and she was beginning to get the feeling that she would never get used to it, that his smile would always unsettle her. Maybe it wasn't his smile, but her guilt that caused her discomfort. She almost wished she hadn't started the charade.

"As long as you don't give me chitterlings and chicken livers, we'll get along," he said. "A good home-cooked meal isn't something I get every day." He tasted the miniature quiche. "If this is a sample of your culinary talent, I can hardly wait for the meal."

He leaned back in the chair, sipped the bourbon (she had bought the best, and she sensed he was aware of that and appreciated it), and focused his gaze on her until it seemed to burn her skin. "Why did you invite me to dinner?"

The question came as a surprise, for she hadn't anticipated it and had no ready answer. She did her best to give him a reasonable explanation. "In the two weeks that I've been back in Woodmore, I've met six people, four women, my married lawyer and you. I was—I didn't feel like spending this kind of evening with any of the other five, and I suspected you'd be a good conversationalist and that you would enjoy a well presented, gourmet meal." She ignored his slightly dropped jaw. "Am I right?"

"You certainly are candid. Where did you live before you came here, and what did you do?"

"I lived in New York City, where I was principal interior decorator for Yates and Crown."

He sat forward. "So that's why your name is so familiar! I know that firm of architects well. Are you married?"

"No. If I was, I wouldn't cheat on my husband."

After staring at her for a minute, a grin floated over his face. "You would call what we're doing here this evening *cheating*?"

She wanted to kick herself for that slip. "Well, you know what I mean."

"I assume your relatives live in the Big Apple, too." He savored another sip of bourbon.

"No. My father died some years ago, and not long after my brother married a Swedish woman. He lives in Stockholm with her and their two children. My mother joined the Peace Corps about five years ago and, ever since, she's been saving Africa."

Concern etched the contours of his face, mirroring his compassion for her. "That's too bad. Do you ever see her?"

"I've visited her twice, once in Nigeria and once in The Gambia. Right now, she's in Sierra Leone."

"I see. Maybe she needs to help others. By the way, why would the chief interior decorator for Yates and Crown architects leave New York and settle in a small town like this one?"

"Because I don't have a life there. Usually, my workdays begin at eight-thirty in the morning and end at midnight. Most Yates clients are wealthy, and when they hire you, they think they own you. If Miss Importance gets an idea at midnight, she thinks she has the right to call me and discuss it right then. I've proved that I can handle the job. Now, I want to smell the flowers sometimes. My aunt's will is what made me consider moving back here."

"You'll find plenty to do here, because there isn't a top decorator in this area. What does your mother think of your plans?"

"Oh, she lives in a different world. For her, living quarters are a matter of providing tin rather than mud structures for poor women, so that their houses won't be washed away in the rainy season. By the way, where's your family?"

He appeared to withdraw, and she wished she hadn't asked him. "You're not married, are you?" He'd have to be deaf, stupid or both to have missed the anxiety in her voice. She might be conniving, but she would not knowingly sleep with a married man, not even if that were the only means of realizing her body's potential.

If he noticed her concern, he didn't make it obvious. "If I was, I wouldn't be here. I also don't cheat." He grinned at that, but a somberness quickly settled over him like fog over a mountain lake. "My mother lives on the outskirts of Woodmore, and I see her from time to time, although I make certain that she doesn't want for anything.

She put her glass on the end table beside the sofa and sat forward. "Don't you like your mother?"

"I like her. The problem is that I resent her for not letting me get to know my father.

"But you're an adult. Couldn't you have contacted him?"

He leaned back in the big overstuffed leather chair and draped his right knee over his left one, comfortable with himself and his surroundings. "Of course I could have, but he's the father, not I, and if he makes no effort to have me as a part of his life, fine with me. I'm not going to beg him, and I don't lose any sleep over it, either."

Without thinking, she reached across the coffee table and pat-

ted his hand. "I'm so sorry. My father was everything to me."
The raw need that she saw in his eyes startled her, and she
jumped up. "I'd better serve dinner. It takes a long time to go
through seven courses."

Lucas savored the first course, *quenelles* of scallops with
Dugléré sauce, without saying a word. After swallowing the last
morsel, he put his fork on his plate and looked straight at her. "If
the rest of the meal is up to this standard, it may take the sheriff
to get me out of here."

Susan thanked God for her brown skin; if she had been
lighter, the hot blood in her face would have betrayed her. "I'm
glad you enjoyed it," she said in barely a whisper.

"That is an understatement." His deep, velvet baritone gave
his words a seductiveness that she assumed he didn't intend to
convey.

She was no expert at the seduction of a man, and she hoped
the food and wine would do their job. After the courses of
sherry-garnished cream of wild mushroom soup; peach sorbet;
filet mignon, lemon-roast waxy potatoes and asparagus that followed, he rested one elbow on the table, fingered his chin and
gazed at her. "If you tell me you feed every stranger you enter-
tain this way, I won't believe you."

If he could play hardball, so could she. "Did I tell you that?
When I do something, no matter what it is, I do it properly. And
you can write that down." She didn't look at him, but busied
herself clearing the table. When she returned with their next
course, she noticed a difference in his demeanor.

"That was impolite," he told her, "and I regret saying it. You
didn't have to go to so much trouble, but you did, and I'm enjoying the fruits of it." Charm radiated from him, and she told
herself to beware. She meant to be the seducer, not the seduced,
whose reward for the evening was a kiss on the cheek and an invitation to dine with him in a first-class restaurant. She served
an assortment of French and English cheeses, French bread and
a smooth red wine. When she stood to clear the table, he said, "I
can do this," and gathered the dishes and headed for the kitchen.

This is working too well. I hope I'm not headed for a let down. When she took the brandy Alexander pie out of the refrigerator and put it on a plate, he whistled sharply. "I guess this is where I open the champagne," he said as he opened the refrigerator door, got the cup towel that hung on the oven door, wrapped it around the champagne bottle and eased the stopper out without making a sound.

"I see you've opened a lot of those," she said. "The champagne flutes are up there." She pointed to a cabinet door, and when he reached for the glasses, his hand managed to brush her shoulder. "Let's have this in the living room," she said, calculating that she would have to sit beside him on the sofa. She put the pie on the coffee table, and as soon as he was seated, she said, "How foolish of me. I have to get plates and some forks," rose and walked back to the kitchen, giving him an eye-full of her back action. Music. That would help get his mind on sex. She sat down beside him, picked up the remote control and within seconds, the haunting music of "Paradise" filled the room. She cut the pie, served it and waited while he poured the champagne.

"Thanks for the most intriguing evening and the most delicious meal I've ever eaten," he said, raising his glass. "The first course alone would have kept me happy for days."

"But you haven't tasted the dessert."

"Any dessert I get will be an anticlimax."

Her nerves seemed to rearrange themselves throughout her body. She didn't know what he meant, and she feared the answer if she asked him. He tasted the pie. "This pie is out of sight, and I'm convinced now that you meant to seduce me to putty."

"Wh-why would I do that?"

"Beats me." He took a long sip of champagne. "Probably for the same reason you're wearing this go-there-come-here dress. I don't know whether to make a pass at you or recite the Twenty-third Psalm."

When she replied, "I'm sure you can figure it out," he put his glass on the table, stood and extended his hand. "Dance with me. I've always loved this song," he said of Percy Faith's recording of "Diane."

Susan didn't need to be coaxed, but she had begun to like the man, and she wondered if she would someday regret what she was increasingly certain would happen between them. She wanted it, didn't she? Hadn't she planned it meticulously? She considered backing out, but his arm eased around her, strong and masculine, and pulled her to within inches of his body. And they danced. Danced until that song and then another one ended. Danced as if they had always danced. She didn't know when she rested her head on his shoulder and his other arm went around her, snug and comfortable as if it had a right to her body.

"Do you realize what's happening here?" he asked after a while. She did, but she didn't answer. "Did that champagne go to your head?" he asked her.

"I'm cold sober," she told him, in a frank admission that she wanted him.

"So am I. I don't want to leave now, but I will if you tell me to go."

"I want some more champagne."

He tipped up her chin and stared into her eyes. "Don't you realize that I want you?"

With her gaze on his mouth, she wet her lips with the tip of her tongue, and he bent to them. She welcomed him with lips parted, took him in. No longer was it a matter of seducing him and using him for her own gain, to have one completely satisfying sexual experience before undergoing a surgical menopause at the age of thirty-four. No longer was he merely a tool, a means of achieving a coveted goal.

Tall, handsome, trim, intelligent, educated, wealthy, charismatic and sophisticated, Lucas Hamilton was precisely what a woman wanted in a man. But in that evening, she had discovered strength in him, compassion, and a vulnerability that ignited in her a need to nurture him. Her arms gripped his shoulders, and he tightened his hold on her until her nipples hardened against his chest.

He stopped the kiss. "Where do you sleep?" She lowered her gaze, lest he see the fear in her eyes. Suppose it didn't work. But in another ten days, it would be too late.

"Down the hall," she murmured.

Minutes later, he stood looking down at her as she lay on her bed clothed only in the burnt-orange bikini panties and bra. "You are one beautiful woman. I wanted you the first time I saw you." With that, he shed his clothes and was soon holding her tightly in his arms as if he thought she would escape. He surprised her with his sensitivity and gentleness, testing and adoring until she wanted to scream for him to join them. When at last he did, it was a homecoming. She didn't know whether the storm howled outside, in the bedroom or merely raged within her like nothing she had ever imagined. She hit bottom before he hurled her into the stratosphere and hung there with her until she thought her heart would stop.

Half an hour later, he raised his head from her breast, stared into her eyes for a second, and then kissed her. But it was a kiss meant to soothe rather than to communicate, and she knew it. He separated them, and she turned on her side, away from him, overcome with emotion as tears trickled down her cheeks. She buried her face in the pillow to muffle her sobs, but she couldn't control the jerking motions of her body. His hands gripped her shoulders.

"My Lord! Are you crying? Look at me!" His voice carried an urgency and something akin to fear. Or was it concern? "I said look at me, Susan." She forced herself to open her eyes and tried to force a smile, though she failed at the latter.

"Are you sorry?" he asked her.

"It isn't that. It's . . . I didn't know I could feel like that. I'm . . . just overwhelmed."

He exhaled deeply, clearly relieved. "I know what you mean."

"Thank you for being so . . . so wonderful," she whispered and hugged him.

He kissed her quickly, almost perfunctorily, rolled over and locked his hands behind his head. "This is a night I'll never forget, Susan, and I have a feeling that you won't either. I have a thousand questions, but I'm not going to ask any of them, because I don't want to spoil this for either of us."

"I have questions, too, Lucas, but they're questions that I have to ask myself."

"I don't doubt it. Will you be upset if I leave? I need to come to terms with this, and I can't do that unless I'm alone."

"No. I want you to know that I enjoyed every minute we've been together, and that I don't regret anything."

"I hope you feel that way when you wake up tomorrow morning. I've enjoyed being with you, and I mean that. I'll let myself out."

When she heard the door close, she got out of bed, locked the door and went into the living room to clear the coffee table, but discovered that he had done that. In the kitchen, she found that he put the plates, forks and glasses in the sink and the remainder of the pie in the refrigerator. She poured a full glass of wine, went into the living room and sat down.

She got what she wanted, but would she be able to live with it? How was she going to reside in Woodmore, see that man and know he thought her different from the woman she was, that his estimation of her would likely be unflattering. He'd said nothing about seeing her again, and he probably wouldn't because he had promised nothing. And she would rather not see him. What on earth had she been thinking? She gulped down the wine, showered and went to bed. Would she have been better off not knowing how a thorough loving made a woman feel?

When Lucas stepped outside the four-unit apartment building in which Susan lived, he turned, locked his hands to his hips and gazed up at her windows. He didn't expect to see her at one; he needed to assure himself that he'd been there, that he was not hallucinating, that he'd eaten that meal and then had the most satisfying sexual experience that he could recall. He walked up Eighth Street East to his car, got in it and drove to his home facing Pine Tree Park on Parkway Street. But he didn't want to go inside where, alone and cloistered within familiar walls, events of the preceding four hours would take over his mind and emotions. After putting the car in the garage, he walked around to the back of the house and sat on the deck.

Lucas regarded himself as a careful, cautious man who did not act impulsively, and he could find no reason or excuse for having allowed Susan Pettiford to seduce him. She attracted him, but she didn't bowl him over. He shook his head as if in wonder. What was more, she had planned to seduce him, and by the time she served that stupefying pie, he suspected as much. Still, like a lemming bound for the sea, he'd let himself coast right into it. A woman with her looks could find an eligible man any day, so why had she done that with a man she'd seen once and rejected summarily?

He got up and leaned against a post. Something was rotten in Denmark. He'd hardly gotten inside of her when he realized she had far less experience than a man would expect of a woman her age. Thank God he'd had the presence of mind to use a condom. Shivers raced through him. He hadn't remembered to examine the condom afterwards to determine whether it broke. He flexed his right shoulder in a quick shrug. Even though he didn't know her, he doubted a woman as accomplished and as proud as she would trick a man into impregnating her. But you never could tell. What was her game?

The dilemma would remain with him for a long time, he knew, because he always sought to understand himself and the events in his life. He unlocked the back door and went inside. What on earth had he been thinking? He didn't have one-night stands with women like Susan.

"That was stupid, and it's over," he said to himself as he headed up the stairs. "No more of that for me." He stripped and got into the shower. "But she sure is one hell of a lover!"

Ever cautious, he called his friend, Mark, the next morning. "Tell me something about Susan Pettiford." To his mind, the request was a reasonable one, since Mark invited him to his wife's birthday party expressly to meet Susan.

Mark's laughter didn't console Lucas. "What about her? You can see as well as I can, man," he said. "All I know is that as executor of her aunt's estate, I had to beg her to come down here and claim her inheritance. She didn't seem particularly interested in the house, car and bank account. Said she was used to making it on her own, that she liked her job and wasn't interested in moving from New York to a town in North Carolina. She finally agreed to come here and have a look at the place, and the strange thing is that the house and its location half a block from Wade Lake really got to her."

"Does the will stipulate that she live here?"

"She has to live in the house for a year in order to inherit what, around here at least, is considered a sizeable estate."

"That's a heck of a job she's got up there in New York."

"I know, but I gather success comes at the expense of everything else. She stood on the back porch of the house, looking out at the lake, took a deep breath and said, 'This is pure heaven. Imagine living in such a peaceful environment!' I wouldn't be surprised if she moved down here."

Although that news revved his engine a bit, his head told him he'd be better off with as much distance as possible between the two of them. Hadn't old man libido kicked into action this morning the minute he awakened with her on his mind?

"You're interested? I thought the two of you didn't get on too well."

"That was on the surface. I had dinner at her place last night. She's an elegant woman, to say the least."

"That's the impression I got," Mark said. "You coming to the club meeting next week?"

"Probably. Thanks."

He hung up feeling that he knew little more about Susan Pettiford, the person, than he did before he called Mark. He didn't intend to get further involved with her, but it wasn't in his nature to leave a problem unsolved.

Chapter Two

"I want another opinion," Susan said to herself as she sat on a log by the lake near her late aunt's house. She threw a small rock in the water and watched the ripples spread outward. "Just like my life," she said of the sinking pebble. "The doctor hands me some bad news and before you know it, I get in bed with a man I've seen once, a man who's given name I used for the first time only a couple of hours before I made love with him." She pulled air through her teeth. "I must have been out of my mind."

A smile crawled over her face. "But what a lover that guy is! Lord, that man is sweet as sugar." She told herself to snap out of her lethargy and contact another of the experts on her list. She wanted to consult with Dr. Chasen in Baltimore, but she doubted he'd speak with her without a high-level referral. What the heck! She could try.

She needed a car, but she couldn't use the one her aunt left her unless and until she signed the papers declaring her intention to reside in that house for a year. Until then, she wouldn't even know the amount of money in her aunt's account.

Suddenly, her mind made up, she stood and headed back to her apartment to call Dr. Chasen. She promised herself that if Chasen said she had to have the operation, she would accept it.

An hour later, she called Mark, her lawyer, with the news that she'd be out of town for three days. "I'll be in Baltimore, Maryland, but I don't have a phone number where I can be reached." From his hesitancy, she sensed that he wanted more information, but she didn't offer it.

She walked into Chasen's office the following Wednesday morning looking as well as a woman could look, with her mink coat, alligator shoes and bag heralding the presence of a successful businesswoman. And she knew she had his attention.

"You made this seem as if you were minutes away from death," he said, shaking hands with her.

"What I'm facing amounts to death."

"Oh, I wouldn't say that."

After examining her, reading the de rigueur cat scans and MRIs that he'd ordered, he said, "There's no escaping it. You have a multitude of tumors inside and outside the uterus. It's best to get it over with as soon as possible. You are very anemic. Who's your surgeon?" She told him. "I'll send him my findings. It's a simple operation, and you should be up and about in a very short time."

"How many children do you have, doctor?" she asked him.

"Why, three. Why?"

"I don't have any," she said, looking him in the eye, "and even if I *am* up and about in a very short time, I'll never have any children. Thank you for seeing me on such short notice."

She turned and walked out before he could reply, and before she lost her poise. The cheerful smile on the secretary's face annoyed her, and she wrote the check for fifteen hundred dollars without speaking, turned and left.

Might as well go on and get it behind her. When she got home, she phoned *The Woodmore Times*, discontinued delivery of the daily paper, packed a few toilet articles and telephoned Mark. "I'll be away for maybe a month. When I get back, I'll let you know whether I'll sign for the house."

"How can you be so lackadaisical about wealth that most people would consider a fortune?"

"I'm not weak brained, Mark. I'm deciding whether to change my life, and I have to consider the positives and negatives. I don't worship wealth. My aunt knew how I lived, and she offered me an opportunity to live a more normal, more satisfying life. I have some unfinished business in New York, and when I've taken care of it, I'll be back."

"All right. Everything will be here when you return."

Five weeks later, Susan walked into her apartment on Eighth Street East, healed after a successful surgery, prepared to begin life anew in Woodmore, North Carolina. Her boss at Yates and Crown had assured her that she could have her job back whenever she wanted it.

"I practically raised you in this business," he said, "and I know what you can do. You come on back, but don't take forever."

Susan thanked him, but she hoped she wouldn't need her old job. With no prospects of marriage and a family, she reckoned that she'd be better off in a small town where she could find real neighbors and friends who wanted more than a lift up the rungs of success. She had to get her business started and renovate the house she'd inherited. While perusing the want-ad section of *The Woodmore Times*, she saw an advertisement for volunteer tutors for disadvantaged children, and called the organization that placed it.

"We'll be glad to have anyone with a university degree, Ms. Pettiford," the respondent told her. "Would you come in and fill out an application? Our semester begins in January, but we've lost a few tutors, and we'd like you to start at once." Susan reported for work the following Monday afternoon and was assigned a group of second grade children with reading and spelling problems.

"What's your name?" she asked the shy little girl who sat far behind the eleven other children.

"Rudy," she said in barely audible tones.

"Come up here with me, Rudy." Snickers from the other children alerted her to the possibility that Rudy was a target of ridicule. She walked back to where the child sat, took her hand and walked with her to the front of the class. "Rudy, I'm going to tell a little story," she said, "and then I want you to tell us one. Something you read, or you can make it up."

"Yes, ma'am."

Susan made up a short tale about pigeons and then asked Rudy to tell her story. When Rudy had trouble beginning, Susan put an arm around the child. "Go ahead. I know you can do it."

Rudy looked at her, and Susan smiled, praying that she hadn't made a mistake. "My story is about the dog that jumped over the fence and got lost," Rudy said, and as she told the story to her hushed classmates, her confidence seemed to grow. When she finished, Susan applauded and Rudy's classmates joined in. Susan hugged the child, and a warm feeling flushed through her when the little girl smiled for the first time.

Now, Susan thought, *I hope these children won't ridicule this child anymore.* As the children began to file out, she beckoned to a boy who hadn't joined those who made fun of Rudy. "You weren't unkind to Rudy," she said to him. "Why did the others laugh at her?"

He hung his head. "I guess it's because she wears those funny old clothes, and the people she lives with aren't her parents. They get paid to keep her."

"Hmmm. But the children were being mean to her."

"Yes, ma'am. And she's kinda nice, too."

"So are you. What's your name?"

"Nathan. Do you think I can learn to read better?"

"Yes, I do, Nathan, because I'm going to help you."

For the first time since she learned that she had to have a hysterectomy, Susan had a feeling of well-being, and she walked out of the building with quick steps and a renewed sense of purpose. She hadn't known what to expect when she saw the old building that had served as Wade Elementary School.

"At least I'll be too busy to moan over what can't be helped."

The next day, Susan looked at three sites as a potential location for her decorating business and, in the process, discovered that Woodmore already had one interior decorator. But she also learned that, because of his volatile temperament, Jay Weeks, the decorator, probably wouldn't present serious competition. Besides, she planned to introduce herself and make him a friend. She rented space on the second floor of a four-story building at 131 Eighth Street West and considered herself fortunate in finding a good address.

She needed an architect, and a good one who she could trust, but she didn't want to contact the only one she knew. Nor did she want to ask Mark for a reference, for he would want to know why she didn't ask Lucas. After stewing over the matter for a time, she told herself that it was business, that she wasn't proposing anything personal. The next day, exasperated at herself for wasting time, she phoned Lucas and asked if he would organize her space, including provision for a toilet and small kitchen.

"Thanks for your confidence, Susan," he said, without inquiring as to how she was or uttering other preliminaries of a personal nature.

This guy's a real piece of work, she said to herself, though she didn't bother to note that she hadn't asked of his health and well-being, either.

"I'll have a look at it and see what I can come up with," he said.

"Before we settle on anything, I'll need an estimate."

"Of course. I . . . uh . . . I hope you've been well."

That took her back a bit and brought to mind her own shortcoming in that respect. "I have. Thank you," she said, her voice losing some of its deliberate stridency. "My shop is at 131 Eighth Street West on the second floor."

"That's a good building and a very good business address. How's one-thirty this afternoon?"

"Good. I'll be there." She hung up and sat down in the nearest chair, uncertain as to whether she had done the right thing. She didn't know another architect, so what was she to do? *Face it, girl, you didn't look for one. Subconsciously, you haven't let him go.* She looked toward the ceiling and closed her eyes. Lucas Hamilton, the man, was water down the drain. She needed an architect, and he was the best in Woodmore.

On her way to meet Lucas at what she envisioned as her shop, Susan stopped at 127 Eighth Street West and introduced herself to Jay Weeks. "I'm Susan Pettiford, and I'm about to open a decorating shop two doors up the street." She extended her hand in greeting. "I wanted to meet you."

Tall, lean, self-assured, good-looking and with a streak of gray at the front of his otherwise black hair, Jay Weeks gazed down at Susan for a few seconds before he let a smile alter the shape of his sensuous lips.

"Checking out the competition, eh? I heard about you. I have my shop here, but most of my clients are over in Danvers where the money is. I don't work for peanuts; I go for the white trade, so you needn't worry about me."

Both of her eyebrows arched, but she quickly smiled. "I'm sure there's plenty for both of us. Since we're in the same business, I'm sure we'll have opportunities to compare notes and maybe even help each other. If you ever need burnt-orange and beige upholstery thread, I'll probably have it."

To her surprise and pleasure, his laughter appeared genuine. "Right. And if you need something too weird for the local stores to carry, I'll probably have that. Let's have lunch sometime."

"Thanks, Jay. I'd like lunch. Bye."

As she rushed to her appointment with Lucas, she told herself she'd sort Jay Weeks out later.

She arrived to find him leaning against the door jamb. "Sorry if I've kept you waiting. Thank you for coming," she said, feeling as if she were talking to someone she hadn't previously met. It was either that stilted conversation or greater intimacy, but she couldn't assert her softer, more feminine self with him for fear of sending him a deeper, unmistakable message. Appraising him from her peripheral view, she hadn't remembered that he was such a big man, but why should she have; she had tried to blot him from her memory.

He stepped aside while she unlocked the door. "I had lunch nearby, so I got here early," he said. Gazing around even as he walked into the vast room, he began moving slowly from corner to corner, paused at the window on the street side and looked out.

"You need a private office, a showroom that takes advantage of this big window, a toilet, storage space with built-in shelves and cabinets, and a small kitchen. I propose the following."

She stared at him as he outlined his idea. The man had been there ten minutes and had envisaged a plan that suited her perfectly.

"I'll get you a contractor who ought to do what you want for two or three thousand."

Shaking her head in wonder, she said, "So far very good, but what about your services?"

When he rubbed the back of his neck, she knew what was coming. "It'll take me all of half an hour to draw up the plans for this." He took a rolled metal tape measure from his pocket, measured sections of the room, made some notes and winked at her. "Willis will divide the space floor to ceiling so that it resembles an apartment. That suit you?"

"Sure it does, but you haven't told me what you charge."

"I'd be ashamed to charge for this, and I won't. Willis will charge you enough. I'll give him the plan, and he'll be in touch with you, or you may call him. I'll give you his number."

When she appeared skeptical, he said, "Don't worry. I'll tell him it's urgent. His work is impeccable."

"I can't imagine that you would recommend him if it wasn't. Thanks."

As he handed her his card on which he'd written the phone number for W. L. Carter, contractor, his hand touched her, and she backed away quickly, bumping against the wall. He stared down at her, and she imagined that he heard the thundering of her heart. She didn't dare shift her gaze.

"Willis will call you tomorrow morning," Lucas said in a voice that had suddenly become hoarse. "It's . . . been good to see you again." He walked to the door, opened it and, as if remembering something, turned back to her. "What's the name of your business?"

"Pettiford Interiors, Inc."

"There's a good sign maker in the Market Street promenade. Be seeing you."

With nothing on which to sit, she leaned against the wall and inhaled deeply. *Was she going to come apart whenever the man came near her? God forbid that he should touch her. Well, what the hell! He wasn't exactly immune to her, either, and he showed it when she backed away from him, but that was small consolation. He had no place in her life.*

She had to stay in Woodmore for at least a year because she had taken a one-year lease for the shop, so she might as well stay in her aunt's house. She phoned Mark and told him she was ready to sign for her inheritance.

"I had hoped you wouldn't make the city a gift of your aunt's property," Mark said when she signed the papers. She left his office with keys to the house, the new BMW, a safe deposit box key and papers allowing her access to two bank accounts. Since she didn't have time to go to her apartment, she put the keys and papers in her purse and half walked, half ran the seven blocks to the old Wade Elementary School building. With five minutes before the tutoring classes were scheduled to begin, she rushed inside and stopped abruptly, as if a ghost suddenly loomed before her. Lucas.

"*You!*" she gasped.

"What are *you* doing here?"

"I tutor a reading class of second graders," she told him.

"Since when?"

"Since the day before yesterday. Why are you grilling me?"

"I didn't know I was. I do have a right to know, Susan, because I'm the principal for this program."

She gaped at him. "Nobody told me that." If she had known it, she would not have answered the ad. She wanted as little contact as possible with him.

Lucas exhaled a long breath and assumed the posture of one resigned. She would have given much to know his thoughts, but he didn't reveal them by gesture or by word. Yet, his very stillness told her he was no more comfortable than she. He pushed back his leather jacket, shoved his hands in his trouser pockets and said, simply, "No one told me about you being here, either."

"I answered an ad in the paper for volunteers," she told him, "but I can occupy myself with my work and my house, among other things. This isn't something I have to do." She turned around and headed in the opposite direction.

"Susan!" It was part command and part plea. Urgent, yet soft.

She stopped, but didn't face him. When she felt the weight of his hand on her arm, she spun around and encountered his body.

Like a deer caught in headlights, she stood transfixed, staring into his eyes. Shaken, she gazed at him, but she didn't see the man; it was the lover who stood before her and the lover's aura that nearly entrapped her. But as quickly as the shadow of their lovemaking returned to haunt them, she backed away, releasing herself from the spell.

"The children need us," he said. "If we don't help them, we'll lose them. Without the ability to read and read well, they'll have a hard life. These children are more important than my emotions and yours."

"Don't worry. I wasn't planning to resign."

"But you said—"

"I know what I said, Lucas. I was telling you that I won't fall apart if you don't want me here."

"I want—" He caught himself. "The children need you. I have almost two dozen fifth and sixth graders down the hall hoping for tutoring in math, so I'd better go. Be seeing you."

Why couldn't I have chosen another man—any other man—for a fling? Why did I have to . . . In spite of her consternation, she laughed. *What am I complaining about? He made it more than worthwhile. He made it beautiful.*

She reached the room in which she tutored and, to her astonishment, a solemn Rudy stood outside the closed door. But when the child saw her approach, she smiled.

"Hi, Miss Pettiford."

"Hello, Rudy. Why aren't you inside?"

"The kids always laugh at me. All except Nathan. He's nice."

She took the child's hand, opened the door, went inside with her, and complete silence immediately replaced the noise and merriment. If she accomplished nothing else, she would teach those children that clothes did not make the individual.

Lucas made his way to his classroom with heavy steps. A casual affair had never posed a problem for him, particularly on the few occasions when the woman made it clear that she was merely taking care of her needs, just as he was. He thought about that for a minute. Susan hadn't said she was tending her needs; indeed, she hadn't said why she decided to go to bed with him, and he made up his mind to find out if it took the rest of his life.

He discovered that he enjoyed the children more than he'd thought he would, and decided to devote a second evening each week to tutoring in physics, since he didn't have a teacher for it. At the end of the class, he stood in the corridor talking with a volunteer and saw Susan leaving the building holding a little girl's hand. *That's strange,* he thought. *The tutors aren't supposed to become involved with the students.* After a moment, he dismissed the thought. Perhaps the child wasn't feeling well.

Lucas drew the plans for Susan's shop and phoned Willis, his friend and partner in W. L. Carter Building and Contracting, Inc. He and Willis Carter roomed together as college freshmen and had been close friends ever since. When the Carter contracting business faltered, Lucas bought a fifty-two percent interest in it, reasoning that a liaison between an architect and a building contractor made sense. They sent customers to each other, but Willis served as the CEO of W. L. Carter Building and Contracting, Inc., and Lucas focused on his architectural firm. Both businesses flourished.

On that crisp November morning, Lucas sat on his deck sipping hot coffee and watching the yellow, orange and brown oak leaves float lackadaisically to earth. He cherished the early mornings when his mind was most active and energy stirred in him. He dialed Willis's number, confident that at six-thirty in the morning, his sleep-loving friend hadn't ventured far from the bed.

"What's up, Lucas? Did you ring me earlier? I was 'sleep, man."

"Yeah? If you were asleep, how do you know the phone rang?"

He heard the sound of feet hitting the floor. "Come on, man. It's still night. What's up?"

"I've got a rush job for you. Can you come over here? I'll even cook you some breakfast."

"Breakfast? Right. Give me forty-five minutes."

He set the table on the deck as the sky's red, blue and gray streaks heralded the coming of the sun. It took him longer than half an hour to lay out the plans for Susan's shop, because he'd added extras that would increase the value of the unit in case she decided to sublet it. When he heard Willis's car stop in front of his house, he poured the coffee and began scrambling eggs.

"What's so urgent about this job, and who's it for?" Willis asked him when he jumped up on the deck.

"Her name's Susan Pettiford, and she's an interior decorator. She rented space in the Halpern Building, which is a co-operative. If everything works out, she'll buy it."

"This stuff is good. I'd like the recipe for these waffles."

Lucas handed him the plans. "Aunt Jesse or Southern Pines. One of those. Look in the frozen food section of the supermarket. What do you think?"

Willis glanced at it. "Looks simple enough, but I won't know until I get there and see what I have to work with. What's this? You want me to rip up half the floor?"

"Well, she didn't ask for it, but a decorator's showroom should be elegant, and that floor is tacky."

Willis put the plans aside, drained the coffee cup and went to the kitchen for more coffee. He returned, sat down and focused his gaze on Lucas. "What am I charging her?"

Lucas flexed his right shoulder in apparent nonchalance. "That's up to you, but when she asked for an estimate, I told her I thought it ought to be somewhere around two or three thousand."

Willis' whistle split the air. "That was before you thought of the toilet, kitchen and storage room, right? Also, you didn't charge her for the plans, did you?"

"Naw, man. Those plans took no time."

Willis sipped his coffee and looked into the distance. "This isn't like you, Lucas. Would you mind telling me what Susan Pettiford is to you?'

He should have expected the question, because Willis Carter knew him as well as he had ever allowed anyone to know him. He rubbed the back of his neck. "The truth? I really don't know exactly what Susan is to me."

Willis leaned back in the wrought iron chair and fastened his gaze on his friend. "Are you aware that this is way out of character for you? You always plot every step you take. With Verna being one strange exception, you've always ordered your life with the same precision you put into your designs for buildings."

"I'm not losing sleep over it, and neither should you. When can you start?"

"I'd like to see the place today."

Lucas took a pocket watch from his shirt pocket, and opened it.

"Man, you still have that watch?" Willis asked him.

"I hope I'll always have it. My maternal grandfather gave it to me when I was about nine. Next to my mother, he was everything to me." Lucas dialed Susan's number.

"You calling her now? It's only seven-thirty, and not everybody gets up at the crack of dawn as you do."

"Hello?"

"Good morning, Susan. This is Lucas Hamilton. Willis Carter, the contractor, wants to speak with you." He could hardly resist snickering at the expression of disbelief on Willis's face.

Willis took the phone. "Good morning, Ms. Pettiford. I've looked at the plans for your shop, and I'd like to see the space today, if possible." He listened for a bit. "Yes, I like the plans. Eleven o'clock is good. I'll meet you there. Till then." He hung up. "Hmmm. She's as business-like as you are. Well, thanks for the best breakfast I've had since the last time you cooked it. I'll call you later and let you know what I think."

"Okay, but come to terms with her, will you? Even if you have to bend a little bit."

Willis raised an eyebrow and then showed his white teeth in a grin. "For that, I'll let you wash the dishes. I have to study this thing before I meet her. Ms. Pettiford must be one hell of a sister."

She is, Lucas thought. *Is she ever!*

Remembering that he had promised to install a microwave oven above the stove in his mother's kitchen to give her more counter space, Lucas phoned her. "I can install that microwave oven this evening, if you'd like, Mama. Tomorrow, I'll be at the school, so I'd rather do it today."

"That's wonderful. I'll fix you a nice supper."

"I could take you out to dinner."

"When did you last have a great home-cooked meal?"

He couldn't tell her about that, so he agreed to eating supper at her table, not that he minded one bit, because she was a good cook by anyone's standards. "All right. I'll be there around five-thirty."

By five o'clock, the weather had cooled, so he put on a three-quarter leather coat lined with sheared lamb, a pair of jeans, and a heavy plaid shirt. In spite of his thirty-five years, Noreen Hamilton hadn't ceased to worry that he might catch cold. He entered the modern house that he designed and built for her and was rewarded with his mother's happy smiles and hugs.

"What're you cooking?" he asked her, sniffing repeatedly.

"Roast pork, candied sweets and collards. Maybe some corn bread."

"Works for me," he said, pulling off his coat. He installed the microwave oven quickly. "Anything else you want me to do?"

"No. You thought of everything when you designed it, and since you pay for a cleaning woman and a man who takes care of the lawn, most of the time, I don't have anything to do except hold my hands and watch TV."

He looked around the kitchen where he perched on a stool. "It's rather big for one person. I'd have thought you'd want someone to live with you."

She wiped her hands on her apron and stared at him. "Such as who? I don't need anybody to make my life miserable. If you're talking about a man, I've told you a hundred times to forget about that. When it comes to men, I've had the best education in the world, and I don't need any further training."

He remained silent for so long that she walked over to him and asked, "What's the matter, Son?

"Mama, I don't want to ruin the evening for us. It isn't often that I eat here with you, so I'm . . . I'd like to drop this. But I have to tell you that I have so many strong feelings around this subject."

"I know." She went back to the stove. "But I did the best I could."

She didn't, and they both knew it. He changed the subject. "I'm thinking of acquiring that land across the river from Pine Tree Park. I'd like to see an upscale retirement village complete with a recreation center and medical facilities."

"Be careful that you don't overstretch yourself. You don't have to make fifty cents off every dollar earned in this county."

"No, but by the time I'm fifty, I intend to be worth more, to be more influential and to have more power than Calvin Jackson ever had. I'll show him."

She didn't respond, as he'd known she wouldn't. He suspected that after thirty-five years, she still loved his father. She had denied Calvin Jackson all parental rights, had never let him see his only son and had not accepted one penny for Lucas's care and schooling. But in Lucas's view, the greater injustice was not to the father, but to the son, and although he loved his mother, he resented her for keeping him from his father.

She shook her head from side to side while she sliced the sweet potatoes, "What is it, Mom?"

"I know what you're thinking. I used to tell myself that when you were older—grown, I mean—I could make you understand, but I know you can't accept what I did. We can't change it now, Son, so please let it go."

"I'm satisfied with who I am right now, with what I've done with my life so far, so don't sweat the past, Mama."

"I'm proud of you. Maybe you could have been more . . . but . . . we'll never know."

"This food is up to your usual high standard," he told her later, changing the subject, as he enjoyed one of his favorite meals.

"There's apple pie for dessert." A grin spread over his face. Nothing anybody cooked tasted as good as his mother's apple pie. "That's pure bribery, mom, and you've been using it since I was three."

He saw her pleasure in the laugh that poured out of her. "As Yogi said, `If it ain't broke, don't fix it.' These apple pies are probably the reason why I'm not very good at making desserts; all I ever had to do to please you was make an apple pie."

Lucas went to the stove, got the coffee pot and poured each of them a cup of coffee. At age fifty-eight, his mother was still beautiful. He imagined that, when she was nineteen, she must have been startlingly lovely. He sat down and voiced his thoughts. "Did you ever stop loving him?"

"No," she said, the word barely audible.

"When did you last see him? In person, I mean?"

"The day I told him I was pregnant."

He put his cup down and looked at her. "How could you handle it? You must have been miserable all these years."

"Not at all. I've had you, and every time I looked at you, I saw him. Whenever I held you, I held him."

He suppressed a whistle. "I realize that I resemble him, because—"

She interrupted him. "Resemble him? You're the spitting image of Calvin."

"This boggles my mind. Always has. You knew he was married; you told me you did. Yet—" He shook his head.

"I fell in love with him practically on sight, son, and a nineteen-year-old-virgin is no match for a thirty-year-old married man."

"Not by a long shot. He should have been ashamed of himself."

She stared at him. "Why? He fell in love with me, too. Your grandfather did everything he could to break it up, but I was of age, and I couldn't stay away from Calvin."

That didn't make sense to him, and he said as much. "You stayed away from him after you became pregnant."

"It wasn't difficult. He wouldn't divorce his wife, and I've learned that hatred is just as powerful an emotion as love. I spent weeks deciding upon the best revenge."

He leaned back in his chair and seared her with his gaze. "Yes, you did, and while you were planning it, all you thought of was yourself. You didn't give your child a thought."

"You're right; I didn't, and I've paid for it every time I've caught you staring at me with your eyes narrowed while you grind your teeth. It hasn't been easy, Lucas."

"Not for either of us." He served the pie and poured more coffee.

"Thanks for this great supper," Lucas told her as he was about to leave, "and especially for the conversation." He winked—which meant he squeezed both eyes, never having learned how to wink one of them—and hugged her tightly. "You shouldn't indict yourself too harshly, Mama. If you had behaved otherwise, you wouldn't have me."

"You are what kept me going."

He kissed her and left. One day, when he had power behind him, he would stand face to face with Calvin Jackson and hear his side of the story. But the man was already seventy years old, and time was running out. Lucas got into his black town car and headed home, but as he drove, he had a struggle trying to keep his mind on his driving. After that short talk with his mother, he understood her less than ever. If she had hated the man, how could she still love him after so many years? Did that kind of inconsistency explain why Susan would have sex with a stranger, and then act as if he'd never been anything to her?

He wanted to rid his memory of Susan, but he didn't expect that to happen—he had to see her at least twice a week when she tutored at Wade School and lately, she appeared whenever his libido revved up. He suspected that he had just begun to pay for that delightful romp with her. If anyone had told him that sex with a woman he'd just met could be so satisfying, even memorable, he wouldn't have believed it. He had to admit that she'd carved a place for herself inside of him, and he didn't know what he'd do about it.

Unlike Lucas, Susan did not permit herself the luxury of reminiscing about their tryst. As she hurried to meet Willis Carter—hurried to the extent that one who carried a folding chair could hurry—color schemes and furnishings for her shop and the house she had yet to enter crowded Lucas out of her thoughts. "I hope this doesn't cost too much," she said to herself, for she intended to put the fifty-three thousand dollars cash that she inherited from her aunt into an interest-bearing United States Treasury account. *And if this works out, I'd like to buy my space in this co-op building*, she thought as she tripped up the stairs.

She opened the door, went inside, sat down and made notes while she waited.

Carter arrived on time. "I hope you haven't waited long, Ms. Pettiford. I'm Willis Carter."

"I figured as much. How are you? Thank you for coming. What do you think of the space?"

"Well, you're across from the elevator, which is good, but you're on the second floor, which is bad unless you air condition the place. In this location, noise from open windows will make this a health hazard. And—"

She interrupted him. "How much is that going to increase the cost of the job?"

He walked around as if he hadn't heard her, and perspiration began to dampen her arms and her blouse. "I said—"

"I know what you said. I'll have to tell Lucas to include air-conditioning in these plans."

She sensed that her temper was about to expose itself, and she didn't think it wise to show anger. "How much will it cost? Mr. Hamilton said it would be between two and three thousand."

"Yeah. He told me that." The man walked over to her, put his hands on his hips—slim hips that complemented his broad chest, long, lean body and handsome face. "What's Lucas Hamilton to you?"

Where did that question come from? Looking hard at the man, trying to size him up, she couldn't decide whether he was indicating interest or merely curious. She angled her head to the side. "I have absolutely no idea what Lucas Hamilton is to me. Anything else?" He continued to look at her, and then he laughed. "Let me in on the joke, Mr. Carter."

He laughed harder. "Sorry. It must be me. I see things strangely sometimes. Don't worry. The job won't cost you a penny more than Lucas said it would. I need a key, and as soon as Lucas includes the air-conditioning in these plans, I'll get to work. I assume you want parquet floors in your showroom. If you want anything else, now's the time to tell me."

"What are my alternatives?" He raised an eyebrow. "All

right, so I've never opened a commercial establishment. The architects I worked for had penthouse offices."

"Hmmm. I'll bet they did. Marble, tiles, cork, cement. I'll put wood in here, but as a decorator, I thought you might want something uh . . . different."

He was right, but she wouldn't let him know that he thought faster than she. "Parquet will be fine. I may put an Oriental carpet in there."

"Fine, Ms. Pettiford. I'll put a contract in the mail, and as soon as you sign it, you ought to be able to move in within thirty days."

Susan thanked him and watched him amble out of the room as if he didn't have a care or a responsibility in the world. Yet, she didn't doubt his competence, for he projected an air of it. Besides, Lucas recommended him. She didn't know why she had such confidence in Lucas Hamilton, but she did. Maybe it was because she had trusted him with her body, and he had treated it as if it were the most precious thing ever entrusted to him.

That night, she wrote her mother:

> *Dear Mom,*
>
> *So much has happened since I last wrote that I don't know where to start. After getting the opinions of three specialists, I had the operation, and I'm fine. I've decided to settle in Woodmore, since I have to live in Aunt Edith's house for a year in order to claim it and the remainder of the inheritance. I'm opening my shop in the Halpern Building. I expect you'll remember it. I wish you'd come home at least for a couple of weeks. It's strange being back here without you.*
> *Love,*
> *Susan.*

She addressed and stamped the letter, wrote out a plan for her tutoring session the next day and got ready for bed. There was something about Willis Carter's attitude that rankled her, and she couldn't quite fathom it. For example, why he questioned her about Lucas. She suspected that he would ordinarily have charged much more than three thousand dollars for that job, but a deal was a deal, and she didn't intend to raise the matter again. She attempted to open the window and had to exert more energy than she thought she would.

"At times like this, I'd like to have a man nearby."

She mused over the idea for a minute, and then allowed herself a good laugh. If the man was Lucas Hamilton, he would be useful for something more than opening a stuck window. She got into bed and went to sleep.

"What's up, Willis?"

"It's a good plan, but you didn't provide for air-conditioning. I'll bring it over, and you can work that in. By the way, you didn't tell me that woman is so good-looking. Man, she's a number ten and change."

For some reason, the comment irritated Lucas. "Why should I have told you? You weren't supposed to be making *her;* you're making her shop. Remember? What time are you coming here with those plans?"

"Leaving now."

Twenty minutes later, Lucas put the plans on his drafting board and began to study them. A roar of laughter from the direction in which Willis sat startled him, and he swung around and stared at his friend. "What's with you?"

Willis stood and walked toward the picture window. "I asked you what Susan was to you, and you said you had no idea. I asked her what you were to her, and she said she had no idea. The more I think about it, the more certain I am that the two of you are fooling yourselves. Hurry up and finish that. If I don't get started, she'll be hard on my tail."

"What're you charging her?"

"Twenty-five hundred for a ten thousand dollar job, and she damned well better mean something to you."

Chapter Three

Susan walked into the modern three-bedroom house and stopped, fascinated. Sunlight streamed through a floor-to-ceiling, wall-to-wall window that faced Wade Lake. What she had thought—from a distance—was the front of the house, was actually a side entrance to the kitchen and laundry rooms. A stone fireplace took up much of the wall to the left of the window, and when she glanced up at the cathedral ceiling, she realized the house had been designed to fulfill her aunt's lifelong dream. She opened her purse to examine the deed, saw that the house was only four years old and that the architect was Hamilton Architectural Designs, Inc.

Awed by that discovery, she dropped to the nearest chair and gazed around her, wondering if fate had entangled her in its net, a fly in a spider's web. At the school, at her shop, and now, whatever joy she found in her home, she would have to attribute to him.

Life is tough, but by damn, I'm tougher.

She got up and wandered into the dining room, and discovered that it had a picture window facing a wooded area and a fireplace smaller than the one in the living room. She preferred a more modern kitchen than the large, airy one she found there. Her bedroom would be the one thing she changed completely, for she wanted off-white wooden furniture in a warm, feminine setting. Fortunately, she would be able to see the lake from her bedroom window and balcony.

After touring her house for the first time, Susan made notes and called the lawyer. "Am I allowed to make changes in this house before the end of the year? I want to renovate the kitchen."

After a minute, he said, "I don't see why you can't. As far as I'm concerned, it's yours as soon as you move in. If you move out before a year's up, the city will be entitled to take the house and sell it at fair market value. That house won an award for design."

"I imagine it did. It's beautiful. I can't wait to move in. By the way, did Lucas Hamilton design this house?"

"He sure did. If I were you, I'd get his advice on the changes you want to make in the kitchen. Sometimes moving pipes can cause real problems."

"Really? Thanks. I'll get in touch with him." She hung up, wondering if Lucas would be sitting in the Baptist church when she got there the next Sunday morning. The man seemed to be every place she turned.

She walked outside, tracing the property, and observed that her land extended to the edge of the lake where a boardwalk used for a pier appeared to be deteriorating. A small rowboat, moored to the pier, lay upside down at the edge of the lake, and she read on it the address, 37 Lake Street, which meant it belonged to her. She looked at her watch and saw that she had about an hour in which to get to her tutoring class, just enough time for a quick stop at her shop to check on Willis Carter's progress.

She met Willis on the stairs. "Were you leaving?" she asked him. "I wanted to see how it's coming along."

"Right now, it's full of dirt, cement and sawdust. Unless you want to look as if you ran smack into a flour mill, don't go in there."

"But I—"

"Suit yourself. I've already put your air-conditioning in, and it's working. You're getting a stainless steel sink and refrigerator and a marble top counter in your kitchen. Tiny, but elegant.

"A marble top counter? That's expensive."

"It's only thirty-six inches square. Besides, it's what Lucas ordered, and that's what you get."

Her eyes narrowed, as suspicion, which she thrust aside earlier, formed in her head. "Who owns this building company? You or Lucas Hamilton?"

"If you want to know something about Lucas, you have to ask him. I'm CEO of W. L. Carter Building and Contracting, Incorporated. That suit you?"

"No, because that is not the answer to my question."

His shrug didn't sooth her nerves. "I asked you what Lucas meant to you, and you didn't answer my question, either. In fact, I asked the two of you the same question and got the same ass-backward answer from both of you." He walked down two steps and stopped. "Lucas is my best friend and has been since we were about eighteen and college roommates. If you trust me to get this job done properly and on time, don't pop by every day to check on me. I don't like it. I usually leave this part of the job to my workers, but this seems especially important because it's yours. See you."

That man is not easygoing, she realized as she pondered his refusal to answer her question directly. She didn't know whether Lucas was underwriting the work on her shop or why he would do that. She took Willis's advice and avoided the shop because of its condition; she couldn't go to her tutoring class wearing soiled clothes. She had only a ten minute walk to Wade School, and she arrived with nearly half an hour to spare. So she wandered down the hall until she saw the principal's office and knocked on the door.

"Come in."

"Hello," she said to Lucas. "May I see you for a minute?"

"Sure. Have a seat."

"I read the deed to my house this morning, and discovered that you designed it. It's beautiful. Congratulations. I want to rip everything out of the kitchen, and make it more modern. You know, with cabinets that have sliding drawers; stove, grill and deep fryer in the center, and so on." She outlined the changes she wanted. "Will this entail any structural or other crucial changes?" She hated talking to him because his gaze unnerved her. His occasional smile only exacerbated the situation, and anger at her vulnerability to him began to rise up in her.

"Look," she said, "I'm not asking you to do the work. I only want to know what kind of problems the person who does it will encounter."

"You seem angry. Did I do something bad?"

He hadn't and he knew it, and she was not in the mood for cleverness. "You'd know that better than I. Can you help me with this?"

He looked steadily at her for a few minutes, propped both elbows on the desk and cupped his chin with his hands. "I presume you're talking about the Edith Greer house. I don't remember those plans offhand, but I have a copy in my office. If you'll come by there tomorrow morning, I'll be glad to give you whatever help I can."

"Thanks." She got up to leave, and he stood and walked with her to the door. "I suppose Willis Carter will do the work." It was a statement.

He didn't react, at least not so that she could tell. "If you want him to. If not, I can certainly recommend someone else, or you could get a kitchen design specialist to do it. Unfortunately, Woodmore doesn't have one of those." Supporting his long frame with the doorjamb, he braced his left forearm against the wall, shoved his right hand into his trouser pocket and gazed down at her. "You may find that you don't like your stove away from your sink, and if you put the sink in the middle of the kitchen, I'm fairly certain that the plumbing will have to be rearranged and reinstalled. Think about it."

"Where is your office, Lucas?" How could he be so nonchalant about everything when her nerves were standing on end? "I can be there around eleven tomorrow morning if that suits you."

He took a small appointment book from his shirt pocket, looked at it and said, "Fine, but twelve would be better. I'm at 1108 Parkway Street."

"All right. Twelve it is."

*　*　*

He watched her as she walked down the corridor, tall, erect and with a set of swaying hips that made his blood rush. He didn't have time to cultivate a meaningful relationship, and if he did, he wasn't sure he'd cultivate one with Susan. He was old enough to know that a man could become preoccupied with an enigma, any kind of enigma, and that if it concerned a woman, he might soon find himself enamored of her. He went to his desk, collected some papers and prepared to go to the classroom where a dozen and a half teenagers waited for assistance with their physics homework.

If I could just figure out why she maneuvered to get me in bed with her and how she can behave as if it never happened. . . . And she doesn't appear to be an aggressive woman. He rubbed the back of his neck.

"Not again," he said aloud when, at the end of the tutoring session, he saw Susan leaving the building holding the same little girl's hand. "He'd explain to her that involvement with the children was against the rules.

His front door chimes rang at precisely twelve o'clock the following day, and it didn't surprise him, because he knew she'd be on time. He met her at the front door and stepped outside. "Hello, Susan. My office is right around here."

"I didn't know you worked at home."

"When I designed my house, I provided for all of my needs." He led her to an office above his garage. "I charge myself rent for this," he said, squeezing both eyes in his version of a wink. "Have a seat over there." He spread the plans out on his drawing board. "I've studied these. With the sink in the center of the kitchen, we'll have to change the plumbing. That's a major job. I suggest you put the grill and deep fryer in the center as well as the sink and the stove opposite, against the wall. You can't have a stove in the center. If you'll step over here, I'll show you what I mean."

She stood beside him as if they were two ordinary people discussing a business project, but he wasn't fooled, for he saw, from his peripheral vision, that her right hand shook almost uncontrollably when she turned the sheet. They had discussed it for nearly an hour when hunger pangs alerted him to the time.

"I'm getting hungry," he said. "I can send out for something. It won't take more than fifteen or twenty minutes. What would you like?"

"Oh, no. I wouldn't put you to that trouble."

He let a grin float over his face, hoping to put her at ease. "It will be my pleasure. After that great meal you cooked for me, I can at least offer you a take-out lunch."

Her face clouded with a frown, and he knew at once that she didn't want to be reminded of that night. He had a mind to tell her that mature adults didn't do things of which they were ashamed, but he didn't voice the thought.

"As you wish. If you want Willis to do this, let me know exactly what you want, and I'll draw up something. Then, the three of us can sit together and work it out. If you'd rather have someone else do it, I can probably suggest a couple of reliable people."

"Thanks. I'd rather work with the two of you, but won't I have to wait until he finishes the shop?"

"Willis hires a lot of workers. Don't worry about that."

"I won't, then. Thanks for your time. Would you please show me the way out."

He stared at her, fighting the urge to shake her. Anger boiled up in him and, with his fists bracing his sides, he growled, "You don't have to run, Susan. You're as safe here with me as you would be in the Vatican. I don't touch a woman unless she invites me to."

No sooner had the words left his lips than he regretted saying them. "I'm sorry. That wasn't called for." He couldn't let it go at that. "But you are the most frustrating . . . Oh, forget it, and let's try to pretend I didn't say it."

"All right. Are you going to see me out? And will you let me know what Mr. Carter says after you speak with him about changes in my kitchen?"

The long breath he expelled didn't reflect a fraction of his exasperation. "Come on. I'll call you as soon as I put something together for Will and me to discuss."

She thanked him, shook the hand he extended, albeit reluctantly, and left. He watched until her blue BMW turned off Parkway Street into Salem Court. One thing was certain: Susan Pettiford had a will of steel. She had made up her mind that nothing more would happen between them, no matter how she felt about him, and she was determined to pull it off. So why'd she do it in the first place?

He took his appointment book out of his shirt pocket and checked the date on which they made love. *If she has a baby around nine months after the eighth of October, I'm going to demand a DNA test, and if she refuses, I'll take her to court and demand my rights. But, damn. I just refuse to believe she lacks integrity, that she would trick a man into fathering a baby. She wouldn't. So where does that leave me?*

He phoned Willis. "Susan wants you to put a new kitchen in the Edith Greer house that she inherited. I'll sketch some ideas, and the three of us can get together and thrash it out."

"As long as you didn't tell her I'd do it for peanuts."

"I didn't mention money, but man, you are not going to bleed her."

"All right. I'll ask a fair price. Have you had lunch?"

"I'm about to phone for it."

"Order me a couple of burgers and some fries, and not to worry. I won't stick it to your girl."

"My *what*?"

"Sorry. Just kidding."

After phoning Sam's Gourmet Burger Castle for an order of four hamburgers, two orders of French fries and two containers of coffee, Lucas put a handful of walnuts in his pocket, walked down to the trellis behind the garage and sat down. What was wrong with going after Susan Pettiford, if he wanted her? He had to admit that he was itching to find out whether what happened between them was an accident, whether they could revisit that special corner of heaven. He'd be a fool voluntarily to live another forty or fifty years and die without ever feeling like that again. He'd had a few women, but the experiences were child's play compared to the way he felt with Susan. And drat her, she made an art of denial.

"I don't care how much she denies it, or how determined she is to forget about it, I know how I made her feel." The two squirrels he'd named Roy and Rob ran up to him and pulled on his trouser legs. He reached into his pocket and got the walnuts that he'd brought, and gave one to each. They accepted the nuts but didn't leave, so he handed each of them another walnut. It was a ritual that they played out whenever he sat beneath the trellis, for Roy and Rob knew that they were entitled to two walnuts each. Occasionally, he gave them peanuts, which they liked, but it seemed that they preferred walnuts.

"Acorns aren't good enough for you," he told them. "I have to buy walnuts to keep you happy. I might as well have two children." Children. He wanted a houseful of them. And suddenly, he wondered whether Susan wanted children. "What the devil is wrong with my head?" He jumped up and went back upstairs to his office.

Between decorating the master bedroom in her new house, planning the furnishing for her office and tutoring twice weekly, Susan found that she didn't have time to be lonely or to wallow in sadness over her inability to have a family of her own. Occasionally, she wrestled with the pain of it, but always managed to dispel the sorrow before she became depressed. And as time passed and she became more accustomed to the truth, those moments of severe pain came even less frequently.

Two weeks before Christmas, she crawled around in her back garden picking up the pecans that littered the ground, looked toward the next house and saw a woman who appeared to be putting something in a bird feeder. On an impulse, she took the half bucket of pecans, walked over to the house and knocked on the front door, holding her breath as she did so. The woman opened the door.

"I'm Susan Pettiford, and I'll be moving into my aunt's house next door. There's a huge pecan tree there, and I'd be happy if you'd like to have some of these pecans. I just gathered them."

"Come in. I'm Cassandra Hairston-Shepherd, and I'll bet my

husband would love to have them. He owns the restaurant Gourmet Corner, and serves as its head chef."

"I'm glad to meet you, Cassandra. I hope we'll be good neighbors. If you have a bag, I'll be glad to leave these with you. Hairston, did you say? Are you related to the newspaper family?"

"Indeed, I am. My parents made that paper what it is, but my sister owns it now. Thanks for the pecans. Maybe we can have coffee after you get settled in," Cassandra said, giving Susan the feeling she'd been dismissed.

"Thanks. I'm having the kitchen gutted and modernized. I'll move in as soon as it's ready. I'd better be going."

"Nice meeting you, Susan, and thanks for the pecans."

"Mmm." Susan strolled back to her house, unsure as to whether her visit had been welcome. Cassandra Hairston-Shepherd's reception was barely tepid, and Susan doubted that she would make the effort again. Too bad. The woman seemed to be about her age, and she would have appreciated a friend nearby. "Oh well, I can always make other friends."

She went into the kitchen, made notes on what she wanted in it and the approximate arrangement. If Lucas's idea didn't complement her own, she figured she would have to give in. He spoke gently, but she had already detected in him a core of steel. Besides, the less she saw of him the better. Deceptively discerning, he had practically accused her of inviting him to make love with her. But to her mind, she hadn't done any such thing. She set the scene, and he responded accordingly.

She ran to answer her cell phone. "Hello."

"Hello, Susan. Lucas Hamilton here. If you're not busy, Willis and I need your opinion on what we've done about your kitchen."

"You mean you already started on the plans for it."

"Unless you have different ideas, we've finished. How about it?"

She looked at her watch. "I need an hour."

"Try to make it in forty-five minutes. Willis has to leave soon."

She told him she'd do her best. "There goes the rest of my day," she fumed, but she walked into his office forty-five minutes later looking her best. She liked their ideas, said as much and focused her gaze on Willis.

"How much?"

He looked her in the eye. "Seven thousand, which means we buy everything from a wholesaler and lug it over there ourselves."

Her gasp didn't escape either of them, and she followed it with, "Should I get on my knees and thank you, or will it suffice merely to genuflect? I need my kitchen remodeled, but I definitely do not need your attitude." She turned to Lucas. "Seems to me you could find a more agreeable partner."

"He's usually milder than this," Lucas said. "Right now, he's mad because I wouldn't let him charge you fifteen thousand. Seven thousand provides seventeen percent profit above costs and labor. It's enough."

"Sure," Willis said, "because I'm going to collect the stuff and truck it over there. I want to be invited to the first dinner you cook in this state-of-the-art kitchen." She whirled around and stared at Lucas, her eyes wide and jaw dropped.

"Easy," he murmured. "I haven't told him a thing."

"What?" Willis asked.

"I was talking to Susan."

Her breathing returned to normal, but if she didn't get out of there, she would begin to hyperventilate, for her undergarments were already damp. "Send me a contract," she said to Willis in a voice unlike her own, grabbed her jacket, and headed for the door.

"You didn't need to do that," she heard Lucas say to Willis. "No matter what you think, she's a client."

The sound of Lucas's steps thudded on the stairs behind her, but she wouldn't look back.

"Wait, Susan." She didn't stop. "You either wait or I'll follow you home or wherever it is you're going." She waited.

"Get this straight, Susan. Unless you tell someone what happened between you and me on October the eighth, it stays between you and me. I don't kiss and tell. I apologize for Willis's childish behavior. He's just begun to make money with this business, and it's been a long, hard pull for him. He's a good guy in every respect, or I wouldn't partner with him."

"He has decided that he doesn't like me."

"That isn't true. He has decided that there's something between the two of us and that we both lied to him when he asked us what we meant to each other. He'd rather we had told him that it was none of his business. Willis and I have different parents, but otherwise, we're brothers."

"All right. May I leave now?"

He held both hands up, palms out. "Ok, Susan. You're the queen of denial. See you tomorrow evening at Wade School."

Susan didn't answer. If he wanted to bend her, he had a lesson coming. She got into her car, ignited the engine and, although she headed home, a wrong turn took her to the underpass beneath the Salem River, and she emerged on Fifth Street at the town's center. She glimpsed an upholstery-fabric store, parked, and went in to introduce herself and examine the merchandise.

"Well, I was wondering when we'd run into each other."

She looked up to see Jay Weeks standing beside her. "Hi. Do you shop here?"

"If I get in a rut. Otherwise, I shop in Baltimore. How's your shop coming along?"

"It should be ready in a couple of weeks. Willis Carter is doing the work." She noticed that his eyebrows shot up and quickly returned to their normal position.

"When are we going to have lunch or something?"

"What about now?" she asked him. "It's one-thirty, and I haven't eaten."

They walked across the street to a mom-and-pop barbecue specialty café. "I hear you're living in the Greer place. How'd that happen? A lot of people would have liked to buy that house. It won a national award." They ordered barbecued pork sandwiches and coffee.

"I know. I inherited it from my aunt. I'm having the kitchen completely renovated before I move in."

"I wish I could have gotten that house. Bon appétit." He bit into the sandwich. "Lined up any work yet?"

"I've just begun to work on my ad material. I hope to get started sometime in January."

"Mmm. Going anywhere for Christmas? If you aren't, you're welcome to come with me to Vermont. I'm going skiing."

She was careful not to show her surprise at the suggestion or to behave as if it implied anything untoward. "Thanks, but I hope my mother will come for Christmas."

"It's hard to find any real fun here in Woodmore. Sometimes I get bored as hell. You'll see."

They spoke of mundane things, passing the time and, after an hour, said good-bye and went their separate ways. She couldn't make up her mind about Jay. She wasn't looking for a man, but if she was, she doubted that she would consider him. Still, he could be a friend, provided he didn't become too competitive. She wanted to stop by her shop, but didn't for fear that Willis would think she was checking on him. Instead, she stopped in a curio store, bought a tiny dancing figure that she saw in the window and went on to her house by the lake.

That afternoon, at the end of the tutoring session and after she left the classroom, Susan gave the little dancing monkey to Rudy. The child hugged her leg.

"Thanks, Miss Pettiford. I'm going to hide this so nobody can get it, and I'll just play with it after I go to bed."

She took Rudy's hand and walked with the child to her car. "It's beginning to rain. I'll drop you home. Why can't you play with the monkey whenever you like?"

"'Cause one of the other children will take it, and my mom won't make them give it back."

"How many children does your mom have?"

"Five, but I'm the only one who isn't hers. I don't have a real mom anymore. A policeman killed her and a man over drugs."

She stopped walking, turned Rudy to face her and asked the child, "Who told you that?"

"My foster sister. I don't like her 'cause she's mean."

What could she say other than a meaningless, "Try not to think that way, Rudy."

She stopped at 316 Salem Court, three blocks from the railroad and let the little girl out of the car. "See you next Tuesday, Rudy."

Rudy slid over and hugged Susan. "I can't wait, Ms. Pettiford. Bye."

Half an hour after she got into her apartment, the telephone rang. "Susan, this is Lucas Hamilton. I need to speak with you urgently. Can we meet somewhere, or may I come to your place?"

Taken aback, she said, "This is a surprise, Lucas. What's so urgent that you need to see me right now?"

"If it wasn't important, I wouldn't deign to take up your time."

Deciding that tangling with him wouldn't be prudent, but feeling nonetheless flippant, she said, "Pick the place."

"Thanks. I'll be over there in twenty minutes."

Gaping at the soundless telephone receiver, Susan felt trapped. She had expected him to refuse her offer and to ask her to choose their meeting place. For a few minutes, she debated whether to look stunning in a red jumpsuit or to greet him in the jeans and cowl neck sweater that she had put on minutes earlier. "I'm not primping for him," she said aloud and busied herself packing belongings that she would take to her house. Her last thought before answering the door was that the evening would not end as it did the one time he'd been in her apartment.

"Hi, Lucas. Come on in and have a seat in the living room. I'll bring us some tea."

"Thanks. You couldn't make that coffee, could you?"

Susan made coffee, glad for the few additional minutes in which to collect her thoughts and emotions before facing him. She put a pot of coffee, cups, saucers, spoons, sugar and milk on a tray, along with some gingersnaps and went back to him. He stood, took the tray from her, put it on the coffee table and sat down.

"It seems that I interrupted your packing."

"There isn't much to pack," she said, rubbing her hands together. "Only a few personal things and linens. Everything else is in New York, packed and waiting to be shipped. What did you want to see me about?"

He ate two gingersnaps. "I like these. Always have." If it were pleasant, she decided, he'd get on with it. She leaned back against the sofa and waited. "It's about Rudy Baxter. You're taking a big risk. The child will become dependent upon you, and that's not a good thing."

"Just because I gave her that little monkey and drove her home so that she wouldn't get soaking wet, I'm making her dependent on me. Don't make jokes." She had a feeling that if he pursued it, she would explode.

He put the coffee cup down and glared at her. "You did what? I didn't know about that. You are not supposed to develop a relationship with these children, because most of them are either from troubled homes and are having a problem with at least one parent. A relationship with you can only compound the problem."

She rested her right knee on her left one and let her right foot swing with vigor. The man knew exactly how to trigger her temper. "I didn't realize that they taught psychology in schools of architecture. That little monkey is not going to hurt Rudy. Besides, she said she'd play with him when she was in bed, so that one of her foster sisters or brothers wouldn't take him away from her. What do you think of that? And as for taking her home, I suppose you would have watched her walk out into that downpour without an umbrella and then gotten into your Lincoln Town Car and driven home dry as a tunnel rat. Well, *not me*."

"Of course psychology is taught in schools of architecture. And you've got a smart mouth. I don't care how you rationalize it, you're out of line. You have the program's guidelines, and I'd appreciate it if you would read them and abide by them. Otherwise—"

"Otherwise I'm fired? You've got a lot to learn, Mr. Hamilton. Nobody pushes me around. My pupils are learning to read, and they are enjoying it. Parents want their children to learn to read and read well. Hold my record up against your stupid rules, and which do you think will win?"

"Otherwise, you may explain it to the school board."

She sat forward. "You wouldn't dare do that." The two hours

weekly that she spent with the children had become the most gratifying, happiest moments of her life. She couldn't have children of her own, but she could enjoy nurturing other children who needed her. "You wouldn't be that cruel." She didn't realize that her personality had practically shriveled as she contemplated the prospect of not being with the children.

He drained the coffee cup and stood. "I signed a form agreeing to abide by the rules, just as you did. That means I gave my word, and if I turn my head and pretend I don't know what you're doing, I'm as guilty of infractions as you are. I'm sorry, because I wouldn't like to hurt you, but—"

"But if I'm nice to that lonely little girl, who goes there in spite of the fact that the other children jeer at her and tease her about her clothes and her living conditions, you'll do your damned duty and drop me from the program."

Realizing that tears had begun to cascade down her cheeks, she jumped up and ran to the kitchen.

"What's wrong? Why are you crying?"

She turned her back to him, walked to the window and pressed her face to the glass. Her flesh remembered the feel of his hard, but gentle fingers and responded to him. Slowly, he turned her to face him, but she wouldn't look at him. Her tears were no longer for the children she might not see again, but for the children she would never have, for the trauma of losing her maternal rights to an ailment that had eventually afflicted her mother and grandmother. His arms went around her, and she clung to him.

Susan knew when his breathing changed; and when he stepped back in order to see her face, but didn't release her, shivers raced through her. The fire in his eyes burned with an unmistakable message and, on the brink of becoming victimized by her vivid recollection of their one-night tryst, she stepped away from him.

"Forgive me for taking advantage of your generosity, Lucas. I rarely cry, but back there, a lot of things crowded in on me. I'm sorry."

Until she made herself look at him, he said nothing. Then, his voice came in something akin to a growl. "That night, you told me that you felt good in my arms. You still do." Before she could respond, he strode to the door and left.

You could have told her that over the phone. Lucas didn't try to justify having gone to Susan's house. He knew she had lunch with Jay Weeks, because he saw them leave the café together. He wasn't jealous, but if she wanted the company of a man, why not him? He admitted to himself that he wanted evidence that she hadn't been able to dismiss making love with him as an insignificant moment in her life. In fact, he told himself, "I'll show her a thing or two."

The next morning, he phoned a butcher and had a turkey sent to his mother for their Christmas dinner. It had been that way all of his life. He shared his life with his mother and his friends and always wondered what home life was like when both mother and father were present. He looked at his latest draft for Hamilton Village, the retirement complex that he envisioned for Woodmore. If he could get the backing for it, both his status as an architect and his financial position would surpass his dreams. Satisfied that he had enough of a plan to attract his targeted investor, he rolled up the draft and went to keep his appointment with the CEO of Muller Furniture, Inc.

"My board and I have considered this carefully," Jack Muller told Lucas, "and I think we can do business. Of course, I'm hoping the people will buy their new furniture from me. We're one of the largest, oldest and finest furniture makers in the state."

"If you give them an attractive deal, you should do well." It hadn't been easy. He'd been dickering with Muller for at least a year before the man encouraged him to draft a basic plan.

"Who's your contractor?"

"Carter. He puts up all of my houses and buildings. We've been working together for a long time."

"All right. Let's meet at the bank tomorrow at ten."

Lucas left Muller's office satisfied that he was one big step closer to meeting Calvin Jackson face to face. He had to go over the blueprints once more with Willis, but didn't expect that his friend would find much to question.

He had the title to the land, the blueprints and the promise of funding. God willing, they could break ground for Phase I in March.

Having finished redecorating the master bedroom in her house, Susan was anxious to leave the apartment that she rented. "Imagine how this living room would look with a big, beautifully decorated spruce tree beside the fireplace," she said to Willis and the two men who were working with him in the kitchen of her house. "Too bad I won't be able to move in before Christmas."

"That doesn't mean you can't enjoy a Christmas tree here," one of them said. "The plumbing will be in order, and we'll have the tiled floor, the stove and refrigerator in place. You can get water from the bathroom."

She phoned her landlord, gave notice and settled into her house three days later. She bought a tree, decorated it, and prepared to have Christmas Eve dinner alone for the first time in her life. On an impulse, she phoned Jay Weeks and invited him to dinner. To her amazement, he accepted, telling her that bad weather was forecast for Vermont, and he'd decided not to go skiing.

On Christmas Eve, she built a fire in the fireplace, scattered pecans in the ashes to roast, and put a goose in the oven. Jay Weeks proved to be the perfect guest, as she had suspected he would be, and she served a near perfect dinner.

"In New York, my friends and I would go to the Cathedral of St. John the Divine for midnight service on Christmas Eve," she told him. "Is that a custom here?"

"At the Catholic churches, but I'm not Catholic. You want to go?"

"Sure. Come on."

Leaving the church after service, she encountered her neighbor, Cassandra Hairston-Shepherd and her husband.

"Susan Pettiford, is it?" Cassandra said. "This is my husband, Kix Shepherd."

"I'm so glad to see you again, Cassandra. Hello, Kix. I moved in a few days ago. This is Jay Weeks."

They exchanged greetings, but Cassandra did not suggest that they get together. Nor did she linger for a brief chat.

Kix glanced at his wife, frowned and then spoke to Susan. "The Greer house is a celebrated house. I was fond of your aunt, and I regretted her passing. I hope we'll be good neighbors, Susan."

"Thank you," Susan said. She noticed that while Kix spoke with them, Cassandra walked on.

"Cassie," Kix called to his wife, "would you please wait." Cassandra stopped, but she did not turn around.

Kix shook hands with Jay. "I hope to see you both again."

Although she couldn't quite put her finger on the reason, it seemed to Susan that Cassandra's marriage needed bolstering.

She liked Kix Shepherd at once, for he seemed more down to earth and was certainly friendlier than his wife. Jay had his own ideas about Cassandra. "That dame's got a helluva estimation of herself."

"You've met her before?"

"Of course I have. She designed my logo and stationery."

"You're not serious."

"Oh, but I am. She's a real piece of work. You'll see."

As she had done for most of her life, Susan went to church Christmas morning, and it pleased her to see there at least one person who she knew: Nathan. The boy came up to her holding the hand of an older woman.

"Miss Pettiford, this is my grandmother."

"How do you do, ma'am?"

The woman, who Susan judged to be about sixty or sixty-five, extended her hand. "I'm glad to meet you, Ms. Pettiford. My name is Ann Price. Nathan talks about you all the time. He thinks you're a saint."

"He's a wonderful boy," Susan said. "Does he live with you?"

"Lord, yes. I have three children of my own. Two of them

have gone about their business and left their children with me, and I have custody of my younger son's child. Altogether, I'm raising five kids. This one's the youngest, and he's a blessing. Never gives me a bit of trouble."

Susan spoke with the woman for a few minutes, wished her and Nathan a merry Christmas and left them. Some people were blessed to have children, but didn't appreciate their good fortune. If she had . . .

"Don't start that, girl," she admonished herself.

Shortly after she arrived home, the phone rang and she rushed to answer it, wondering who her caller might be. "Merry Christmas, Susan. This is Lucas Hamilton. I hope you're enjoying your home and that you're feeling more chipper than when we were last together."

"Merry Christmas, Lucas. I am indeed in better spirits."

"Glad to hear it. All good things for the new year."

"Thanks. Same to you."

"Bye for now."

She hung up. Surely he hadn't called only to tell her merry Christmas! She lifted her shoulder in a shrug. It seemed that he had.

The next time the phone rang, Susan answered it and heard the voice of her mother, Betty Lou Pettiford. "Honey, I'm so sorry I couldn't get there for Christmas, but so many people here need me, I just couldn't make myself leave. I hope you've found someone to share the holiday with. I do miss you."

"I'm so glad you called, Mom. It's just as well you didn't come. I moved into Aunt Edith's house, and I'm remodeling the kitchen, so it's torn up. I know you can't stand chaos."

"Don't joke. That was then. Over here, there's nothing but chaos. I think I'll go back to the States after this tour is over. It's time I started living in realty. Your father's been gone for five years now, and escaping over here hasn't helped. I have to deal with it there."

"You know I'll be here for you, Mom, whenever you get back."

"I know, child, and it means everything to me."

Later, as Susan mused over their conversation, it occurred to her that she'd heard that decision from her mother several times in the last four years—whenever her mother had a fit of depression about her father's death.

School resumed after the first of the year, and Susan could hardly wait to see her pupils. When she saw that all of them had returned, a wide grin spread over her face, and she could hardly contain her joy. Rudy and Nathan sat beside each other, the only children to sit in the front row, and she suddenly understood Nathan. He was not a foster child, but he lived separately from his mother, and he sympathized with Rudy.

The children's apparent delight in returning to her class made her giddy with happiness and, when the tutoring session ended, she stood in the corridor beside the door of the classroom surrounded by them as they laughed and chatted. However, she had a sudden twinge of discomfort when Lucas Hamilton walked past her accompanied by an attractive woman who was not one of the volunteers. And it angered her that he didn't speak, but half smiled and winked at her instead. That is, if you could call squeezing both eyes tight a wink.

"I don't care what he does or who he does it with," she reminded herself as she drove home.

But that proved to be only the beginning. One of Lucas's girl-friends dropped by Wade School on Tuesdays and Thursdays and left along with him with such regularity that one would have thought he feared leaving alone. "The devil with him," Susan murmured one Thursday evening.

Chapter Four

Lucas left the Woodmore Bank in high spirits, his steps quick and his purpose sure. During the past two weeks, he had hired a secretary, a junior architect and an accountant. Most importantly, he had the financial backing of Jack Muller and Muller Furniture, Inc. and the right to break ground for Hamilton Village. He slid into the driver's seat and knocked his right fist into his left palm. "I'm on my way." And he'd managed it without investing a dime of his own money.

Using his cell phone, Lucas phoned Willis. "It's all set. The money's in the bank, and the papers are in my briefcase. Get busy." This was his chance to ensure that Woodmore, North Carolina, registered his name for posterity, and when he finished, Hamilton Village would do for him what Fallingwater did for Frank Lloyd Wright.

"We've just put the floor in Susan's kitchen," Willis said, "and I have to tell you, we ought to photograph this place for *Architectural Design*. It's exquisite. I've never been so proud of anything I've done. Man, it's perfect."

"I'm on my way home. I think I'll drop by and see it. Is she home?"

"I don't know. She gives me a wide berth."

"I hope you haven't done anything else to upset her."

"Aw, come on. I pull her leg a little bit sometimes, but—"

"You'd better say what you mean." The sound of Willis's laughter did not amuse Lucas.

"Weren't you trying to upset her when you decided Wade School was the place to interview women for the secretary's post?" Willis prodded. "Huh? Man, I'm not stupid."

"I'll see you in a few minutes." Lucas had not bothered to examine his motive in interviewing the women in his office at Wade School half an hour before the tutoring sessions terminated. On those days, he scheduled his own class half an hour early. If seeing him with four different, attractive young women had impressed Susan in any way, she'd kept it to herself. He'd like to know why she cried when he was last in her apartment. Certainly the possibility of losing her appointment as a volunteer hadn't triggered that level of misery. And miserable was the only way he could describe Susan's tortured demeanor. Then, when he opened his arms to her, she went to him with the eagerness of a bride to her wedding. Yet, the minute they became aware of their feelings, she gathered that iron will of hers and moved. But he was not willing to give up just yet.

I haven't been inside of you for the last time, girl. You liked what I did to you, and as sure as salmon go back to the place of their spawning, I'll be back there.

He parked in front of her house, got out and would have gone inside if he hadn't seen her in the garden trimming boxwood.

"Hello, Susan." He could see that he'd startled her, for her head jerked up as if he'd frightened her. "Sorry if I'm intruding, but Willis wants me to look at the kitchen."

"Hi. Go on in. They're working on the floor."

"He said they've finished the job, and I'm anxious to see it."

When she struggled to get up from her squat position, he jumped over the fence, grasped her shoulders and lifted her to her feet. His fingers caressed her softness, but she didn't look at him. Neither did she move away.

"Why can't you look at me, Susan? I'm here, and I am not going to disappear like a ghost." And the more she tried to behave as if he were just another man, the more determined he was to make her admit that he was special to her because she wanted him.

As if his words triggered her consciousness, she stepped away from him. "Thanks for the lift up. If I gain any more weight, you'd need a crane to lift me."

He didn't allow her to derail his thoughts. "You haven't gained one ounce since I lifted you and put you on your bed."

"Please, I—"

"You want to forget it, but I don't and I can't, so don't expect me to cooperate."

She leaned down, picked up her pruning shears and started toward the back door. "If you told Willis you were on your way, I'm sure he thinks you got lost," she said over her shoulder.

"Listen here, woman. All you're doing is making me more determined to find out if what went on between us could happen again and why the hell it occurred in the first place. You said you didn't regret it. Were you lying?"

She stopped walking, turned around and stared at him. "I'm a free woman, thirty-four years old. Until now, I've made an enviable living for myself that has given me a measure of independence. I don't have to lie to the president." With those words, she strutted into the house and did not hold the door open for him. Nor did she lock it.

A cool way of telling him she still didn't regret it. He didn't want her to see him laugh, so he coughed instead. "I'll bet she fanned my tail," he muttered to himself. No one knew that house better than he, so he opened the back door and headed for the kitchen. The house remained one of his stellar achievements, an award winner, and pride suffused him as he strode through it.

"Say, man, what took you so long? How do you like it?" Willis asked him.

"Fantastic. You've done a superb job. I think I'll use this model for kitchens this size. It really is great. What did she say about it?"

Willis began cleaning his hands with a brush that he kept for the purpose. "She hasn't seen it with the floor installed."

"When will you finish her shop?"

"In a couple of days. They're working on the storage room. I'll be glad to make some real money. These peanut jobs are a pain in the ass. Say, my dad wants to visit me next week. Do you think Aunt Noreen would invite us to dinner? I'm still tasting that food she cooked for Christmas. I always said you were lucky, Lucas. My mother couldn't cook worth a cent."

"And neither can you. I'll ask Mama, or you can. Let me know the dates."

He wanted to see Susan again before he left there, but he couldn't stroll around in her house as if he belonged there, even if he did design it. "I've got to get out of here," he told Willis. To the men working with him, he said "Great job."

He whirled around and knocked Susan against the dining room table. "Good Lord!" he said, grabbing her shoulders. "Did I hurt you?"

"Uh . . ." One of his arms eased around her, and the fingers of his other hand stroked her bare arm. "I don't think so," she said so softly that he almost missed the words.

"I'm sorry, Susan. Stand up, and let's see if you're all right." He kept his arm tight around her and eased her into a standing position.

"I'm all right. Honest." But she didn't move from the curve of his arm.

"What's the matter? What happened?" Willis asked.

He cared a lot for Willis Carter, but at the moment, he wanted to strangle him. "It's okay, Willis. I ran into Susan and knocked her against the table. She says she's fine."

"Yeah, man. That's a sneaky way to get next to a gal." He wondered at Willis's lack of sensitivity. Couldn't he see Susan's embarrassment, and wouldn't a savvy man have guessed that they remained locked together for a reason and left them alone?

"You'd know," Lucas said, not bothering to hide his irritation. "Back off, man."

"I hope you don't get any bruises from this," Lucas said to Susan. She stared at his mouth and then shook herself as if bringing herself out of a trance. He had to get out of there. "I'll be in touch," he said and brushed past Willis on his way to the back door.

"What's wrong? You two can't get together?" Willis asked Susan.

"We don't want to, Mr. Carter. It's as simple as that. We do not want to become involved."

Lucas didn't stop. A minute earlier, he could have demonstrated her error to anyone who cared to know it.

Susan did not believe the words she'd uttered to Willis, but she wanted them to be true. His renovation of her kitchen so pleased her that her attitude toward him softened. When she arrived at her shop the next morning to ask when she could occupy it, she found him having strong words with Jay Weeks.

"Man, no one comes in here but my workers and me. You're snooping around, and it's illegal. You're trespassing. How do I know you won't cause some damage?"

"Susan and I are friends," Jay said.

"Yeah? You're also the only other interior decorator in Woodmore. You stay out of here, or I get a warrant that says you do."

What was Jay doing there? She turned around and went across the street to the barbecue café, where she bought a container of coffee and a scone, killing time until the two men settled their disagreement. She didn't want to takes sides with Jay because he was wrong, yet she didn't want to embarrass him by agreeing with Willis. She would remain friends with Jay, but she would keep a careful eye on him.

When she returned to the shop, Jay had left. "How long was Jay Weeks here?" she asked Willis.

"Maybe twenty minutes. I went out to get some coffee, and when I returned, he was walking around as if you'd hired him to inspect the place. What do you think so far?"

"It's wonderful. I had no idea it would be so elegant, though I hoped for the best. If I put a couch in my office, it can be my second home."

"That's what I thought you had in mind. For instance, it's

supposed to snow tonight. If you were here, you wouldn't have to go home."

"When I get it all dressed up, I'll call you, and you can see how great it will look. I realize you didn't make any money on this, and I'm grateful. The kitchen in my house is out of sight, too. You're the best, Mr. Carter."

"Since I'm such a great guy, Susan, you may call me Willis. And if you happen to bake some buttermilk biscuits sometime in that oven back there, give me a call. The only time I get any is when I drop in on Lucas's mother. He really is a nice guy, Susan."

She threw up her hands. "I know that. End of topic."

She went home, bent over her catalogues, and selected fabrics, trimmings and accessories that she would order from the dealer she used in New York. A pain in her neck alerted her to the fact that she had worked for several hours, through lunchtime and into the late afternoon. She got up, stretched her arms, walked over to the dining room window, looked out and gaped at the solid mass of snow. After checking her refrigerator for food supplies and discovering that she needed nothing, she went back to work.

Suddenly, darkness enveloped her. Tests of the lights confirmed her worst fears: the blizzard had caused a power outage. Her cell phone rang.

"Susan, this is Lucas. Electricity is off in your house, but in case you aren't aware of it, you have a generator. Just inside the door leading to the basement is a switch that glows red in the darkness. Push it to the right, and the generator will kick in. I'll hang on while you do it."

After fumbling her way to the basement door, she found the switch and did as he directed. "I found it, and the lights are on. I can't tell you how much I appreciate your calling to tell me that."

"My pleasure. Have a good evening."

Silence followed the click on the other end of the wire, and she stopped herself as she was about to throw the cell phone across the dining room. "I'd give a lot to know what goes on in that man's mind," she said. "He can make me madder than anybody else on God's green earth."

The next morning, awakened by a loud banging on her front door, Susan pulled on a robe, slipped her feet into her house slippers and ran down the stairs. The banging was of such urgency that she expected the worst. She opened the door to find Cassandra standing there with a shopping bag in her hand.

"Hi, Susan. I noticed that you have electricity, and I was wondering if I could put these eggs, milk and butter in your refrigerator until I get some electricity."

She had expected anything but a visit from Cassandra Hairston-Shepherd. "Of course. Come in. Do you have time for some hot coffee?"

"I sure do. I can't get started without my coffee. Hope I didn't wake you up. I thought that since you work—"

"Oh, that's all right. I worked here until after two this morning, and with all this snow, I figured sleeping in was the most productive thing I could do." She led Cassandra to the living room. " Have a seat. I'll be back in a couple of minutes."

She brushed her teeth, dressed in a pair of jeans and a sweater and hurried back to her guest. "I haven't changed anything down here except the kitchen," she said. "Let's get that coffee started, Cassandra."

"Thanks. Call me Cassie. My goodness, this is a real gem. I wouldn't cook in this place. I'd just stand here at the door and gaze at it."

"They did a good job, all right." After putting on the coffee, Susan stored Cassie's groceries in the refrigerator, quickly microwaved bacon, scrambled eggs, and toasted two bagels. She set the kitchen table and looked at Cassie. "I hope you don't mind eating in the kitchen."

"I'm lucky that I'm getting coffee, not to speak of a hot meal. Kix only had orange juice. He usually cooks breakfast for me before he goes to the restaurant. He spoils me, you know."

"How long have you two been married, Cassie?"

"Eight years. I can hardly believe it."

"And no children yet?"

Cassie's fair skin bloomed from a rush of blood, and Susan suspected that she had pushed the wrong button. She became more certain of it when Cassie said, "Don't ever ask that question around Kix. I don't know why it is that men think fatherhood is the only way to prove their masculinity. Seems to me that being able to take a woman to bed practically every night ought to be proof enough."

To Susan, that sounded like bragging. "I thought most women wanted children, too," Susan said. "But . . ." She flexed her right shoulder in a shrug. "Different strokes for different folks. Do you work away from home, Cassie?" she asked in the hope of changing the subject.

"I certainly do. I'm a graphic artist at Cutting Edge Stationers and Engravers."

"Of course. Jay said you designed his logo and stationery. I'm going to need some stationery and maybe a logo. Where's Cutting Edge Stationers and Engravers?"

"A block and a half from the Rose Hill School on Fourth Street East. You can't miss it. I'm on the second floor. I'd better be going. Thanks for storing my groceries and especially for breakfast. I'm going to speak to Kix about a generator this very night."

Cassie left without mentioning the possibility of their getting together socially. "If she doesn't want to be friends, it's no skin off my teeth," Susan said to herself. She straightened up the kitchen, phoned her supplier in New York City and ordered what she needed for her shop. Then, she sat in her living room, studying it to decide the changes that she would eventually make.

A phone call from Cassie was the last thing she expected. "Hello, Susan, this is Cassandra Hairston-Shepherd." *Why did the woman insist on presenting herself as if she were royalty, or a trumpeter heralding the arrival of a sovereign?* "Kix wants us to get together as soon as we get electricity. So please come, and do bring your SO. Uh . . . he said we're due to have electricity by tomorrow morning. He's off on Mondays, so how about Monday around six for drinks and snacks?"

In other words, Susan thought, *come for an hour and a half, and be sure to bring a man. Suppose she didn't have a significant other?*

"I'll have to check, Cassie, and call you later. Sounds like a great idea. Thanks." Maybe she bared her teeth; she wasn't sure. One thing, though; she didn't like that kind of sloppy invitation. She could be wrong, but she had a feeling that Kix had *urged* Cassie to make friends with her neighbor.

Susan had guessed correctly. Cassie did not relish the company of women, and especially not good-looking, independent-minded, career women. "Why is Kix so anxious for us to make friends with her?" she asked Drogan, her brother. "We'll get to know her eventually, and that's good enough for me. I don't buddy-buddy with women."

"Maybe he's hoping some of her femininity will rub off on you."

"As usual, you're a big help."

At six o'clock, dressed in her elegant, black velvet cocktail suit, Cassie drove to Gourmet Corner to meet Kix. The waiter led her to a small private dining room, the table of which contained a large vase of tea roses, her favorite flower and, within a few minutes, Kix joined her. She appreciated that he'd dressed in an oxford gray pinstriped suit rather than his chef's uniform; the world didn't need to know that her husband worked as a chef, even if he owned the famous restaurant.

After kissing her on the mouth, he sat down and gave her a box that was wrapped in silver and tied with a silver bow. "Happy anniversary, sweetheart," he said.

"Oh, dear. Should I open it now? You're so thoughtful. Thanks." Even as she spoke, she put the small package into her purse.

The waiter brought a bottle of Veuve Cliquot champagne, filled their glasses and waited. Kix tasted it, looked at the man and winked. "First class." The waiter left, and Kix raised his glass to his wife. "Here's to the next eight. I'm praying that by then, we'll have a child in the second grade, if not further on."

"Oh, Kix. You always manage to spoil every occasion with that. Please stop pressuring me. I'm going to do it."

"You've been promising me for the last six years. I want a

family, Cassie, and if you don't give me one, another woman will gladly do it."

Shocked at words she hadn't previously heard from him, her shaking hands caused the champagne to spill on her new velvet suit. "See what you've done," she sneered. "My new suit is ruined. I want to go home."

He called the waiter. "Cancel the dinner, Ray. We're going home."

How skillfully she maneuvered every incident to her advantage. One day, and soon, he'd be fed up with that and her other shenanigans. He looked at her expensive velvet suit and couldn't see a single blemish.

He drove the car into the garage at 39 Lake Street, turned off the motor, leaned back in the driver's seat and looked at his wife. "You didn't get hysterics over three drops of wine on your suit; you freaked out because I mentioned your starting our family. You do it every time. I want you to get this straight. I am not working my ass off twelve hours a day, six days a week so that you and I can engage in conspicuous consumption. I want children. I want them to have a good, useful and productive life, and I am doing what I can to ensure that. But you are not planning to honor your commitment that you made to me before we married. You agreed to have two and if we could afford them, three children. We can afford half a dozen, but I'm not asking that. I'm asking right now for one. If you won't do it, I'll find a woman who will."

"I can't get pregnant right now. We're starting a school to give graduate level instruction to graphic arts students, and I want a shot at the deanship. Can't you wait just that long?"

"First, you wanted a promotion from level one to level two. You're at level five. You wanted to attend an international conference. You went, came back, and so what. I have accepted a dozen excuses from you. This is the last one. Whether you get that deanship or not, it's ante up or I'm out of here." He got out of the car, opened the kitchen door and went inside. She sat there for a few minutes. For the first time since they'd married, she was certain that he had not made an idle threat, that he would leave. She pushed the passenger's door open and retched.

When she finally went inside, a glass once filled with milk and a part of a sandwich remained on the kitchen counter, remnants of her husband's supper on the night of their eighth wedding anniversary.

"He's not fooling now," she said aloud, remembered to open her gift and stared at the heavy gold chain from which hung a gold heart pendant. "I've got to fix this right now," she told herself and sped up the stairs. The sound of water streaming in the shower of the master bedroom foiled her, but only temporarily. She kicked off her shoes, stripped and hesitated. He had always wanted them together in the shower, but she put him off, fearing that he might see a blemish, a ridge or some other imperfection on her body. But she had never seen him in that don't-give-a-damn mood, so she had to do something. Why, he hadn't even opened the car door for her. She glanced at her size D breasts, standing straight out with their nipples glistening. He loved to suck them until he drove her out of her mind. She reached for a robe, thought better of it, and knocked on the bathroom door.

"I'm showering. Can't you use another bathroom?"

She opened the door, pushed back the shower curtain and stepped into the tub.

"What the—what are you doing?"

She let her hands do the talking. With one arm around his waist, she pressed her jutting nipples to his back, and with her other arm, she began to massage his penis. Slowly at first and then with all the vigor she could muster.

"Wait a minute. As long as I've wanted you to do this . . . ohh . . . stop it!"

"You don't want me to stop it. You love it, and you know it." Water streamed down on her naked body, and every nerve came alive. He groaned aloud, and a wild wantonness beset her.

"Turn around and suck my nipples," she said.

"No. You finish what you started."

"I will if you turn around."

He turned to face her, and she knelt before him. Uncertain as to what to do or how to do it, she looked up at him. He bent down, lifted her and, with the water still streaming down, got out of the tub. He dried her and then dried himself. She looked down at him, fully erected and pulsating with eagerness for completion, and began to stroke him again. If men loved it so much, she'd try. Still stroking him, she knelt in front of him again and kissed the tip of his penis. His groan sent shivers through her, and she sucked him into her mouth. It wasn't bad. He tasted sweet. She grasped his buttocks and began pulling on him, enjoying the feast.

"Oh my God, baby. Stop it!" He pushed her back from him. "I was a second from losing it, and you're not that sophisticated."

He picked her up and carried her to bed. Flat on her back on the bed staring up at Kix, she wondered what else they'd missed as a couple because of her prudishness. Ashamed, she opened her arms to him, spreading her legs as she did so. Lying beside her, he leaned over her, and she waited for the moment when she'd feel his tongue circle her nipple. He stared down at her until she squirmed.

"You she-devil," he said and pulled her left nipple into his mouth. Gone were the days when she lay still and prim beneath the onslaught of his mouth, fingers and penis as they tried to command her body to orgasm. Her one adulterous act had taught her to appreciate what her husband's body offered her.

Maybe he wanted to subdue her. She didn't know. She didn't care. His fingers snaked down beyond her belly, found her folds and began their talented dance.

"Get in me," she moaned, but he ignored her until, exasperated and not a little angry, she pushed him over, straddled him and rode him until they were both spent. She collapsed on him.

When at last he separated them, she resisted going to the bathroom, as had once been her habit, and lay beside him, quiet and a little ashamed, for she had taken advantage of him and, clever man that he was, he would one day remind her of it. Still, whatever sorrow she felt didn't go very deep, she realized, because she knew she would do it again if seducing him would take his mind off fatherhood and her shilly shallying about getting pregnant.

"You're going to pull that trick one of these days, and it won't work," he said, as she was about to doze off to sleep. "I'm glad you've finally learned to like sex, but get it into your head that sex is not the equivalent of a guided missile; it's been known to miss the target."

"I'd say I was sorry, if I didn't enjoy it so much."

"You don't think you used me?"

"In a way, I guess I did. But I learned something, too, and that was a good thing."

He rolled closer to her and locked her fingers with his. "Just remember what started this. You hear?" She remembered. How could she forget?

The next afternoon when Susan visited Cassie's office to order stationery and a logo, Cassie greeted her effusively.

"I'm so glad to see you, Susan. Have a seat and I'll send for some coffee. By the way, you *are* coming over at six on Monday, aren't you? Here have a look at these. What is the name of your outfit?"

Who is this chameleon? Susan wondered. "My company is called Pettiford Interiors, Incorporated." She handed her a card on which she'd written her company's name, address and telephone number.

"Great," Cassie said.

"Now, in my experience—and I've had a lot of it—either pearl gray or sand makes a more elegant paper than white or cream." Cassie smiled. "But of course, it's up to you. Would you like a sewing machine in your logo?"

"A sewing machine? I don't sew. My taste runs rather to an elegant house and a bolt of fabric. See if you can work that in somehow." One put-down deserves another, Susan said to herself and refused to feel remorse for having been nasty. Nonetheless, she was relieved when Cassie ignored the stab.

"All rightee. I ought to have a draft for you by Tuesday. I don't usually offer drafts, but you want something different. I'll call you when it's ready."

Susan thanked her. "I'll see you Monday evening, Cassie, and thanks again for the invitation." She dialed Jay as soon as she got out of the building.

"Jay Weeks speaking." She asked if he would go with her to

Cassie's house for cocktails. "It'll be a pleasure. I can't wait to see what a cocktail party here in good old Woodmore is like. Either I'm persona non grata at these affairs or Mrs. Hairston-Shepherd is just showing off. Everybody I know, including His Honor the Mayor, hightails it to The Watering Hole, guests and all, if they want a drink and don't have any booze at home. Thanks for inviting me."

Susan dressed in a royal blue velvet dress, nipped in at the waist and flattering her five feet, nine and a half inch, svelte figure, put her hair in a knot at the back of her head, stuck a pair of six-inch ivory-knitting needles in it and got downstairs just as Jay rang her doorbell.

"You're working the hell out of it, babe," he said in what he considered an appreciative remark on her looks. "That's a classy dress."

He handed her a long sprig of white orchids, and it didn't surprise her that he would choose novel and exotic flowers. She thanked him, put the orchids in a tall vase half-filled with water and went back to him.

"If we leave now, Jay, we'll be right on time." She handed him her coat, a street-length black mink that she hadn't expected to use in North Carolina, but which had come in handy, and strolled with him next door to the Shepherd home.

In response to Jay's ring, Kix opened the door. "Thanks for coming," he said, shaking Jay's hand. "I'm glad to see you both again. And Susan, thanks so much for those pecans. You won't believe how many times I've eyed those nuts over there on the ground rotting. I made some pecan pies that were very popular with my guests."

"Let me know when you make some more," Jay said, "and I'll be there. I love pecan pie."

"Who is it, darling?" Susan didn't want to believe that Cassie was a phony, but the woman was expecting them at six o'clock, and Jay rang the bell at one minute past six. She walked into the foyer just as Kix said, "Susan and Jay." Cassie's disappointment was unmistakable, and Susan couldn't understand why.

However, Cassie quickly recovered, and allowed her face to

crease in smiles. "Oh, it's so good to see you both. Come on in the living room."

Jay looked at Susan, but spoke for the group's benefit. "Don't you have any pecans stashed away over there? If you have, I'll take 'em out to Kix. I can practically taste that pie."

She had several bushels. "I do have some, and I had already planned to give them to Kix, but not with the proviso that he make pies for you or anybody else."

Cassie left them and returned with a tray of hot hors d'oeuvres. "Darling, that pie is so fattening. You shouldn't serve it too often."

Kix took the tray from Cassie and put it on the coffee table. "Sure it is, but I don't force anyone to eat it. Having those nice fresh pecans made my last pies very special." He looked at Susan. "If you have too many next year, say the word, and I'll gather the extra ones."

"Give me a call and I'll help you," Jay said.

Cassie sat down, crossed her knee and assumed a queenly air. "Oh, for goodness sake. Much ado about nothing."

Susan selected a marguerite from the tray of drinks, sipped it and said nothing. If Cassie needed to show off, the next time, she would have to do it with different guests. As a decorator, she had spent a good deal of time in homes and observed many couples interacting with each other. Something was wrong in this marriage, and her mind told her to keep her distance.

The long hour and a half approached its end, and at seven-fifteen, Susan stood, smiled at Jay and said, "I think we'd better be getting on to dinner."

"Right," Jay said, stood and extended his hand to Kix. "I've enjoyed the opportunity to get to know you better, and I look forward to you and Cassie being my guests."

Susan's eyebrows shot up. Jay had said the perfect thing, as smooth and as affected as Cassie. She hadn't wanted to overstate her "pleasure" at being Cassie's guest. "Yes," she said. "Thank you both so much." To Kix, she said, "I'll bring those pecans over to Cassie."

His smile didn't reach his eyes, so she knew that something—or someone—had displeased him. "I wouldn't hear of you dragging a bag of nuts over here. Let Cassie know, and I'll come get them."

Susan and Jay had hardly reached the street when Cassie said to Kix, "She's not fooling me. Jay Weeks is not interested in Susan Pettiford or any other woman."

"What do you mean, 'She's not fooling you?'" he asked, staring down at her. "What business is it of yours who she dates? If you want to talk about this evening, we'll do that. You were not one bit gracious to her, and I was embarrassed. She'll call you about those pecans, and see that you don't forget to tell me."

"You don't need her pecans. You can buy as many as you can use."

"Of course I can, but I also appreciate her neighborliness, and I wish you would. How about going out to Moe Robinson's place for some pizza and beer? I want something different."

"I'm dressed up like this to eat pizza and drink beer?" she asked him, looking aghast.

"You're always dressed up, sweetheart. Tonight, you're just a bit more so. Let's go." He knew he'd gotten to her, for she prided herself in always looking as perfect as possible. He pressed his finger against her right nipple and made a rotating motion. "You blush beautifully, and you look good, too," he said, ensuring for himself an hour of good loving when they returned home.

"Do you think she's better-looking than I am?"

So that was it. "Who? You mean Susan Pettiford? Baby, you've got to be joking."

Cassie couldn't know that Jay Weeks's sexual preferences were of no interest to Susan. She needed a date, and Jay was an acceptable man who she knew. "Let's take my car," Jay said to Susan as they walked away from the Shepherd residence. "If it wasn't Kix's night off, we could go to Gourmet Corner."

"I've heard so much about that place," Susan said. "Let's plan to go there."

"It's definitely not over-rated," Jay said.

They went to Sam's Gourmet Burger Castle after Jay said that, in view of Cassie's estimation of herself, it was unlikely that they would encounter her and Kix at a hamburger restaurant, gourmet or not. Instead, they met Lucas and Willis, who appeared to be having a "working" dinner. Susan waved to them and, although she couldn't figure out why, it annoyed her that Jay pretended not to see them.

"You could have said hello to my friends," she said to Jay.

"That's right. I could have," he replied.

This man can be bitchy, Susan thought. *He and Cassie would make a fine pair.* She decided then that she shouldn't spend too much time in Jay Weeks's company. *Lucas has been more than nice to me*, she thought, recalling his Christmas greeting and his thoughtfulness the night the snow storm caused a power outage.

"What was that all about?" Willis asked Lucas. "I thought she'd at least come over to say hi."

Lucas rapped the table lightly with his pen. "Unless she wanted to make a scene, how could she? Weeks continued walking when she tried to get his attention. I never did cotton to that guy."

"Me neither," Willis said. "I could do without that dude forever. Don't tell me that something's going on between those two."

"All right. I won't. She couldn't be that stupid."

In spite of her reservations about Cassie, the woman's invitation to cocktails provided an opportunity for socializing, for doing something other than working and sleeping, and Susan supposed she should be thankful for that. In New York, she'd enjoyed an active social life, although she couldn't claim many women friends.

She usually shunned women who were insecure about their men, as Cassie was about Kix. Nonetheless, she phoned Cassie the following morning and asked her to tell Kix to come for the pecans.

"Thanks, I'll let him know," Cassie said and added, "Darling, you looked smashing last night, much to lovely to be in the company of a man who has no interest in women."

Stunned by the woman's temerity, Susan stammered, temporarily at a loss for words. "Wh—what did you say?"

"You're wasting precious time with Jay, darling."

Best to ignore that. If I give her a taste of my razor tongue, we'll never be friends. "Let me know when Kix is coming over for these nuts," she said. "I've got to get to my shop. See you."

Tuesday afternoon at the end of the tutoring session, Susan walked with Rudy and Nathan down the corridor toward the front door. She noticed that Rudy's coat was not properly buttoned and stopped.

"Wait a second, Rudy. I'll button your coat." She knelt in front of the child and was securing the bottom button when Lucas entered the front door. Rudy opened both arms to Susan, who hugged the child, relishing the feel of that warm little body in her arms. As she released Rudy, she looked up into Lucas's censoring gaze.

"May I see you in my office, Ms. Pettiford, after you excuse the children?" His words, and especially his tone, brought to her mind a tongue-lashing she received from her third-grade teacher for having spread her arms and embraced a heavy spring rain.

"Uh . . . of course," she said, wondering what had displeased him this time. "I'll be there in . . . uh . . . five minutes."

"The door isn't locked," he said. "They can let themselves out of the building."

Didn't he understand that someone meets the other children and takes them home, and that Rudy has to walk that distance alone in the winter twilight?

Without responding verbally, she grasped the childrens hands and walked out of the building with them. "Wait a minute, Rudy," Nathan said. He climbed into his grandmother's car, spoke with her and got out of the car. "Miss Pettiford, you don't have to worry about Rudy. My nana and I will take her home."

Susan went around to the driver's side of the car and spoke with Ann Price. "Thank you so much for taking Rudy home. It's dangerous for her to be alone in the streets after dark."

"No problem, Miss Pettiford. Somebody doesn't care about her, and it's a pity."

Susan walked back inside, preparing herself for what she expected would be Lucas's fury. He waited for her a few steps from where she had left him. With his fists at his hips, and in a voice so quiet and calm as to be frightening, he said, "What do you think you're doing?"

"What do you mean?" He starting walking toward his office, so she stepped in stride with him.

"You're making that child dependent on you, and that little boy, too. They always leave with you, holding your hands."

"You need a course in humanness," she said as they entered his office. "I told you how these children treat Rudy. Nathan is the only one who doesn't, and he seemed to empathize with her, so I put them together in the front row. They have become friends, and Nathan is protective of her. She is the only one of these children who has no one to meet her and take her home. Imagine that six-year-old little girl walking from here to Salem Court and Market Street in the dark. I've been driving her home but, thanks to you, I couldn't do that tonight, so Nathan asked his grandmother if they could drive her home."

"I don't need a course in humaneness, Susan. I'm trying to do this job according to the rules. Even so, she will become too attached to you. I saw her hug you after you buttoned her coat."

"You can hardly call that rag a coat. It's almost threadbare, and two of the buttons are missing."

"I suppose you're planning to buy her another one."

She'd thought about it, and by damn, she'd do it. "Come to think of it, that wouldn't be a bad idea." His gaze softened, and his eyes took on that same haze that she saw for the first time when he released himself into her. A feeling of dizziness unbalanced her, like a sudden attack of vertigo, and she closed her eyes and grasped the arms of the chair.

"Susan, are you all right?" His voice had that same huskiness, that same loss-of-control tremor that she heard the first time he had her in his arms. Why was this happening to her, now that she had no right to embrace it? She reached down, picked up her pocketbook and briefcase and stood, praying that she could make it as far as the corridor.

"What is it? What's wrong?" he asked. But even as the words left his lips, he bounded out of his chair and rounded the desk.

"Don't. Please don't touch me. I . . . I have to go. I'm in a hurry."

"Don't lie to me. You're afraid of the way you'll feel in my arms. Aren't you? Tell me you've never remembered the way I made you feel. Say you don't ever think of the way you went wild beneath me. Tell me you don't want to have me buried to the hilt inside you. Tell me that, and you'll be a liar."

"Please. Let me go."

"Not until you tell me you haven't thought about it once since that night. Tell me, and you may go with my blessings!"

"All right. Damn you! I think about it all the time. But that's all I'm ever going to do about it. Think. Now—"

His hands gripped her shoulders, and seemingly of its own volition, her body moved to him, and she was tight in his arms. He stared down at her, and she couldn't stop the trembling of her lips and chin. Would he never . . .

"What are you waiting for?" Susan said in a voice she didn't recognize.

His mouth was on her then, hard and strong. And so sweet. She parted her lips, and he possessed her with one thrust of his tongue deep into her mouth, anointing every centimeter, testing and thrusting, simulating lovemaking, until her nerve ends seemed to ignite and hot blood raced to her loins. Suddenly, he moved away from her, though he didn't release her.

Annoyed and ashamed of the way she kissed and caressed him, she broke away, grabbed her bag and briefcase and ran to the door, but when she would have opened it, his hand closed over the knob.

"There's no point in running, Susan. This dance is not over."

She brushed a few strands of hair away from her face, an act that she knew betrayed her nervousness. "What you don't know, Lucas, is that it never started."

A half smile flashed across his face. "You're fooling yourself, and I just proved it."

Chapter Five

Lucas sat with Willis in his mother's living room after having consumed one of his favorite meals. He knew his mother pampered him, and he knew she did it not just because he'd built a beautiful, modern home for her and contributed to her support, although she worked at the post office as she had for years. Love overflowed from Noreen Hamilton, and apart from himself and Willis, who she had embraced when Lucas brought him home from college the Thanksgiving weekend of their freshman year, and himself, she had no one on which to lavish it. He had stopped hinting that she should find someone who loved her and who she loved and marry or affect another suitable arrangement, for he had come to realize that his mother still loved Calvin Jackson, and would never commit to another man.

Willis went into the kitchen, returned with two mugs of coffee and placed one in front of Noreen. "The coffeepot's on the counter," he said to Lucas. "I don't have but two hands."

Lucas got the coffee and returned as Willis flipped on the television and tuned in the evening news. "Stay tuned for today's financial tips," droned the blonde female with pale pink lips, flawless makeup and hair in stiff strands framing her face with its ends meeting under her chin. "Good evening, Mr. Jackson," she said minutes later. Welcome to *Piedmont News*." She turned to face the camera. "We're delighted to have with us this evening Forsyth County's own success story. As a black American who made it big, what advice would you give to young blacks who want to follow in your footsteps?"

Lucas sat forward, as alert as a bulldog who'd caught a stranger's scent. He'd seen the man on television and his picture in newspapers and magazines a number of times, and always that tenor of resentment surfaced in him. Yet, he had an unexplainable sense of pride in the quality of his origins, in knowing that he had probably inherited from Calvin Jackson the skills and the mother wit that propelled him to success as an architect at the young age of thirty-five.

The condescending smile on Calvin Jackson's face and what he was sure it portended reminded Lucas of himself when he was about to put someone in his place. He watched, transfixed, as Jackson leaned back in his chair and appeared to get comfortable. It was a trait he recognized in himself. "As a plain old American who fought his way to the top in spite of the social obstacles in my way," Jackson said, "I advise any young person to get an education, adopt high moral values, especially integrity, and work hard. If society, or any of its members, puts a stone in your path, move it, and keep going. Avoid alcohol, except for modest amounts on social occasions, and don't use drugs. They'll eventually kill you."

Lucas laughed aloud. The red-faced woman obviously didn't want to hear that. When he would have commented to his mother, he became aware that she had left the room.

"Something wrong with her, Lucas?" Willis asked him. "I mean, does your father still get to her, or is she mad at him?"

"Both."

"That's too bad. You'd think that after all these years, they could at least be friends," Willis said.

"Not a chance, man. She loves him, and she hates him."

Willis went to the bar and helped himself to a snifter of cognac. "That's tough. You look so much like him, that she must have been miserable whenever she looked at you."

"That's what I thought, but she said holding me was like holding him."

"Damn! I don't want any part of that love business."

Lucas flipped off the television and prepared to leave. "I

wouldn't say that. It's hell when it goes sour, but when it swings right, there's nothing like it."

Willis put an arm on Lucas's shoulder. "Would it hurt you to give your old man a call and have a drink with him? He must be at least seventy years old by now."

"Would it hurt him to do the same? He's seventy-one, and that day will come as soon as we complete Hamilton Village. I want to meet him as an equal."

"You may be his equal now."

Lucas kicked at the carpet. "Not yet. I keep tabs on every step he takes, and I've done it for years. I'd better find Mama and tell her good-bye so we can go."

"Willis and I are leaving, Mom," he said to Noreen when he found her in her bedroom, sitting on the edge of her bed with her back to the door. "Say, what's going on here? Seeing him on the air didn't upset you, did it?"

"You're so much like him. You stand, sit and walk like him. I don't want you to ruin some girl's life like . . ."

She didn't finish it and she needn't have. He sat beside her. "I'm as much a part of this and as much a victim of it as you are. I see the results maybe more clearly than either you or he, and I have no intention of fathering a child that I don't raise. Unless death intervened, it would never happen. Period. So don't let that enter your head. Now, cheer up. I'll call you." He kissed her cheek and loped down the stairs where Willis waited.

"Is she upset?"

"A little, but she'll snap out of it."

"Do you think it's a good time for us to leave?" Willis asked Lucas. "Right now, when she's upset?"

"She's not that distraught. Go tell her good-bye."

Later, sitting in the comfort of his own home, Lucas couldn't help focusing upon Susan and their strange relationship. When the weather warmed up and she didn't wear a coat or a suit, would he see her belly protruding? And what if he did?

"Hell! I don't even want to think about that possibility. I'd hate to take her to court, but that's where we'd go."

* * *

It occurred to Lucas that he could ask Susan if pregnancy was a possibility, since the passing of three months following their sexual romp was sufficient to verify the presence or absence of conception. His opportunity to do so came sooner than he expected.

One Sunday morning in late January, believing that pools would be empty or nearly so at that time, Susan decided to swim at one of the local hotels. She prided herself on being an excellent swimmer and enjoyed the water, but she had low tolerance for crowded pools. She adjusted the straps of her red bikini swim suit, threw the white terry cloth robe on the white-slatted chaise longue and prepared to dive when she glimpsed Lucas, who was about to do the same.

Like a stalking Adonis, he walked over to her, cataloguing her assets, his gaze ablaze with unmistakable desire. She struggled to shake off the effect of his unexpected presence. Surely the fact that he'd made mind-boggling love to her just once shouldn't send shivers throughout her body every time he came near her. She swung around, grabbed her robe and started for the exit, but he placed a heavy hand on her arm.

"Don't let my presence deprive you of an enjoyable swim. What do you say we dive in together? I'll race you one length."

Susan loved a challenge as much as she loved to swim. She threw the robe back on the chaise longue. "Let's go."

She didn't beat him to the end of the pool, but she arrived there only a few strokes behind him. "You're first class," she said.

"So are you. Coffee's pretty good in that coffee shop over there. Want to?"

She was out of breath and didn't pretend not to be. "All right. I guess I have enough air to walk fifty feet."

"You'd better. Otherwise, I'll carry you."

It occurred to her that they hadn't previously bantered with each other. Maybe less seriousness would make them less sexually aware. But Lord, looking at him almost bulging out of those bathing trunks wasn't doing a thing to cool off her libido. At the coffee shop, she sat down quickly, knowing that he would sit and take temptation away from her eyes. Instead, he strolled over to the counter and alerted the waiter.

"I'm glad I ran into you," Lucas said. "I've got something I want to ask you, and I should have asked you some time ago."

Her antenna shot up. He had already asked her at least twice why she went to bed with him. *What could he have in mind?* "What's the question?" she asked him.

He shifted in his chair a little, as if he were preparing himself for a long session. And maybe he was. She realized that, in spite of their intimacies, she knew almost nothing about him, and when his gaze penetrated her with dagger-like sharpness, she began to feel uncomfortable, sliding deeper into his orbit than was good for her.

"What's the question?" she asked again.

"Is there a likelihood that you could be pregnant?"

Her gasp must have shocked him, for his eyes widened. The likelihood was so remote that his concern about that possibility had not occurred to her. She hastened to put him at ease. "None at all, but thank you for asking. I'm sure it's a relief to you."

His slow, barely perceptible shrug did not confirm relief. "I don't know. It would have meant a substantial readjustment in my life, but I certainly would have made it."

She didn't try to disguise her reaction, and a deep frown altered the contours of her face. Yes, she thought. He would have proposed that they marry and raise his child together. He'd do the gentlemanly thing even if it destroyed his chance for happiness with someone else. And she had to meet such a man when he could never be more to her than an acquaintance or, at best, an occasional bed mate.

"Well," she said. "That won't be necessary. How do I get to Winston-Salem?" she asked, hoping to change the subject lest he ask her if she wanted children.

"Highway 52 West. If you've never been there, allow yourself time to visit Old Salem. It's an authentic living-history town and has an interesting and important African American story very much unlike that elsewhere in the state or in all of the Antebellum South."

"I take it you've visited Old Salem."

"I have," he said, "and if you can go on a Saturday, I'll be glad to show you around there. The place has always fascinated me."

"I'd like that very much. Tell me, Lucas," she said, for the thought plagued her. "Would you really marry a woman you hardly knew just because you discovered that she carried your child?"

"Damn right I would. That's more than my father did for my mother after a four-year affair."

"I know. You told me. But should you feel bitter toward him? Was it entirely his fault?"

"No, and I never said it was. But he was years older than my mother and far more experienced, a married man, and she was no match for him. She loved him. Still does, for that matter, although she hasn't seen him in person since before I was born."

"Good Lord! That's . . . that's frightening. Have you ever had the urge to find him and—"

"Flatten him?" He socked his left palm with his right fist. "Plenty of times. Funny thing is that I resent her more than him. She wouldn't allow him any parental rights, not even to see me, and she moved from Danville, Virginia to Woodmore before I was born, to prevent either of us from having any contact with him."

"Don't judge her too harshly. Can you imagine going through that alone, without the support of the man you loved? Even the thought gives me chills."

"Is Willis related to you and your mother?"

He laughed. "Sometimes I think he wishes that he was. I brought him home from school with me when we were college freshmen, and they've been tight ever since. She mothers him, and he tries to be a son to her. Why didn't your mother come home for Christmas? Doesn't she get leave?"

"At one point, she said she'd be home for the holidays, but someone needed her. I think she can't face being here without my father. She's escaping reality. I miss her, but I've been alone so long that I . . ." She'd said more than she planned to say. "Oh, well. It's getting late."

"Is that why you spend time with Jay Weeks? I'd be surprised if you had a lot in common with him."

"I don't, and he annoyed me when he wouldn't wait while I said hello to you and Mr. Carter at Sam's Gourmet Burger Castle." She made the mistake then of looking him in the eye, and at that moment, their real and personal contact shook her. She had a feeling that her limbs would sever themselves from her body, and her once warm flesh shivered as if caught in a draft of north-winter wind. She took a deep breath and composed herself. Making love with a man who knew what he was doing created a bond whether or not a tie with him was wanted. She'd been foolish not to have realized that.

"Hmm. I wondered about that," he said. "What do you say we visit Old Salem next Saturday? If it's a nice day, we'll see it as it was in the eighteenth century with townspeople dressed as they did in those days, going about their daily lives, with transportation by horse and buggy. Back then, most people were Moravians. African Americans who converted to that faith worshipped with the Europeans and were buried in the same cemetaries as they. After several outbreaks among African Americans, they established their own church in 1822, and the Moravians mandated racial segregation in 1823. The place is steeped in history."

"I shall definitely look forward to it. I haven't seen any of the places surrounding Woodmore."

"Winston-Salem is about forty-minutes from here."

Susan stood. "Coffee's on me."

When Lucas seemed startled, she laughed. "Next time you'll pay, and it will be much more expensive."

"I imagine it will," he said dryly, as if she'd just said "checkmate" in a hard-fought game of chess.

At nine o'clock the following Saturday morning, when Susan opened the door of her house to Lucas, she wore her coat and boots, her scarf wound around her neck, and her pocketbook hung from her shoulder.

"Are you always so punctual?" he asked after she greeted him, "or are you telling me you don't want us to linger here?"

Candid, was he? Well, honesty never hurt anyone. "Since you mention it, possibly some of both. You ready?"

He squeezed both eyes together in his version of a wink, a gesture that she found increasingly endearing. "I'm ready. I hope you trust me to drive. Would you mind if I detoured past Pine Tree Park East? We won't stop, or at least I hope we won't have to."

"I don't mind. What's over there? You don't mean the marshlands, do you?"

"No. It's northeast of the marshlands. I'm building a village there that has health and recreation facilities. It's designed for retirees."

He drove along Wright Road, took the underpass beneath Bakers Bridge to the east bank of the Salem River, and she marveled that he waited calmly while a pair of equestrians trotted their horses leisurely across the road, and did the same minutes later when a dog-lover strolled in front of the car with half a dozen identical terriers. In neither case did he display an eagerness to move on, but waited with evident patience.

She commented on his sangfroid, and he replied, "What's the point in getting shook up? I couldn't run over them. Whenever I can repair a situation that's not to my liking, I do it. If I can't change it, I either accept it or walk away from it. I try not to stress myself attempting the impossible." Those words told her much about him, but they seemed to belie his dogged tenacity about their night together. "Well, what do you think?" he asked her of the structure rising on the river's east bank.

She hadn't imagined a retirement village with the potential for elegance. "I'm impressed. I'd like to see it again six weeks from now when the brick walls are up."

"So would I. I think Woodmore is the perfect place for a retirement village, and I can't believe no other builder has considered it."

"You're the architect as well as the builder?"

"Willis is the builder. I own a share of the building company."

Yes, she thought, as it dawned on her that Lucas's part ownership of the building company explained the modest amount she paid for the work on her shop and her kitchen. *If I want this day to pass smoothly, I'd better not allude to that*, she told herself.

It surprised her that Lucas had such a wealth of information about Old Salem, and she eagerly encouraged him to tell her about the lives of people who might have been her ancestors.

"This is God's Acre," he said of the graveyard. "The first burials here were of Moravians in 1771. In its oldest section, African American and European Moravians were buried side by side. As I told you earlier, segregation took place in the nineteenth century. You know, it seems to me that the Moravians gradually adopted the attitudes of other southerners. They opened a school for girls in 1772, and in 1785, admitted an African American student, daughter of a baptized Moravian. Today, it's known as Salem Academy and College.

He drove down Main Street to the corner of West Street, parked and walked with her past houses, former schools and churches that were once a part of African American life, institutions that helped to spawn the new-world African American culture.

"I wouldn't have missed this. It would be a nice excursion for my students," she said. "But I don't know if they could grasp it. Junior high level might be more appropriate."

"They would probably enjoy seeing the old method of weaving, and making other hand crafts, and they would certainly enjoy being back in the eighteenth century."

They walked back to his car, seated themselves, and he drove through Winston-Salem slowly so that she could acquaint herself with the city. "You really enjoy the tutoring, don't you?" he asked her.

"I do. It surprises me that I never considered teaching."

"Don't get too attached to them, Susan. They belong to someone else and can be snatched from you at any time. So be careful."

His words had the impact of a sculptor striking stone. They and children like them were the only children she would ever have. She didn't respond to him. She couldn't.

* * *

The following Tuesday afternoon, as Lucas entered Wade School, he saw Rudy and Nathan standing beside their classroom door holding hands. He remembered Susan having said that the children abused Rudy because of her outdated and tattered old clothes, so he stopped and greeted them, hoping to make them feel special.

"Hello, I'm Mr. Hamilton, your principal. Are you waiting for your tutor?"

"Yes, sir," they said in unison.

Rudy's smile revealed one captivating dimple. "We always wait for her right here," she said.

Nathan seemed uneasy. "Can we stay right here and wait for Miss Pettiford, Mr. Hamilton?"

He let his gaze roam over Rudy, taking in her red coat, obviously new and very elegant. "You don't want to wait in the classroom?" he asked them.

The children looked first at each other and then at him. "She'll be here soon," Rudy said.

Without a guard at the door, he didn't think it a good idea for them to stand in the hall. "There's a cold draft from that front door. Come down to my office and wait there. I'll let her know where you are."

Nathan showed reluctance, and to encourage the child's cautiousness, he took his badge from the pocket of his jacket, and handed it to the boy. "That satisfy you?"

It amused him that Nathan scrutinized both him and the badge. "Yes, sir."

The children walked on either side of him holding his hands, and he had a strangely protective feeling toward them, an emotion that he had not previously experienced. And how odd it was. His thoughts of fatherhood hadn't gone beyond the joy of holding and nurturing his own son or daughter. But as he walked with two vulnerable children who were not his own, but who trusted him to care for their well-being, it occurred to him that fatherhood didn't necessarily involve a man's genes.

In his office, the children sat together in a big leather chair, still holding hands as if they needed each other. He dialed Susan's cell phone number. "This is Lucas. Rudy and Nathan are waiting for you in my office. It's rather cold on that end of the corridor." He listened for a second and then said to the children. "She'll be down here in a few minutes."

He stood to greet Susan when she entered his office, and both children jumped up from the chair, ran to her and hugged her. Susan's expression of joy at their welcome made his heartbeat accelerate. "Thanks for taking care of my charges," she said to him and opened the door to leave.

However, Rudy ran back to him and hugged his leg. "Thank you, Mr. Hamilton."

"You're welcome." He watched the three of them leave, holding hands with the children skipping happily along.

"Both of those children love Susan, and she loves them," he said to himself. Furthermore, Rudy's new coat was a gift from her. He'd bet anything on it. They needed her, and he was beginning to suspect that she needed them. *It's irregular. What the hell am I supposed to do?*

Somewhat bemused and suffering a rash of internal conflict—a rarity for him—Lucas excused his class five minutes before the scheduled time and went down to Susan's classroom, arriving there as her pupils jumped up from their seats and bolted for the door. When he entered, Rudy and Nathan smiled and rushed to him, and he experienced an attack of guilt about what he was obliged to do.

He greeted the children with a pat on their shoulders, but that did not satisfy Rudy, who reached for his hand. He looked down at the child whose trusting smile planted a seed somewhere deep in him.

"Who's taking these two home?" he asked Susan.

"My grandmother," Nathan said before Susan could reply.

"We'd better be certain that she's here," he said to Nathan.

The boy took Rudy's hand. "She always comes," he said.

They left the children in Ann Price's care, and stood in the darkness on the barren acreage of what had once been one of Woodmore's most vibrant social and educational centers. For the first time in his life, his emotions interfered with his head. He ought to tell her that further involvement with her pupils would result in her being asked to withdraw from the tutoring program. Reason told him to back off from her, that she didn't plan to level with him and answer the question that had begun to haunt him. She looked at him, expectantly, he thought. *Oh, no. The thing for him to do was get into his car and go home.*

"Drive carefully," he said. "Be seeing you."

He was safe then, but he soon had reason to wonder if agreeing to volunteer his time as principal of the tutoring program would have a lasting affect upon his personal life. Fate seemed determined to lock him into her clutches. He arrived at Wade School for the next tutoring session to find Rudy standing alone at the door of Susan's classroom.

"Hello, Rudy," he greeted the little girl, whose face immediately bloomed into a smile. "Where's Nathan?"

At his question, the child's eyes clouded with unshed tears. "He didn't come to school today. His grandmother said he has a real bad cold."

"Want to wait in my office until Miss Pettiford comes?"

She reached for his hand. "Yes, sir."

"You didn't walk all the way from Rose Hill School, did you? How'd you get here?"

"I used to walk, but Nathan's grandmother brings me along with him. She brought me today. That's when she told me he's sick."

"She seems like a wonderful lady."

"Yes, sir. She loves Nathan."

He heard the unspoken message. Someone who loved her was lacking in Rudy's life. "That's a pretty coat you're wearing."

She rubbed the sleeves and patted the pockets. "I love it. Miss Pettiford bought it for me. It's nice."

"Do you have brothers and sisters?" he asked her, hoping to learn more about her life.

"No, sir, but I have foster sisters and brothers. I don't like my oldest foster sister, 'cause she's not nice. She told me someone found me in an alley, and that my real mother left me there 'cause she didn't want me."

"You're a lovely little girl," he said, feeling helpless to comfort her. "I don't believe that anyone wouldn't love you. Try to ignore your foster sister if she says unkind things."

"But she's mean all the time, Mr. Hamilton."

He leaned forward and had to resist cradling her when tears spilled down her cheeks. "Some day, she will regret mistreating you. Try not to be angry with her." What else could he say without fanning the coals of an ugly situation. "What is the name of your teacher at Rose Hill?"

"Miss Brown."

He looked at his watch. "Let's see if Miss Pettiford has arrived." It didn't surprise him that Rudy reached for his hand as soon as he stood. She seemed to enjoy emotional security from the comfort and warmth of his hand. No wonder Susan paid her special attention.

He left her with Susan, and the next afternoon, went to Rose Hill to speak with Rudy's teacher.

"I don't think she needs tutoring any longer, Mr. Hamilton. It's worked wonders. The child's making A's and B's in all her classes."

"She's improving as much for emotional as academic reasons," he told the woman. "She has a new friend in Nathan, a six-year-old boy who is very protective of her, and most especially, she's in a tutoring class of only twelve children with a tutor who mothers her. She's responding to that little friend and to the mothering that she's apparently never had. If she leaves the tutoring session, her grades may drop."

Ms. Brown pursed her lips, pushed her glasses higher on the bridge of her nose and looked hard at him. "Are you saying she's not happy at home?"

He frowned and didn't care if she saw it. A teacher should know about a child's home environment. "Ms. Brown, Rudy is a foster child who has lived in a series of foster homes, and she is not happy in this one."

The woman's eyes widened. "What's wrong in that home?"

"I questioned Rudy, and her answers suggested that love wasn't something she received there. Moreover, I'm sure the State provides money for her clothing, but you know how she's dressed when she comes to school."

"Yes, but I thought she was from a poor family. I'll look into it. But . . . she just got a new coat."

"Yes, her tutor bought it, because the one she wore was a rag."

"Yes," the woman released the word slowly. "This explains a lot. Thank you for coming, Mr. Hamilton. I'll watch this more closely."

After the end of the next tutoring session, Lucas stood with Susan beside the concrete steps of the old schoolhouse. "Do you have any plans for this evening?" he asked her and was immediately aware that his question had unsteadied her. "I'd like us to talk for a few minutes, Susan, but if you don't want to do that in more apt surroundings, we can talk right here."

He could tell that she anticipated his concern and the reason for it. "I don't want to hurt you," he began, "but it's my duty to tell you that you're overstepping the line with Rudy. You bought her a coat. I know she needed one, and I can't blame you for doing that, but she's becoming emotionally dependent upon you, and you've been cautioned against that."

She turned her back to him, and he walked around to face her, certain that she was at that moment experiencing emotional turmoil. "What if you become deeply attached to her and she's suddenly taken from you? Don't you see the danger in this?"

She nodded, but didn't speak, and he supposed that she couldn't for fear of breaking down. He strove hard not to take her into his arms and comfort her, for if he did, it would be tantamount to pouring oil on a fire that he was already having trouble extinguishing.

"Do you want to eat somewhere?" he asked in an attempt to put her at ease.

"Thanks, but I think I'll go on home."

"But you haven't eaten. Follow me to Gourmet Corner. The place is homey and attractive, and the food would enliven the most dour saint."

She smiled at that. "All right. You're a very persuasive man. I'll follow you."

He couldn't help laughing at the thought that flickered across his mind. If there ever was a woman who didn't fit that mold, it was Susan Pettiford. *Where are you going, how are you getting there and how long will you stay?* were the words a man could expect from an independent woman such as Susan.

"I'm honored," he said, aware that she wouldn't understand the full meaning of his words. "Let's go."

They entered the anteroom of the restaurant, where a waiter served patrons a complimentary glass of wine, just as Cassandra Hairston-Shepherd seated herself in a big chair near the fireplace. She accepted a glass of white wine from the waiter, lifted it to her lips, and at about the same time as her gaze captured Susan, she smiled and waved.

"She lives next door to you. Is she a friend of yours?" he said to Susan.

"Not yet, and I have my doubts as to whether she intends to be."

At his raised eyebrow, she continued. "And I haven't decided that I want her for a friend. I generally avoid women who are insecure about their husbands."

"She's smooth-looking. Why should she worry about other women? Does he have a roving eye?"

"Not that I noticed. But something isn't quite right with them." At that moment, Kix came into the room, walked directly to his wife at what Lucas figured was her usual seat and kissed her cheek. He sat down, but didn't accept wine. They exchanged a few words, and he looked in their direction.

"I think he's going to invite us to join them," Lucas said. "Do you want to?" She only had time to lift her right shoulder in a quick shrug.

"It's great to see you here, Susan," Kix said as he came to stand beside her. "It's been a while, Hamilton. I hope you'll come more often. Would you two join my wife and me for dinner?"

He looked at Susan for her reaction, and when she smiled, he said to Kix, "We'd love to."

"I'm still waiting for those pecans," Kix said to Susan at the end of the meal. When Susan looked at Cassandra and didn't say a word, Lucas couldn't miss the distaste in Cassandra's stare; it had the force of an electric charge. Kix leaned back in his chair and censored Cassie with a glare. "You didn't tell me that Susan had the pecans ready for me."

"Honey, I forgot. You know how busy I've been with my efforts to get that deanship." She looked directly at Lucas. "My company, Cutting Edge Stationers and Engravers, is opening a school of fine arts, and I'm up for the deanship. I don't have any real competition, but you know how it is when one contender is a man and the other is a woman. It's the story of my professional life.

The woman was sharp. She had skillfully changed the subject from her failure to give her husband a message to her campaign for a promotion. But Kix Shepherd had not been distracted. "When will it be convenient for me to get them, Susan?"

Susan didn't look at Cassandra, and Lucas didn't blame her. "I leave for my shop at eight-thirty weekday mornings, so any morning between eight-fifteen and eight-thirty will be fine. No need to call first; I'll be ready to step out of the door."

What a woman! Lucas thought, translating Susan's words to mean: No need to worry about your man where I'm concerned. He could see why a woman who wasn't sure of her man wouldn't want him with Susan. Because Susan was a knockout. But he'd be very surprised if Kix Shepherd was a womanizer. Still, something wasn't right in that marriage.

"How about tomorrow morning?" Kix said. "And I'll leave a pecan pie at your front door Thursday morning." He looked at Lucas. "I hope you have a chance to taste it, and if she has whipped cream for it, so much the better."

"Thanks. If she doesn't share it with me, she'll be in trouble. Thanks for a delightful dinner. Next time, it's on me." He looked at Susan. "Shall we go?"

If he'd ever seen a manufactured smile, Susan wore it. "Of course. Thanks so much," she said, not looking at either of them until she smiled at Kix. "I'll look forward to that pie. Good night."

"I figured some things out," he said to Susan as they stood beside her car. "You gave her a message for Kix, and she didn't deliver it, right?"

"Exactly. And she didn't forget it, either. I don't know what her problem is, but she needn't worry about me. I don't want her man or anybody else's."

"You rammed that at her so hard that I almost felt sorry for her. I'm coming over for some pecan pie. I love that stuff."

"If it's up to the standard of that dinner we had tonight, it will be worth the calories," Susan said.

Lucas cocked his head to the side and looked down at her. Her eyes sparkled in the moonlight, the vapor of her breath curled skyward as she talked, and the tip of her tongue moistened the center of her upper lip. He imagined that even in the crisp winter night, her lips would be warm and her body a furnace that could heat him to boiling point. Damn his treacherous thoughts!

He winked at her. "If you know it's not good for you, it's rarely worth the consequence. This time, I'll trail *you*."

"They make a nice couple," Cassie said to Kix after Lucas and Susan left. "At least he's a man, which is more than I would say of Jay Weeks."

Kix looked at her as if he were scrutinizing her for evidence of a deadly disease, a certain sign of his displeasure. "I had no idea that you were so familiar with Weeks that he confided in you his sexual preferences," he said.

"Well, anybody can see it, and in addition, he's a decorator."

"Yeah. Pure gospel. Jerry Mulligan was a great jazz saxophonist. Did that make him black? He was as blond as they get. Let's stick to the truth. I knew you weren't anxious for me to go to Susan's house for those pecans, and that is precisely why I asked her to let you know when they were ready. I'm sure you know you lost some points with her, though I suppose you don't care. But you lost some with me, too, and turning the sex on tonight is not going to fix it.

"I've never given you reason to distrust me." She winced at that reminder of her infidelity, a one-time act that he suspected she would give anything to erase. "And those pecans—wonderfully plump and fresh—are for my restaurant," he went on, "yet you don't care if I don't get them."

"I know it's hard for you to forgive what I did, but—"

"I forgave you ages ago, so let's not harp on that. We're talking about your failure to give me a message."

"Well, you'll have your pecans tomorrow morning. What do you think of Lucas Hamilton?" she asked her husband, expecting confirmation of her conclusion that she had misjudged Susan Pettiford. The woman wasn't on the make; indeed, with a man like Lucas Hamilton hot for her—as he apparently was—what other man did she need?

Kix flexed his right shoulder and beckoned a waiter. "Hamilton's a solid citizen. Why do you ask?"

"No special reason, except that he seemed more interested in her than she was in him."

"Really? I didn't pay that much attention to him. Shall we go?"

"Sure." *He'll make the first move tonight*, Cassandra thought. *He accused me of using sex to smooth out our differences. Well, not tonight. I won't, no matter how much he wants it. He doesn't hold the trump card; I do.*

"Has a decision been made about the head of that fine arts institute or whatever it's called?"

"Not yet. They're still interviewing. I'll—"

He held up both hands, palms out. "Just checking."

"You know I'd tell you," she said.

"Hmmm. And if you don't, *The Woodmore Times* will."

"Oh, Kix," she said, needing to have again the sweet and loving man who catered to her every whim and to whom she had once felt superior. But she made one mistake with a man who wore brogans, and had at least a hundred keys dangling from the pocket of his jeans and had never had a manicure, an arrogant electrician. She wished it hadn't happened, but she couldn't say she was *Godly* sorry, because the man introduced her to her raw, sexual potential, and from then on, Kix never had to beg her. She *was* Godly sorry that, until then, she'd been a prude and hadn't allowed her husband to teach her all that lovemaking could be for the two of them.

Lord, I've been a fool! She reached over and patted her husband's hand, and he glanced at her, but didn't reciprocate.

Her moment of contrition forgotten, concern for self reasserted itself. *Nothing will placate this man but to see my belly sticking a yard out in front of me.*

Cassie was not the only one with concerns about what Lucas meant to Susan; the more he saw of Susan, the more anxious Lucas became to learn if their pairing could be duplicated. Indeed, getting a satisfactory explanation as to why she orchestrated that evening was becoming a priority for him. She parked in front of her house, and he stopped directly behind her, got out of his car and walked with her to her front door.

"You don't want anything else to happen between us, and at first I didn't either. Now, I'm not so sure. You built a fire in me, and I suspect you're the one who'll have to put it out." Her face distorted itself into a deep frown. "You seem horrified at the thought? Why?" He put his hands on her shoulders and eased her body closer to his. "I'm the same man you made wild love to. What's so different now?"

"Please . . . I—"

"Don't tell me that a gentleman wouldn't mention it. Hell! Any man would. I told you once that this dance is not over. Well, I'm telling you now that it has just begun. And if I have to play dirty pool, I damned well know how." Her lips quivered, he didn't know whether from anger or passion, and he didn't let his mind linger on it, but bent to them and let her feel the force of his own passion.

"I'll see you Thursday, if not sooner."

He waited until she was inside her house and he heard the lock turn. Then, he walked down to the lake, desolate and haunting in the moonlight. *She gets to me, but is that because she's a challenge? Or is it because she's . . .* He looked for the word and decided that mysterious most aptly described her. "Naaa!" He picked up a stone, tossed it into the lake, went back to his car and drove home.

The blinking red light on his answering machine was the first thing he saw when he walked into his bedroom. He sat on the chair beside his night table and picked up the receiver. "This is Attorney Arnold Baumann. My client, Calvin Jackson, asked me to be in touch with you. Would you please call my office at this number?" By the time he heard that last sentence, Lucas was standing up. He replayed the message to be sure he'd heard correctly, wrote down the phone number and prepared to spend a sleepless night as hundreds of questions filled his thoughts, the most distressing of which was whether his father had died.

Chapter Six

Daybreak finally came, and Lucas dragged himself out of the disheveled bed, an unfriendly parking place in which he had struggled for sleep throughout the night, but to no avail. He fumbled his way to the bathroom, showered and then opened his eyes fully. He had two long hours in which to wonder whether he'd waited too long, and would never meet his father face to face, never question him as to why he didn't overrule Noreen Hamilton, and never tell him how a boy felt growing up without the care and guidance of a father.

"Hell, I'm not going to get maudlin here," he said aloud. Growing up with only his mother had been heaven compared to what Rudy was experiencing without either parent. He shook his head as he tried to imagine living as a child with complete strangers whose interest in you was limited to the income earned for taking care of you. At least, he had not suffered that. He had an urge to telephone Susan, but for what reason and what would he say to her? Anyhow, why should he dump his anxiety on another person?

Two hours and five cups of coffee later, he went to his den, sat in his Barcelona chair, the only thing he owned that his favorite architect, Mies van der Rohe, designed. He bought the chair with money from the first building that he designed, and sitting in it always brought to the fore his pride in what he had managed to achieve. He dialed Arnold Baumann's telephone number.

"Good morning, Mr. Baumann. This is Lucas Hamilton returning your call. What may I do for you?"

"Thanks for getting back to me so soon. I'm Calvin Jackson's attorney. He asked me to call you."

A streak of annoyance shot through Lucas, and he made no attempt to hide it. "I understood that much from the message you left me."

"He said he hoped I'd be able to persuade you to come to see him."

"Really? I don't suppose it occurred to him that had he made the call himself, he'd stand a better chance of speaking with me."

"He's ill, Mr. Hamilton, and he wants you to go to the hospital to see him. Today, if you can make it."

Lucas sat forward, every nerve in his body tingling with anticipation. "What's wrong with him, and how serious is it?"

"I'd better let him tell you. He's at General Hospital, suite A-6. May I tell him to expect you?"

Lucas was standing now, his left fist balled and eyes narrowed, grinding his teeth. "What do you know about Calvin Jackson's relationship to me, Mr. Baumann? Why the hell should I go running to him the first time since the day I was born that he makes an effort to get in touch with me? All he's ever done for me was shove me into my mother's womb. Period. In all of my thirty-five years, he's never said one damned word to me, although he's always known where I was. I'll visit him when I damned well please. If at all."

"He said this would probably be your reaction. He knows everything about you, all you've done and what you're doing now, and he has always known. He asked me to tell you that he had never excused himself and never forgiven himself, and that he wants to hear whatever you have to say to him."

"*You don't say,*" Lucas sneered. "Well, I hope he doesn't have a heart condition. I'll think about it."

"I do hope you will visit him soon. If you don't, you may regret it."

Lucas hung up and dropped himself into the chair. All his adult life, Lucas swore he'd meet his father on his own terms; but now he had to meet the son-of-a-bitch on *his* terms. But he wouldn't make it easy for him. After a few minutes, Lucas composed himself, went to the kitchen, drank another cup of coffee and phoned Willis.

"Sorry, buddy, but I can't meet with you and the engineer this afternoon. I have to go to Danville."

"No problem, Lucas. We've finished the wiring and plumbing, and today we'll be working on the windows and flooring. If I don't have to deal with the next unit for a couple of days, I won't mind a bit. We can step up the advertising for this unit."

"You're that far?"

"Yeah. We can put the floor plans on the Internet."

"Right on, Willis. You don't know how good that makes me feel."

"I don't? You didn't expect us to blow it did you? Anything you know that I don't? That I ought to know, that is?"

"That depends. Let's meet for dinner. You're paying. I always pay, but you're making money now, so you pay, and I want to go to a first class restaurant."

"If I'm paying, we go to the joint of my choice. See you at your place around seven."

He hung up, went to his office above his garage and switched on the lights. The low-hanging dark clouds and the dreariness of the morning robbed him of the eagerness with which he always approached his work. He put on a CD hoping that Mozart's joyous music might lift his mood, but it gave him no relief. He didn't want to talk with his mother, because she would immediately advise him to do or say something that reflected her thoughts and feelings rather than his. He reached up, yanked his old mackinaw jacket from a hanger, put it on and headed across the street to Pine Tree Park.

The place offered for him a comforting isolation from the people, problems and concerns that weighed upon his mind and soul, and it was his love for that park that had prompted him to build his house facing it. He found peanuts in the pockets of his jacket, threw out a couple near the base of a pine tree and almost immediately two squirrels found them and came to him for more. He couldn't hear his footsteps as he walked, for the earth's heavy blanket of leaves cushioned the sound. He ambled along until he reached a man-made stream whose source was the Salem River and which, after a few loops in the park, ended in the river. He sat for a while on the trunk of a fallen tree, letting the cold air seep through his jacket and into his body.

I've never felt as if I were a victim, and I am not going to sink into that now. My mother wasn't a victim either; she had an affair with another woman's husband. My father was the age I am now, and he had a wife who he was living with and deceiving. So I don't see how the hell he could be a victim, no matter how vindictive my mother was. He shook his head as if in wonder.

He got up, hunched over against the wind and made his way back home. Never one to procrastinate for long, he shaved, polished his black shoes, and dressed in a gray pinstripe suit, light-gray shirt and red and gray paisley tie, got into his town car and headed for Danville, Virginia. What would he say to the man? After all these year's of dreaming of a confrontation, of clever sayings and examples of a curt one-upmanship, his mind was blank. As he mused over his absence of pertinent ideas, it occurred to him that he was responding to the situation as a mature man, rather than as a wounded child who, in his subconscious, he may have regarded himself.

"I'll take it as it comes," he said to himself. "At least he's still alive." But he would have preferred to meet the man when he was on his feet, and they stood toe to toe, measuring each other.

Susan opened the stationery that Cassie designed for her and gaped at the exquisite letterhead: tiny bolts of fabric lying across an elegant brown sofa beneath the name and address of Susan's company. A beige border with gold flecks enlivened the sand-colored paper. She telephoned Cassie.

"Mrs. Hairston-Shepherd speaking."

Each time she heard Cassie say that, Susan had trouble resisting a rude response. "Hi, Cassie. This is Susan. I've just opened the stationery, and I'm practically speechless. This is the most gorgeous . . . it's fantastic. I love it."

"I'm glad you're pleased. I figured you wanted something that was both feminine and very professional."

"I did, and that's what you sent me. I couldn't be more delighted."

"Thanks for letting me know, Susan. I'm always happy when my work pleases. Your shop isn't too far from Cutting Edge Stationers and Engravers. Would you like to meet for lunch. I usually bring a sandwich, since there's nobody here that I like to socialize with."

This woman was a chameleon if one ever existed. A doll today and a witch tomorrow. "Great. Let's meet at Sam's Gourmet Burger Castle, unless you know a better place. How about one o'clock?"

"Fine with me," Cassie said. "See you there."

"It's ten o'clock in the morning, so I know I'm not dreaming. Why would Cassie want to eat lunch with me? She doesn't even like me," she said to herself after she hung up.

"Oh!" She whirled around.

"Sorry if I alarmed you," Jay Weeks said. "You ought to put a bell or something on your door, so you'll know when someone enters or leaves."

"I have one on it," she said, her voice humorless and unfriendly. "What may I do for you, Jay?"

"You could sound a little friendlier. I need half a yard of black naugahyde. I'll give it back to you Monday. I'm going to Baltimore Sunday to shop for supplies." She cut a piece and gave it to him. He raised an eyebrow. "Hmmm. I see you're using top of the line material."

"What would you expect me to use?" she asked him, cross and not bothering to hide it. "I charge top prices, so I use the best materials."

"Done any jobs yet?" he asked, and she didn't miss his attempt to sound casual.

She forced a grin. "Jay, my daddy always said, 'Never let your right hand know what the left one is doing.' I've learned that, in most things, he knew his onions."

"Yeah. How about lunch?"

"Thanks, but I have a date."

"With Hamilton?"

"No," she said, deciding that the identity of her luncheon companion was none of his business.

He waited for a long minute, realized that she wouldn't say more and nodded. "See you soon."

If he's not careful, I'll learn to dislike him, Susan thought as she put the roll of black naugahyde back on its shelf and went about drawing an arrangement for a teenage female's bedroom-*cum*-sanctuary. She worked better for a client when she liked the person, and she did not care for that girl, so catering to her taste was proving a struggle. Much to her relief, a woman entered who wanted her entire house redecorated.

"My husband and I divorced," the woman explained, "because of something he did. That was two years ago. We've made up and we're remarrying in about a month. I want the whole house redone, so nothing in it will remind me of that other time when I was miserable. We're starting fresh, house and all."

Susan wanted to ask the woman why she didn't sell the old house and buy another one, but she had learned never to pry.

She folded the file on which she had been working, walked over to the velvet sofa and sat beside the woman. "I always begin with the question, what are your favorite colors in woods, fabric, and porcelain."

"Good, because I think that way," the woman replied. "You and I will get along beautifully."

Susan completed a satisfying meeting with the woman, signed a contract, and arrived at Sam's Gourmet Burger Castle with several minutes to spare. However, to her delight, Cassie waited at a corner table. *Hmmm, so she wants to talk privately. I wonder about what.*

They had barely begun to eat their gourmet hamburgers when Cassie blurted out, "How is it being single? I mean, is it . . .

do you get invitations to places? You know . . . do you get left out of things like receptions and fundraisers, and do people invite you to their homes?"

What on earth brought that about? She decided to respond as if the questions did not seem strange coming from a married woman. "I expect people will be more charitable here than in New York, though being single in New York posed no problems for me. If you're well known and have connections—as you have, for example—it shouldn't pose a problem anywhere. I haven't done much socializing here, but I'm just realizing that I haven't seen too many single women alone in the evening." There! She could take either end of the stick. "Why? Do you have a sister or a friend who's unmarried?"

"I, uh, just wondered what it's like. I've been married a good while, out of circulation, you might say, and . . ." She leaned her fork and knife against the edge of her plate. "If I don't agree to get pregnant, Kix is going to leave me."

"*What*? Is there a reason why you can't conceive?"

Cassie picked up her fork and toyed with her salad, before putting a fork full of it into her mouth and chewing it slowly. Finally, as if it pained her to do so, she lowered her head and said, "Nothing that I know of. The problem is that I don't want to be pregnant. I hate the thought of it." Susan's fork fell to her plate, and she stared at Cassie, wide-eyed. "Don't tell me you think a woman has to have children in order to legitimate herself and to justify her existence," Cassie said with a grimace.

"I certainly do not." *Better tread carefully here, girl.* "But it seems to me that if you love your husband, you'd want to have some children. Don't you feel . . . uh . . . secure enough to . . . to take a chance on it? He seems like a sturdy man."

"He is, and I do love him. It's just that . . . I don't know."

"Won't he agree to your continuing your career if you have a child?"

"He probably would, but I . . . I can't even contemplate it."

Susan folded her arms, leaned back in her chair and looked at Cassie. "I'd give anything if I had your problem."

"Well don't bother to feel superior. If you marry Lucas

Hamilton, you'll be in the same boat. He's the same type as Kix—a dependable, hardworking, and successful family man. That type has to have children."

The words were as daggers in her heart. Of course, Lucas would want children. However, her feelings about him were her own business, so she neither affirmed nor denied an interest in him. Instead, she said, "Didn't you and Kix discuss children before you married?"

"That's part of the problem; he asked if I would, and I said yes, but I would have said most anything he wanted to hear." She took out a linen handkerchief and blew her nose. "Susan, if I don't get pregnant, he's going to leave me. He deserves better than I've given him. A lot better."

"Perhaps you both deserve better. Don't underrate yourself or what you mean to him, Cassie."

Cassie smiled through her unshed tears. "Thanks, Susan. I'm sorry I dumped on you, but you can't imagine what a weight this is. Sometimes, I feel as if I'll go bonkers."

Back in her shop, Susan mused over her conversation with Cassie. Would the woman risk losing something so precious because she couldn't contemplate doing what to most women came naturally? *If only she knew how gladly I'd change her prospects for childbearing with mine.* At three o'clock, she closed the shop, got into her BMW and headed for Wade School to begin the most enjoyable hour of her day.

Driving past Children's Village, a store that specialized in clothing for children six and younger, Susan impulsively stopped in front of the store, put a quarter in the parking meter and went inside. Almost at once, she saw a blue knitted cap, scarf and mitten set that she thought would become Rudy.

Why can't I buy it for her? she thought. *I won't hurt anyone, and Rudy doesn't have a hat or mittens.*

"May I help you, madam?" an eager salesperson asked her.

"How do you think this would look with that red coat over there?" She pointed to the same red coat she bought for Rudy.

"It will look lovely."

"I think so too, and I'll take it." She put the set unwrapped in her briefcase, aware of the consequences if Lucas saw her carrying a package with Children's Village printed on it. She found a gray sleeveless sweater for Nathan and rushed back to her car. Rudy and Nathan waited outside her classroom door as usual and ran to greet her as she entered the school's front door. She hugged them both, opened her briefcase, put the cap and scarf on Rudy, handed her the gloves and gave Nathan his sweater. The children hugged and kissed her, giggled and danced with joy. When she thought her heart would burst with happiness, she straightened up and looked into the eyes of Lucas Hamilton.

Lucas neither smiled nor spoke to Susan, but patted the children's shoulders and walked rapidly to his office. She couldn't know the drama of his life from nine o'clock that morning until the minute he found her breaking the Department of Education's rules, drama that he had raced to Wade School to share with her. He closed the door, sat down at the principal's desk, leaned back in the chair, closed his eyes and relived those awesome moments.

As he was about to enter General Hospital, he stepped away from the door and gazed at the world around him, aware that no matter how their meeting went, when he stepped out of that hospital, his life would have changed. At the desk, he asked for a visitor's pass to suite A-6, identified himself and got the pass. Why didn't he feel anything? Not happiness, sadness, nervousness, or anger. Nothing. He knocked on the door, didn't hear an answer, cracked the door and peeped in.

"Come in." The voice was strong enough. He walked in, looked toward the bed and the man who was half sitting and half lying in it. He walked over to the man who sired him.

"I'm Lucas Hamilton. Why do you want to see me?" Of all the words he might have uttered, those were perhaps the most benign. They were also the most impersonal, without any reference to the man's health and well-being.

"I'm Calvin Jackson," the man said. "Have a seat. This may take a while."

Lucas nearly laughed. He'd said only ten words, and Calvin Jackson had sized him up as cut and dried. No nonsense. Lucas was a replica of the man who sired him. He sat in the only available chair, crossed his knees and leaned back, comfortable and projecting it.

It was his father's turn to be amused, and he half laughed. "You're so damned much like me that it's frightening, and I'm not only talking about your looks, height and bearing. It's like watching myself. Don't sit there and give the impression that you have nothing to say to me. If I wasn't in this bed, you'd probably consider slugging me."

"Why do you think I still won't do it?" Lucas shrugged. "You're right. It wouldn't be the least bit gratifying. I have nothing to say to you until you say something to me, and I'm sure you appreciate the value of time."

"You're a gentleman. I know all about you. I have a box this high"—with both hands he suggested an interval of about thirty inches—"full of clippings, photographs, and letters about you and the things you've done. They are among my most precious possessions."

That hadn't moved him. "So, what does that tell me?"

Calvin braced his hands on the bed and propped himself up further. "I'd be the last one to speak to you against Noreen. I should have stayed away from her, but I didn't. I loved her." He closed his eyes and shook his head. "I was older and wiser, and I knew better than she the consequences."

"But you took advantage of her anyway."

"Yes, and she told me that if I ever contacted you for any reason, she would tell my wife and my daughters everything about our affair and about you. I was the age you are now—though not as far advanced—building a name for myself in Danville, and I didn't want to break up my family. So, like a fool, I stayed away from you."

"I didn't know you had any other children. Where are your wife and daughters now?"

"We'll get to them later. A few weeks ago, I got tired of the secret and told them about Noreen and about you. I had to tell them, because of what I want to do now. I could have done it years ago, because Marcie—my wife—said that she had been suspicious of Noreen and me and that the first time she saw your picture in the paper, she guessed. And to think I let all those years pass without knowing you or contributing in any way to your growth and development. Believe me, I am sorry. I would be so proud of you, if I had the right."

Lucas looked his father in the eye. "Don't think for a second that I'm a victim. I'm not. And yes, there have been times when I wanted to dismember you, but I resented my mother more than you, because she told me that she forbade you to see me and moved away from Danville so that you and I wouldn't be near each other. I could have contacted you, but doing so never once entered my mind." He rested both feet on the floor, leaned forward and covered his knees with his hands. "I always planned to get my revenge by besting you at what you do best, and without any help from you."

"And you're practically there, if you're not actually ahead of me."

Lucas looked at his watch. "We've talked a long time, but you haven't told me why you wanted to see me."

"I need a spinal operation that will incapacitate me for months, maybe years, and I want you to run my business enterprises."

"*What*? You can't be serious. What about your daughters? Why can't they do it?"

"Neither of them has ever showed the least interest in business. Besides, a woman's place is in the home, and they're both married . . . and childless, I may add."

"A woman's place is in the home? You're a century behind the times. Some of the Fortune Five Hundred's top CEOs in this country are women, and I say right on."

"We disagree, but that isn't important. Will you do it?"

"I don't have time. I'm focusing on a new development opposite Pine Tree Park, and I want it to be outstanding for its class. I haven't finished the design."

"But what you've done is fantastic, miles ahead of Scenic

Gardens. You can do it. You'll have ample staff who know their jobs, but they need guidance."

"What will your daughters say? I get two half sisters who'll hate my guts before they meet me. I don't like it."

Calvin took the pitcher from his night table and poured a glass of water for himself. "My daughters are not in the habit of disobeying or confronting me. They've always been happy to accept the environment of wealth that I provide for them, and they don't question the source."

He stared at the man whose supine position in a hospital bed in no way diminished his aura of authority. "Pretty authoritarian, aren't you? I imagine you know that doesn't work with me."

"Will you do it? I'll give you the reins, and you'll be amply compensated."

Imagine being at the helm of Jackson Enterprises, a conglomeration of real estate holdings, media outlets and transport facilities. Wasn't it rightfully his duty and opportunity? "What will you do if I refuse? I have to look after my own business."

"Hire an architect to assist you."

Pride suffused him for he could truthfully say to Calvin Jackson, "I have an assistant, but I'm the chief architect, and I develop the original plans from my own ideas. I'll think about it."

"And some award-winning ideas you've produced, too. I want you to do more than think about it. My operation is scheduled for the day after tomorrow. Only God knows whether I will survive it. I've drawn up a contract, and all my lawyer has to do is type your name in the appropriate place. This is important, Lucas. I am not trying to make amends; in my view, that isn't possible. I want to preserve what I've worked so hard for over the last forty-six years, and you will do that, and more."

"How do you know that I wouldn't deliberately destroy it?"

When Calvin Jackson laughed disparagingly, Lucas had to wonder at the power of human genes. How frequently he allowed his laugh to make an unspoken statement. "You're too proud. Your ego would drive you to succeed if only to show me that you're as capable as I am, or more so. I'm not concerned about that."

Lucas thought of his mother and what her reaction might be if he told her about his meeting with his father and what his father had offered him. Would she be angry and distressed if he told her that he wanted to accept the challenge of managing one of the most successful African American conglomerates in the country? He leaned back in the chair and gazed at his father. Both of his parents had let him down. He had succeeded beyond his dreams, and he would go farther. His mother lived in a house that he designed and built for her, and he gave her a sizeable monthly stipend. He didn't owe either of his parents anything.

"Do you have a copy of the contract here?"

Calvin reached over, opened the drawer of the table beside his bed, grimacing as if in pain. "It's in there." He pointed to the drawer.

He walked over to his father's bedside, gazed down at him for a full minute during which their gazes locked. He hadn't counted on the emotion that welled up in him, and he couldn't describe the feeling. He did know at that moment that he was not immune to his father, to his evident pain or to what could happen to him. He picked up the paper, went back to his chair and sat down to read the contract.

"Well?" Calvin said when he folded the paper. "What's the verdict?"

Lucas narrowed his eyes. "Surely, you don't think my decision is contingent upon the terms of this contract. Far from it. Money has nothing to do with it, though you're dangling a sizeable amount of it. You're giving me carte blanche. I answer to no one, and I return the company to you whenever you ask for it, but in not less than one year. Why the guarantee of a year?"

"Because you can't accomplish anything in less time. If you take the job, what will you do first?"

He was testing him. Lucas knew his smile said that the question pleased him. "Announce the appointment and call a meeting of all unit heads and assistant heads."

"You're a smart man. If you have the assistants and deputies there, the chiefs can't mislead them. What do you say, Lucas? I would be so relieved and content knowing that it's in your hands."

He got up, walked over to his father for the second time and looked down at him. "All right. I'm obligating myself to do this because the role is rightfully mine, and not for any other reason."

Calvin Jackson's face bloomed into a smile as he extended his hand. "That's all I need to hear." When Lucas grasped the proffered hand, he knew that it was more than a handshake. For the first time in his life, he was touching his father, feeling the warmth of his flesh, and he wondered if his father felt the tremors that raced through him."

"This is one of the happiest days of my life," Calvin said. "Do you have a pen?" He took the pen Lucas handed him, wrote the name of his son in the proper place and handed Lucas the contract. "Sign it, please." Lucas signed the three copies and handed them to Calvin who also signed them.

"You're head of Jackson Enterprises, and I can give in to this awful pain and get some morphine or something to ease it."

"Do you want me to ring for a nurse?" Lucas asked him, stunned that the man showed no sign of discomfort except when he reached over to open the drawer.

"I have a pill here," he said, "but I couldn't take it because I didn't know when you would come, and I didn't want to be in a stupor when you got here."

Lucas poured a glass of water and handed it to him, aware that it was the first thing he had ever done for his father. "Take it now."

Calvin's eyes widened and a half smile flashed across his face. "You're not bad at authoritativeness yourself." He swallowed the pill. "Your office is in the Jackson Building at 18 Tiner Street, about four blocks from here. Your secretary, Miriam Payne, will give you the folder that I prepared for you."

"Pretty certain, weren't you?"

"Yeah. My scout told me that you are just like me. Good luck. My regards to Noreen."

"Thanks for your good wishes, but I'm not going to tell my mother that you mentioned her name."

"I don't b . . . blame you."

The morphine seemed to be doing its job. Lucas eased out of the room. He hadn't been wrong in thinking that his life was about to change. He covered the four blocks in ten minutes, looked up at the twenty-story Jackson Building and shook his head. With the help of the receptionist, he found Miriam Payne on the nineteenth floor.

"Hello, Mr. Hamilton," she said before he introduced himself. "Come. I'll show you to your office."

"How do you do, Ms. Payne?" he said, after entering an office three times the size of his own. "How did you know who I am?"

"Oh, it was easy," the matronly woman said. "Mr. Jackson told me that you're the personification of him, that you look precisely as he did when he was your age. I couldn't possibly make a mistake. I'm glad you agreed to take over, because he needs that operation, and he's put it off for at least five years." She handed him the folder. "I'm here to help you in any way that I can."

He liked her at once. "Thank you." He opened the folder and began to read. At two-thirty, hunger pangs alerted him to the passing of time, and he put the folder in his briefcase, looked around at the spacious and elegantly furnished office, walked out and closed the door.

"I want a meeting of all unit chiefs, deputies and assistants," he told Miriam Payne, "here in my office at nine o'clock Monday morning. Can you manage that?"

Her smile was like a brilliant light, and he couldn't help wondering why she was so pleased. "Yes, sir. Yes, sir. They think they can do things their own way now that Mr. Jackson is going to be laid up for a while, but I am going to be happy to tell them that they shouldn't even think it."

He felt the smile forming on his face as he looked down at her. "You don't know how right you are. Here are my cell numbers and the number at my office in Woodmore. I'll be in touch."

* * *

"Mr. Hamilton, are you tutoring today?"

He raised his head abruptly, jerking himself out of his reminiscence. What a day it had been. "I'll be there in a couple of minutes," he said to the man who tutored in romance languages. A glance at his watch told him that he was seven minutes late for his class, a waste of the allotted time that hardly ever proved adequate, considering the help the children needed. Most of his pupils wanted help with math problems, but when he questioned them, he learned that even more needed coaching in chemistry, but they didn't consider it an important subject. All of them regarded math as their nemesis. With so many thoughts and problems whirling around in his mind, tutoring that day proved difficult, and when it was over, he breathed deeply, recalling that on many days, he thought the time passed too swiftly.

He hurried down to Susan's classroom hoping to waylay her and to say good night to Rudy and Nathan both of whom he'd barely acknowledged when he entered the school earlier that afternoon. He arrived as Susan and the two children were leaving the classroom, the last ones out as usual. As soon as Susan saw him, he sensed her fear.

"Hi," Susan said, though she knew he had to guess the word from the way in which her lips moved. Her fear that he would recommend her dismissal was such that she could barely open her mouth.

Nathan's exuberant greeting saved him a response. "Mr. Hamilton, look at my new sweater." He opened his coat. "It's brand new, and Miss Pettiford gave it to me today."

"It's beautiful," he told the boy, for he didn't want to dampen the child's enthusiasm.

"Hi, Mr. Hamilton. I finished reading my favorite story," Rudy told him, reaching up for his hand and smiling happily.

He hunkered between her and Nathan. "What's the name of your favorite story?"

"*Puss 'N Boots,* and I read it three times last night when I was supposed to be in bed," she told him.

"I'm glad you read it three times, but remember to obey your foster parents," he said and turned to Nathan. "Do you have a favorite story?"

"Yes, but I'm writing a story. My story's gonna be about Miss Pettiford. Everybody should have a teacher like Miss Pettiford. I love Miss Pettiford."

"I love her, too," Rudy said.

Unknowingly, the children had provided a defense for her, telling him that they needed her. But she didn't hope that their needing her would placate Lucas; he would consider what she'd done against the rules. But she loved Rudy, and the child needed love and attention. Even if he had her dismissed, she would find a way to fill that gap in Rudy's life.

"We'd better get out of here before your grandmother thinks you're not coming," Lucas said to the boy, and he took Nathan's hand and walked ahead of her and Rudy. Ann Price waited for them in her old Ford Taurus. Each child hugged first Susan and then Lucas and jumped into the backseat. She felt bereft when the car drove away, for she knew she had to face a tongue lashing.

"I suppose you drove," Lucas said.

"I did."

"We have to talk. Is it your house or mine? Either place, I'll order us some food. What do you say?"

She thought for a moment, and it occurred to her that she didn't trust herself alone with Lucas in her house, but what would he think if she said she preferred going home with him? "Let's get a pizza at Moe's, and go to my place. You're getting off cheap."

His scowl suggested perplexity. "What do you mean?"

"I bought coffee last time, and this is your turn."

"Oh, yeah? A pizza costs more than coffee."

"I was hoping that when your turn came, you'd have to shell out for something fancier."

"You only have to say the word."

In other words, don't say it if you don't mean it. "I'll settle for pizza tonight."

At Moe's, he ordered an everything pizza to go. As she drove home, she wondered at his calm and agreeable manner, as if she hadn't broken the rules, hadn't annoyed him.

He followed her to the kitchen, put the pizza in the oven and set the oven to low. "This is a truly elegant kitchen, if I do say so," he commented.

"And so easy to work in. Would you prefer red or white wine or beer?

"I prefer beer with pizza, but I'll take red wine, if it's convenient. Beer makes me sleepy. Let's sit over there." He pointed to the table in a corner by a window. "No point us taking this to the dining room."

She cut the warm pizza, poured white wine for herself and red for him and sat opposite him at the small table. They had nearly finished eating when she couldn't take the suspense any longer.

"What do you want to say to me, Lucas? I know you don't like what I did today, but the children are so dear to me, and Rudy needs attention and some sign of love so badly."

He leaned back and closed his eyes. "I'm asking you for the second time, what will you do when she's taken away from you? I know it will hurt her, but she will recover before you will. Can't you see that the rules serve a good purpose? I am not going to report you, because I know that if I do, you will find a way to maintain a relationship with Rudy, and you may do more damage."

"Damage? How can you say that? I love her, and I would never do anything to hurt that child." She fought back the tears. "That was a cruel thing for you to say."

"I meant damage to *you*. I know she's lovable; she gets to me, too. Both of them do. Have you considered the possibility that Rudy's foster parents might make an issue of the gifts you give Rudy?"

"Yes, I've thought of that, although they don't seem to care that much. But if they do, I'll ask what they do with the money the State gives them for her clothing. I kept her old coat. It's in the trunk of my car."

"I see."

"According to Rudy, her foster mother hasn't asked where she got the coat, and she hasn't told her."

"That's not a healthy environment for a child, but at least she let her keep the coat. I have something else to discuss with you. I need to talk about it, and I don't want to discuss it with my mother or Willis. At least, not yet."

Chapter Seven

Susan wouldn't say that Lucas looked worried; what she saw went deeper than concern, and she didn't think the matter centered on her. She perceived of Lucas as a man sure of himself and of his ground. But bemusement? That seemed out of character for him. He had told her about his background, and she listened with interest, but she hadn't questioned him about his personal life; indeed, she didn't think she had that right.

When it seemed that he couldn't bring himself to broach the subject pressing on him, she asked, "Is something bothering you, and can I help?"

He rubbed the back of his neck in a familiar gesture that she had yet to decipher. "This morning, I spent almost two hours with my father." When he said the words, the air seemed to belch out of him.

"*What!* How did that happen?" Of all the possibilities that crossed her mind, she would have least expected that.

She listened as he related the unlikely story, obviously still astonished and awed by the experience. "You can't imagine what it was like to talk with him, touch him, hear his voice unaltered by electronics, and most stunning of all, to see myself in him."

She wanted the answer to one question, for she knew that his response to it would tell her who Lucas Hamilton really was. "Did you feel any empathy for him? Any at all?"

He adjusted his position in the chair, the seat of which was too short for his long body, eased his right trouser leg and crossed his knee. "I couldn't help it. When he extended his hand to me for a handshake, I knew he was asking more than to seal an agreement, that he wanted even a small measure of forgiveness. I did hesitate for a brief moment, but I . . . somehow, I felt for him."

Although his answer surprised her, it also pleased her. "It amazes me that you weren't harsh with him."

"I was . . . at some points, but I wasn't rude. Even lying in a hospital bed, covered in those thin white sheets, he had an authoritative manner." Lucas locked his hands behind his head and leaned back. "Calvin Jackson is not a man who begs or crawls any more than I am. At first, we didn't fence with each other, and I think each of us recognized the futility of that. He spoke his mind, and I did the same. Susan, it's damned eerie how much like him I am, not only physically and in gestures, but in attitude."

"How do you feel about that? Being like him, I mean." His right shoulder flexed in a shrug, but she didn't believe the implication that it didn't matter or that he didn't care.

"How *should* I feel? The man's public behavior has been exemplary, and he has a record of honest achievement that any man would be proud of. He fell in love with my mother, didn't exercise self-control, and wronged her and his wife; but that's not my business. If he'd behaved differently, I wouldn't be here."

That he had mixed feelings about it did not surprise her, nor did his obvious admiration for his father. "And he turned his enterprise over to you, giving you total control?"

Lucas nodded. "Right, and he said he hadn't the slightest reservation about doing it."

Of course not. The man saw himself in Lucas. "Knowing you, neither would I," she said. "Have you told your mother?"

From his facial expression, she could see that he regarded that as a chore. "Not yet. I'm not ready to deal with her attitude. He asked me to give her his regards, and I told him I wouldn't do it. And I won't."

Susan felt her lower lip sag. "Why not?"

"Because she still loves him, although she hasn't seen him in person since before I was born."

"Good Lord! Do you think he—"

He interrupted her. "I don't know, I don't want to know, and I don't intend to facilitate any contact between them. He was married then and he's married now. Besides, it's over. Period."

She had never thought of herself as being overly sentimental, but she hurt for the woman who had loved futilely for over thirty-five years. But . . . "Can't say I blame you; she must have suffered."

"Of course she did. I'd better be going. I have a mountain of material to read, and I want to be on top of it for my meeting Monday morning."

"And you will be," she said. "Thanks for sharing this with me; this must have been one of the most exciting days of your life. I'm happy for you."

He leaned toward her, his grayish-brown eyes gazing intently into hers. Beautiful eyes that she would lose herself in if she wasn't careful. "I needed to share it, Susan, and I realized that you were the only person I wanted to discuss it with." His gaze softened and seemed to bore into her. "What am I to you, Susan?"

He had a way of coming up on her blind side and stunning her with the unexpected. "You are my guest," she said, finessing the question, but forcing a grin to suggest that she was teasing him.

But he apparently did not find her jest amusing, for his soft gaze abruptly became a glare. "Don't give me that crap. Who and what am I to you other than the man you inveigled into your bed with the smoothest, most artful seduction I have ever witnessed. Do you dare to answer?"

Her heartbeat accelerated, and she had a feeling that, if he touched her, she would incinerate. "I . . . you said you had work to do, so maybe you'd better leave now."

"You're asking me to go?"

"I think it's best."

"You're scared to be alone with me *now,* but you once had the nerve to invite me, a stranger you'd seen once, to your home, serve me an exquisite meal in an atmosphere guaranteed to stimulate a man's sex drive and then take me to your bed and into your body. I want to know why you did it, because I'm aware now that it was way out of character."

"Please, Lucas. That's over and done with. I don't want to re-hash it."

He sprang up from the chair. "You don't want to . . . Woman, you used me. Tell me you didn't. And whatever you were after, you damned well got it. Well, let me tell you what I'm after. I in-tend to find out if what happened to you and me in that bed was a fluke, if—"

She didn't want to remember. "Please. I want you to leave."

He loomed over her, a human magnet that she didn't dare touch. "You're enjoying another first, as the only woman ever to order me out of her home." He headed for the door.

"Lucas!" She went after him. "I didn't mean it like that."

"How did you mean it? You can't give a man what you gave me and expect him not to want more. I want more, and I need more. Right now, I need you." His voice lost its harshness. "When I awakened this morning, I wanted to call you, to tell you how I felt about the prospect of meeting my father for the first time. I was scared, anxious and eager, wound up tight as a ball of twine. All of that. I didn't want to dump on you; I needed to hear your soothing voice. I've needed you all day."

He was getting to her. What she lacked most in her life, and what she longed for was someone who needed her. Not the wealthy men and women who were her clients and whose busi-ness sustained her financially, but a loving husband and chil-dren—children that she could never have. If she opened up to him, she would be lost. Didn't he know that she needed him as much as he needed her?

"I hope there're no hard feelings," she said, bluffing.

She looked at him then, and his gaze caught hers. "No," he said softly and, she knew at once, deceptively. "There aren't any hard feelings." He braced his palms against the wall above her head, pinning her between the wall and his body. "At least I can have this," he said and brushed his lips over her mouth and nibbled on her bottom lip.

"Take me in," he murmured. "Susan, I need you."

She wanted to push him away, to banish the temptation to make love with a man she couldn't have and with whom she feared she would fall in love and ruin her life. But heedless of her warning to herself, her hands gripped the back of his head, and her lips parted. Oh, the feeling of him inside of her again, caressing her and loving her. Flushed with heat, her whole body welcomed him.

With one arm around her shoulder and the other clutching her buttocks, he locked her to him, twirling his tongue in her mouth, shoving it in and out to show her what he wanted to do to her, possessing her until her senses reeled. Holding and caressing him, she couldn't get enough, and when he bulged against her, she tried to straddle him. He lifted her to fit him; nearly out of her mind with desire, she undulated wildly against him.

"You want me as badly as I want you," he said. "Tell me I'm lying." He slipped his left hand into her cleavage and stroked her right nipple. "Say it," he taunted.

Without thought, she caressed the hand that covered her breast, symbolically asking for more. "Say it," he repeated.

"Kiss me. I want to feel your mouth on me."

"And then you'll send me home hard and aching?" The words came out of him as a sneer.

"Lucas. Don't. Don't do this to me."

"What do you want me to do to you? Tell me."

No more. She couldn't take the loneliness, the longing, the pain of knowing she could never have him or what he represented. "I want you to make love to me. I need you, Lucas."

He eased her down until her feet touched the floor, and then he stared wordlessly into her eyes, his own eyes burning with desire. When she thought he would deny her, that he'd staged that scene to exact revenge, he spoke in a gentle voice, "Are you sure?"

"I'm sure."

Minutes later, skin to skin in her bed with him, her eagerness to know again what she had experienced only with him nearly overwhelmed them both. "Easy, honey," he said. "I'm going to enjoy you, and I intend to make certain that you'll welcome me anytime I knock."

He started at her forehead and made his way down slowly, deliberately, kissing, sucking and bathing her with his tongue until he reached his goal and hooked her legs over his shoulder.

She waited, panting for breath, until he plunged his tongue into her and sucked, nipped and licked until she screamed for relief. Finally, when she thought she would die, she exploded in orgasm, exhausted.

"Don't you want more?" he asked her, and on his face she saw a soft and loving expression that she would remember as the moment in which he cultivated the seeds of love that he'd planted within her months earlier.

"Yes. Oh, yes," she said. "I want to feel you inside of me." Within a few minutes, he drove her to climax again, weakening her resolve to stay away from him, marking her for all time.

When at last he separated them, he lay beside her stroking the back of her hand. "It definitely was not a fluke. You and I are a hell of a pair together. Are you going to tell me why you seduced me last October?"

Was he never going to stop beating that dead horse? She hated lying, but she didn't intend to tell him the truth. It wasn't his business. He leaned over her and gazed into her face. She squeezed her eyes shut. "I . . . uh, because I had been held but never truly touched, and I had to know what I was missing."

He released her hand and sat up, exposing his firm chest and hard, thick biceps. "And you thought you would find fulfillment with a stranger you'd seen once and for whom you didn't feel a damned thing? I don't believe you."

"Well, I did feel something. I felt plenty." Having come as close to telling him the truth as she ever would, she turned on her right side, away from his knowing gaze and fought the tears that threatened to spill down her cheeks. The beauty of their mating definitely was not a fluke; it was a life-giving stream, nourishment for her existence. She was its victim, because she needed him, and there could be nothing more for them than an occasional sexual encounter.

"Believe it or not, that's your right," she managed to say.

"Are you aware that I didn't use a condom? What do you say to that?"

"What's there to say? You already told me you wouldn't let a woman have an out-of-wedlock child of yours."

"That's right, I did." He released the words like a growl.

The tears came then, and they quickly turned to sobs. He gathered her into his arms. "Why are you crying? What did I say?"

"Nothing. Crying is what women do. Didn't you know that?"

He pulled air through his front teeth. "Listen here. If you're sorry, I don't want to know it, because I am not. I needed you, and I don't want you to ruin the experience with your flippancy. Something's going on with you, and one day I'll know what it is. And if you miss your period, I want you to tell me at once. No child of mine is going to be looking for a man to serve as a role model for him."

She heard all that she could stand. "Please let it rest, Lucas. I should have let you go home."

He pulled her closer, as if to make certain that she heard every word. "No two people who make love to each other the way you and I do will *ever* let it rest, as you put it. The minute I was inside of you the first time, deep down, I knew that no matter what kind of lie I told myself, I'd be back for more. And I'll be back again. I know that, and so do you."

Hours later, alone and unable to sleep, she sat up in bed. *What have I done to myself . . . and to him? What on earth have I done?*

Lucas also spent the night in mental disarray. After thrashing in bed for hours, he got up, went to his bedroom window and pressed his nude body against the window frame. As he peered at the darkness, the silhouettes of the trees in Pine Tree Park loomed before him like undulating ghosts, cold, eerie and wind-blown in the night's bleakness.

Why had he opened himself to a relationship in which he saw no future for himself? She wanted him, but would take him only when her libido forced her to it, for she obviously did not want a loving relationship with him.

"I could love that woman," he whispered, "and I could love her forever." He stood there for a long while staring at the dark-ness and seeing nothing. "The hell with it. I've had worse to con-tend with. I've got work to do, and neither she nor any other woman is going to derail me."

He went into his den, removed the cover from the painting that he began four years earlier when he walked away from Verna. Looking at his idea of Pine Tree Park in early spring, Lucas wondered why he suddenly decided in the dead of winter that he wanted to paint spring scenery. Dabbling at the painting occasionally with no urge to finish it was hardly gratifying. He realized that he didn't even want to finish it, that it served as a repository for his frustrations. He painted a few strokes, but the red and pink flowers that the ground cover at the bottom of the painting required held no interest for him at the moment. Indeed, he couldn't imagine how the flowers should look.

He returned to bed, slept for about an hour and got up earlier than usual that Monday morning. Not in years had he greeted a day with more enthusiasm. He loved a challenge, and he expected to get a few. Precisely at nine, he walked into his office at Jackson Enterprises, noticed three vacant seats at the conference table, sat down and turned to Miriam. "To whom do those seats belong?" She told him, with what he noted was no small measure of glee. "Is this their usual pattern?" She shook her head, and he smiled in delight. The boys were testing his mettle.

"Good morning," he said. "First, I'll hear the status reports that I requested. Mr. Montague, you're first," he said to the chief of the transport unit.

"Are we going to have these reports every Monday?" Monta-gue asked Lucas.

"As often as I request them. Let's have it." He thought the report a good one and said as much.

At about a quarter past nine, three men entered and took their seats. Lucas made a show of reaching into his pocket, removing the pocket watch that his maternal grandfather had given him and putting it on the table in front of him.

"No one comes late to these meetings. Is that clear? Let this be the last time. I'll hear your report now," he said to the man among the latecomers who headed the real estate division.

"I wasn't sure what you wanted," the man said.

So he hadn't prepared a report. "Here's an example of what I want," Lucas said. "At number 2101 Rovine, the halls are filthy, the elevator doesn't work, several hall lights are out, and the entire hallway plus the stairs, laundry rooms and elevators need painting. It's a slum building. I want to see the receipts and expenditures in this office tomorrow at ten o'clock."

"But I can't—"

"That's what you get paid for."

"If you don't mind my asking," the man said, "are you Mr. Jackson's nephew or his cousin?"

"Yes," another one said. "I'm assuming that you're the manager."

So they want to know by what right I'm telling them what to do, do they?

He leaned back in the tufted, maroon-leather high back chair and looked from man to man, straight in the eye. "Neither. I'm Calvin Jackson's son. His only son." He heard the gasps, but continued as if he hadn't. "And I am not the manager. According to my father's signature, I am CEO of this enterprise. I answer to no one, not even to him, and everyone answers to me. Is that clear?" He looked at the man who first questioned his authority. "I want that building in pristine condition a week from today. I'm an architect, and I know pristine when I see it."

Deciding to put them all on notice, he said, "By the end of this month, I will have personally inspected every building and those three bus lines. That gives you a month before I get to your unit, Mr. Pearson. For now, what can you tell us about the media holdings?" He listened with interest to what he regarded as a well planned, carefully structured report.

He questioned the chiefs and their deputies without regard to status, and at precisely ten o'clock, he closed the meeting. "See you all here next Monday at nine."

"Brother, are they hot under the collar!" Miriam said. "I'm proud of you. I'd better warn you, though, that they're mild compared to what you'll get when you tangle with Enid Jackson."

"Thanks, Miriam. I appreciate the support. Does my father know how poorly some of his properties are kept?"

"No. And if he did, he'd have a fit. Matt Logan, he's unit chief, gets away with murder because he's Mr. Jackson's golf buddy. Something tells me you ought to make him bring in his books."

"I will, and in the future, all books will be kept in your office in a safe. I can't imagine company books in the hands of the person in charge of collecting and disbursing funds."

"Shall I tell them to bring their books next Monday?"

"Yes, but don't tell them until late Friday."

A smile spread over her face. "Gotcha."

Hmmm. She knows something that Calvin Jackson doesn't have an inkling of. He got into his car and headed for Woodmore and Hamilton Village. He meant to return to Calvin Jackson a thriving business free of the problems that currently beset it, but he didn't intend to neglect his own business.

"Say buddy, you're scarce as hens' teeth these days," Willis said to Lucas when he arrived at the building site. "What's up?"

"Wait'll after work. Man, have I got a story for you!"

Unable to find the carpets she wanted for her client's house, Susan decided to make a short trip to New York. After contacting her suppliers there and determining that she would be able to choose from a number of Tabriz patterns, she made plane reservations, packed and telephoned Cassie.

"Hello, Cassie, this is Susan. I have to be in New York for a couple of days, and I wanted to ask that if you see lights on or anyone moving around, please call the police."

"Of course, I'll look out for your place, Susan, and I'm sure you'd do the same for me. When will you be back?"

"I plan to return on Monday. If I have to stay longer, I'll call you."

"Safe journey. Let's have high tea when you get back."

Susan laughed at that, for she doubted Cassie ever did anything simple. "Please, no mayonnaise or butter on the sandwiches."

"I wouldn't think of it. Do you think I want to get fat? Not on your life."

At that comment, Susan's amusement disappeared like shadows in the noonday sun. Cassie would go to any lengths to keep her stomach flat, including risking her husband's affection. She bade Cassie good-bye and hung up. *I'd be stupid if I let myself be jealous of her. She could have it all, but she's too selfish to realize that.*

After showering and eating a sandwich, she phoned the New York limousine company that she always used. "This is Susan Pettiford. Please meet me at LaGuardia Airport at twenty minutes after six today. I'll be on Delta flight 187."

She dressed and, with an hour and a half to kill, she sat down at her drawing board to sketch window treatments for one of her clients and nearly swallowed her tongue. She had forgotten to tell Lucas that she would be out of town for the weekend. He had no special right to know, but if by chance she didn't return in time for her Tuesday tutoring session, he would be irate. She dialed his cell phone number.

"Hamilton speaking."

"Lucas, this is Susan. I wanted you to know that I'm leaving for New York in a little over an hour, and that I expect to be back Monday. If I'm not, and if I miss my Tuesday class, you'll know why."

His silence told her that he was adding two and two and getting nine. "Is this an emergency trip?"

"In a way. I can't find what I need here, and I can get it in New York."

"I see. When did you decide to make the trip?"

"About . . . oh, four hours ago." She decided not to wait until he delved methodically into every step she'd taken all day, but to bring it to a head. "What's the matter? Should I have called you earlier?"

"If you had, I could at least have offered to drive you to the airport."

"If you're in Woodmore, and if you're not too busy, you may still do that."

"I'm out at Hamilton Village, and I'm wearing a hard hat, brogans and soiled jeans. When is your return flight? I can meet you then."

She gave him the flight number and time. "If I'm not on it, I'll call you."

"Thanks for letting me know. I have a feeling that you came close to forgetting it. Good luck shopping."

In New York, she found what she wanted immediately—a tan patterned Tabriz and matching silk pillows for her client's living room sofa—bought a ticket to the Metropolitan Opera House to see *Madame Butterfly* and headed for Fifth Avenue. She didn't want anything in particular, only to be among beautiful, elegant things, to smell the myriad designer perfumes when she entered the upscale department store, to see models parading in beautiful dresses, and all the skinny young men with their perfectly cut and shaved hair, diamond studs in at least one ear and dressed in their tight, slim-legged black pants and black T-shirts.

After strolling around the first floor where the cosmetics companies competed for the opportunity to put makeup on her face, she went up to the designer floor and wandered from one over-priced designer to the next. *What did I ever see in all this? Just think of all the money wasted on staying ahead of the Joneses. Woodmore is a blessing. If you want to show off, at least it costs less.* Having reacquainted herself with what she'd left behind and remembered why she didn't miss it, Susan went to her hotel on Fifth-Seventh Street. Later, she attended the opera and enjoyed the one thing she missed about New York.

The following morning, she telephoned her suppliers and visited some of them, making certain that she kept her contacts, and that she would remain a favored client. On the way to her hotel, she passed a store that featured children's clothing, and although she admonished herself not to go in there, she went, and came out with two large bags filled with gifts for Rudy and a book bag for Nathan.

"Lucas is going to blow a fuse," she said to herself, "but I don't care. I have to do this."

He awaited her at the airport Monday afternoon as he'd promised, and to her surprise, he kissed her when they met, and he did it as if it were his right. "What's in those shopping bags?" he asked casually.

She refused to lie. "I don't think you want to know."

He said nothing more about the gifts until they reached her house. "Don't you realize that Rudy's foster sisters and brothers are going to be jealous about the gifts she's getting, and that, as a result, they will mistreat her, perhaps even destroy some of her things? Apart from breaking the schoolboard's rules, you may unwittingly cause Rudy unhappiness."

"Why can't I befriend her? She . . . you don't understand."

"Yes, I do. And what I'm beginning to understand worries me."

She looked at him hoping that her unspoken plea would suffice, and that he would not have her dismissed. "I'm not going to hurt that child, Lucas."

"I know. You love her too much to hurt her intentionally, but one day, you'll lose her, and it will tear you apart. I'd hate to see that. Look, I'd better get back to work. Be in touch."

"Thanks for meeting me."

A grin formed around his lips, exposing his even white teeth. "Don't mention it. It was my pleasure."

What had come over him? He hadn't been severe with her, yet she knew he didn't approve of her giving gifts to Rudy. She went inside, called Cassie to let her know she was back home, sat down and wrote a note to Rudy's foster mother.

Dear Madam,

I would like to take Rudy and Nathan—another of the children I tutor—to the museum on Wright Road next Saturday afternoon. If this meets with your approval, please

write me a note giving your permission. You may write it on
the back of this letter and let Rudy bring it to me Thursday.
Yours truly,
Susan Pettiford

She addressed the letter, sealed it, put it in her briefcase, and telephoned Ann Price. "Mrs. Price, this is Susan Pettiford. I'd like to take Nathan to the museum Saturday afternoon around one o'clock. I hope Rudy will join us."

"That's a wonderful idea, Ms. Pettiford. I don't have time to give these children the care they need, much less expose them to art, music and things like that. Do you need a note or anything?"

"I need your written permission. You may send the note with Nathan on Thursday. Thanks so much."

"What you're doing for little Rudy is a blessing to her. She told my Nathan that, until she started your tutoring class, she was planning to run away. Poor thing gets nothing at home but scraps. Scraps of attention, scraps of clothing, and scraps of food. The State ought to supervise these foster homes more carefully.

"That's why I'm raising my grandchildren. My youngest son and his wife are so messed up, and their two kids suffered so that I went to court and got legal custody of them. Sometimes I think people ought to be forced to go to a school for child rearing before they can have a baby. Bring these poor little things into the world, and don't have the slightest idea how to raise them. No sense of responsibility. Well, I bent your ear enough. I may see you tomorrow when I come for the children. Thanks for calling."

Susan hung up feeling as if the wind had been knocked out of her. Was Ann Price saying that Rudy's foster mother didn't feed her as well as she fed her own children? A kind of heaviness settled in the region of her heart. If she had a child or the exclusive care of one, she would shower it with love and attention. Was this a sample of what Lucas insisted she would encounter for having become involved with Rudy?

She opened the shopping bags that contained the gifts she bought for the children, arrayed the items on her bed, and gazed at the colorful jeans, sweater, blazer and the two pleated dresses for Rudy, and the navy blue and beige book bag she bought for Nathan.

"I'm dumping my disappointment, my longing on this child," she said aloud. "But what can I do? She needs me . . . and I suppose I need her. What if . . . if the State moves her from this foster mother to another one far from here?" *I wish there was someone I could talk to, someone other than Lucas, who thinks I'm wrong because I didn't abide by the rules, never mind the child's needs.*

Suddenly, feeling claustrophobic, as if the world were closing in on her, she donned an old tweed coat, went out the back door and down by the lake. In the still of the cold but windless air, she sat on the stump of a pine tree and gazed into the water. What if Rudy's foster mother refused to allow the child to go with her on Saturday? *Am I boxing myself in, guaranteeing misery for myself?* She took a deep breath, blew it out and watched the vapor rise slowly upward and disappear. She got up and started home.

"Oh, Susan. I was calling you. You promised we'd have high tea when you returned. Remember?" Cassie said as she stepped off her front porch. "If you're busy, we don't have to drag it out."

"All right, but let me stop home for a minute. I'll be right over." In the house, Susan got the little parcel that she bought for Cassie and hurried over to her neighbor's house where Cassie had set out the tea in the den.

"I love to sit in front of the fireplace," Cassie explained. Susan handed her the small box wrapped in silver paper and tied with a gold bow. "This is . . . I wasn't expecting you to . . ." She opened it with trembling fingers. "Good grief, you brought me some split-nib dip pens and . . . what's this? India ink." She jumped up and hugged Susan. "I haven't seen any of these pens in years, not since the last time I went to an artist convention. Susan, I may cry. I'm so glad to have these. You can't find them within miles and miles of Woodmore. How'd you know they're a prize for anyone who does what I do?"

"I asked a friend who's also an illustrator and design artist. How's everything?" She asked because she knew Cassie had a reason for pursuing the idea of tea.

Immediately, Cassie's demeanor darkened like a cloud over

bright moonlight. "I don't know. I love Kix, but he's . . . He has always let me do whatever I wanted, and . . . and even when I messed up royally, he forgave me, or at least he says he did. I don't see how he could have."

"Was what you did so bad? I'm not asking out of curiosity— I want to understand, and I suspect you're too hard on yourself."

"It couldn't have been any worse. Still, as awful as it was, things are better, entirely different with Kix and me because of it." She reached out and took Susan's hand. "I hurt him terribly. Susan, I had sex with another man, an electrician handyman at the company I work for. Imagine! *On the floor in my office.* I wanted him so badly that I would have swum Wade Lake to get to him. He was . . . exactly the kind of man I look down on, rough, ungentlemanly, coarse . . . and a walking ad for sex. Every time I saw him or thought about him, my mouth watered. He did it to show me I was no better than he."

Flabbergasted, Susan stared at Cassie. Speechless.

She managed to close her mouth and ask, "All right, so you made a mistake, but you didn't have to tell your husband and make him as miserable as you were, did you?"

"I didn't tell him. We had never had a satisfactory sex life because, as I learned after my adulterous affair, I was too much of a prude to allow my husband the liberties to do what that guy automatically did without asking me. For five years, I had faked and pretended with Kix. I was ashamed of myself.

"After that, I wanted sex badly, and the first time Kix made an overture, I was ready, and he realized it."

"And then, you told him?"

Cassie shook her head, and unshed tears glistened in her eyes. "No way. *He told me.* I'll remember his words as long as I live. He was lying on top of me, staring down in my face, and I couldn't look left or right. He said, 'So someone beat me to it. All these years, I tried to teach you, but you wouldn't let me. This is what I wanted for us, Cassie.' Then, he rolled off me and turned his back.

"He's such a good man, Susan, and he deserves so much better than he's gotten from me." Tears trickled down her cheeks. "I'm not going to get pregnant, all disfigured, throwing up every morning, waddling around like a duck with swollen feet and legs. I can't. I just can't."

She felt sorry for Cassie, but only because the seemingly worldly woman was, in fact, juvenile in important ways. "You're willing to give up the man you love because you'll lose your figure for about five months? If he wants a child as badly as you say, he'll be eating out of your hand from the minute you tell him you're pregnant."

"In the best of all possible worlds, sure. Have you looked at Kix? That man isn't a number ten—he's a number twenty. Gorgeous. I walk down the street with him and every woman we pass, no matter her age, does a double take. And when he turns on that smile, he lights up a room."

"Cassie, if he heard you say this, he would probably think you're talking about another man. Maybe you should talk with a psychoanalyst or a spiritual advisor. If you let him slip through your fingers, you will never get over it."

"It won't help. I just don't want it, and I'm going to lose him."

An hour later, as Susan headed home, she stopped suddenly and looked up to the sky. *Why me, God? I want a child so badly, and it's impossible. She has a man who loves her and wants to father her children, and she's too vain and too scared to spend nine months of her life giving him what he wants so badly. I'd give anything to have her problem.*

Deciding to make herself as busy as possible, so as not to focus on herself, she sketched the interior of a cathedral ceiling living room, penciled in an arrangement of modern furnishings and, on an impulse, added a Louis XVI style, kidney-shaped love seat upholstered in avocado-green velvet. She sat back and stared at it. Every other item in the room was of contemporary design, and all other fabrics were of brown or an autumn color. She pictured the tan Tabriz carpet she ordered while in New York that would be the only pattern in the room, and clapped her hands. "I'm on to something here. If only Mrs. Burton likes this, I'm going to submit photos of the finished layout to *Architectural Design*. It could be the break I've waited for."

In her joy at what she had created, she had no appetite and, for dinner, ate a toasted bagel and drank a glass of milk. When she went upstairs to her room, she pushed the gifts for Rudy and Nathan into the shopping bags, hardly looking at them for fear that what they represented would precipitate a rush of melancholia. "I refuse to think about it," she said to herself in a fit of bravery, but throughout the night, sleep eluded her.

Half an hour after they finished work for the day, Lucas sat with Willis in Sam's Gourmet Burger Castle enjoying cappuccino and a cinnamon donut. "Okay, so what was it I waited all afternoon to hear?"

"You won't believe this. I'm CEO of Jackson Enterprises."

"Get outta here, man. It's me you're talking to."

"Right." He told him the story beginning with the call from Calvin Jackson's lawyer and ending with his second meeting with Jackson's unit chiefs. "They tried to screw me this morning, but you know how I enjoy a fight. Miriam, my father's secretary, is an ally, fortunately, and considering the antics those guys are capable of pulling, I'm glad she's there."

Willis scratched his head, hailed the waiter, and ordered two vodka comets. "Man, this calls for something stronger, but I have to drive."

Lucas accepted the drink with a raised eyebrow. "How much stronger do you need it?"

"Here's to a solid year," Willis said, and frowned. "Say, you didn't mention an accountant."

"That's because he uses consultant accountants. I intend to hire an accountant and use consultants to verify his work. I'll bet I find half a million dollars that ought to be in the bank."

"Your old man will be happy. How's he doing?"

"He's having surgery tomorrow morning. I hope to get there before they anesthetize him."

"Yeah. What does Aunt Noreen say about this?"

"I haven't told her." He held up both hands, palms out. "I dread dealing with her attitude."

"You gotta tell her, and you ought to do it before he has that operation."

"I hadn't planned to see her tonight."

Willis seemed skeptical. "Suppose he doesn't make it through the operation? You ought to tell her. Call her and tell her I'm pestering you to ask her to invite us to supper."

"She won't buy that. You drop by there whenever it pleases you and head straight to the kitchen. I'll tell her we're coming over, and if she doesn't feel like cooking, I'll order take-out from Sam's." He took out his cell phone and dialed his mother's number.

"Hi, Mom. Feel like putting up with Willis and me for a couple of hours this evening?"

"How are you, Son? Come around six-thirty or seven, and I'll feed you."

"That's what we were hoping you'd say."

They walked into his mother's house at a quarter of seven. She hugged both men and then looked at Lucas. "I sure hope you don't have any bad news. My left eyelid's been jumping all day."

Chapter Eight

After dinner, Lucas stood before the fireplace in his mother's living room, stirring the fire and watching the sparks bump into each other. Why was it so difficult to tell her? Maybe she'd be happy that the two of them finally met and found common ground. Well, he'd soon know.

"What are you doing, Lucas?" He turned around and took a seat near the fireplace. He had never been able to fool her; indeed, he hardly ever managed to surprise her. "Something is going on. I just know it," she said.

Willis cleared his throat. "Lucas saw his father, and he's afraid you won't like it."

She gasped. *"He what?"*

"I'm not afraid you won't like it," Lucas said. "Having access to his father is any child's right, but I've been reluctant to upset you. Yes, I saw him. He sent me a message that he wanted to see me, and I went. I spent two hours with him a little over a week ago."

"And you didn't tell me?"

"I'm telling you now, Mama. He turned over Jackson Enterprises to me, and made me its Chief Executive Officer until he's able to return to work, but for not less than one year. I have contractual rights to run the company as I please."

"Why'd he do it? To get even with me?"

He took a deep breath and let it out slowly. This was what he had most dreaded telling her. "He's having surgery tomorrow morning, and he expects a long period of convalescence."

She jumped to her feet, her face ashen and her lips trembling. "What's wrong with him?"

"It's a spinal operation for two dislocated vertebrae."

"But that's dangerous! Suppose something . . . I mean . . . just a little slip of the surgeon's hand could make him an invalid for life or . . . God forbid, even kill him."

Willis walked over to Noreen, draped an arm across her shoulder, and held her close. "Don't worry about that, Aunt Noreen. That man can afford the best doctors, and you bet that's what he has. Come on. Sit down."

"Where is he?"

When Lucas didn't respond, Willis glanced at him and, as if Noreen meant the same to him as she did to Lucas, Willis said, "He's in Danville's General Hospital. If you want to see him, I'll take you."

She patted Willis's hand. "Thanks. I knew I was going to get news I didn't want to hear." She looked at Lucas. "Is he still married?"

"Evidently. He didn't say he wasn't, and you can bet I didn't ask him." He leaned forward and braced his forearms on his thighs. "I'm not dancing on the ceiling because I'm doing what, by my birthright, I *should* be doing. Furthermore, I did not absolve him, although he sought it, and in those short two hours, I saw what I missed as a child and as a youth growing into manhood. But in spite of everything, I am just like him. I don't intend to be sandwiched between the two of you. You've been a wonderful mother, and I don't doubt that he would have been a wonderful father if he'd had the chance. You didn't allow him access to me, but he didn't demand it or circumvent the fences you erected, either. You were both wrong. Those are my last words on the subject."

For a while, the silence shouted at the three of them. Then, Lucas went to the fireplace, stirred the fire and the sparks crackled again, the only sound in the room. At last, Willis said, "Aunt Noreen, do you want to see him before he goes under?"

After a minute, she shook her head. "No, Son." She had called Willis "Son" since he was eighteen and Lucas's college roommate. "I don't dare do that, but . . ." She looked at Lucas. "When you see him, tell him that I'll keep him in my prayers."

He looked her in the eye. "Ask Willis to do that, Mama. I am not going to carry messages between the two of you. I'd do anything for you, but not that. I don't want to hurt you, so please don't ask me."

He watched in amazement as his mother drew herself up, squared her shoulders and asked him, "Have you met your half sisters?"

His lower lip dropped. "You knew Calvin Jackson had children, and that I had two sisters, but you never told me? I haven't met them, but I expect to soon."

"They're both older than you are, so why didn't he turn his business over to one of them?"

He didn't like mind-wrestling with his mother, though she was good at it, but he was going to enjoy his answer. "Because he's a male chauvinist, and admitted as much. He thinks women are incapable of running a big company, and I enjoyed letting him know I thought he was a century off." He walked over to where she remained standing with Willis's arm supporting her and kissed her cheek. "I'm going now. Thanks for that great supper."

"I think I'll stay here with Aunt Noreen for a while," Willis said. "In a few minutes, I'll be able to eat some more apple pie."

Lucas told them good-bye, got into his car and headed home. It wasn't the apple pie that kept Willis there; his friend didn't want to leave Noreen alone for fear that she would worry or become depressed. Willis loved her as much as he loved his own mother, and Noreen reciprocated the feeling.

Lucas hoped Willis would discourage his mother if she indicated she wanted to contact Calvin Jackson. "If he wants to help her pile one stupidity on another one, I'm having nothing to do with it. The man's still married, and she still loves him."

At five o'clock the next morning, Lucas dragged himself out of bed, exhausted from a night of wrestling with the sheets and blanket and praying for the sleep that never came. He opened the blinds and stared out at the bleak darkness. He didn't have to go to that hospital, and he doubted that anyone—including his father—would blame him if he didn't. Yet, he couldn't justify staying away.

"Visiting hours begin at twelve noon," the guard informed him when he asked for a visitor's pass. "It's six-fifteen in the morning."

Lucas eyeballed the man, almost daring him to refuse. "My father is having spinal surgery in an hour and a half, and this may be my last chance to see him alive."

The guard handed Lucas a pass. "This is irregular, buddy, but if it was my dad, I'd do what you're doing."

"This is a pleasant surprise," Calvin Jackson said when Lucas walked into his room. "I didn't expect anyone this morning, and especially not you, but I'm glad you came. It's something I won't forget."

Lucas dragged the chair close to the bed and sat down. "It was the right thing to do."

Calvin laughed. "I see you're not ready to bend, but you're here, and that's what matters to me."

He hadn't been in the room more than a few minutes when a nurse breezed in. "I'm sorry," she said to Lucas, "but I have to anesthetize him now, so you'll have to excuse us."

Lucas raised one eyebrow. "I'm old enough to watch, and I plan to stay with him until that thing takes effect."

Calvin didn't flinch when she administered the hypodermic with a jab, but Lucas narrowed his eyes. "I didn't dream that sticking a needle in a sick man could give a person so much pleasure," he said between gritted teeth. "Can't you find a more humane way to get your kicks?" he asked the nurse. The woman reddened and hurried out of the room.

"I've been thinking that one is sadistic," Calvin said, "and it seems you agree." He held out his hand, and Lucas grasped it. "At least, I'll be out of this pain no matter what happens." He squeezed his son's hand and gave in to the drug's effect.

* * *

Susan arrived at Wade School early that Tuesday afternoon, for she knew that if Lucas found Rudy and Nathan waiting for her in the hall beside her classroom door, he would take them into his office, and she would have to go there for them. She didn't want to arouse Lucas's concern further about her relationship with the children and, she especially didn't want him to know about their gifts. After carefully considering her options, she left the gifts in the trunk of her car and went inside, where the echo of her steps reverberating throughout the empty hall gave her a sense of unease. It was as if someone were walking behind her. She looked back and saw no one, but nevertheless, she accelerated her pace, as if that would banish her suddenly terrible feeling of aloneness.

The door slammed, and she whirled around as Rudy and Nathan ran toward her. "Miss Pettiford. Miss Pettiford," Rudy sang, "I made a A in reading. I made a A." Susan bent down as the child launched herself into her arms.

"I did, too," Nathan said. "Look what I got." He opened his arms, and Susan knelt and hugged both of the children to her breast. They smothered her face with kisses, and when tears trickled down her cheeks, Nathan asked, "Is something wrong with you, Miss Pettiford? You aren't crying, are you?"

Rudy stepped back, and her eyes seemed twice their normal size. "Gee. Are you sad, Miss Pettiford?"

She forced a smile. "No, I'm not sad. I'm crying because I'm so happy that you got A's. That's what we've been working so hard for."

"I'm glad you're not sad," Nathan said.

Rudy, who had begun to ape Nathan, smiled and hugged Susan's leg. "Me, too."

Overwhelmed with emotion, Susan knelt again and wrapped both children close to her body. In the happiness of the moment, she closed her eyes and enjoyed the gift of the children's love.

"Good evening."

She opened her eyes and stared at Lucas Hamilton. Speechless. No words that she could muster would take away the censorship of his gaze. He patted the children on their shoulders.

"We'll speak later, Miss Pettiford." With that pronouncement, he headed for his office.

I'm in for it. He's either going to report me or move me to another class. Unmindful of the tension between Susan and Lucas, Rudy ran after him and grasped his hand to get his attention

"Mr. Hamilton, I made a A in reading, and my foster mother said I'm going to the museum with Miss Pettiford next Saturday. I've never been to a museum. Is it big?"

He looked down at the child and smiled. Susan turned away. "Nathan, wait here for Rudy and come to class along with her." She reached for her classroom door and stopped when Nathan tugged at her hand.

"I almost forgot to give you this note from my grandmother. She told me that God is going to bless you. Is he?"

The simplicity of children's thoughts, and their uncomplicated way of viewing the world and its contents made her wish that adults could occasionally revisit their childhood. Nathan gazed up at her, open and trusting, as refreshing as a cooling spring rain.

"I hope so, Nathan. I could use a blessing."

Nathan took her hand. "My grandmother talks to Him all the time. I'll ask her to get one for you."

She leaned down, kissed the boy's forehead and went into the classroom to await the children she tutored. At the end of the class, she left the building with Rudy and Nathan quickly in order to avoid an encounter with Lucas. She opened the trunk of her car, got the gifts and handed them to the children.

"Thank you, Miss Pettiford," Rudy said, reaching up to hug Susan. "I'm going to be just as pretty as LaToya. I love you a lot."

"Me, too," Nathan said with his arms tight around Susan.

"Who is LaToya?" Susan asked Rudy, although she suspected that she knew the answer.

"One of my foster sisters. She said she's prettier than I am."

Susan took them by the hand and walked toward where Ann Price had parked her car. "Children love to say things like that, Rudy. Don't pay any attention to it." They reached Ann Price's car and, after greeting the older woman, Susan turned and headed for her own car.

Lucas leaned against the driver's door of the car. "Are you trying to force my hand? I pride myself in doing properly anything that I undertake. You know I'm supposed to report you for your behavior with these children. What was in the bags you gave them?" He held up both hands. "Don't bother to answer. You're going to make me choose between my feelings for you and my obligation as principal. One more infraction, and it will be no contest."

She walked around to the other side of her car, opened the door with the key and stood beside the open door. "Rudy needs care, but you don't see that. You see the rules, the impersonal rules that don't take into account children like Rudy. You—"

"Or women like you. Are you sure you don't need that child more than she needs you?"

She tightened her lips to control their trembling and blinked back the tears. "Everybody needs someone, Lucas. Everyone but y-you, it s-seems."

"Look, I'm just—"

She interrupted him. "Doing your duty? Right." She got in, slid across the seat, ignited the engine and revved it. He moved, and she drove off. However, when she got out of her car in front of her house, he stood there, waiting for her. She didn't want to see him, or anyone else. Yes, she needed the children; each time she looked at them, hugged them or watched them smile was a reminder of what she would never have. They brightened her life, not completely, but sufficiently to ease the emptiness.

"Good night, Lucas," she said, without looking directly at him, and walked on to her front door. When she put her key in the door, his hand covered hers.

"I hurt you. I know I did, and I'm sorry. Something isn't right with you. What can I do to help?"

"Nothing. You . . . Please . . . Suddenly, the weight of it settled on her, shattering her, and she was back at that moment when the last doctor she visited told her that there was no alternative to a hysterectomy. Her head moved from side to side as she groped, mentally, for a way around it.

"What is it? Susan. Let me help you." He took the key from

her hand, opened the door and walked in holding her arm. "This is somehow mixed up with the reason why you went to bed with me, isn't it?"

She wouldn't tell him. It was her business, and she would deal with it. "You're way off. I'm fine."

"You're not, and I can prove it," he said, easing his arms around her and tightening his hold on her.

"There's not going to be anything between you and me, Lucas. What happened between us is . . . it was great, and it's over."

"You think so?" His mouth covered hers and, for a minute, she gave in and took from him what she needed. When he turned down the heat and began to cherish her, it was as if he set off an alarm reminding her that each time she was with him, she wanted him more. She moved away from him.

"If you have to report me to the board, there's nothing I can do about it. I appreciate your leniency."

He stared at her. "How can you respond to me like a nail to a magnet one minute and in the next act as if you never saw me before?"

"I'm tired. I'd offer you some supper, but I don't have the fixings of one."

"I get the message." He started toward the door, turned and walked back to her. "You may not believe this, but I really don't want to hurt you. Still, I know it's better that I do it now, than it happens later when you've grown to love that child more than you love yourself. Good night." She didn't try to detain him.

Susan changed her clothes, slipped into a pair of corduroy pants and a turtleneck sweater and sat down to review her plans for the Burton woman's house. Her client had kept the sketches for several days and then telephoned her approval. Susan decided to decorate the downstairs first. She listed the items that she would purchase the next day for delivery to Mrs. Burton's house, closed her notebook and went to the kitchen to search for food. The telephone rang, and she considered not answering it, for she did not want to speak with Lucas. However, a glance at the caller ID window told her that the caller was Cassie. "Hello, Cassie. How are you?"

"Uh . . . fine. Kix is working tonight, and I was wondering if you'd like to eat with me. We could get a bite at Sam's or maybe over at The Watering Hole, but that's so crowded."

Susan agreed to Sam's. "We don't have to eat hamburgers." She didn't feel like driving, but she offered.

"Oh, we can take my car, since it's my idea. I don't get dressed up to go to Sam's. Twenty minutes?"

She'd never seen Cassie when she wasn't dressed up, but it didn't matter; she didn't plan to take off her clothes again until she was ready for bed. "I'll be over to your place in twenty minutes," she said.

If Cassie wanted sympathy for her refusal to have children, she could forget it. "Tonight, I'm telling her just like it is," Susan said to herself.

Susan's eyebrows rose when Cassie told the waiter, "I'll have a shot of vodka."

"What's wrong, Cassie?" she asked after ordering a glass of wine. "Do you want to talk about it?"

"My husband walks around the house smiling and whistling— he can't sing, you know—and being a perfect gentleman, but he's treating me the same way he'd treat you. Maybe not as warmly. Last night, he kissed me on the cheek, turned over and went to sleep. On the cheek, dammit."

Susan thought for a minute. "You don't have to tolerate that. After living with him for years, you know where he's vulnerable."

"Yes, but Kix has a will of iron."

The waiter brought their drinks, and Cassie stunned Susan by putting the vodka to her lips and draining the glass. "That's not the way to go, Cassie." she said.

"That's all men think we're good for," Cassie said, "and half of them get another woman as soon as your belly starts to protrude. I'm not doing it." She knocked her fist on the table.

"I don't believe that's what really worries you, Cassie. If you don't want to tell me, at least be honest with yourself. You're experiencing a genuine crisis, and I think you ought to get help."

Cassie signaled for the waiter. "Not another vodka, Cassie, unless you plan to let me drive us home. I do not want to be the subject of a front page story in *The Woodmore Times*.

A waiter brought their food. "Did you want something else, madam?" he asked Cassie.

She looked first at Susan and then at the waiter. "Not right now. Thanks."

Susan reached over and patted Cassie's hand. "I may not have sounded friendly, Cassie, but I meant well."

"I know. You're the only person I can talk to. My sister's so righteous and so wound up in Rafe McCall—he's her husband—and the paper, that she doesn't give a hoot about anybody or anything else." She speared a shrimp and slid it between barely parted lips.

"Cassie, why don't you see a psychiatrist? You need professional help with this."

Cassie rolled her eyes toward the ceiling. "You're joking. In this town? In two days, everybody would know my business. Everything they didn't know they'd fabricate. All they'd need would be to see me walk into that doctor's office."

"What will you do if Kix leaves you? Will you ever forgive yourself?"

"My problem is whether *he's* ever forgiven me."

"Oh, come on now. That isn't what's bothering you. You haven't forgiven yourself for sleeping with that other guy. Forget that. It's in the past. Concentrate on keeping your marriage intact."

Tears pooled in Cassie's big brown eyes. "I love him, Susan. He's everything to me."

"Then go home and make him feel good about himself."

"I will, if he'll let me."

"He's not going to kiss me on the cheek and turn his back tonight," Cassie said to herself as she walked into the house. Susan was right. She'd been married to Kix long enough to be able to get him to do whatever she wanted him to do. She showered, put perfumed lotion all over her body and donned a transparent royal blue nightgown and negligee. Kix loved a quiet, restful environment. So, she lit candles in the bedroom, put on a CD of Mozart's early violin concerti and chilled a bottle of wine. He wasn't strong on alcoholic drinks, but he'd join her if she wanted a glass of wine. When she heard his key in the door, she hurried and opened it as she'd had a habit of doing during the early days of their marriage.

"Hi," she said. "I thought you'd never get here."

He glanced at his watch. "Same time as usual. What's the urgency?" He bent down to kiss her cheek, but she turned her face and met his mouth with her lips parted. Apprehension stole over her when he hesitated, so she gripped his shoulders and was rewarded with the feel of his tongue sliding into her mouth. When he broke the kiss, his quizzical gaze reminded her of the night he discovered her infidelity, the night on which she was so eager for sex that she forgot how she normally behaved with him and allowed him every liberty that she'd given to her lover.

"Let's have some wine," she said, hoping to cloud his memory of that fateful night. "I had an exhausting day, and I expect you did too."

"Mine was about the same," he said. "What happened to you? I called a couple of hours ago to suggest we have dinner together at the restaurant. Where were you?"

"At Sam's with Susan. I'm getting to like her. Too bad I didn't know you wanted me to join you."

He poured two glasses of wine, handed her one, and she walked ahead of him into the living room, intent on making it a romantic evening, and that meant not drinking the wine while standing in the kitchen.

He knows what I want, and he's planning to make me ask for it. All right, dammit, I'll ask. She exchanged the Mozart CD for Duke Ellington's "Mood Indigo," walked over to him, held out her hand and said, "Let's dance."

"I thought you were exhausted."

"I'm not too exhausted for what I want."

He stretched his arms out on the back of the sofa, spread his legs and let his gaze drift from her head to her ankles. "What do you want, Cassie? You can work up to it with first one ruse and then another, or you can come right out and tell me."

"That's not the feminine way, Kix. I want to dance with my husband."

Kix stood, opened his arms, and she walked into them. She realized almost at once that he intended to make her show her hand, for he held her as loosely as he would a woman he barely knew. She moved closer, locked one hand to his buttocks and tightened her hold on him. As if by reflex, his genitals moved against her body, and she let him feel the print of her teeth on his ear, something she always did after he ejaculated into her. If he wanted to play hard to get, she didn't mind playing dirty in order to get him. She took his left hand, rubbed it against her erect nipple and had the pleasure of hearing him suck in his breath. When she undulated to the beat of the music, he bulged against her, put a hand behind her head and shoved his tongue into her mouth.

She let the negligee drop to the floor, so that his eyes could feast on her body through the lace that covered it, and slipped down one strap, to expose a turgid nipple. She knew she had him when he swallowed so heavily that his Adam's apple bobbed furiously. He licked it slowly, teasing her.

"Take it in," she moaned. "I want you to suck it."

His hot mouth covered it, and when he started to suckle her, she reached down and began stroking, squeezing and fondling him. He picked her up, carried her up the stairs and put her in bed. Minutes later, he was storming inside of her, almost frantically driving her and himself to climax. As soon as she exploded around him, he released himself—grudgingly, she thought, realizing that neither of them had enjoyed it.

He lay above her, still locked inside her body, his gaze penetrating her. "Sex is not a substitute for love and devotion, Cassie, and it won't solve problems, at least not the one that you and I have. When you give us a family, *that* will solve our problems. All of them."

"You promised to wait till things were settled at my job."

"And how many weeks ago was that?" He rolled off her, lay

on his back and locked his hands behind his head. "At the end of six months, I will either be an expecting father or filing for a divorce. That's final."

She said nothing, for any promise she made would fall on deaf ears. In her scheme to bind him to her with sex, she had succeeded only in hastening their day of reckoning.

After a mental wrestling as to whether she should prepare a picnic for herself and the children and take them to Tanglewood Park after a visit to the Gallery of Art on Main Street in Old Salem, Susan decided that a restaurant was more appropriate, given the cool weather. She drove first to the home in which Rudy lived, hoping to meet the child's foster mother and establish a relationship with her, but when she rang the doorbell, Rudy opened the door.

"Hi, Miss Pettiford. I'm ready."

Susan concealed her disappointment in not meeting Rudy's foster mother. "I'm glad to know that you're punctual. Since you're not twelve yet, you can't sit up front with me," she told her, "but I'll strap you in the backseat."

At Nathan's house, his grandmother opened the door. "Come on in, Ms. Pettiford. Nathan's going crazy waiting for you. For the last couple of hours, he's been looking out of the window every two or three minutes." She followed Ann Price into the living room of the neat bungalow.

"I've got coffee ready, if you'd like some."

"I'd love some, Mrs. Price, but I can't stay. Rudy is sitting in the car, and I couldn't bring her in with me, because I have permission to take her to a museum, but not into anyone's house, including mine."

"I understand. You go on back. Nathan will be there in a minute."

"I'm coming, Miss Pettiford." At the sound of Nathan barreling down the hall, she wondered about the joys of a home filled with the voices and laughter of children playing and making noise.

"Hurry," she said. "Rudy is waiting for us." He caught her

before she reached the car and climbed in beside Rudy. She strapped them in, and immediately the children began to sing "Row, Row, Row Your Boat." She was certain that she had never been happier.

"I'm wearing my new jeans," she heard Rudy tell Nathan. "Miss Pettiford gave them to me."

"What did your foster mother say about them?"

"Nothing. I put my coat on. She never bothers about what I wear."

She listened to their chatter, talking to each other like adults, and the time passed swiftly. Very soon, they reached Winston-Salem, and she found her way without difficulty to the Children's Museum in Old Salem, where children could explore life as it was long ago. Rudy's and Nathan's excitement told her that she had chosen the right adventure for them. At one-thirty, exhausted from following them from one eighteenth-century adventure to another, and hungry, she had to plead with them to go to eat.

"We'll come again if it's all right with your guardians, but please. I'm starving," she said.

"I don't want any hot dogs," Rudy said. "I eat that all the time at home. That and peanut butter sandwiches."

"I like peanut butter and jelly sandwiches," Nathan said.

Rudy wrinkled her nose. "I don't."

"Then it's settled. We'll go to a real restaurant, and we'll have ice cream for dessert."

The three of them enjoyed crab cakes, French fries and grilled sweet peppers at Mazie's, an attractive restaurant that welcomed children with a menu especially for them.

"I want peach ice cream," Rudy said. Nathan wanted chocolate and strawberry. "You can't have two kinds, can he Miss Pettiford?"

"Sure he can, and so may you."

Rudy clapped her hands and a grin spread over her face. "Then I want peach and strawberry."

Susan realized with a pang that she would gladly give them the moon, if it were hers to dispense with. As they drove back to Woodmore, it occurred to her that, as a financially solvent person with a good job, she could adopt a child. The thought jarred her to the extent that she caused the car to swerve and barely managed to control it before it went off the road and into a ditch.

Calmer now, she said to herself, "Maybe that's the answer for both of us."

They entered Woodmore, and the children immediately recognized the familiar landmarks. "We're back home, Miss Pettiford," Rudy said. "Can we go to your house?"

"Where do you live?" Nathan asked.

"On the other side of town," she answered, opting for vagueness. "I'd love for you to visit me, but I didn't get permission. Maybe one day we can do that."

"But I had so much fun I don't want to go home," Rudy said.

"It's okay," Nathan assured Rudy. "If we stay away too long, your foster mother might not let Miss Pettiford take you out anymore."

She parked in front of the house in which Rudy lived. "I'll be right back Nathan." One of the children opened the front door, and she had to leave Rudy without having seen her foster mother. Etched in her mind was the thought that the woman had no interest in Rudy beyond the money she received for the child's care.

After leaving Nathan with his grandmother, she drove homeward thinking that what she was about to attempt would, if she succeeded, change her life forever. With her mind on that possibility and not on her driving, she turned off the Market Street underpass before reaching the exit leading to her house. Finding herself only two blocks from her shop, she decided to stop there for a short while.

As she sat in the storage room checking the fabric for Mrs. Burton's dining room chairs, the buzzer on the front door rang. Asking herself why Jay would come to her shop on a Saturday afternoon when he knew she was normally closed at that time, she opened the door with what she supposed was a question on her face.

"Hi, Jay. This is a surprise. Come in."

"I saw your car out there. It's a little chilly. Want some coffee? I got us some at Pinky's down the street."

She wondered at his motive. "Pinky's? I wouldn't have thought Pinky's served food to carry outs."

"If you're the chef's first cousin, you can take out anything but the tables and chairs. You like sugar and cream or milk?"

"Just milk." She led him to the showroom, sat down in a chair and took a few swallows of coffee. "I didn't realize I wanted any coffee. This hits the spot."

"You still seeing Hamilton?" he asked without preliminaries.

Taken somewhat aback by the abruptness of the question, she gulped. "Uh . . . I see him at Wade School where we both volunteer as tutors. Why?"

He looked her in the eye. "That's not what I mean. Do you have a personal relationship with him?"

She took a few more sips of coffee, using the time to figure out Jay's motive. "I really don't know what my relationship is with Lucas Hamilton. He's my boss at Wade School, and he's not happy about my relationship with some of the children. I'm probably too motherly. On the other hand—"

"Yeah," Jay said, his voice laden with disgust. "He wants to take you to bed." Her bottom lip dropped. "Don't look so surprised. Of course he does. You're a helluva good-looking woman. What man wouldn't want you?"

She wondered then why she'd been so certain that Jay's interest in her was purely professional. Cassie's summation of him had probably helped her to discount Jay as a man but, in addition, he possessed a streak of deceitfulness that caused her to beware of close ties with him.

She pinned her gaze on him. "Why are we having this conversation?"

His half smile should have warned her, but it didn't. "Because I'm like any other man. I want you, and Hamilton is in my way." She saw in him neither regret nor wistfulness, but the arrogance of a man exercising his God-given right.

"Well," she said, annoyed at his brazenness. "I'm glad you only see in me what every other man sees, because that means

I'm not special to you, and you and I can be friends. I'm not looking for a man, Jay."

He drained the coffee cup and tossed it into the wastepaper basket. "You do like men, don't you?"

She ground her teeth, a sign that Jay Weeks was about to get a sample of her temper. "Do ants like sugar? You bet I like men, but I'm beginning to not like you. Until you walked in here, I would have asked if you liked women. Thanks for the coffee."

"Look. Don't get hysterical. I didn't mean to upset you."

"Why would I allow you to upset me, Jay? Close the door when you leave."

He stood and stared down at her. "Women can be such bitches. See you around."

He sauntered out of her shop, and as her gaze followed him, he would have been stung with arrows if her eyes had been capable of it. "If I was going to get involved, it wouldn't be with a man who swings both ways," she muttered to herself.

She suspected that Jay might be trying to temper his competition, and she had proof of that when she arrived at Mrs. Burton's house the following Monday morning and found Jay standing at the front door talking with her client.

Lucas, too, had discovered an adversary, and he set about immediately to isolate the man, neutralizing his influence with other unit chiefs. "I haven't decided to fire Logan," he told Miriam, "at least not until the accountant inspects his books. Nothing has been done at 2101 Rovine. If he's calling my bluff, he'll be sorry."

Miriam patted his arm. "Logan tended to boss Mr. Jackson. He always told Mr. Jackson what his unit needed, how it was prospering and what kind of profits it made, and Mr. Jackson trusted him."

"Why? That's not the way to run a business as big as this one."

"Logan's been with the company from the first, even before

Mr. Jackson built his first building. They were in school together."

He had no idea as to his father's education, and he didn't
want to show his hand, so he asked her, "Which school?"

"University of Minnesota, and after all these years away
from there, whenever the two of them are in my presence, Logan
manages to mention the word, *gopher*."

This would be more difficult than he had thought. "I have no
sentimental attachment to the University of Minnesota or to
Logan, and if he doesn't shape up, he's out of here. From now
on, I'll deal with his deputy. Get Landon on the phone, please."

"Mr. Landon, this is Lucas Hamilton. As you know, I ordered
that 2101 Rovine be brought up to standard within a week. The
week has expired and not one thing has been done there."

"I know, Mr. Hamilton, but I can't move unless Logan tells
me to."

"I'm removing that building from Logan's responsibility. As
of this minute, you're in charge of it, and I am informing Logan
accordingly. Can you handle that?"

"Yes, sir. I'll get right on it."

He dictated a letter to Miriam, informing Logan of his re-
duced responsibility, signed it and headed back to Woodmore
for a conference with Willis about the next unit of Hamilton
Village.

"Oh, what the hell! I ought to stop in and see how he's getting along." He turned off Highway 52 and headed back to
Danville. Not much later, he stood beside the bed gazing down
on the man who sired him, a man asleep, but nevertheless wan
and seemingly fragile. He tried to push aside the emotion
welling up in him, but to no avail. Slowly, he lowered his body
into the chair beside the bed and closed his eyes.

"How long have you been here?"

Lucas jerked upright. In the quiet that surrounded him, he
had dozed off. He looked at his watch. "About twenty minutes.
Seems I fell asleep. How are you?"

"They insist on giving me painkillers, and I don't want them,
but I don't know which one of those pills is the painkiller. I

walked yesterday with crutches, but only a few steps. It's going to be a long haul. How do you like your new job?"

"It's a challenge. They tried to put the screws on me, but that lasted exactly fifteen minutes, or until I let them know who and what I am. I may have to fire Logan if he doesn't shape up." He studied his father's face for a reaction, and saw none.

"I'm not surprised. Logan's been cheating me for years. He thinks I don't know it."

"Why did you tolerate it? A couple of his buildings are in disrepair. I won't stand for it."

"You're young, vigorous, full of the future, willing to deal with problems. I got over that. My family enjoys my wealth and the status it gives them, but if I went off to Mt. Everest for a year, they wouldn't miss me as long as the checking account had plenty of money. So I stopped knocking myself out, and stressing over everything that went wrong with Jackson Enterprises. Logan knew my feelings about . . . about things, and he took advantage of it."

Lucas looked hard at his father, making certain that the man heard and understood his words. "I wouldn't like to interfere with Logan's relationship with you, but if he doesn't straighten up *now*—he emphasized the word, *now*—he'll need another job."

Calvin's half smile reminded him of his own trait. "You're the boss, Son, and you don't know how glad I am to have that load off my back."

"Is it very painful?"

"It's worse since I got up. I think it was too soon, but nothing gets me down. I'm glad you came. It's good to have a visitor."

Lucas mused over that for a minute, reluctant to ask whether his wife and daughters had visited him. But he should know, shouldn't he? "What about your daughters? I'd . . . like to meet them. I didn't know I had sisters."

"Luveen, my younger daughter, was here once right after my surgery. She lives in Johnson City, Tennessee. But I don't expect to see Enid. She's mad because I put you in charge of the business, even though she knows she can't manage a bunch of five-year-olds in kindergarten. Anyway, she lives over on the Outer Banks."

No point in skating around reality; they were both adults. "What about your wife?"

Calvin breathed deeply and expelled the air slowly. "Marcie has never taken an interest in what I do. She has her book clubs, bridge club, sorority, alumni association, the NAACP, the Urban League, and hell knows what else. A little real work would kill her."

Now, he knew where he stood. His main opposition would come from Logan and his older sister, Enid. He wanted to ask Calvin how long he'd had that peculiar relationship with his wife, but he didn't. It wouldn't have been much of a stretch from that to an explanation as to why he had an affair with Noreen Hamilton, and Lucas didn't want to hear about that.

He was therefore unprepared for the advice his father gave him. "I want you to listen to me, Son. Don't let concern for what people will think or greed for material things interfere with your happiness. If you do, as Eugene O'Neill said, it will be a 'long day's journey into night.' I know what I'm talking about."

"I don't want to tire you out," Lucas said, hoping to avoid comment on what amounted to a confession on his father's part.

"Will you come back? I don't need any reports on the business. I don't even want any, but I'll be glad to see you whenever you can make it."

I'm not his judge-penitent. God will take care of that. I haven't done what he did, but I'm not perfect, either. "I have staff meetings every Monday morning at nine, so I can stop by on my way back to Woodmore." A loud, soul-cleansing kind of laugh erupted from Calvin Jackson's throat and, as painful as it appeared, he rolled over and let himself enjoy his happiness.

"What's so funny?"

"I can just see Logan dancing to your tune. It does my soul good. Right on, Son."

"You didn't have regular staff meetings? No, I guess you didn't."

"You keep up the good work. It won't hurt those guys to earn their pay," Calvin said.

"I'd better go. I have a meeting with my builder. I'll see you next Monday."

"I'll look forward to it. Tell me this. Do you think you will ever be able to address me as your father? I know it will be strange for you, but will you try?"

He'd already thought about that, and it wouldn't come off his tongue. "I'll try. It may take a while."

"I know that, and I'm grateful for what you've given me."

Chapter Nine

Susan sat in her office at home going over her finances. As a single woman, any shortcoming would weigh heavily against her chance of adopting Rudy. She should be able to say that she was solvent and debt free with a substantial income. She had no debts that couldn't be paid at the end of the month, and her contract with the Burton woman would satisfy the financial requirements. Her shaking fingers transformed her handwriting into unreadable strokes, so she stopped making notes, got her recorder, and dictated her ideas. Perhaps she should talk with her mother and brother about adopting a six-year-old child, but she knew that no matter what they said, she would proceed with the adoption until she either succeeded or failed irrevocably.

She mused over her obligation to her family and decided to telephone her brother, who lived in Stockholm. The six-hour difference meant that the time in Stockholm was ten in the evening. She dialed his number. "Hello, Jack. This is Susan."

"Susan! How are you? Everything all right?" He asked that each time she called, reminding her that he had always been protective of her.

"Fine. I'm settling down here, and the more I see of this town, the better I like it. I'm glad I decided to stay. Jack . . . You remember about my operation. Well—"

He interrupted her. "There's a problem with that? You just said you were fine."

"I'm fine Jack, but . . ." She paused, for once she heard herself say the words, there would be no turning back. "There's a little girl that I want to adopt. She's six, in foster care, and she's not getting much love. Jack, she's so lovable."

"You're planning to do *what*? Whoa there. You don't know what you'll be getting into. Now, if you were married—"

"But I'm not, and I won't be, Jack. The man who married me wouldn't have children of his own, unless he was already a father. So, I'm not counting on getting married. Furthermore, I'm not going to get involved with anyone and start hoping. I've accepted my inability to have children, and I'm going to do the next best thing. I love this child, and she loves me."

In her mind's eye, she could see him frowning and pulling on his left ear as he did in a moment of frustration. "What can I tell you, baby girl? That's a tough one. Have you spoken with Mama about this?"

"Not yet. She's wrapped up in the children of Africa. I'll tell her when it's a fait accompli. I don't feel like agonizing with her. She said she was coming home for Christmas, but she changed her mind."

"I know. We want her to come here as soon as it warms up. She can't escape reality forever. Mama has to face the fact that Daddy is dead. I know it's hard for her, and we want to help her, but . . . you know how she is."

They spoke at length, but after she hung up, it bore heavily on her that he hadn't told her to go on and follow her heart, that he would welcome her adopted child into the family.

What would be the point in discussing her plan with Betty Lou Pettiford? Her mother had enough of a burden in trying to adapt to widowhood, something she hadn't managed in almost five years. She closed her ledger just as the phone rang.

"Hi, Susan. This is Cassie. Would you like to come over for a cup of coffee? I bought some scones on the way home, and they're very good."

"Give me fifteen minutes." She didn't want Cassie to lean on her, because she thought it unhealthy. To her mind, Cassie's problems didn't even merit discussion. She went into the basement, filled a small bag with pecans and struck out for her neighbor's house. *I'm fortunate in having a friendly neighbor, even if she does get on my nerves a little sometimes. I hope she doesn't want to gripe about her husband's insistence on being a father. Poor thing doesn't know how lucky she is.*

Cassie opened the door before Susan knocked. "Hi. Come on in. I want to show you this ad I did for a guitar maker in Bristol." Her face glowed with the rapture of success. "It's my first out-of-state job." Cassie grasped her hand and pulled her into the dining room where the design leaned against a vase on the table. "Well, what do you think? Kix never sees any faults with my work. I want your honest opinion."

Susan studied the ad. As a graphics designer, Cassie knew her business. That much was clear. "Would it make me want to buy that guitar? I don't know, but it would definitely encourage me to learn to play one."

Cassie's grin blanketed her face. "That's exactly what I want. They're opening a school for beginners in the hope of boosting local sales. Oh, I'm so happy, I could dance." She went into the kitchen and returned with coffee and scones. "I had to show it to someone, Susan, and I don't think Kix is interested in my work anymore." She held up her hands as if in defense. "Don't say it. I know it's my fault."

As usual, Cassie's conversation returned to her unstable marriage. But this time, Susan did not plan to indulge her. "If you persist on reneging on your promise to have children, you'll have to accept that there are many women who will willingly give him three or four children."

Cassie lowered her gaze. "I know that, and I know he's a man any woman would be fortunate to have."

"Then don't gripe to me, Cassie. You've got him, and he loves you. I'd be happy for you if you could make yourself do what you know is right. I'm going to tell you something that I've not told anyone other than my mother and my brother. In January, after years of pain and discomfort, I had a hysterectomy." She ignored the expression of horror on Cassie's face. "You cannot imagine what I would give to be able to have a child. I don't sympathize with you, Cassie. I can't."

Tears pooled in her eyes when Cassie rushed to her, eased her arms around her and tried to comfort her. She hadn't allowed herself to cry about the operation, possibly because she hadn't shared the experience with anyone face to face. But Cassie's compassion moved her deeply and, within minutes, tears sprang from the eyes of both.

"I could kick myself," Cassie said after a few minutes. "Mama always said that I don't think about anybody but myself. I ache for you."

Susan wiped her face with the back of her hand, her one thought being that, at last, they would be genuine friends. "It hurts, but I'm getting used to it."

"Does Lucas Hamilton know about this?"

She shook her head vigorously. "No, and I don't want him or anybody else to know."

"Well, he sure won't learn it from me. I won't even breathe it in my prayers. Guess who I saw trying to catch up with Jessica Burton this afternoon? Jay Weeks. She heard him call her, because she was closer to him than I was, but that dame tossed her head, quickened her steps and gave him the wind from her back."

So Jay was trying to steal, was he? That's what she'd suspected when she found him at the Burton home a few days earlier. "I'm redecorating her whole house, and I suspect Jay is trying to get a piece of the business, but I have a contract with her, and I expect her to honor it."

Cassie refreshed her coffee cup and sat down. "Not to worry. Jessica Burton is a lady from the old school. She can see straight through Jay."

Susan thought for a minute. Cassie had lived in Woodmore all of her life. Perhaps she'd have some insight into the enigma that Jay Weeks represented. "Jay stopped by my shop Saturday afternoon and hit on me. Real hard. I thought—"

Cassie's eyebrows went up sharply. "First indication I've had that he goes both ways. Jay's gay. He had a lengthy liaison with a guard at Gourmet Corner, but he carries himself so well that nobody thinks about his sexual preferences. He decorated that lovely reception room at Kix's restaurant, you know, the one where you wait for your table."

"That's elegant. Somehow, I never doubted his competence. If he's going to be competitive, though, I wish he'd come out in the open with it."

Susan rolled her eyes toward the ceiling. "You're joking. It's Jay's nature to be foxy. He's crooked, too. I'll bet he doesn't even go straight home."

That comment brought a giggle from Susan. "Now, that's what I call crooked."

As Susan rose to leave, she realized that she felt lighter, less heavily burdened, though she hadn't solved a problem. Maybe knowing you had a friend helped. But as she waved good-bye to Cassie, she noticed that a worrisome expression had replaced the woman's smile, that her bravura of minutes earlier had slipped away. Indeed, Susan hadn't reached her house before Cassie collapsed in a living room chair.

Cassie buried her face in the soft leather of the overstuffed chair. Was it too much to ask that she have the life she wanted, a career and the man she loved? Kix could have any woman he wanted, and the damning thing was that the older he got, the better-looking, more masculine, more distinguished-looking he became. It wasn't fair. The older a woman got, the older she looked, and if a woman had children, her breasts sagged, her belly bulged, and her hips began to look like oversized biscuits. Visions of herself with bumpy cellulite thighs and legs puffed up with varicose veins brought tears to her eyes.

"It's not right. I won't do it. I won't. Underneath, he's like other men, and they all want their women to look great." Her gaze landed on the ad for the guitar. "I'm good at what I do. It's good enough for me, and if it isn't good enough for Kix, I'm sorry." She didn't believe her own words, and tremors shot through her as she faced the truth.

He's my whole life. I loved him when we married, but after I learned how he could make me feel, I fell in love with him. God forgive me for what I did with Judd, but if I hadn't done it, I probably never would have discovered the man Kix is and what he means to me. I just don't know what I'll do.

* * *

Susan walked into Wade School that Tuesday afternoon with her heart aglow, overjoyed that, in a few minutes, she would see Rudy and hold the little girl in her arms. Her feet seemed to sail down the hall to her classroom. Abruptly she stopped, and her heartbeat accelerated. Nathan waited beside her classroom door. Alone. She ran to him.

"Nathan, honey, where is Rudy?"

He gazed up at her with sad eyes. "I don't know, ma'am. My grandmother and I waited for her on the corner from school where we always wait for her, but she didn't come. So, my grandmother went inside and asked somebody about her, and they said Rudy didn't come to school today."

Susan draped an arm around him, opened the door and let her feet take her into the classroom, but neither her mind nor her heart was in that place. She endured the long hour, helping the children as best she could and, at its end, she took Nathan by the hand and walked with him to Ann Price's car.

"If you learn anything about Rudy, Mrs. Price, please let me know." She handed the woman a business card. "Here's my number. Rudy must be sick, because she wouldn't willingly miss tutoring."

"She sure wouldn't," Ann Price said, her voice laced with concern. "That child can't wait till she gets here. Poor little thing is ready to jump out of this car before I can stop it. And my Nathan's in the dumps, too. I sure hope she comes on Thursday."

However, on Thursday, Susan's fears materialized, for Rudy did not come to the tutoring class, and Nathan reported that she had not been at school all week. Devastated, Susan waited beside Lucas's town car after saying good night to Nathan and his grandmother. But when she saw Lucas strolling down the steps, she ducked around the car, hurried to her own and drove home. *Come here, go there* was not her style. He said that she used him, and she did. He couldn't do anything about Rudy that she couldn't do, and in the morning, she would urge the principal of Rudy's school to find out why the child was not in school.

At home, she drove into the garage, got out of the car and

walked around to her front door. "Oh!" she said just short of a scream, at the sight of a lone male figure standing beside her front door. "Hello, Susan."

She relaxed at the sound of the familiar voice, but didn't hide her irritation at having been frightened when she asked him, "What are you doing here?"

Lucas strolled down the stone path to meet her. "Waiting for you. You wanted to see me, but you either got cold feet or decided not to risk an encounter with me, and since I'm curious as to which it is, I decided to find out. Is that a good enough explanation?"

She didn't feel like matching wits with him. "Rudy hasn't been to tutoring this week, and she hasn't been to school, either." Her voice broke, and he moved closer to her, almost automatically as if it were his duty and his right. But he wasn't going to tell her ever again that she used him for her own ends, so she squared her shoulders and stepped back.

"Are you telling me you haven't seen her since last week?"

She nodded. "I saw her Saturday when I took her and Nathan to the museum in Old Salem."

"You did what? Now you wait a minute. You know that's against the board's rules and probably against the law, too."

"I had written permission from Nathan's grandmother and Rudy's foster mother. I took them to the museum, to a restaurant and back home. I didn't even take them to my house."

He pushed back the front of his leather jacket, shoved his hands into his trouser pockets and kicked at the stones beneath his feet. "Now what the hell do you expect me to do with that information? You want me to report you when I know what that will do to you? Are you putting me to some kind of test?"

"Suppose she's sick," she asked him as if she were oblivious to his words. "Lucas, that child does not have an easy life. There's no telling why she's not at school or what could be wrong with her." She whirled away from him and made her way to her front door.

"Give me that," he said when her shaking fingers couldn't insert the key into the keyhole. "I'll get on it tomorrow morning."

He opened the door, took her hand and walked with her into the house.

"Will you, please? That's a strange house she lives in. I went to get her Saturday hoping to meet her foster mother, but Rudy answered the door, and when I brought her home, a small child opened the door. I wouldn't allow a child that young to open the front door."

"All right, I'll get on it," he said, "but you worry too much."

"You'd worry about her, too, if . . . if you loved her as much as I do." She turned her back to him. "If anything happens to that child, I'll—"

His arms went around her, and the tears spilled from her eyes. "Don't worry. You're jumping to conclusions." His hand stroked her back. "She's fine, and by this time tomorrow, we'll have proof of it. Sweetheart, please don't cry."

"She doesn't have a real mother to look after her, just somebody who gets paid to do it."

His arms tightened around her. "You don't mean that. Many foster mothers love their charges as much as if they gave birth to them. Let's not hang the woman before we have proof that she's committed a crime."

She only knew that, until she gave Rudy a new coat, the child wore a threadbare one on one of the coldest days of the year in spite of the generous clothing allotment provided by the State. "You don't understand how I feel. You can't."

"Why can't I? I care for that little girl and for Nathan, too, and I am not a callous and unfeeling man."

His heat warmed her, and she felt her body begin to relax against him. "You don't know what that little girl means to me," she told him with her face buried in the comfort of his chest.

"I'm beginning to understand, and I'll do what I can to help."

Grateful for his considerateness, she kissed his cheek, not thinking that she might set off the desire that always simmered between them, a serpent waiting to strike. Immediately, she knew she'd done the wrong thing. He stared down into her face, lowered his head and slipped his tongue between her waiting, parted lips. They tightened their arms around each other, and he pressed her back to the wall, giving her more and more of him, until her arms dropped to her sides, her panting could have been heard across the room, and her breasts heaved against his chest.

Slumping in surrender, she whispered, "You can take me to my bed if you want to, and I'll let you, but it wouldn't work for us tonight. I'm too miserable."

He startled her with a gentle hug, stroking her back as he did so, almost as one soothes a baby. The gesture bore no sign of passion, but communicated to her a deep caring. And it frightened her, for it brought home forcibly to her that they were both deeply entrapped in the web she'd spun.

"Keep your cell phone on," he said, "and as soon as I know something, I'll call you. Don't worry, and try to sleep." His kiss on her mouth stirred in her far more than she wanted to acknowledge.

Lucas couldn't help being uneasy as he held Susan, feeling more for her than was healthy and wary of asking her the question that burned in his mind like kindling soaked with kerosene. She was vulnerable right then, and he might hurt her, but he had to say it. He drew a deep breath. "It's strange to me that you haven't married and had children. You're beautiful, desirable, and you love children. Why is this?"

She seemed to fold up before his eyes, to wilt like a water-starved flower so visibly that her pain seeped into him. Hardly able to bear the suffering that he saw in her, he folded her close. Susan Pettiford had a hook in him, one that he expected to carry for a long time. As soon as he could extricate himself without giving her cause for concern, he left.

"Don't worry about this anymore. I'll call you as soon as I know something," he said, and ambled down the cobbled walk, shaking his head at the feeling he identified in himself.

On that Friday morning, he would ordinarily have met with Willis and his team of builders at Hamilton Village, but he'd promised Susan that he would find out about Rudy, and he would. He telephoned Willis.

"I have to take care of some personal business this morning, so I have to cancel our meeting."

"Too bad, buddy," Willis said. "I need to go over a few things with you. Call me when you're free. Nothing's wrong with your old man, I hope."

"No. He's doing fine."

He dressed in a business suit, drove to Rose Hill School and found Nathan's teacher. The two of them questioned the boy as to Rudy's whereabouts. "I don't know where she is, Mr. Hamilton. One time, she told me she was going to run away, but that was a long time ago."

That revelation disturbed Lucas, and after speaking with Rudy's teacher, the principal and the social worker, he left the school and went to the Department of Child Welfare, which had responsibility for children in foster care. Finally, around three o'clock, he had the answer and telephoned Susan.

"Hello, Susan. Rudy is right now in Ann Price's home under the protection of the Department of Child Welfare."

"Thank God." She seemed to breathe the words. "What happened?"

"Seems the foster mother went to Alabama to see her sick mother and left her seventeen-year-old daughter in charge of the house. When Rudy wouldn't let one of the children wear her red coat and fought the child to prevent it, the older girl banished Rudy to a closet and kept her there since Tuesday morning. She gave her nothing to eat, not even water or milk, except peanut butter and grape jelly sandwiches, which she knew Rudy hates.

"Rudy refused to eat them. When I got there and I saw her, she was thin and hungry, and she ran to me crying. The agency is looking for a more permanent home for her, because Mrs. Price already has four in her care."

"I want her," Susan blurted out. "I want to adopt her, and I'm going to try to get custody of her. I can't tell you how much I appreciate what you've done."

She wouldn't have stunned him more if she had hit him upside the head with a baseball bat. "Don't thank me, Susan. I did it as much for myself as for you. The suggestion that she stay with Mrs. Price came from Nathan, and I supported the idea, but I don't think she'll be there long. You may imagine how happy that little girl is right now. I'll be in touch."

He knew without being told that Susan would be at Ann Price's house as soon as her car would take her there, and he was not going to interfere. Fate seemed to have taken a hand in the matter. According to his watch, workers at Hamilton Village would quit work in half an hour, so he saw no point in going there.

He phoned Willis. "It's too late for a conference. Where can I meet you?"

"How about The Watering Hole? It doesn't get noisy until after nine." Half an hour later, he waited for his friend and business associate in a far corner of Woodmore's most famous gathering place. Willis joined him almost at once.

"Sorry, but I forgot to ask how's your old man," Willis said almost as soon as he sat down.

"You didn't forget, Willis. You asked me this morning. You know, I'm beginning to think we ought to put some upscale green and black tiles—I mean heavy duty ones—in the lobbies of those buildings. I want them to have an atmosphere of elegance."

"Yeah, man," Willis said, "and think of the behinds of those senior citizens kissing that tiled floor regularly."

"Point taken. Then, it's parquet floors and Royal Bokhara carpets. I'm sick of that combination," Lucas said.

"But it's damned classy, if you ask me. Uh, say, Aunt Noreen's pretty pissed at you."

Lucas supposed that his frown would give Willis his answer to that. "She told you that?" He shrugged. "I don't have to ask why, but I'm enjoying my work with Jackson Enterprises, and I'm not going to stop it to please her."

Willis propped his elbows on the table and leaned forward. "I think she can handle that. The problem seems to be that you see him regularly and won't tell her anything about him. You don't even mention his name to her."

Lucas banged his fist on the table. "He's married, dammit, and if he let her down before, she shouldn't be in such a hell-fired hurry to get back with him."

Willis stared at him. "Don't be so hard on her, man. At least she can't get pregnant."

Lucas jumped up and gazed down at his closest friend. "You must be rowing with one oar. We're talking about my mother. She's old enough to know right from wrong, and so are you."

Willis didn't flinch. "But, man, after thirty-six years of misery, she deserves to grab whatever happiness she can get."

His hands gripped his hips, and if the small-town gossips sitting at the next table had suddenly taken an interest in his business, he didn't much care. "Willis Luther Carter, you are about to torpedo twenty-eight years of friendship. I know you love Mama, but love doesn't mean you have to be stupid. I am not going to be their go-between, and neither are you."

"But, Lucas—"

"If Calvin Jackson ever finds himself a single man, they're on their own. But he can't have his cake and eat it too a second time around, at least not with my help. If he wants her, let him get a divorce. My last word on this subject."

"Sorry, man. She never said she wanted to get together with him. She . . . uh . . . needs to know how he's doing."

He felt for her. He always had, but he had to stick with the principles that she had instilled in him. "Don't encourage her, Willis. Let it lie."

As Lucas anticipated, Susan drove immediately to Ann Price's home. "I'm so happy that you have Rudy," she told Ann. "Do you mind if I see her for a few minutes?"

"Come right on in, Ms. Pettiford. Rudy's upstairs with Nathan and Dolly, my youngest granddaughter. That child was so happy when she saw me. I wish I could keep her, but I can't."

"I hope I can adopt her," Susan said, causing Ann Price's eyebrows to arch, "but it may not be easy."

"If you decide to do it, I'll speak for you. Rudy loves you, and you love her, and if you two get together, you'll both be blessed."

As the days passed, Nathan and Rudy became a fixture in Susan's life. Not only was Child Welfare slothful about finding a permanent home for Rudy, since the child appeared happier and content where she was. But Ann Price encouraged Rudy's fondness for Susan. Consequently, she allowed Susan to take Rudy and Nathan on excursions and picnic outings or to her home every Saturday and Sunday.

"I know I'm playing with fire," Susan told Cassie one April morning as she raked cut grass from around her lavender bushes. "But that little girl is so dear to me. I want to adopt her, and I think I have a chance, but—"

"File the papers. She's a darling child, and she and that little boy seem devoted to you." She looked away, as if her next words wouldn't be pleasant. "Those two seem inseparable. What's she going to do if you adopt her and take her away from him?"

"I've thought about that. I think they'd be happy as long as they could see each other often. I'd take him too, but I know Mrs. Price would never agree to that."

"Probably not, from what I've seen of her."

"Cassie, I've been thinking of sending photographs of my work at Mrs. Burton's house to a national magazine. She's given permission, and if the magazine accepts the story, I'll be able to call my shots. But I need a top flight photographer and a layout artist. Would you do the layout?"

"Would I . . . Nothing would please me more. That's right up my street. I'll get you one of our photographers. He's the best. When do you want us to start?"

Three weeks later, Susan sat in her shop gazing at the photographer's glossy pages and Cassie's layout complete with artistic captions and notes. "Well, it's the best I've ever done, and I'm going with it." She packaged it along with a cover letter and mailed it. Later that day, she telephoned her mother and told her what she'd done.

"I'll be a wreck until I hear from that editor," she told her mother.

"Don't be. If you're sufficiently satisfied with something you've done to willingly expose it to professional criticism, consider yourself a success no matter what anybody else says. When can you take a vacation and come to see me for a week or so?"

"Later on in the summer, maybe, but right now, my business is moving nicely and, until I can afford an assistant, I don't want to go away."

"That makes sense. Now tell me, have you met any nice men in Woodmore? You're too young to miss the best that life can offer you."

"Mama, I can't encourage a man, because I, well, you know I can't have children, and it wouldn't be fair for me to become involved . . . I mean, to lead a man on when I—"

"Don't be ridiculous, Susan. Not every man needs to prove his masculinity by fathering a brood. Besides, you can find one who's already a father."

"Yes, ma'am." If only it were that easy. But it wasn't, and it wouldn't be. Lucas Hamilton was the man she wanted, and he had already indicated a desire for children. From the time Rudy went to live with Ann Price, she had avoided Lucas as much as possible, for she feared testing his professional integrity and wanted to spare him the dilemma of choosing between her and what he saw as his duty.

Lucas knew how involved Susan had become with Rudy and Nathan and chose to pretend unawareness of it. He realized that Susan needed the children, and especially Rudy, although he could not understand why her maternal instinct expressed itself as it did. She had given him a wide berth recently, and he had allowed it, for he had questions about her that disturbed him, and he didn't want to care more for her than he did. He'd had a satisfying meeting with his team at Jackson Enterprises that morning, and he'd rather not alter his mood with his concern about Susan.

"I'd give anything to understand women," he said to himself. Calvin Jackson had let his mother down when she needed him most, but after more than a third of a century, she still cared for him. Susan Pettiford loved children, but she was thirty-four years old and still had none of her own. Verna, the woman to whom he was formerly engaged, could lie like a stick under him in bed, and yet, he'd walked in on her thrashing like a wild woman beneath a man she'd just met. If there was a man who could explain to him the mystery of woman, he wanted to meet the guy.

He parked in front of General Hospital, got out and headed for his weekly meeting with the man he still couldn't manage to address as Father, though he found that being with him became increasingly easier.

Calvin sat in a recliner beside the window. "I'm glad you could come today." He said that on each of Lucas's weekly visits, as if he didn't expect him. When Lucas commented on that, Calvin said, "I take nothing and no one for granted, least of all you. Have a seat." He glanced toward the nearby window. "I see you drive a town car. It doesn't surprise me. A man should carry himself according to his means."

He observed that his father sat in a chair, rather than the wheelchair. "You're making progress. When do you think you'll go home?"

"Tomorrow morning. You're right. I'm moving along much faster than the doctors thought I would, and I only take a pain-killer at bedtime. I'd like to go to Stewart Mineral Springs for a couple of weeks."

"You can't do that," he heard himself say. "It's in California. You'd have to fly across the country. Sitting upright for five hours would put you right back in the hospital. Why not Warm Mineral Springs, Florida? It's so much closer, and you could travel in a limousine rather than a plane. You'd be more comfortable."

He could see the man studying him, evaluating his ideas while sizing him up. "I don't doubt that you're right on all counts, but the springs in California have special healing properties. That place is more than a spa; a Native American healer guides you through the healing ceremony."

He didn't expect his father to take his advice, but he expressed his view nonetheless. "It's too far," he said flatly. "You'll reverse all the gains you've made. What's the point in sweating through those strenuous exercises only to do something foolish and land back here in this bed?"

Calvin's laugh surprised him. "You don't bite your tongue, do you?"

"No, and from what I've observed, neither do you. Why not rest at home for a couple of weeks and then decide whether you need to go to one of those places."

"The pampering I'd get in a spa would certainly be more pleasant, but you're right, and I'll take your advice. You don't happen to play rummy, do you?"

Surely, his shock registered on his face, in fact, in his whole person. Calvin Jackson did not want to recuperate at home, because he would be alone there with nothing to do. A man who had everything . . . and nothing. "No, and I'm surprised that you do."

"That was what I did on cold nights while in college. You couldn't have paid me to go outside. That town was like a deep freezer."

He sat forward, anxious to know about his father's youth. "Where did you go to college?" According to Miriam, his father went to college in Minnesota, but he wanted Calvin Jackson to confirm it.

"The University of Minnesota. I had a choice, and I went as far from Georgia as I could get."

"Can't say that I blame you. Fifty years ago, Georgia was no place to be. Are either of my grandparents living?"

Calvin looked hard at him, as if he needed to gauge the impact of his answer. "Yes. My mother is alive. She's eighty-eight and still very active."

He gasped, but quickly gathered aplomb and asked him, "What's her name, address and telephone number? I'm going to see her."

Calvin reached toward him, but quickly dropped his hand. "You're serious? You do intend to visit her?"

"Of course I do. This coming weekend, if it's all right with her. I wouldn't miss this for the world."

"Well, I'll be damned. You're a man and a half." He gave Lucas the information. "Would you like me to tell her to expect a call from you?"

"That would be good. I wouldn't like to shock her too much."

Calvin lifted his right shoulder in a careless shrug. "You won't shock her. She told me just yesterday that she wanted to meet you. I told her that could take time. She'll be pleased to know that you're the one who raised the matter."

He'd stayed much longer than usual, but he didn't mind; he'd enjoyed the visit, and he had certainly learned more about his father in that hour and a half than he had on any previous visit with him. "I have to leave now. By the way, is it going to upset your wife if I visit you at home?"

"No more than handing my company over to you upset her. But as long as the money rolls in, she couldn't care less. I hope you'll spend some time with me Mondays as usual."

"Right. I'll phone you before I head for Georgia."

"I want you to know that this past hour has brought home to me forcibly what I've done with my life, and I don't deserve your magnanimity."

When the plane touched down in Athens, Georgia, that Saturday morning, he could hardly wait to get to the end of his journey. Not since he knocked on Susan Pettiford's front door for the first time had he experienced such a sense of excitement or been so worked up about the approaching unknown. He hailed a taxi and half an hour later he rang the bell at Alma Jackson's front door. He hadn't wondered how she would look, but it surprised him when the diminutive, light-brown-skinned woman opened the door. She looked up at him, and her face brightened into a smile.

"I'm Lucas. Are you my grandmother?"

She nodded and opened her arms as she smiled through her tears. "I never even dreamed that this day would come."

He bent down and wrapped her in his arms. "Neither did I."

Arm-in-arm, they walked into the house, and he realized immediately that Calvin Jackson took good care of his mother.

"Until Monday of this week, I didn't know about you," he said, "or I would not have let so many years pass without getting to know you." They sat opposite each other in chairs upholstered in brown velvet.

"I understand, Lucas, because I didn't know about you either until Calvin decided he'd better get his house in order before undergoing that surgery. Imagine keeping a secret like that one for thirty-five years. Let me look at you. I would have recognized you anywhere, because from head to toe, you look exactly as Calvin did at your age. He told me the story." She leaned forward. "Can you ever forgive him?"

"He's no more at fault than my mother. What I resent is being deprived of his guidance as a child and, especially, as a teenager." He rubbed his right cheek almost absentmindedly, a certain sign of awe. "In spite of that, I find that I'm like him in many ways."

"You certainly are. Do the two of you get along?"

"Things improve each time we're together. I realize that I'm increasingly less inclined to be a smart aleck with him."

"Good. If you accept him as your father, you should respect him." She stood, and it continued to surprise him that she wasn't a bigger woman. "I've got dinner ready, so I hope you're hungry."

"I was too excited to eat on the plane," he said, following her to the kitchen. She bent to get a pan out of a bottom cabinet. "This is a really nice house, but we have to do something about these cabinets."

She straightened up. "Like what?"

"Shelves that pull out like a drawer, and you won't have to break your back every time you want a pot or a pan."

"That's right. Calvin said you're an architect. Your mother must be very proud of you. Do you take good care of her?"

"Yes, ma'am. She wants for nothing. We don't have to eat in the dining room," he said when she headed that way with a platter of barbecued chicken. "What's wrong with this table?"

That seemed to please her. She held his hand while she said the grace. "Lord, I never dared to pray for this blessing. I thank you from the bottom of my heart."

He barely tasted the food, although he realized that she was a good cook, but the entire experience seemed surreal. Overwhelming. "You're the only one of my grandchildren who's ever visited me."

He stopped chewing, put his fork down and looked at her. "But what about your granddaughters?"

She focused on her plate. "I don't remember what they look like. I've only seen them when I visited Calvin, and it's been years since I was in Danville. Calvin comes to see me about once a month. I haven't seen my daughter-in-law in twenty-six years."

He gave up eating and leaned back in his chair. "What's the problem? Don't you get along with the family?"

"We've never had a misunderstanding. At least not to my knowledge. I used to send them presents regularly, and I'd get a thank you card from them, but I stopped that when I realized that I didn't hear from the children and their mother unless I sent them something."

"That's almost unbelievable."

"You can't imagine what your coming here means to me." She shook her head as if in wonder. "My grandson. I feel as if my heart will burst."

They finished the meal of barbecued chicken, grilled tomatoes, string beans, rice, buttermilk biscuits and apple cobblers, and she rose to clear the table.

"I'll do this, Grandmother." He looked at her and grinned, suddenly flushed with happiness. "What do you want me to call you?"

"Whatever you feel like calling me."

"Grandmother is too formal. I think I'll call you Nana."

When he walked into the living room a few minutes later, she sat in a big chair, leaning back with her hands covering her face. "What is it?" he asked her, fearing that she might be emotionally overwhelmed by his presence there. He knelt beside her chair. "Are you all right?"

She moved her hands and looked at him. "I couldn't hold you in my arms when you were a baby or enjoy you in all the little ways that grandparents enjoy their grandchildren. I never got the chance to teach you to love me."

He moved closer, put his arms around her and his head in her lap. "It's all right, Nana. We'll make up for it."

Her thin arms eased around his shoulders. "I've been lonely for my family. Oh, I have a lot of friends, my church and my work with the library and the local aid society, but I miss having someone close that I belong to. Your grandfather died when Calvin was four, but he left me with a good insurance policy, and I saved it and used it to send Calvin to school. I made a decent living as a high-school math and physics teacher."

He sat up and leaned against her chair. "I've always done well in math and physics. Maybe it's in my genes." She laughed, and he relaxed, grateful that she was apparently off that emotional high. "Don't let me forget about your kitchen," he said, knowing that he wouldn't forget, but doing his best to shift her attention to a less emotional topic."

"You mean the drawers?"

"Right. That and any other changes that will make life easier for you. Would you like a ride up and down those stairs?"

"Well, I do get tired of hiking up those stairs sometimes."

"I'll see what we can do."

"I always wanted my grandchildren to be an intimate part of my life," she said, "but I didn't even ask the Lord for a grandson like you. Whatever you do for me, I will appreciate, but all I need from you is love. I'll be happy with that."

Later, he went through the house. "Who did this?" he asked her of a large landscape painting.

"I did," she told him. "Painting is my hobby."

"This is interesting, and it's good work," he said. "I'm getting a better idea of who I am and why I do what I do."

"Do you paint, Lucas?"

"I sure do, and I love art." He smiled and draped an arm around her shoulder. "Seems I've inherited a lot from you." She smiled up at him and blinked rapidly, but he had already realized that she valued her composure and was unlikely to lose it.

After going through the house, he walked around the outside, admired the blooming spring flowers and the crepe myrtle trees heavy with red blooms that gave the grounds a festive air.

His thoughts went to Susan who also loved flowers and femi-nine surroundings. In recent weeks, he had neglected her, and at the moment, he wanted to share with her all that he'd experi-enced with his grandmother. The day passed swiftly, and at dusk, he prepared to leave.

"I brought this for you," he said. "I wanted to give you some-thing valuable, not financially, but of real value, so I brought you these." He reached into his briefcase, pulled out a portfolio and handed it to her.

She opened it and looked through several pages. "Oh, dear. These are houses that you designed?"

"Yes, ma'am, and further on, you'll see some other build-ings."

She closed the folder and clasped it to her breast. "I'm going to study it carefully and put it on my coffee table. Nothing you could have given me would have meant this much to me. You're smart, and I'm proud of you."

"Thanks. I . . . I'm glad you like it. Well . . . I'll see you again as soon as I can."

"Don't make it too long."

She stood at the door, tiny and frail in the twilight, and he put his arms around her. "I'm good as my word, Nana. I'll be back, and before that I'll call you. This has been one of the most won-derful days of my life." He kissed her cheek.

"For me, too, son. Go with the angels." She handed him a small shopping bag and he got into the waiting taxi, waved and was soon out of sight.

He walked into his house at seven-thirty, threw his briefcase and jacket on a living room chair, put the little shopping bag on a counter in the kitchen, and headed up the stairs to his den. Suddenly, he realized how disappointed he would be if Susan were not at home. He dialed her number. "Hi, this is Lucas."

"Hi. You do not have to tell me who you are; by now I recog-nize your voice. How are you?"

"I'm on some kind of high. So much is happening to me. I wish we were together so I could talk with you."

"If it's so important, we can fix that," she said. "What's a friend if she's not there for you when you need her?"

"It's important," he said, and waited.

"Okay. We can meet at Sam's, or you can come here; but I can only offer you shrimp salad, hard rolls and coffee."

Maybe he was begging for trouble, but if that's what he got, he'd deal with it. "I'll take the shrimp. May I bring you anything?" When she declined the offer, he told her he'd be there in twenty minutes. "I'll bring along some delicious apple cobbler for dessert."

"Great. I won't ask where you got it, but I'll enjoy it, because I love it."

She greeted him with a kiss on his cheek, generating in him a feeling of emptiness, and he realized he needed greater intimacy with her. He hugged her, and watched her face mold itself into an expression of uncertainty. "The food is ready," she said, and he knew he had undermined her self-assurance.

As they ate, he told her about his grandmother and how he happened to learn that he had one. "It's been an unbelievable day for me, Susan. She . . . she's such a sweet woman, warm and feminine, yet composed and accomplished like you. She's softer than my mother, but I understand why: she had the love and support of her husband, and my mother didn't have that."

"Are you going to see her again?"

"As soon as I can. And I'm going to redesign her kitchen. She's eighty-eight, though she neither looks nor acts it, and those stairs must be a burden for her. I'm going to put a chairlift on those steps. It's amazing how much she and I have in common. I learned a lot about my father, too. You know, he's really good to her, calls her a couple times a week and goes to see her at least once a month. That surprised me."

"Why should it have? Isn't that how you treat your mother? You've made your grandmother happy, and I'm glad for both of you. What does your mother say about this?"

"I haven't told her yet. I suspect they'd like each other."

"When will you see your mother?"

"Tomorrow." He put the bag containing the apple cobbler on the table. "Let's try this for dessert."

"Your grandmother made it?" She bit into a piece. "Mmmm. This is wonderful."

He nodded. "Sure is. Do I dare ask about your relationship with Rudy?"

She looked past his shoulder. "I guess you know that I haven't taken your advice. Mrs. Price lets her spend some nights with me, and once, Nathan stayed with us. I was almost in tears when I had to take her home that Sunday night."

It was going to backfire, and he wouldn't be able to help her. "Have you done anything about adopting her?"

"I engaged a lawyer, but he apparently didn't think it urgent, so I fired him. I'm looking for another one."

"I know you love Rudy, but what I can't understand is why you'd settle for adoption. You're young."

"Who said I'm settling for it?" she asked in whispered tones.

He wasn't foolish. She had a love affair with children, and yet gave no indication of concern that her biological clock ticked away her chances of childbearing. He didn't want to hurt her, so he said. "You'll make a wonderful mother. The child who gets you will be fortunate indeed. Thank you for this evening. I needed to share this . . . what's going on in my life."

"What about your father? How is it with you and him?"

"I don't know. The more I learn about him, and the better I get to know him, the less animosity I feel toward him. He . . . uh . . . his life is empty. He's in a loveless marriage and has been for many years, and his daughters, especially the older one, are less attentive to him than I am."

"Maybe he deserves it."

"Somehow, I'm not so sure. He put everything into making it big, ensuring his family a good life. They have that, and that seemingly is all they want from him. There's no love in that family."

He could see that something was on her mind, and that she was reluctant to voice it. "Go ahead," he urged. "I can take it."

Leaning forward and in a softer, sympathetic voice she said, "Did he love your mother?"

So she hadn't wanted to hurt him. "Yes, I'm almost positive of that. What I can't figure out is why he didn't get a divorce and marry her. He could have paid off his wife."

"Oh, that's easy. In those days, divorce around here was frowned upon. Don't forget, this is still the Bible belt. He wanted to get rich, and that meant being a good boy if he wanted to keep his grip on local patronage. It's a pity."

"Yeah. It cost him a lot." The memory of his father warning him against doing that flashed through his mind. He stared at Susan, wondering why, after leaving his grandmother with love and joy churning in him, he'd felt such a driving need to share it with her. One thing was certain: he'd better watch his step.

Chapter Ten

Lucas parked the town car in his mother's two-car garage, got the lawn mower and mowed the grass on the front lawn. Then, he found the pruning shears and trimmed the boxwood. By the time he pulled all the weeds from the tulip patch, he figured he'd had enough exercise for the day. His mother wouldn't be home from church for another forty minutes or an hour, so he went in the kitchen to see what he could cook. He found a roasting hen in the refrigerator, seasoned it, stuffed it with herbs, put it on the spit, set the rotisserie, got his mother's Sunday paper and a cup of coffee and made himself comfortable. It would be either a good day or a bad one, and he was prepared for both.

"Yoo-hoo! Where are you, Son?" His mother burst into the house like a curtain billowing in the breeze. "The front yard looks great"—he wondered why she always referred to the lawn as the yard—"and the shrubs look as if you manicured them. Did you get something to eat?"

He rested the coffee and newspaper on the table and went to greet her. "Hi. I'll bet you turned heads today. You look great," he said, hugging her.

She patted the back of her dark-green suede hat. "When I was your age, I had all of 'em doing double takes."

He looked down at her and grinned. "I'll *bet* you did. I seasoned your chicken and put it on the rotisserie."

"Good. Put some sweet potatoes in the microwave. Everything else is cooked. Let me change my clothes. By the way, you didn't tell me you were coming today. Anything special going on?"

"You may think so. Go on and change."

She glanced at him over her shoulder, but said nothing, for although she easily figured him out, she treated him as the man he was, and never tried to force his hand. With a half laugh, he recalled that she used her wiles on Willis rather than on him, possibly because she scored better with Willis.

"I was down in Athens yesterday," he told her after she changed. It didn't surprise him that she set the plate down on the table almost hard enough to shatter it.

"Who do you know in Athens?"

He walked over to her and put both arms around her. Her body communicated some resistance, but she didn't move away. "After I questioned my father, he told me that his mother, my grandmother, was living in Athens, so I called her and went to see her. I'm glad I did, Mama. She's a youthful eighty-eight. Did you know that she taught high school math and physics—my best subjects in school—and that she paints? She's pretty good, too. Dad is her only child."

Shock reverberated throughout his body when he realized he had referred to his father as Dad. "He takes good care of her," Lucas continued in awed tones. "I learned a lot about myself and why I'm like I am. It's a pity you never met her, because you would have loved her."

She moved away from him then and looked into his eyes. "Because *you* love her?"

He shrugged. "Yes. I suppose I do. It's impossible not to love her. Having her grandchild with her in her home made her so happy."

A frown covered her face. "But she has two granddaughters."

If she was fishing, he was not going to bite. "She didn't know she had a grandson until several weeks back when Dad discovered he had to have that surgery. I told him I was going to see her, but I haven't spoken with him since I got back."

She turned back to the table and resumed setting it for their noonday meal. "Back then, I would have given anything to meet her, but after things went sour between Calvin and me—"

"Why did it go sour? Couldn't you both have admitted that you made mistakes and parted friends?"

"Never!" she spat out. "That man loved me, but he loved money and status more. I'm no longer bitter, though, because you've been such a blessing to me, but I'll love him as long as I breathe."

He didn't know what to make of it. "What do you want from him, Mama? He's still married."

"I know." Her voice had a wistfulness that surprised him. "I can't have him, but I long to know that he's contented, that he's well and . . . and comfortable. I know he's not happy, because he loves me and he's living with her."

He shoved his hands in his trouser pockets, walked to the other end of the dining room and back to her. "You're telling me that love is that powerful, that it can last so long with nothing to fuel it?"

She stared at him. *Nothing to fuel it?* We fell in love on sight, and for four years, we gave it all the fuel it needed. Haven't you ever been in love?"

"I'm beginning to wonder."

Susan looked through her mail and suddenly her heart seemed to stop beating. She clutched the envelope with *Architectural Design* in its return address, opened it with trembling fingers and read: "We'd like to do a story on you for publication along with photos of the wonderful house you've decorated. We love your ideas and the way you put colors and styles together."

She couldn't read any further, for tears blurred her vision. She put the letter aside, went into the living room and sat down. Suddenly, she jumped up and whooped for joy. She was going to be featured in one of the country's leading design magazines. She twirled around and around, ran to the phone and dialed Cassie's number.

"I just got a reply from the magazine, Cassie. They're going to run the story, and they want to interview me."

"Oh, goodness, Susan. I'm so excited. I bet Jay will be a spot of grease on Market Street when he sees that."

Several days later a reporter arrived at Susan's house along with a photographer, and Susan breathed deeply when at its conclusion, she had managed to get through the interview without relating personal facts that she would hate seeing in the years to come. She had no way of knowing the powerful impact that article would have on her life.

In the meantime, Jessica Burton was so delighted in having her home featured in a national magazine, that she introduced Susan to her friends, several of whom clamored for her services, although their homes did not need redecorating.

"You're gonna fall flat on your ass," Jay Weeks told her one afternoon while browsing in her shop. "You can't maintain that standard, because anything you buy here is second rate and you can't run to New York every time you need a yard of trimming. Then everybody will know you're in the class with the rest of us."

Deciding not to lose her temper, she forced a grin. "Not to worry, Jay. If I land on my fanny, I'll find good company, because you'll be down there sitting on yours. Now, would you please excuse me so I can stitch this braid?" He sauntered toward the door, and she called after him. "How'd you like the piece in *Architectural Design*? I thought it was rather elegant."

"What piece? You can find all kinds of junk in magazines these days."

Her bottom lip sagged. Why had she ever thought she could be friends with Jay Weeks? *I don't care what he thinks. It wouldn't be junk if it was attributed to him.* She picked up the remote control, turned on the CD player, changed her mood with Ray Charles's "What I Say," and was rocking to it when the telephone rang.

"Pettiford Interiors. This is Susan."

"Hi. You sound happy, and well you should. That's a spectacular piece *Architectural Design* has on you in this month's issue. Congratulations."

"Thanks. Coming from you, that's a real tribute, Lucas. Do you really like what I did with Jessica Burton's house?"

"Absolutely. It gave me an idea. How'd you like to work with me at Hamilton Village? I need someone to decorate model apartments. It'll take you a while, because the village consists of three buildings, each with a different design. If you're willing, let me know your fee, and I'll get my attorney to draw up a contract."

He was serious? She hadn't dreamed of such a plum of a job. "You mean you'll pay whatever I charge? I've never done anything like that. I'll have to look at the apartments, and I need to know what age and income level you're shooting for."

"But you'll do it?"

"If we come to terms, definitely, and thanks for thinking of me."

"Thinking of you is something I do with remarkable regularity."

I'd better ignore that remark, she thought. *What is it about this man that the sound of his voice can set me on fire?*

"Aren't you going to respond?" he asked, and she thought his voice carried the sound of hope, something that she had not associated with him, for he was a man who wore self-assurance the way judges wear their robes.

"I can't encourage that sort of talk, Lucas. I've told you there can't be anything between us but a platonic friendship."

"You're joking. Surely you don't make love with all of your buddies. Anyway, you don't believe that yourself. There's already more between you and me than many married couples can boast of. You respond to me as no other woman has, and I'd better not get into what you do to *me*. The question is what we'll do about it. Frankly, this unresolved relationship is getting to me. Someday you're going to tell me why you started it."

"I told you—"

"Oh, sure, you told me something, but the better I know you, the less I believe that explanation."

"I'm sincere in what I said, Lucas. It's true that I cave in sometimes when I'm with you—"

"Stop it, Susan. Mislead anybody you like, but tell yourself the truth.

"If you can, I'd like you to start in the first building of

Hamilton Village in about two weeks. I want the model rooms on the eighth floor."

"I need to see the plans for that floor so that, from the beginning, I can design each apartment differently. I hate redoing anything. What about the public rooms?"

"These apartments are intended mainly for retirees. I suggest you do the lobby and recreation rooms last. I'll bring the floor plans to your office tomorrow."

Shortly after one o'clock the next day, Monday, the shop door opened and she looked up from her drafting board to see Lucas stride in carrying a roll of plans. "How about some lunch?" he said. "I can go across the street and get a couple of barbecued pork sandwiches, or we can waste a lot of time on an elegant meal."

She put the pen aside and took off her smock. "Hi. Make it barbecued chicken, and let's eat here. I'll make some coffee and open two cans of soup. Thanks to you, I have a nice kitchen over there."

After lunch, they sat down to discuss her ideas for decorating the retirement village. "I think light colors, and a focus on comfort and safety should attract seniors," she said, "so I won't use ultra modern furniture, or low slung chairs."

He leaned over the drafting table, too close, and he knew it, but she wouldn't give him the satisfaction of knowing her reaction to his nearness. "That would make a nice room for a child," she said, "but since we're dealing with seniors, I'll put a big television in there."

"That's what I intended it for, a den," he said. "Speaking of children, what's happening with Rudy?"

"I was going to tell you. I've become friendly with Harris, my lawyer, and his wife, and so I didn't want to use him for something personal like this, but it was moving so slowly that I called him and told him my problem. He brought the papers over this morning, I signed them, and he's filing them. Now, I have to wait. He said it could be a month or ten months.

"Lucas, I don't know what I'll do if they turn me down. I love her so much, and she loves me."

"I know. I've always known. Well, now's the time to send up some prayers. What are you going to do about Nathan?"

"I'll just have to make sure that they stay in close contact. They need each other."

"Yeah," he said in a manner that seemed absentminded, at least for him. "Funny how easily a person can become a habit."

Lucas left his regular Monday morning meeting with the senior staff of Jackson Enterprises feeling that they had finally accepted him as the boss, although he'd had to roll heads in order to achieve that. He drove to Calvin Jackson's house, an imposing brick Tudor on the edge of Danville, parked in front of it, strolled up the walk and rang the bell. He'd never cared for the Tudor style, because most of the houses contained space that wasn't easily put to good use.

"Good morning. I'm Lucas Hamilton," he said to the woman who opened the door.

The woman's eyes widened. "Yes, I can see that. He's in the library." Considering the draft of cold air that came from her, he didn't have to imagine who she was. He'd finally met Mrs. Calvin Jackson.

The library. And where the hell is that? he wanted to ask her when she left it to him to find his way. But as an architect, he knew the Tudor design, and walked directly to the room in which his father sat reading *The Woodmore Times* and drinking coffee.

Calvin looked up at him, smiled and pointed to a chair facing him. "I wanted to call you and ask how it went, but I decided to leave it to you. I don't have the right to intrude in your life; I'm thankful for whatever you give me."

He ignored that last part, recognizing the truth in it but prepared to move on from the past, to the extent that they could. "You mean my visit with Nana? I'm still awed by it." With his forearms resting on his thighs, he leaned forward. "Dad, she's so tiny and frail, and at the same time, she's so strong."

Calvin Jackson closed his eyes and leaned back in his chair while his lips trembled. "Do you know what you called me?"

He hadn't planned to say it, but it came off his tongue easily, and maybe it was time. "It shocked me when I said it to Mama yesterday. I didn't force it. I think it has something to do with Nana. I fell in love with her. It's as if she's a present you gave me."

"Thank you. She called me, and I never knew her to talk so fast and so much. She is enchanted with you. Are you going back to see her?"

"Of course. As often as I can. I saw a couple of things I want to do there."

"She told me. I get a sense that you take good care of your mother."

"I do, indeed. And you take good care of Nana. It amazed me that she and I have so much in common. My visit with her was a homecoming for me. I'm so glad I went."

Sitting with his father in the house that he should have called home, looking at the wealth that substituted for happiness, he thought of his own life. He didn't need to be wealthier than he was; he needed a family and time in which to smell the flowers.

He observed his father, strong and with the appearance of a capable man. "You're up and around now, so in a month I should be able to hand the company back to you. What do you say?"

Calvin donned his corporate demeanor and looked hard at Lucas. "Your contract is for a minimum of one year. That aside, I had something else in mind."

Lucas held up his hand. "Before we get to that, tell me what you think the CEO of your company is worth for a year."

Calvin let him know that, in business matters, he did not shilly-shally. "In your case, about three hundred thousand more than the contract stipulates. Now, to what I have in mind. I want you to add Hamilton Architectural Designs to Jackson Enterprises, and—Lucas bolted upright. "Hear me out. You would continue as CEO of Jackson Enterprises as newly formed, and I would retire completely. I want to travel while I still have my health and enough energy. I've dreamed of seeing Europe, Africa, Asia, the world, in fact. I don't want to die without having seen the Taj

Mahal, the world's most beautiful edifice. Can you appreciate that?"

Lucas nodded in a perfunctory manner. "Sure I can, but I want to give my architectural business my full attention."

"Hire an architect whose ideas are similar to yours. Think about it. In five years, you'll double the value of our holdings, something I can't do. You're young, and you have vision and ideas. Old men dream dreams."

Lucas got up and began walking from one end of the room to the other, and his father remained quiet, as if allowing him the freedom to think. He stopped in front of the man he had called Dad for the first time three minutes earlier. "This is bizarre. I spent all of my professional life working my tail off to equal you in status and accomplishment, and now you're handing it to me. I'm not sure I want to accept. I have to think about it."

"Fair enough. I'm sure you'll arrive at the right decision. By the way, can you come over Sunday afternoon? My daughters will be here, and I want you to meet them."

"What about your wife? I assume it was she who opened the door for me. Will this be a family conference?"

Calvin lifted his right shoulder in a lazy, uncaring way. "Who knows? I don't doubt that you can hold your own in any setting. And yes, that was my wife."

Lucas looked hard at Calvin. "Why are you doing this? You've known me less than six months. How do you know I won't steal the company or worse, destroy it?"

A smile settled around Calvin's eyes. "Do you think I got where I am today by being stupid? I'm a good judge of human beings, and I damn well know the difference between copper and tin. You won't do any such thing. You're too proud, and you're honest. I admire your character, and I know that I am not taking a risk. Hasn't it occurred to you that you're only getting what's due you?"

Lucas held up one hand. "Slow down, Dad. Has it occurred to you that your family may make it impossible for me to run this operation as I see fit?"

"I'll take care of that." A laugh floated out of him. "You're safe from them as long as they don't have to work. Promise me you'll give this serious thought."

The following evening around seven-thirty, Lucas left an old movie, *The Color Purple*, with Susan—having given her seven yards of silk velvet as a bribe for going with him—took her hand and walked with her to the corner ice cream stand. "I've got so much on my mind, Susan. Let's get some ice cream and go sit in the park and eat it. It's too nice an evening to go inside."

As they sat on a bench in Pine Tree Park eating the ice cream, she wondered about his inattentiveness. "If you want to talk, I'm listening," she said.

"I don't know where to start." With apparent effort, he told her of his father's proposition. "Why should I turn my life around for a man who didn't recognize me as his child?"

"Wait a minute. That's not what you told me. Your mother had a hand in that."

"Oh, all right, but he didn't bust his butt demanding his rights." His fingers brushed his forehead, as if ridding it of the memory. "Okay. You have a point. His company is solid, and in the six short months that I've run it, I've improved it, but I'm not a business administrator; I'm an architect, and that's the work I love to do."

She didn't spare him. "If he had married your mother, you would not be complaining; you'd do what you were expected to do. Don't act hastily, Lucas. You're beginning to care for your father, and he obviously admires and respects you. I suspect he loves you, too. Get to know him. You may learn to love him."

"You're right. He's a warm, decent man, and he's had over a third of a century in which to suffer for his misdeed. Say, would you like to go with me to see my grandmother this weekend? I think I'll drive. Flying is such a hassle these days."

"You're sweet," she said in an effort to minimize the pain that his question stoked in her. "But Lucas, a man does not bring a woman to see his grandmother unless he's contemplating permanent ties with her. Your grandmother will get the wrong impression, and I will be embarrassed."

He looked at her. "You said I'm sweet. So why would it embarrass you to be seen with me?"

She slapped the back of his left hand. "You can be very thick headed when it suits you."

"I was hoping for company. It's a long drive. You could keep me from falling asleep."

"Take Willis Carter. Your grandmother won't make any mistakes there."

His features became animated, and he crossed his knees and leaned against the back of the bench. "You've given me an idea. I'm planning to change some things in her kitchen, and if Willis goes with me, we may be able to do it together. What's wrong?" he asked when she appeared to sulk.

"Oh, nothing. I'm disappointed that Willis can replace me so easily."

"In your dreams, maybe." He indicated a desire to leave the park, and she wondered at his sudden shift from light-heartedness to seriousness.

"I really enjoyed sitting there and eating ice cream. Do you like picnicking in remote places? I do, and I took Rudy and Nathan picnicking over near Scenic Gardens. They were so excited and so happy. Oh, Lucas. I love those children so much."

"I know you do, and I hope it works out well for all of you."

She had attempted several times recently to ask Lucas about his half sisters, but hadn't followed through for fear that he might not want to talk about them. After all, they had been raised in comparative luxury. She grasped his left hand and knew at once from his reaction that he anticipated an unusual move on her part.

"What's on your mind?"

"I was wondering whether you've met your . . . uh . . . sisters and if you have, what you think of them."

She was always so sensitive about his feelings. He squeezed her fingers. "Not yet. We're meeting at Dad's house next Sunday. He warned me that the older of the two can be a cuss, but that doesn't bother me."

She thought for a moment. "You would be in a strong position if your father could tell them that you will be in charge of his business. If you're going to agree to his proposition, why not tell him now? You trust him, don't you?"

"Absolutely."

"Then why don't you accept his proposition. You'll still have Hamilton Architectural Designs, and you'll gain so much more. You won't get revenge by refusing him; you'll only have to watch someone else, maybe a stranger, get what is rightfully yours. If you want to punish him, this is not the way."

They reached his car, and after opening the door for her, he went around to the driver's side and got in. "That's just it. I have no desire to punish him. And you're right. I'm going to call him and take him up on his proposal. It isn't what I've envisaged doing with my life, but maybe his plan is better than mine."

Susan arrived at Wade School that afternoon simultaneously with Ann Price. She parked the BMW and walked toward Ann's car as the children jumped out of it and raced to meet her. When she knelt to hug them, they launched themselves into her arms.

"You children go on inside," Ann said. "I want to talk with Ms. Pettiford for a minute." They kissed Susan's cheek and ran toward the school's front door, holding hands as they went.

Susan stood and faced Ann. "Hi. What do you want to talk to me about?"

"Well . . ." At the woman's hesitancy, Susan experienced a moment of anxiety. "I . . . uh . . . Well, how are your plans for adopting Rudy coming along?"

After remembering that Ann had offered to help in the adoption, she decided to confide in her. "I've signed the papers, but I don't want Rudy to know in case it falls through. She would be as disappointed as I."

Ann Price nodded. "That's good. I'll be glad to speak for you. You'll need good references. I'll be glad to send an affidavit to the agency."

"I appreciate that, Ann. I don't know what I'll do if they turn me down."

"I don't think they will."

Susan didn't see Rudy and Nathan when she went inside the building, for she was already a few minutes late and, assuming that the children were either in class or with Lucas, she went on to her classroom.

Occasionally, Lucas walked the halls to assure himself that nothing untoward occurred at Wade School while he was in charge. As he stepped out of his office, Rudy and Nathan ran up to him and tugged at his hands, one on either side of him as they usually did.

He put his arms around their shoulders. "Why aren't you in class?"

"We have to ask you something, Mr. Hamilton," Nathan said. However, it was Rudy who seemed worried.

"Mr. Hamilton," she began. "Mrs. Price gave us a dollar and fifty cents to give to the tsunami children, but I want to buy Ms. Pettiford a present with mine."

"Me, too," Nathan said. "Do the tsunami children need it real bad?"

"You mean the children in Asia who are victims of the tsunami? Yes, they need it badly."

Rudy hung her head. "Gee, I just gave everything in my piggy bank to the New Orleans children. Now I have to send—"

He hunkered between them. "You have a home, food and clothing, but those children don't."

"Okay," they said in unison.

"Tell you what," Lucas said. "Give your money to the tsunami victims, I'll take you shopping and you may buy something for Ms. Pettiford." When they hugged and kissed him, the pangs in his heart became almost unbearable. *If I don't hurry, I'll miss the opportunity to have a family.* "We won't mention this to Ms. Pettiford," he told them. "It will be a surprise."

At the end of the tutoring session, he walked out of the building in time to see Susan hugging Rudy and Nathan, as if she would never see them again and detaining Ann Price, who looked on, smiling like a benevolent grandmother.

Susan loved those children as much as if she'd given birth to them, yet she was thirty-four and seemed to make no effort to have any of her own. Scratch that. She hadn't told him to wear a condom and hadn't asked if he might have impregnated her. Hmmm. One day, I'll make her tell all, even if I have to get her in bed in order to do it.

The next afternoon, he waited for Ann Price at the Rose Hill School when she arrived for Rudy and Nathan and told her of his promise to the children. "I'd like to take them shopping now, if it's all right with you. I'll have them at your place within a couple of hours."

"The smaller the store, the better it will be for your nerves," she told him. "They'll be so happy they'll drive you crazy."

"Maybe, but I doubt it. We get on well." Rudy and Nathan ran to them, stopped and gazed up at Lucas in wordless question. "We'd better get started," he told them. "I promised Mrs. Price to have you home in a couple of hours." He strapped the excited children in the backseat of the town car and headed for Market Street.

In Annie's Souvenir Shop, Nathan picked up a yellow necklace and showed it to the clerk. "Can I buy this for a dollar and fifty cents?" he asked.

The clerk shook her head. "No, dear. I'm afraid not."

Nathan's face sagged. "How much more do I need?"

"Wrap it up nicely for him," Lucas said. "It's for his teacher."

Nathan turned to look at Lucas. "Thanks, Mr. Hamilton. Miss Pettiford is my friend." He looked up at Lucas with eyes that shone with happiness. "You are, too."

"What can I buy her?" Rudy asked. "I can spend a dollar and fifty cents, too."

The sales woman looked at Lucas, who said, "Pick out something, Rudy."

"I want . . . everything is so pretty," she said.

Lucas ran his fingers over an amber bracelet that matched the necklace Nathan chose. "This looks nice."

"Oooo. It's beautiful, Mr. Hamilton. Can I give her this one?" He nodded, and she wrapped her arms around his legs. "I love you, Mr. Hamilton."

With their packages in little bags, the children thanked the clerk. "You are welcome," she said, "come back to see me again."

To Lucas, she said, "They're such charming children, so well mannered and obedient. It's been a pleasure to have them here."

"Thanks," he said, realizing how proud of them he was and how happy he would be if he could take his own children shopping. He took their hands and headed down Market Street.

"Don't we have to be home now?" Nathan asked him

"Not yet. We have time for ice cream."

"I love ice cream," Rudy said. "I never got any before, but now I do. I hope I don't have to go back to those families anymore."

Nathan's arm slid around Rudy, and he whispered something to her. "That's not likely," Lucas said. "Mrs. Price, Ms. Pettiford and I will do all we can to make sure you're happy, Rudy."

"Everybody loves me now, Mr. Hamilton. Before, nobody did."

"All of us love you, Rudy, and we love Nathan, too. Don't forget that."

Sunday afternoon at four o'clock, Lucas pushed the button at the door of Calvin Jackson's big Tudor house and listened to the chimes play the tune, "Row, Row, Row Your Boat." He liked the warmer welcome than one received from the sound of a buzz. The door opened, and he looked into the eyes of Luveen Jackson. He knew it was Luveen, because he doubted that Enid, the older of the two sisters, would have greeted him with a smile.

"So you're Lucas," she said with a broad smile. "I'm glad I know you're my brother. Papa's waiting for you. I'm Luveen."

"I gathered as much. I'm glad to meet you, Luveen."

He followed her to the den, and when he walked in, Calvin rose and went to meet him. "Welcome, Son. As usual, you're right on time," he said in a tone that suggested he was making a point. He gestured toward the woman who sat farthest from him. "This is Marcie Jackson, my wife."

Lucas walked over to her and extended his hand. "How do you do, Mrs. Jackson?" He waited for her to show him and everyone present what she was made of. She let him wait, and a grin altered the contours of his face. It wasn't nice, but he couldn't help it.

Visibly shaken, she extended her hand. "We met a couple of times."

His grin widened. "Did we?" He walked back to his father.

"This is my elder daughter, Enid," Calvin said. "You'll find that she's very much like her mother."

"Hello, Enid. Dad has spoken of you quite a bit. I've been looking forward to meeting you." He'd been waiting for an opportunity to slip in the word, Dad.

Her eyes seemed to bulge. "Uh . . . hello."

"I'm sure Luveen introduced herself to you already," Calvin said.

Lucas walked over to Luveen and kissed her cheek. "She did, indeed, and I appreciated the welcome."

"There's only one person missing," Marcie said, with what to him sounded like a sneer.

"Don't worry. I haven't told her about this yet," Lucas said. "If I had, she would certainly have wanted to come." He ignored the look of panic on Marcie Jackson's face. "But my mother has a great sense or propriety, and she would have restrained herself, just as she's done for the last thirty-five years." A glance at his father told him that the man appreciated his ability to duel.

"You may imagine that I didn't arrange this meeting as some kind of side show," Calvin said. "I've always wanted my children to know each other, but Lucas's mother denied me any paternal rights, and I had to live with that." He ignored the gasps from Marcie and Enid. "I saw him in person for the first time six months ago. I'm proud of the man he's become.

"He's been running Jackson Enterprises and doing an outstanding job. Tomorrow I will retire. Lucas has agreed to add Hamilton Architectural Designs to Jackson Enterprises, and he will run the company as CEO, owner and manager." Enid jumped up from the chair and slowly dropped back down. "Proceeds from Hamilton Architectural Designs belong to Lucas, and half of Jackson Enterprises belongs to him." Marcie stood and turned to leave the room.

"Only those present to sign this document will get anything from this estate," Calvin said. "For years, I have tried to interest my family in my business, tried to make them see that if I died, they would lose the company because they didn't even know what constituted it and weren't interested. Not even in those awful days when I thought I'd lose it and could have used help, if only someone to answer the telephone. When I faced that surgery and couldn't manage the business, I asked Lucas to do it. He agreed, and after six months, he knows it as well as I do and has even improved some of the properties. I am happy to place it in his hands. You may stay, Marcie, or you may leave. The choice is yours." She sat down, as Lucas knew she would.

"As I was saying," Calvin continued, "we will all be taken care of. Income from the other half of Jackson Enterprises will be shared by the three of you and myself."

Lucas could see Marcie Jackson slowly shrink. "You can still hang out with the Jack and Jill folks, Marcie," Calvin said. "For the last few years, the company's been netting about two million a year. With Lucas at the helm, it will do much better, because he won't tolerate half the foolishness from some of the employees that I put up with."

"How could you?" Marcie hissed. "This is what you've always wanted, isn't it?"

Calvin leaned toward her. "If you had paid one-tenth as much attention to me as you paid to your clubs and charities and to any organization that asked you to be a board member; if you had spent two evenings a month at home with me; if—in those days when I was poor—you hadn't spent money I hadn't even made and kept me ridden with debts; if you had been a wife rather than an ornament, believe me, Lucas Hamilton would not exist. He's here, and he has a special place in my heart. End of topic."

Luveen appeared to be the peacemaker when she smiled at Lucas and said, "Will I get income monthly or annually? Now, I just tell Papa I need some money, but at my age, I suppose I should organize my affairs better."

"However Dad arranges it," he said, "although I think it

should be according to your wishes and based on the previous year's records."

"Right," Calvin said. "Each of you arrange it with Lucas."

Marcie glared at her husband through pursed lips that seemed to have shriveled into a thin line. "You've got your millions, and you're cutting us loose with a measly two hundred thousand a year. How do you know this man will do right by us?"

Calvin's smile could only be described as pitying. "It's too late for pretense, Marcie. We can only deal with what we have left. Besides, I haven't said a word about cutting anyone loose. If you'd been paying attention, you'd have noticed that Lucas is a gentleman. I'd trust him with my life."

"I want mine annually in advance," Enid said.

Lucas didn't know why, but Enid stuck in his craw like ground glass. To show her that she hadn't struck a blow, he reached down for the briefcase beside his chair, took out a pad, and made a note of what she'd said. *"Once a year means exactly that: once a year,"* he said, looking directly at her.

He checked his watch. A quarter to six. If he hurried, he could see his mother and get a decent meal. He stood. "I have to run, Dad. I want to have dinner with my mother. I'll see you Monday morning around the usual time."

Calvin opened a drawer and took out some papers. "I'm going to sign this above my name, and date it, and I want each of you to do the same." He read it aloud to assure them that the content was as he had discussed. "Is there anyone here who doesn't want to sign it?" Since he got no response, he signed it and passed it next to Lucas.

When they had all signed, he stood, shook Lucas's hand and handed him a copy of the document. "You're owner and CEO of Jackson Enterprises. As soon as I'm up to it, I'm going on a safari. I've wanted to do that for years, but I never could get away."

Lucas didn't feel triumphant, only sad for the man whose life had churned in an unhappy marriage for over a third of a century. He patted his father's shoulder, a barely noticeable gesture, as they stood head to head. "Thanks for everything. See you tomorrow."

"I'll walk out with you," Luveen said.

He wasn't going to lie and tell Enid and Marcie that he was glad to have met them; he could have done without ever seeing either of them. Forcing a smile, he said, "Good-bye, all. See you again."

"I hope we get to know each other better," Luveen said as they walked to the door. "Your existence was a shock to me. Papa told Enid and me about you together, and he didn't spare the details. He's very impressed with you. When you were growing up, did you know about Enid and me?"

"Not until Dad told me after he and I met. Discovering sisters who are older than I rocked me a bit, I must say I'm glad at least one of them is friendly."

Luveen's laughter tinkled like a bell. "Enid and Mama don't knock themselves out making people comfortable. Have a nice supper with your mother."

"Thanks. She's a great cook."

Half an hour later he parked in front of his mother's house. "Hi," she said when she met him at the door. "I'm just putting the barbecued pork on the rotisserie. It'll be ready in about an hour. I can give you—"

He kissed her cheek. "Slow down, Mama. You know I'm going to wait for that barbecued pork. I just left Dad's house. He had a family conference with his wife, his two daughters and me."

She clutched his arm so tightly that he felt the print of her nails. "You were at Calvin's house?"

"Sure," he said, as casually as he could. "I go there every Monday."

"I see. And you met Marcie?"

"Why . . . yes, and his daughters, too."

She looked away from him and spoke in a softer than normal voice. "How did Marcie treat you?"

"She was testy, but that will be the last time. You know I can hold my own. I don't expect any trouble out of her. I'm not so sure about Enid, the older daughter, but I suspect she'll stay out of my way as long as the money's rolling in."

"You put Marcie in her place right in front of Calvin?"

He jerked his shoulder in a slight shrug. "She got out of *her* place in front of him. Anyway, he didn't seem to mind, and if he had, that wouldn't have bothered me. Don't worry about it, Mama. I'll tell you this much. He told them in my presence that I have a special place in his heart."

She let out a long breath. "So I didn't ruin things for the two of you after all. Thank the Lord. What did he want a family conference for?"

He went into the kitchen got a bottle of beer for himself and a glass of wine for his mother, sat facing her in the living room and told her of his arrangement with his father. "I've managed his and mine separately and done a decent job of it, it ought to be a little easier this way."

"You're sure you want to do this?"

"I gave it plenty of thought, and I'm satisfied that I've made the right decision." He showed her the agreement signed that afternoon.

"You got the lion's share," she said. "He's been very generous."

"I'll earn everything I get, Mama. Nothing in this life comes free, and I'm preparing myself right now for some family skullduggery led by Enid Jackson-Moore."

She shook her head from side to side as if unable to contemplate what had happened. "I know you can take care of yourself, Son. Just watch your back."

Chapter Eleven

"The wheels of progress move so slowly," Susan said to Ann Price on a Monday afternoon late in May. "That agency still hasn't acknowledged receipt of my application to adopt Rudy."

"It's been that way all my life," Ann said. "People say patience is a virtue, but if you ask me, it's a blessing if you got it. I sure hope they do something soon." She stopped peeling apples for a pie and looked at Susan. "Not that Rudy's any trouble, but I'm just so worn out lately."

Susan sat down and leaned against the back of the chair. Ann's sluggishness had worried her for days. "Can't they stay with me?"

"I wish they could. Yesterday morning early, one of the social workers was here claiming she just dropped by. If Rudy hadn't been here, they would probably have taken her away from me. So I guess she can't stay away overnight again."

"I can at least do the laundry and grocery shopping for you. It won't be much of a help, all things considered, but it's something I can do."

Unshed tears glistened in Ann's eyes. "I ought to say no, thank you, Susan, but it would be such a relief. God bless you."

As Susan drove to her shop, she thought of her good fortune compared to Ann's problems. The woman was not well, and yet she had the burden of raising her four grandchildren on a pensioner's income. She had desperately needed the income from

Rudy's foster care, but she treated the child as one of her own. *I would give anything for a family with a . . .* she hesitated—*with the man I love. But I can't have a family, so I can't have him. He deserves his birthright. But I have my health and a good life, something that Ann would love to have.*

With the tutoring program nearing its end, she wouldn't see Rudy unless she went to Ann's house, and if she did that too often, would she wear out her welcome? But if she didn't have to see Lucas twice a week maybe she would finally get him out of her system. *Foolish thinking. I'll never get him out of my system, and maybe that's the price I have to pay for using him.*

She parked in front of her shop, went inside and checked her mail. Who was Enid Jackson-Moore? She read further. The woman wanted her summer house decorated before hot weather set in, and the house was in Nags Head, on the Outer Banks of North Carolina. She could do that, provided the place wasn't too large. Her priority at present was Hamilton Village. She telephoned the woman.

"Mrs. Jackson-Moore, this is Susan Pettiford. I've just received your letter. I have a commitment, but I may be able to decorate your house if it isn't too large. What do you need?"

"I appreciate your calling. With your reputation, you must be very busy. Jessica Burton is singing your praises, and I saw your work in *Architectural Design*. I'm facing the ocean, almost right on the beach, and I want the house to reflect that. I mean, no reds. I have five rooms."

"I have to see it. If I decide to do it, we'll sign a contract. I can get over there this coming Sunday."

"Great." She gave her the address and her cell phone number. "I'll be there all weekend. I can't tell you how happy I'll be if you'll do it."

Susan finished the call as quickly as possible and hung up. She'd bet anything that the woman was only interested in staying even with Jessica Burton. "It will cost you," she said aloud.

She walked into the neat, two-bedroom house that Sunday and stared out at the Atlantic Ocean through the glass wall that was the back of the house, a challenge to any interior decorator.

The large deck beyond it put a limit on what she could do with that living room without ruining the setting and the view.

"Well, what do you think?" Enid asked her. "What can you do with that glass wall?"

"Wall-to-wall accordion Chinese screens that stand folded in each corner. When you want privacy, you close them and cover the window."

"Won't they be too heavy to pull around?"

"They'll be on a track. Not to worry."

"And you figured that out just like that? Where's the contract? I fixed us some lunch."

While Enid set the table and served the lunch, Susan looked around the remainder of the house and filled in the blanks in the contract. Enid signed it and motioned to Susan.

"Come on, let's eat. It's already one o'clock. I usually spend the entire summer here, straight through the hurricane season and sometimes a good part of the winter. I have a small apartment in Danville, but this is my preferred residence."

"Do you live alone? As your decorator, I need to know whether anyone lives with you. Comfort for men is not the same as comfort for women."

Enid rolled her eyes toward the ceiling. "My husband and I separated four years ago. I don't need a divorce and don't plan to give him one. I've had my fill of men. My own father just threw a sack of shit in my face."

Susan's eyes widened at that unexpected descent into street language.

"All of a sudden," Enid continued, "six months ago he announced that he had a bastard son from a four-year adulterous affair that neither my mother, my sister nor I knew anything about. Two weeks ago, he got us all together—and turned over everything he owns to his son—everything, including his business."

Susan could only hope her surprise wasn't written on her face. She couldn't believe her new client was Lucas' half sister. "What will your father do now that he doesn't manage his own business?" she asked, hoping to get off the subject of Lucas.

"He told us he's going to see the world, do all the things he's always longed to do."

"Will your mother travel with him?"

"I can't imagine them doing anything together. They'd kill each other. One of them says something, and the other doesn't even respond. Their marriage is worse than mine ever was."

"That's a pity." She looked for a way to end the conversation, for she suspected that if Enid had a listener, she would talk incessantly until midnight. "I'd better be getting back to the airport. I'll e-mail you my sketches, and I'd like you to let me know what you think as soon as you can."

"All right. It's been wonderful getting to know you. I'm sure I'll be pleased. If you'll wait two or three minutes, I'll drive you to the airport." When she smiled, she resembled Lucas, Susan realized. "I hope we're going to be good friends."

"Thanks so much," Susan said, "and thank you for the wonderful lunch." She ignored Enid's offer of friendship, because she didn't think a friendship with her possible in the circumstances. Furthermore, she suspected that Enid thought mainly of her own words and needs, and not of anyone's consideration of them or response to them.

When she returned home a few minutes after seven, the light on her answering machine was blinking. She returned Lucas's call first. "Hi. I just got in. What's up?" she asked him.

"Have supper with me," he said, "Unless you've already eaten."

She shouldn't do it. Nothing but misery could come of a deepening relationship with him. "I . . . uh . . . all right, but not any place fancy."

"But I want a decent meal," he said. "I was thinking of Pinky's."

"Pinky's in the evening means I have to put on a decent-looking dress."

"You have to do that anytime of day. Besides, are you suggesting that I'm not worth it?"

She detected the laughter in his voice, but ignored it. "Sweetheart, you're worth far more than a dress." At his long silence, she added, "Aren't you?"

"You're flirting with me, but I rather like it, and especially since I know you never offer what you won't deliver."

"You're full of it, Lucas Hamilton," she blustered. "What time do you want us to meet?"

"I'll be there in forty minutes, and keep yourself in check. I'm in the mood to believe everything you say and do."

She waited for him just inside her door with her raincoat on and her pocketbook on her arm. "Now, if I can keep him at a distance when he brings me home, I'll pat myself on the back. Through the dining room window, she watched him dash up the walk with his lips positioned as if he were whistling. She licked her lips as she watched his sexy gait. "He is some man," she said to herself. "Everything about him screams *man*." He rang the doorbell and, without thinking, she answered it at once.

"Hi," he said. "Hmmm. I certainly hope you were expecting *me*."

"What do you mean? Of course I was expecting you."

He raised one eyebrow. "I'm glad to know it. From the expression of welcome on your face, I'd be happy to stay here and call out for supper."

She didn't have to wonder what he saw on her face, because she knew what she'd been thinking. "No, thanks," she said. "I dressed for Pinky's, and that's where I want to go."

He leaned down and kissed the side of her mouth. "Pinky's, huh? You break my heart. Where's your key? I have a lot to tell you. My life's moving like a spinning top."

"Mine, too. Which one of us goes first?"

He parked across the street from Pinky's Restaurant, got out and headed around to the passenger door, but she had it open when he got there, held out her hand to him and eased out of the car only slightly hampered by her short, narrow skirt. "You tell your story first," he said. "Mine will probably last all evening." They followed the maître d' to their table.

"I dunno," she said. "My story may be your story. I just left Enid Jackson-Moore." His eyes widened and a frown replaced the smile he'd worn seconds earlier. "She wrote, asking me to decorate her house on Nags Head, so I went to see it. I'd just left there when I returned your call. I didn't know who she was until she began complaining about her father, and his having given you ownership of his business. Lucas, that sister can talk. She told me all about the family meeting, her parents' relationship over the years, and how her father feels about you."

Lucas leaned back in the chair. "And how did she say he feels about me?"

"That you're special to him, and she said any fool could see that that's because your mother is his one great love."

"I suppose that should make me feel great," he said, "but it doesn't. Both of my parents have been miserable ever since mama told him she was expecting."

"Enid suggested that she'd like the two of us to be friends, but I don't want that. I don't want a running account of her fights with you and her attitudes toward you and her father. She's a bitter woman, refuses to give her husband a divorce although they've been separated for four years, and I got the impression that she's developed a negative attitude toward men in general. So, I'm going to keep her at arm's length, as my dad used to counsel. I don't want a personal relationship with her."

"How will you avoid it?"

"What? You're not serious. If I don't want to associate with her, I won't."

"If you tell her we're lovers, that ought to nip it in the bud."

She glared at him. "We are not lovers."

"Don't be silly, Susan. You're the most wonderful lover I've ever had. If you don't remember the first time—and considering how . . . er . . . impassioned you were, I don't see how that's possible—you've *got* to remember what you did to me the second time. I'm human. Are you trying to destroy my ego?"

"Don't make jokes, Lucas. Nothing I say will affect your ego."

He reached across the table and grasped the fingers of her right hand. "I was joking a minute ago, but I'm serious now. You are the only woman who can take the edge off my ego, so be careful, will you?"

She hadn't been prepared for that. "Look, I . . . hadn't we better order?"

He tightened his hold on her hand. "Why are you afraid of me now? I was a guest in your home and in your bed when you didn't know one thing about me other than that I wore pants and was a few inches taller than you. Susan, I can solve $E=mc^2$. You intrigue me far more, so you can bet that I will figure you out, too."

She withdrew her hands and searched for another subject, anything that would remove his focus from her. She should not have agreed to have supper with him, but she had wanted to tell him of her contract with Enid Jackson-Moore before he learned it from someone else.

"Thank you for the lovely presents that Nathan and Rudy gave me. I was flabbergasted. How did you know that I love amber?"

His facial expression told her that she hadn't fooled him and that he would question her again about her reason for making love with him that first time. He explained how he happened to take the children shopping. "Nathan fell in love with that necklace, and I helped Rudy select something that matched it." He reached into his pocket and handed her a small box. "This is from me."

She opened the box and looked at the oval shaped amber earrings that matched the children's gifts. She hardly trusted herself to look at him. "You're . . . these are beautiful." *Why would he do things like this to me? I'm not going to get weepy.* "I'll wear them often. Thank you."

"You started to tell me something about myself. What was it? I need to know, Susan."

She shook her head. "I—"

"May I have your order now, sir?"

After they gave their orders, Susan asked Lucas to excuse her and ignored his raised eyebrow as she left him to go to the women's lounge to collect her presence of mind. *He can do things like this, things that endear him to me even more, and I lose my resolve to get him out of my life. I won't cry. I won't. I swear it!* She reached for the box of tissues that rested on the marble-top counter in the lounge and put a wad of it into her mouth, dampening the impulse to give in to her feelings. Calmer now, she applied some eye drops to clear her eyes, dabbed beneath them with a tissue and went back to the man who could upset her, electrify her, and put her on the defensive as no one else could. He stood when she returned to the table and walked around it to seat her. She would have preferred to seat herself without any assistance, but if she had so much as hinted at that, she would have incurred his annoyance.

"You were gone a while. Everything all right?" he asked her, and to her surprise, his voice contained neither mockery nor sarcasm, but genuine concern.

"I'm fine, thanks." She thought she would force a smile, but when she observed his relief, as if sunshine enveloped him, her smile came from her heart.

"I love barbecued anything," he said, after savoring a forkful of the barbecued short ribs of beef. "My mother can barbecue a sparerib until it dances. If you want to assure yourself an eternal niche in my heart, learn how to barbecue."

She itched to ask why she should have a niche in his heart, but restrained herself and didn't ask him. Instead, she said, "I have other attributes."

With his fork suspended between the plate and his mouth, he said, "You're damned right you have."

She gave up. "I don't want to josh with you right now, Lucas. I don't know why, but that doesn't suit me right now."

"I wasn't teasing. Okay? Have you thought of what you'll do with Enid's house?"

She let her eyes tell him how grateful she was for his having opened a subject into which she could enter with pleasure. "The back of the house is a glass window with nothing between it and the ocean except the sandy beach." She told him of her plans for it. "What do you think?"

"Sounds good to me. It's both decorative and functional."

"As to the rest," she went on, "white walls and white floors, light or white wood and all upholstery and fabrics in sea green, pale blue and aquamarine. To break the monotony, the master bedroom will be in yellow and sand. I'll make the sketches after I see what's available in Woodmore and Winston-Salem and e-mail them to her."

"How long will it take you to sketch the plan?"

"I'll do it one evening at home. While I'm in Winston-Salem, I'll finish shopping for Hamilton Village I. My biggest problem is that older people like velours, velveteens and velvets, but the most comfortable furniture around these days comes in leather. I'm looking for a good mix."

"And you'll find it. Did it ever occur to you that we'd make a great team?"

She held up her hands, palms out. "Don't expect the truth out of me when you ask such questions, Lucas."

"So you *have* thought of it. At least I'm not crazy."

She declined his offer to lengthen the evening with a stop at The Watering Hole, pleading a long and taxing day. "But I enjoyed supper with you."

He parked in front of her house, a white edifice shrouded in moonlight. "What's that sound I hear?" he asked her.

"Fish jumping in the lake. They do that on nights like this when there's a full moon and no wind."

"Walk with me to the lake," he said. "I want to see it in the moonlight. He took her hand and strolled with her to the water's edge. Standing against an old pine tree and with her back to him, he wrapped her in his arms.

"Today, my life changed forever. Enid told you that my dad gave me Jackson Enterprises to operate as I see fit." He explained the conditions of his agreement with his father. But that enormous gift meant less to him than his father's sentiments. "But you don't know what it meant to me to hear him say that I'm special to him. You know . . ." He paused and looked into the distance. "I'm beginning to love my dad."

"I'm so happy for you, Lucas. Does he know?"

"I haven't told him, but at least I've begun calling him dad, and that seems to make him happy. If anybody had told me a year ago that I'd call Calvin Jackson dad and put my arm on his shoulder, I would have called that person a liar." With his arms draped across her shoulder, he walked with her to her house.

He held out his hand for her key, opened the door and stood in the foyer gazing down at her. "Aren't you going to invite me to have a cup of coffee?"

He stood too close to her. She could almost taste his breath. "You just had coffee."

"But I didn't have this," he said, and his mouth was on hers, his arms around her and the heat of his aura began seeping into her. "I need this. I need you!" He broke the kiss. "What was it that you didn't say when you looked at those earrings? I'm not releasing you until you tell me."

Susan didn't want him to release her. "That you're wonderful, that you're so loveable, that—"

He swallowed her words and pushed his tongue into her mouth. She heard her moans and knew that she would capitulate to him. Right then, she didn't care about anything but the way she felt in his arms. When he trembled, shaking her to the core, she held him tighter, and when she felt him hard and bulging against her, she grabbed his hips, the better to feel him.

"Let me go, sweetheart. If you don't want me inside of you, tell me right now."

She locked one hand behind his head and the other on his buttocks, sucked his tongue into her mouth and wrapped her left leg around his right one. He lifted her into his arms and raced up the stairs to her bed. An hour later, he separated his body from hers and fell over on his back, exhausted.

"I wish I knew how this will end," he said. "You can't tell me that you'll be content for us to go our separate ways, that you'll be satisfied if I decided to spend my life with another woman. I sure as hell don't want to see another man within ten feet of you." Suddenly, as if driven, he bolted off the bed and stood beside it. "You didn't get pregnant. Why did you pick me to go to bed with? You are not the kind of woman who . . . How many men other than me have you been in bed with since the first time you made love with me?"

"None." She put the corner of the sheet into her mouth to muffle the sounds that she knew would follow the tears that rolled down her cheeks.

"Right. That's what I thought. You're damned near puritanical. I have a right to know why you did that."

"I t-told y-you, but you don't believe m-me."

"That's because it . . ." He rested one knee on the bed and

leaned across it. "Good Lord. You're crying. I didn't mean to . . . Baby, for goodness sake, don't cry. I wouldn't hurt you for anything." He wrapped her in his arms, kissed her eyes, her cheeks, her lips, and within minutes he was deep inside of her again, driving her to ecstasy. She cried out, oblivious to her words or what they meant.

The following Saturday morning at daybreak, Lucas sat in the backseat of his town car pretending to sleep while Willis took his turn driving on their trip to Athens, Georgia. He had ordered the cabinets for his grandmother's kitchen weeks earlier, and he hoped that the chair elevator would be installed before he and Willis left Sunday afternoon. If not, he would make another trip down there to inspect it before he accepted the job as finished. He stretched out on the backseat to the extent possible.

He couldn't get Susan off his mind. His hearing was perfect, and he understood the English language. Still ringing in his ears was the sound of her moaning, "I love you. I love you. Oh, Lord, I love you!" at the moment when she pulsed around him, squeezing and thrilling him until he thought he would go out of his mind. He couldn't be wrong about that. If she loved him, why did she protest so adamantly that there could be nothing between them, that they were not and could not be lovers? According to Mark, his friend and Susan's lawyer, she was not and never had been married. So what was her problem? Whatever it was, it definitely was not simple, and his mind told him he ought to connect it to something else, but he couldn't figure out what. He'd get it, though.

"We're almost in Athens, Lucas. Let's stop for some coffee or something. I don't want to walk into that lady's house and ask her what she's got to eat."

"Don't eat too much, though. We're going to my grandmother, and food comes with the title."

When Willis parked in front of Alma Jackson's house, she stood on her porch, her face enveloped in smiles. "I'm so glad to see you, Son," she said to Lucas with her arms open to welcome him.

He hugged and kissed her, then moved aside and said, "Nana, this is my best friend from my freshman college days, Willis Carter. Willis is my brother in all ways except blood. He's a builder, and we work together."

He watched, delighted, as Alma Jackson opened her arms to Willis and hugged him. "You're welcome, Willis. I've got a big house and a big heart. You come see me any time you feel like a little change."

"I sure will, Gramma. I hope you don't mind my calling you that."

"Oh, that's wonderful. I like it. I haven't heard it enough in my life. You all come on in. It's not quite time for dinner, but I'll give you some waffles and sage sausage. How about some nice fresh strawberries, just picked this morning?"

Lucas looked at Willis. "I told you so. That will suit me perfectly, Nana. Can I help you? We didn't come down here for you to wait on us."

She patted his back. "Sausage is cooked, and I'll just warm it up. We'll cook the waffles at the table."

He set the table, put the waffle iron on it, and sat down. While they ate, she told him that the cabinets were in the basement, and that the chair elevator had been installed the day before, but as he'd cautioned, she didn't use it. "I'm waiting for you to inspect it. Have you seen Calvin since he had that family conference?"

"Yes, ma'am. I've gotten into the habit of visiting with him every Monday after I have my staff conferences. He's well now, but . . . well, it's a nice habit."

She looked at Lucas. "I suppose you can keep a secret."

Lucas raised his hand. "I can, but if you don't want my mother to know it, don't say it in front of Willis. They're very close, and when it comes to her, he doesn't always use his best judgment."

She looked at Willis. "Well, isn't that sweet. She's got two sons for the price of one."

Willis savored the waffles as if he hadn't eaten for a long while. "I'll make a good grandson, too."

A smile brightened Alma's face. "I've already adopted you, Willis,"

By the time Lucas and Willis were ready to leave late Sunday afternoon, the new cabinets gleamed in Alma's kitchen, they had transferred the contents of the old cabinets to the new ones, and Lucas had satisfied himself that his grandmother could ride up and down the stairs in safety.

"I'll see you as soon as I can, Nana. If you need anything or have any problems, let me know. I'll be extremely unhappy if you don't."

She thanked him. "But I want to see you whenever you can make it, even if I don't have any problems." She hugged Willis. "You can't be stressed down here with me, Willis, so if you need rest, remember that I'm good at pampering."

Willis kissed her. "You're precious, Gramma. I'll be back here with or without Lucas. Here are my phone numbers. Call me if you need me, or if it's storming and you're scared of lightning."

Alma laughed. "Somebody's been tattling on me. With summer coming up, you may be sorry you said that." She put an arm around Lucas. "I've never met your mother. She raised a fine son, and I want to meet her."

He hadn't counted on that. "I told her she'd love you, Nana."

"And I'll love *her*, too."

As they headed back to Woodmore, Lucas said to Willis, "I can't accept that all these years, I didn't know this wonderful woman, and all she wants is to have me around so she can pamper me and love me."

"Don't blame Aunt Noreen, Lucas. If I'd been in her place, I'd have probably done worse than she did. At least she didn't fill your head with a lot of unpleasant things about your dad, and that's more than I can say."

Lucas switched off the cruise control and glanced over at his friend. "I've known you for seventeen years, and you never even hinted at that before."

"Because I was ashamed. Anyhow, after you got together

with your dad, I called mine and talked with him, and I'm going out to Colorado to see him. Would you believe he sent me a first-class air ticket? Like I can't afford to go anyplace I want to. My mother's sorry now, and it's pretty late, but I'm . . . he seemed so nice, man. It's a pity she laid all that crap on him."

"They had issues, so don't get into that," Lucas told him. "Deal with your dad, and keep your mother out of it as much as you can."

"Yeah. She's finally got somebody else, and I'm happy for her. Would you believe she's a completely different woman?"

"Sure, I believe it."

"What did Gramma tell you that was such a secret?"

He couldn't help laughing. "That's the point, Willis. She told me not to tell anyone." He didn't plan to tell his mother, either. His father had confided to Nana that he intended to will one-quarter of all he owned to Noreen Hamilton, one quarter to her, one-quarter to Lucas and one quarter to be shared by his wife and daughters, explaining that his daughters already had substantial trust funds. He didn't need the inheritance, but his mother needed the confirmation that Calvin Jackson loved her above all women.

Susan leaned against the edge of Enid's kitchen counter drinking ginger ale and talking to Fred, her helper. "I'm glad we got through this today, Fred. We have a lot to do at Hamilton Village, and we haven't even started."

"I know. This was a cinch because we had the place to ourselves, and it looks fantastic, not one bit like the old-fashioned place I walked into this morning. I wouldn't mind living here myself, but my wife is skittish about the water."

She changed into street clothes, packed her personal things. "I want to be gone when Enid gets home. I don't have time for a personal visit."

Fred's chuckles amused her. "I gather that dame ain't to your taste. I'm ready to go."

She arrived home after nine, exhausted but happy with what

she'd done with Enid's house. She had no doubt that the woman would be pleased, and especially because she finished a thousand dollars under budget. The red light flashed on her downstairs phone, and she saw Cassie's number in the caller ID window.

"I'm sorry, old girl, but I'm starved, so you'll have to wait till I heat a can of soup and make myself a sandwich."

She prepared the meal and sat down to eat, but the doorbell rang before she could bite the ham sandwich. She went to the window, saw Cassie standing at the door and rushed to open it.

"Hi, Cassie. Come on in." She saw the woman's mottled and tear-stained face and her eyes red from weeping and pulled Cassie into her arms. "What is it? What's the matter?"

Through the sobbing and tears, she couldn't understand anything that Cassie said. Finally, she took her by the hand, led her to the kitchen and gave her a glass of water.

"Now. Slowly. What happened?"

"K . . . Kix. He's left me. He packed up and left while I was on a trip for the office. My first trip since I was promoted to dean of our school."

"Wait a minute, Cassie. I didn't know you got the promotion. When was this?"

"About three weeks ago. I meant to tell you, but I never saw you."

"I don't care about that," Susan said. "Didn't you promise Kix that you'd start a family as soon as your boss decided who would be dean of that institute?" Cassie nodded.

"Sit down, Cassie. You don't have the right to be unhappy. I'm in love with a man, and I can't give him a family, so I try not to let him get too close. If he falls in love with me, he risks giving up his birthright, and I won't be responsible for that. You willingly deny Kix that right, and yet you claim that you love him. I don't feel for you, Cassie. Give him a divorce, and let him marry a woman who loves him enough to give him a family."

"I know I sound awful, but I can't do that. I love him."

"You can't prove it by me, or by Kix either, I suspect. Do you have a health problem?" Cassie shook her head. "Well, if you want that man, girl, you have to change your act, because he means business. And if you don't keep your word this time, he's gone for good."

"I know. He left me a note that he intends to file for a divorce, but I'm not giving him one, you hear?"

"If he states his grievance to a judge, you won't have a choice."

Lucas's insistence in knowing why she invited him to her apartment and seduced him into making love with her came to mind, and she thought . . . "Cassie, are you scared to have a baby? Scared of being pregnant and having those pains?"

"It's something like that, but not exactly."

"Why can't you share your fears with Kix? He'll help you deal with them."

"I . . . uh . . . I don't want him to know that . . . I mean, to see me ugly and sick. Oh, Susan, he's so handsome . . . and he can have the most beautiful woman—"

Susan's hands went to her hips. "I can't believe you said that. Girl, get off your behind and straighten things out with your husband. That man loves you. Go home and call him. Do you know where he is?"

"He said he's staying in his office at the restaurant." She hugged Susan. "You think I'm a bad person?"

"No, but I think you're not very wise. Give Kix a chance to show you what you mean to him. Nothing is certain in this life but death and taxes, so you have to have faith."

"Maybe you're right," Cassie said in a softer than normal voice, mostly to herself. "If it doesn't work out, At least I'll have a child."

"Atta girl. Now get busy. I'm starved, and my soup's getting cold."

Cassie jogged home deep in thought. *Had she been so wrong all this time? Would Kix really love her more if she had a child? She hardly remembered her father, and she grew up thinking that men wanted children because kids gave them bragging rights. Well, anything was better than that empty house that had creaked and rattled ever since Kix moved out.*

She walked into her house, locked the door and dialed Kix's cell phone number. "Kix, this is Cassie. I want you to come home. Please. I can't stand it here without you."

He was silent long enough to unnerve her. "All right, Cassie. I'll be there in an hour, but not to stay. I'm through begging you for a family. I'm going there in order to hear what you have to say. Don't bother to try getting me into bed, because sex is the last thing you'll get out of me." He hung up.

He could get home in half an hour if he wanted to, so he was letting her know that he was in no hurry to see her. She had intended to look as elegant and sexy as possible, but his words brought her up short. He didn't want veneer or polish, but the real thing, warts and all, and wasn't that the problem anyway? He'd never seen the real Cassie, except maybe when he had her strung out in bed. She was always perfect from her toes to her hair; perfection was her crutch and her assurance that she was superior. "My Lord, have I always been so shallow? It's been years since Kix told me I looked nice," she said aloud, "and I hadn't even noticed." She walked from the kitchen to the living room and back, then retraced her steps. What would she do if he didn't want to hear all that she had to say?

She heard his key in the front door lock and tremors raced through her as she stood rooted in the spot. Kix walked into the house, went straight to the living room and sat in a chair that had never been his favorite. At a loss as to what to do or say, she looked around, feeling helpless.

"I'm in here," he said, as if she knew the exact location of "here." She walked into the living room and stood before him, much as the accused stand before a judge, awaiting sentencing. That she had wronged him was paramount in her thoughts, for she couldn't deny that she had not lived up to her promises, promises that she made before their marriage and many times thereafter.

"I'm waiting for what you have to say." He didn't sweeten his harsh manner with a smile or a gentle voice, and she had a feeling that she was about to drown.

"I'm . . . I'm scared, Kix."

He spread his arms out on the back of the big chair and narrowed his eyes, but said nothing.

"I'm . . . I can't . . . I don't know where to start."

"Start with why you've been content to welsh on your bargain." She twisted her hands over and over, and she hated seeing anyone do that. "Sit down, Cassie, and calm yourself, because this is your last chance to tell me anything."

"If I'm . . ." She dropped on the sofa and buried her face in her hands. "If I was big, fat, out of shape, my feet and legs swollen and nauseous all the time, would . . . would you be able to stand being around me?"

"What? What in God's name are you talking about? Have you gone out of your mind?"

She wiped her tears with the back of her hand. "I'll be ugly, because maybe I won't feel like fixing up. I always try to look nice so you'll love me and be proud of me."

"Have you been drinking?"

"Kix, please don't joke. This is hard enough for me. I walk down the street with you and almost every female we pass, even teenagers, ogle you. I know you can have any woman you want, so why should you be satisfied with a miserable-looking—"

He interrupted her. "I can't believe you're serious. You want me to believe you have an inferiority complex, when you look down your nose at half the people you know?"

"I don't. There's so much about me that you don't know and wouldn't believe." The tears met beneath her chin, and she stopped wiping them. "All those years when I pretended to have orgasms, although I really didn't because I wouldn't let you teach me. I was scared you'd think I was inadequate, that I wasn't much of a woman, but I pretended just the opposite. I told myself all kinds of lies about why I couldn't afford to get pregnant. I want a family, Kix, but I'm scared you'll . . . that if I'm huge and ugly and unfeminine-looking you won't feel the same way about me, and . . . and maybe you'll get interested in somebody who—?"

"Don't say it. If all these years, I didn't know you, you don't know me, either."

She didn't know when he left his chair, for her hands covered her face, and the feel of his arms around her had to be a hallucination. She trembled from the loneliness she felt.

His words startled her. "You will always be beautiful to me, Cassie. In spite of all your foolishness, I love you. If you're telling me that you need my assurance that I'll love you no matter what, you have it. I've loved you, sweetheart, from the day I met you. You've made it difficult at times, but I've never wavered. I . . . Woman, I'd worship you on my knees if you were big with my child. "

He moved away from her. "Are you willing to make love with me without a condom?" He asked, his voice unsteady and his eyes squeezed tight.

"Yes."

He opened his eyes and looked hard at her, as if to confirm with his eyes what his ears heard. "Are you taking the pill?"

"I've never taken it."

He gazed at her until her breathing accelerated, but she could do nothing but wait for his response. "Tell you what," he said. "Let's run upstairs, pack a few things, and go to Winston-Salem and spend the night in a luxury hotel."

"But you said—"

"I don't give a damn what I said. Go ahead and get your things. I'll make a reservation. We're going to do this thing right."

Chapter Twelve

Susan looked at the caller ID on her ringing telephone and couldn't decide whether or not to answer it. She wanted to know what Enid Jackson thought of her work, but she dreaded an encounter with the woman, whether by phone or in person. Loose-tongued people were to be avoided, and Enid's tongue was looser than most.

She lifted the receiver. "Hello. This is Susan."

"I'm ecstatic. I never dreamed my house could look like this. It's just fabulous, and cheaper than you said it would be. I'm going to give a reception and invite about twenty-five or thirty people. You have to come, so I can show everybody my decorator. Girl, this place makes me look rich. I'm hiring a landscaper tomorrow; I want the outside to look as elegant as the inside. I'm putting your check in the mail today. Jessica Burton thinks she's such hot stuff, but her place doesn't look any better than mine. I'll send you an invitation to the reception."

Susan thanked her, marveling that she hadn't had to say a word. Enid was happy listening to her own voice. She hung up and gave herself a gentle pinch. Life was good.

With the tutoring session at an end, Susan welcomed the chance to spend a few minutes with Rudy and Nathan when she went to Ann Price's home to collect Ann's laundry and get her shopping list. Maybe an iron deficiency accounted for Ann's lethargy, but the woman seemed also to have lost weight. From

what Susan could discern, the three older grandchildren did little to relieve Ann of the housekeeping chores.

"Your grandmother is not well," she said to Yolanie, Ann's
fourteen-year-old granddaughter. You should at least keep the
kitchen clean for her. A lot of grandmothers would have let the
city put you children in a foster home, and you'd have had a
much different life. Ask Rudy what a foster home is like. Come
on. Let's clean this kitchen."

To her surprise, the girl worked along with her and didn't
seem to mind. "If you clean after every meal and if you don't
allow the other children to make a mess, you can keep this
straight, and your grandmother won't have to do it. If she has to
go back to the hospital, you may have to go into foster care, so
help her all you can."

Yolanie looked at Susan. "Okay, but you tell them they have
to obey me. Rudy will want to go live with you, and Nathan
wants to be with Rudy. He stayed to himself until Rudy came.
His mother was my aunt."

Susan's antenna shot up. "Did you say was?"

"Yes, ma'am. She was living in Philadelphia with some guy
who was selling hash, and she got killed in a drug bust. He's
doing time."

"Is he Nathan's father?"

"No ma'am. Nathan's father was killed in Iraq. He was a ma-
rine. He sent Grandma money every month." Susan detected
pride in Yolanie's voice when she spoke of Nathan's father, as if
he, and not Nathan's mother, had been her relative.

"I'll speak to the children and ask them to help you relieve
your grandmother while she's not feeling well."

Susan put the laundry in the trunk of the BMW, went back inside to Ann's room. "Did you make out your grocery list?"

"I made it out, but I don't feel right. Last week, you didn't
take the money, and if you won't let me pay, I can't let you shop
for me. How's it coming with the adoption papers?"

"I've been waiting three weeks for that case worker to tell me
whether my volunteer work for the school board can be considered as a job. Since I'm self-employed, I need a job reference."

"Those people are geniuses at creating obstacles. I'll keep on praying for you."

"Thanks, Ann. I'm praying, too."

Already an hour behind her daily schedule, she went to her shop where she found a message to call Willis. Her heart stuck in her throat as she dialed the number.

"Hello, Mr. Carter. This is Susan. What's up?"

"Call me Willis. This is a ten-story building, and I just wanted to remind you that on each higher floor, an apartment may have a few inches less space in certain important places. Which floor are you using for a sample?"

She blew out a long breath and let herself relax. Willis Carter hadn't previously called her, and her first thought was that something had happened to Lucas. "I measured on the second floor, but I haven't ordered furniture, although I've selected it."

"If you can come over, I'll show you where you may have a problem. It won't complicate things too much, but you need to anticipate it."

"Thank you, Willis. I want this to be my best job ever, and I appreciate your help."

"I want the same. The three of us ought to make a great team."

She hung up, closed the shop and headed for Hamilton Village. "Yes, we would make a wonderful team, but it would never happen. Lucas thinks I'm something that I'm not, and if he casts his lot with me, he'll come to hate me."

As she drove along Parkway Street, past Lucas's house and alongside Pine Tree Park, she recalled the evening she sat on a bench with Lucas eating ice cream under a star-filled sky. Why couldn't life be like that? If she was lucky, Lucas would be in Danville, and she wouldn't have to deal with his presence or with the fact that when she was last with him, she told him over and over in a moment of ecstasy that she loved him. They had talked since, but he hadn't mentioned it, and she had tried to forget it. But it was her moment of truth, and he had to know it.

*   *   *

Lucas was about to have a moment of truth of his own. He left his Monday morning staff meeting and stopped by his father's house for a short visit with him as had become his weekly custom.

"Good morning, Marcie," he said to Calvin's wife when she opened the door. "Where's Dad this morning?"

"Calvin's in the den," she said, as if she denied his right to call Calvin Jackson Dad.

He walked into the den and, for the first time, his father greeted him with a hug. Startled, he didn't return the gesture, and when his father stepped back and looked him in the eye with an expression of sorrow, he opened his arms to the man against whom he'd held a gripe for so many years and enveloped him in an embrace. He parted his lips to tell his father that they should bury the hatchet for all time, but when he saw the tears that rolled unchecked down Calvin Jackson's cheeks, the words wouldn't leave his tongue. He simply held his father in an embrace.

"Is it . . . all right between you and me now?" Calvin asked him.

Lucas fought to rid himself of the lump in his throat. Finally, he was able to say "I've buried the hatchet, Dad, and I don't waste time thinking about what used to be."

"Calvin, I want to see you a minute, but if you can't tear yourself away, I can say it right here."

Lucas glanced toward the door, looked steadily at Marcie's pursed lips and furor-mottled face, then at his father's troubled visage.

"Excuse me, Son," Calvin said.

Lucas jerked his shoulder as if to say he had no interest in Marcie, and indeed, he didn't, except to give her the time of day when he entered her home, a courtesy that she didn't bother to reciprocate.

"Listen," Lucas heard Marcie say from an adjoining room. "You have to wash my face with your philandering by bringing that man into my house whenever it suits you. Wasn't it enough that you slept around with his mother for years, and now you throw the evidence in my face and in my children's face. What's worse, you fix it so that I have to get my allowance in a check with his signature on it. If our friends knew—"

"Would you please lower your voice? You didn't have to tolerate my affair with Noreen. You didn't once mention a divorce. Many is the time when I would have gone out of my mind if I hadn't had her, but you didn't even know I was suffering. I had eighty dollars in the bank, and you wanted me to replace your mink with a sable because that was what everybody was wearing. I knew damned well that *everybody* couldn't afford a sable coat.

"Let me tell you something, Marcie, and I want this to be the last time we have this conversation or one like it. When I married you, I was besotted with you, crazy about you. I'd leave home to go to work, and I could hardly think about anything all day except getting back home to you, and maybe that would be the day you would welcome me with love. You knew how I felt about you, and Lord knows you took advantage of it. If I tried to kiss you, you presented your cheek. If I kissed you on the mouth, I'd ruin your lipstick. Sex? Once in a while, you opened your legs and allowed me to relieve myself. Then, you went to sleep. I can't remember a single time in all these years when you initiated a kiss, not to speak of sex.

"Oh, you were a master at dribbling out your affection. When I needed you—to talk with you, to have a little assurance that you'd be with me no matter what—where were you? Off someplace building your social kingdom. I hit rock bottom. My business was thirty days from changing hands. I completely lost my self-confidence. If you knew it, you didn't let on. You sent our children to me with foolish requests for in-line skates, video games. Hell, Enid asked me for a shearling coat with a fox trim when I could hardly afford to pay the electric bill. Why should a seven-year-old have that kind of coat when, a year later, it will be too small? The day I might have given up and declared bankruptcy was the day I met Noreen Hamilton. I told you I didn't feel like going out, that I was out of sorts and having trouble with the business, but you nonetheless dragged me to a fundraiser at somebody's house and then ignored me as usual.

"I was standing alone in the hallway away from the noise

and the smell of liquor, Marcie, trying to figure out what I'd do after I watched ten years of my hard work slide down the drain in a bankruptcy court. What would I do with my life? I'd never been so miserable, so far down.

"This woman walked up to me and asked me, 'What's wrong? What's the matter?' I looked down into the face of the first person, other than my mother, who had showed any concern for me in years, and I heard myself pouring my soul out to her. That stranger opened her arms, and said, 'I'm so sorry. I wish I could help.' I went into those arms, held her and soaked up the compassion she offered. I fell in love with her. I've been in those arms ever since, and I will always be in them.

"To her credit, because she knew from the start that I was married, she avoided me as long as she could, but I pursued her. I didn't help her raise Lucas, because out of vengeance—because I was hell bent on getting rich and staying atop the social set, and marrying her would have interfered with that—she denied me any parental privileges. She moved to another town to be sure I never saw him or her, but I always knew where they were, how they were getting on and how his life was shaping up. I would give him the heart out of my body if he needed it. And that's that. You say one more word to me about him, and I'll give him the key to this house."

"Where does that leave me?"

"That's up to you. You got what you wanted out of this marriage—financial security and social status. It's foolish to hope for anything else."

Lucas dropped himself into a chair, leaned back and closed his eyes. He had been conceived in love, and his parents had then suffered an unfulfilled love ever since. He'd rather face a question about the foundation of a skyscraper building than decide what to do about his parents, and he knew the ball was in his court.

"I'm sorry," Calvin said when he returned to the den. "Things aren't so good between Marcie and me these days. Where were we? Oh, yes, I meant to tell you that my mother told me she was enchanted with your friend, Willis. Later, she called to say he sent her a box of live crabs and two pounds of shrimp from someplace on the Chesapeake Bay. Did she tell him how she loves those things?"

"If she did, I didn't hear her. Willis had an unpleasant childhood. My mother spoils him, and Nana sure did her bit."

"You're never going to tell me how Noreen is? I'm so hungry for any news of her, but I don't question your integrity in this."

He sat forward, facing his father, spread his knees and rested his forearms on his thighs. "I . . . over the years, I've judged you both, sometimes harshly, but for different reasons. I suppose I've been harder on her because she kept me from you."

Lucas leaned back, draped his right ankle over his left knee and looked at his father. "I heard every word you said to Marcie, and I realized that my parents have suffered from an unfulfilled love all of my life." Calvin jerked forward. "What makes me happy right now," Lucas continued, "is knowing that I was conceived in love. My mother loves you still, and she wanted so badly to visit you before you had the operation and after, but I prevented it, and I wouldn't let Willis take her. I told her that you were still married and that contacting you would be improper. I'm sorry I did that, and I'm going to tell her so."

When Calvin could control the trembling of his lips, he said, "I know that she never married, and I always felt guilty about that. I . . . I don't know how to thank you for telling me this. Will you tell her I love her, and that I'm sorry I wasted so much of her life and mine, years we should've lived together? Will you tell her?"

It's not for me to judge. I'll leave them to heaven. "Yes, sir. I'll tell her."

He watched as his father's countenance shone with the happiness he felt. "After all these years. How does she spend her days?"

"For years, she worked as a clerk in the superintendent's office at the post office. She doesn't need to work now. She volunteers at the library, goes to church on Sunday mornings, and—"

"Did she encounter any social problems because she wasn't married when she had you?" Fear of the answer clouded his eyes.

Lucas thought for a minute about the implications of that question. "I don't know. She's never said."

"Is there someone who you love? You've never even hinted."

It was a question that a father would ask his son, and he didn't find it intrusive. "There's someone I care about, quite deeply, in fact, but she insists that there can't be anything serious between us, and I fail to understand why. There's already been some serious stuff between us."

"I see. Maybe she has a secret, something she can't share with you," Calvin said. "Does she love you?"

"Yes. She does. She told me at one of those times when only the truth comes out. Does she have secrets? Probably; now that you mention it. I wouldn't be surprised."

"If she loves you, you can overcome any reservation she may have, that is, provided you want to. Do you like her as a person? What does she do?"

"She's an interior decorator and yes, I like her, but I can't figure out what makes her tick. I will, though."

"Be careful, Son. If you push her too hard, you may push her away from you. An interior decorator, huh. That works well with an architect. "

"I know. It's a relationship with great potential, although I've only recently realized that." He stood to leave. "Thanks. Talking about it has been helpful. I've never discussed my personal affairs with anyone, not even Willis, who's my brother in every sense but genetic. I'll see Mama this evening."

For the first time since he'd met his father, he didn't feel awkward leaving him, but put an arm around Calvin's shoulder, hugged him and left. As soon as he got into his car, he telephoned his mother.

"Hi, Mama. What are you cooking for supper?" He listened while she made it as interesting as she could. "Smoked pork shoulder, turnip greens cooked with some good old ham hocks, baked sweet potatoes, jalapeño corn bread and bring my own dessert?" He couldn't help laughing. She was in a good mood, a playful mood, and he could hardly wait to tell her what she wanted so badly to know. "I'll see you at about six."

"Did you visit Calvin today?"

"Why, yes. I just left him. See you later." He hung up. How on earth had she handled that unhappiness for over thirty-five years? He wondered what she'd do now. He drove slowly, far more slowly than usual, whistling a favorite tune as an unfamiliar kind of joy suffused him. He hoped Willis was at the building site, because he couldn't wait to tell his friend what he'd just learned about his parents. He didn't know when he'd been so happy.

Susan stood atop a four-foot ladder, measuring the space between the window and the adjoining wall for the drapery that she planned to hang there. "I should have put this ladder closer to the window," she said to herself when she discovered that she could barely reach the ceiling.

"Let me do that for you." She whirled around, startled by Lucas's voice, lost her footing and tumbled backward. He caught her, looked into her startled face, grinned and said, "It's a good thing I'm here to catch you. If I hadn't been, you'd have hurt yourself."

How easy it would be to put her arms around his neck and cuddle up to him while he held her as one holds a baby. The feel of his big hands cradling her so gently almost lulled her into a complacency that she could ill afford. Oh, how she longed to give in to her feelings and enjoy that moment in his arms! Reminding herself of the price they might both have to pay, she said, "If you hadn't walked in here, I wouldn't have lost my balance. Would you please put me down?"

She wished he'd stop grinning, but he didn't. In fact, his smile broadened. "What way is that to talk to the man you love?"

"What? What on earth . . ." Her voice tapered off as she remembered the moment when she had exploded in orgasm as he lay buried deep within her. That moment when the words, "I love you," tore themselves out of her.

"I'm glad you haven't forgotten, Susan, because I will never forget it. And don't deny it. I'm in a good mood, and I don't want anybody tampering with it."

"What brought on this good mood?"

"I just left my father. How many times have you hugged your father?"

"I don't know. Maybe hundreds."

"I hugged mine for the first time, and I meant that hug. Later, I heard him tell his wife that he'd give me the heart out of his body if I needed it. He really loved my mother. I am not going to let avarice and hunger for power ruin my life. He realized too late what he'd done. Imagine, loving someone for so many years and not being able even to see that person." He looked past her. "You know, I'm beginning to suspect that I'm capable of feelings equally deep and lasting."

As if he had unwittingly exposed an intimate part of himself, he shook his head slowly. "Is Willis around?"

"He was. In fact, I'm here because he suggested that I get the exact measurements on this floor."

"Good idea, because certain space can lessen a bit the higher up you go."

"By the way, Lucas, Enid invited me to a reception she's giving to show her redecorated house to her friends. I'm obligated to go, so please don't think I'm being disloyal."

"Of course not. If she invited me, I'd go, but there's not a chance." His lips brushed hers, and the tip of his tongue probed their seam, startling her, and they opened as if of their own volition. Within seconds, he was possessing her. One of his hands gripped her buttocks and the other plunged into her shirt. His fingers teased and pinched her nipple, and with his other hand, he pressed her body to his own, sending rivulets of heat throughout her nervous system. When, wanting and needing more of him, she twisted against him, he put both arms around her and kissed her eyes, her cheeks and the tip of her nose.

"I'm trying to work and you—" she sputtered before he interrupted her.

"I need some loving. If I had you someplace private, I'd go at you till you gave me the loving of a lifetime. That's how I feel right now."

"You're playing with fire, and you're inducing me to do the same. And I've told you—"

"I know what you've told me. But then you kiss me and hold me the way you did a minute ago. You can't convince me, because you either don't believe or you don't want to believe there can't be anything between us. Your words are incompatible with your actions, and when I finally know why—and I will—you and I won't have a problem."

"We don't have a problem now," she said barely loud enough for him to hear it, because she didn't believe her words.

Lucas found Willis in the second building conferring with his head plasterers. "I don't want stucco. That's as outdated as art deco. This is a modern building, and it's going to have modern finishes. If you're enamored with stucco, it can go in the basement recreation room. And make it cream colored." He looked up at Lucas. "How's it going, man?"

Lucas leaned against a wall and regarded Willis with brotherly affection. It wasn't necessary to call a conference in order to say, "I don't want that." No. Willis had the meeting in order to explain every crossed T and every dotted i. He shrugged. That made the man one of the best builders in the region.

"I'm going out to see Mom this evening. If you're interested in smoked pork shoulder, turnip greens—"

"Speak no further. What time did you say we'd be there?"

"I said I'd be there at six. You may call her and tell her you're coming, too. I'll leave my car at home. Pick me up there at five-thirty."

"Right. See you then."

Lucas and Willis greeted Noreen as the precious person she was to both of them. "I smelled food the minute I got out of the car," Willis said when they walked into Noreen's house.

Lucas picked his mother up and twirled her around. "So did I."

She gazed knowingly at her son. "You're in a wonderful mood. I'd like to know what's got you so high."

"Me, too," Willis said. "He definitely hasn't been drinking."

"I never drink enough to get high. If you want to know my business, feed me first." He looked at Willis and winked. "This has been *some* day!"

"Did you happen to see Susan?" Willis asked Lucas.

"Who's Susan?" Noreen asked.

"Our interior decorator," they said in unison.

"Well, did you see her?" Noreen asked.

Lucas couldn't keep the grin off his face. For a woman who wasn't fond of bodies of water, his mother was a genius of a fisherwoman. "Yeah, I saw her. When I walked in there, she was standing on a stool. I was just in time to catch her when she fell backward."

"Sure," Willis said. "Susan is no klutz, so that means you frightened her or something like that." He finished setting the table. "You know what I'm saying?"

Noreen put the food on the table. "You're both trying to talk over my head, but I see right through you. Lucas, please say the grace. I don't want you to forget the words."

"What did you bring for dessert?" Noreen asked Lucas after he and Willis cleaned the kitchen.

"Yipes, I forgot about it," Willis said. "We bought cheesecake, but I'm too full to eat it."

"So am I," Lucas said. "Maybe later."

Willis made coffee, and Lucas put a coffee service on a tray and carried it to the living room. "Come in here. I have something to tell you, Mama."

She sat facing him. "About Susan?"

"About my father."

"If . . . if it's not pleasant, I don't want to hear it," she said clutching her stomach.

"It's got to be pleasant, considering how he's been acting," Willis said.

Lucas lowered his eyelids, picturing in his mind's eye the events as they had unfolded. He began with Marcie's failure to greet him that morning and, told her how he felt when he hugged his father and of Calvin's tears. He omitted nothing that happened in Calvin Jackson's house from that time to the point when Calvin said, "Tell her I love her, and that I'm sorry I wasted so much of her life and mine, years we should've lived together." He didn't mention their discussion of Susan.

Noreen's sobbing brought him back to the present, and he opened his eyes to see that Willis sat on the arm of her chair with his arms around her. "Don't cry, Mama," Lucas said. "I wish now that I hadn't interfered, that I'd let Willis take you to the hospital to see him, and I told Dad that. He knows you love him and that you wanted to be with him."

"Thank you so much for that," she whispered. "Wh-what about Marcie?"

He told the truth. "I don't know, Mom. There is absolutely nothing between them, and hasn't been for years, over thirty-five of them, I suspect. I'm out of it now. Whatever happens between you two is your business."

"Did you tell Calvin that?"

"I didn't have to. I told him you loved him, and that was in response to his saying to me that he was so hungry for news of you. When I told him that, he knew that I was moving out of the way." He looked at her. "You don't know how wonderful it made me feel to know that he always loved me because he loved you so much, that I was conceived in love."

"You were. Oh, you were."

"What will you do, Aunt Noreen?"

"I don't know. I long to see him but, well, as Lucas has reminded me many times, he's still married."

"Yeah," Willis said, "but in name only."

"I forgot to . . . no, I *neglected* to tell you, Mama, that Nana told me she wants to meet you. Next time Willis and I go down there, I'd like you to go with us."

"Oh, I'd love that. I want to meet her, too."

"I can't stay too late, Mama, I have a stop to make."

"I'm so glad you finally have a real relationship with Calvin. He needed you in his life, and I—"

"That's over, Mama. Come on, Willis. Man, I've got some fish to fry."

"Give my love to Susan," Noreen said.

Lucas hugged her. "You must be hallucinating. I'll call you."

Susan told Lucas good night and hung up. Learning details of his parents' great but tragic love had brought about a change in him, barely evident, but a difference nonetheless. It seemed to have strengthened his confidence in his ability to nourish a relationship, but she didn't plan to let him drag her into the misery that she foresaw. He longed for a family—he'd hinted as much during their conversation that evening—and she could not give him one. She finished ironing Anne Price's laundry, mended Rudy's jeans, and sat down to watch television.

"What am I thinking?" She jumped up, got her address book and telephoned Mark, her lawyer. "Hello, Mark," she said when he answered the telephone. "I went to the agency and inquired about my application to adopt Rudy, and the case worker told me she'd check whether my work as a volunteer for the school board could be used as an employment reference. Said she'd call me the next day. That was three weeks ago. Rudy is temporarily with a woman who is sick and has the care of her four grandchildren, in addition to Rudy. The people at that agency are not doing their job."

"I agree, and I'll call them on it even if I have to take the case to family court. Give me ten days, and I'll have it settled."

Susan left work shortly after three o'clock the next day and drove to the temporary box office in Pine Tree Park to buy tickets for the summer concerts that would be held there. The box office closed at four. Clutching her tickets proudly, she sat down on one of the park benches to put them in a compartment in her pocketbook.

"Mind if I join you? I walked from my atelier, and I'm pooped," Jay Weeks said. "This is a hot day. How's the business coming? I heard you decorated Enid Jackson's summer place over on the Outer Banks. Is that so?"

"Yes. I did it a few weeks back."

"She asked me last year, but I flatly refused. I can't stand the woman. She's got the tongue of a viper. She's already had the damned place redecorated twice. But . . . if that's what floats your boat . . ." He let it hang.

Susan couldn't decide whether to answer him or simply get up and leave. She did not believe Enid had asked Jay to decorate her house or that redecorating had been on Enid's mind until she saw pictures of Jessica Burton's house in *Architectural Design* magazine. Enid was a copycat and unlikely to step out in front of the crowd.

"I'd better be going, Jay. I'm way behind."

"What do you expect? You grab every job offer, people know you can be had, and you don't have time to lead a normal life. That kind of greediness has been the death of a lot of people. You can't take the money with you, toots, 'cause there ain't no pockets in shrouds. See you around."

She stared at his back. The man had deliberately halted her departure so that he could leave her sitting there. Something about Jay Weeks made her mad enough to chew glass.

The next evening, armed with a picnic basket containing smoked salmon sandwiches, cheesecake, grapes, spring water and a bottle of white wine, Susan strolled into the concert tent and sat on a fourth-row bench. The early June breeze wafted through the open tent, and she let herself enjoy it and the sound of musicians offstage tuning their instruments. She had arrived early in order to get a good seat, but she soon realized that, unlike New Yorkers, the local people didn't rush to a concert and were as likely as not to arrive late. The tent's canvas top rattled as the wind seemed to gather velocity, and she thought that a storm might be eminent. Never having experienced a southern storm, she feared the worst.

"Hi. I hadn't thought I'd see you here." She looked up to see Lucas accompanied by her lawyer, Mark Harris, and his wife. "Mind if we sit with you?"

"By all means, have a seat," she said. "I'm glad to see you all."

When Lucas's eyebrows shot up, she knew he took exception to sharing her greeting with his companions. To placate him, she asked, "Did you bring your supper, Lucas?"

"I didn't have a picnic basket, so I figured I'd leave when I got hungry. Did you bring enough for two?"

"If you eat part of mine," she said, attempting to be friendly in an impersonal way. "It'll be an appetizer for us both, and I'll have to eat dinner later." As soon as the words left her mouth, she recognized them as a request for an invitation to eat dinner with him.

"I'm not dressed for Pinky's," he said, "but how about Sam's?" At her lengthy silence, Mark watched them closely.

"Come on, Susan, don't let the poor guy eat alone."

"I'm outnumbered," she said as the lights dimmed and the conductor walked onstage.

Susan closed her eyes and enjoyed the rare performance of Duke Ellington's sacred music, commissioned by the dean of Grace Cathedral Church in San Francisco a few years before Ellington died in 1974. Lucas's hand slipped beneath hers and tightened around it, but she wouldn't let herself look at him.

At the intermission, he said. "Any wine in that basket?"

She put the basket between them. "Help yourself."

"This basket's almost big enough to be a bassinet," he said, devouring a smoked salmon sandwich. "Now, if—" She tuned him out. He put a hand on her arm and shook her gently. "Where'd you go?"

"What do you mean?" she asked him, grateful that the members of the orchestra were returning to their seats, tuning their instruments and giving her an excuse not to answer him.

"I assume you drove," he said at the concert's end.

"Yes. I parked right at the corner of Parkway and Glade Streets."

He gazed down at her, his eyes telegraphing what she didn't want to see or hear. "That's less than a short block from my house. Want to go home with me and let's call out for some real food?"

"That . . . uh . . . sounds great," she said, fumbling for words, "but my head hurts so badly that I think I'd better go home and crawl into bed."

She thought she would shrivel beneath his intense and accusing stare. "Whatever you say. I hope you improve."

She thanked him, told the Harris couple good night, and headed for her car, grateful that the wind had subsided and the stars occupied their usual places in the sky. Lucas was either angry, hurt or both, so she knew he wouldn't follow her. She couldn't help it. It was as if her life was at stake. He didn't telephone her that night, and she had known that he wouldn't. Her picnic basket brought to his mind the image of a bassinet. Lately, he alluded often to the prospect of his being a father, but when she'd looked down at that basket, she saw an emptiness so vast that she nearly cried out. She had to get him out of her system and out of her life.

As she was preparing for bed, her mother called. "Honey, I'm coming home for a couple of weeks. They're telling me I have to take a vacation. Can I bunk with you?"

"Of course you can, Mom. This is wonderful. When are you coming?"

"Sunday, the tenth. I'll e-mail you my itinerary. If you have anything planned, go on with it. I know how to get a taxi. After five years in this place, I could flag down a camel."

"Thank heaven you still have your sense of humor. I can't wait for you to get here."

A more practical woman than Betty Lou Pettiford probably hadn't been born, so she'd better watch it. Her mother would adore Lucas, and she would go to great lengths to mend their relationship and make it permanent.

Chapter Thirteen

Lucas went home, ordered a pizza and a green salad from Sam's, changed into Bermuda shorts and sneakers and ate his supper on the deck of his house, occasionally washing the food down with Pilsner beer. He'd give anything to know what he said or did that caused Susan to withdraw so completely and abruptly. He refused to believe she had a manic-depressive personality. If he could just get a finger on it. . . . He swallowed the last of his beer, threw the bottle into the recycle bin and went inside.

"I'm not calling her tonight. I might aggravate her sudden headache," he said aloud in a voice that sneered.

The next day, giving himself time to cool off from Susan's slight, he avoided Hamilton Village I, where he knew she would be working. Instead, he made an unplanned inspection of an office building in Woodmore that he'd recently learned belonged to Jackson Enterprises. Pleased with what he found, he telephoned Landon, chief of the real estate unit—he had fired Logan several weeks earlier—and congratulated him.

"The building looks great, but I think we ought to replace those vending machines and spruce up that lounge in the basement."

"Yes, sir. Thank you, sir. I'll get on that right away." That was what he liked to hear.

He went to his office and opened his mail. *Another fundraiser.*

Why can't I just send a check? But that's not good enough. They want me as well as my check. Well, it's for handicapped children, so I shouldn't complain. But why do I have to wear a blasted tux?

He saw her the minute he entered the grand ballroom of the Scott Key Hotel, and if he didn't watch himself, he'd pant. What a siren she was in a one-strap, floor-length melon-red gown that hugged her body—a body he knew well. His libido kicked into high gear.

"Hello, Susan."

She swung around, a little off balance, as if he'd startled her, but she immediately became the essence of poise. "Hello, Lucas." And he didn't doubt that she liked what she saw.

"You're lovely tonight, as always," he said.

"Thanks. You're a knock-out," she breathed as if being able to express her feeling afforded her immeasurable relief.

He hadn't known what she thought of his looks, and he did a little inner preening. "Thank you, Susan. We seem to have some more interests in common—concerts, the Girl Scouts, the children's repertory theater. You'd think we'd be able to get together."

"Life is rarely logical, Lucas."

"Feel like a drink and a snack later?" he asked her. "Unless you're with a date."

"I didn't come with anyone. Tongues will wag, but I'd rather have come alone than with a man whose company I didn't relish merely to satisfy convention. I'm sick of that."

He decided to shake her up a bit. "You could have asked me."

She didn't give in. "I know. But I didn't."

"Can we meet right here at, say, nine-thirty?"

She seemed to mull over the idea, and then she smiled. "All right. My watch says eight-twenty-three. See you later."

As she walked away, it hit him. Children! Rudy, Nathan, the tutoring, the Girl Scout Fundraiser, the Repertory Theater and this. But there had to be something else. He leaned against the doorjamb. Bassinet! He'd said her picnic basket resembled one, and sometime back, he'd boasted that he'd be a good father. She clammed up each time. But what lay behind it? Did she try to get pregnant the first time they made love and fail?

Nine-thirty couldn't come fast enough. They went to The

Watering Hole and, for the first time in his life, he felt like getting stoned. "What am I doing?" He asked himself. "I love this beautiful witch sitting in front of me."

"Are you drinking tonight?" Susan asked when he ordered the second margarita.

Instead of responding to her query, he dealt with the question that burned in his own mind. "Why did you invite me to your apartment for the sole purpose of getting laid?" he asked her as anger rose up in him. "Any man would have done that for a beautiful woman like you. I deserve the truth, and I want it." He emptied the drink down his throat.

"I like you better when you're drinking lemonade," she said. "Please excuse me."

He stood and had to fight himself in order to keep his hands off her. "You're excused, madam!" He sat down, finished his drink and ordered another one. "*Damn her!*"

"What's with you, man?"

He looked up into Willis's anxious face. "Of all the women I could have fallen for—"

Willis interrupted him. "You mean Susan? What's wrong with her? She's perfect for you, man."

He drained his third drink. "A hell of a lot you know. Miss Pettiford doesn't want me. She wants single motherhood."

"That was a low blow, but maybe I asked for it," Susan said to herself as she walked into her house. She never would have believed he'd say something like that to her.

She met her mother at the airport the following Saturday morning. "My, but you look wonderful," her mother said when they met. "I hope we don't have far to go, because I'm a wreck and I'm dying to fall into a bed."

Susan went into her mother's arms, the haven that never failed to comfort her. "You look good, too, Mom, though you're three shades darker. You remember Aunt Edith's house, don't you?"

"Sure do." Betty Lou leaned back, rested her head against the headrest and was soon asleep.

"I have to attend a reception this afternoon, Mom," Susan

told her mother when they reached her home. "A client is showing the house I decorated for her, but you don't have to go."

"What do you mean, 'I don't'? I want to see your work. Will a long-sleeved peach chiffon do?"

"Absolutely. Now get some rest."

They arrived at Enid's house a few minutes after five, and the reception had already become noisy and crowded.

"My goodness!" Susan said minutes after introducing Enid to her mother. "That man must be Lucas's father. I've never seen such a resemblance, and right down to height and bearing."

She saw Enid take the man's hand and walk toward her. "Papa this is my wonderful decorator, Susan Pettiford. Susan, this is Calvin Jackson. Susan introduced her mother to Lucas's father as if she'd never heard of him or of his son.

What a figure of a man he must have been in his youth, she thought. He handed her his card. "Your work is wonderful, really commendable. You have very good taste," he said. "I may need your services, so please remember that you met me."

Forgetting him would not be possible, but she didn't tell him that. "Thank you, sir." She shook her head in wonder: this was proof positive of the power of genes to mold a person. They even walked with the same lilting stride.

When she caught her mother checking out Calvin Jackson's assets, Susan experienced momentary alarm. "Don't even think it, Mom. Don't go anywhere near there. He's completely taken. Besides, I'm in love with his son, and he's in love with his son's mother, who he never married because he's married to someone else."

Betty Lou blinked several times in rapid succession. "*What*? Run that one by me again."

"You heard me correctly, Mom. Enid doesn't know about me and her half brother and neither does Calvin Jackson."

Betty Lou rolled her eyes toward the ceiling. "How do you know what his son may have told him? This is a bigger pile of manure than the one I left in Nigeria. Why haven't you met the father of the man you're in love with?"

"Because we haven't committed to each other, and we won't. Let's drop this right here."

"Hmmm. Whatever you say." But Susan knew she'd hear more on the subject.

When Susan left home Monday morning to go to her shop, her mother still slept. She waved at Cassie as she backed out of her garage, and when Cassie walked out to the street, Susan knew that her friend wanted to tell her something.

"I did as you told me, Susan, and he's back home. Oh, Susan, I didn't know I could be so happy."

"Do you think you're expecting?"

"I haven't seen any evidence of that, but we're definitely working on it."

Susan drove on. At least that relationship had a future. If only she could say the same for herself. She found a message on her office phone and returned Mark Harris's call.

"Good news, Susan," he said, and she nearly sat on the floor when she groped for a chair. "All that stands between you and instant motherhood is a letter of recommendation from the person who served as principal of the Wade School tutoring program. The letter must verify good character and good work habits. The agency would prefer that you'd had local paid employment, but I gave them an affidavit about your business. So see Lucas and tell him I said you need the letter pronto."

She phoned Lucas and, in between expressions of joy and exultation, told him what she needed. "Oh, Lucas, I'm so overwhelmed." And so ecstatic was she that, at first, she failed to notice his silence. When he didn't respond, she asked him, "Aren't you happy for me?"

"I'm speechless. Can you come out here to my office? It adjoins my house. Remember?"

"Sure," she said, bubbling with happiness. "I should be there in about twenty minutes."

He stood in the doorway, his hands in the pockets of his khaki Bermuda shorts. She'd never seen him so casually dressed, with a short-sleeved T-shirt hanging out of his shorts, and a pair of sandals on his otherwise bare feet. She checked her gasp at his raw virility. "Hi," she said and hoped she sounded normal.

"Come on in."

She thought she detected a chill in his manner, but in her

delirium over the status of the adoption proceedings, she dismissed the thought.

"Mark said all the agency needs now is a character and job reference from you as principal of the Wade School tutoring program and I can sign the adoption papers and take Rudy home with me."

"Have a seat." Her antenna went up, and the bottom dropped out of her belly. She didn't like his formal manner with her. "What's wrong, Lucas? Are you still angry with me?"

He leaned back in his chair. "I have never been angry with you, Susan. Disappointed in you, hurt, even miserable because of you, but never angry with you. I am sorry that I can't write that letter for you, at least not as things are."

She jumped to her feet. "What? You know how important this is to me. It's everything to me."

"Yes, I do, and I'm sympathetic, but I'm not going to perjure myself." He didn't bat an eyelash at her loud gasp. "I cannot attest to your good character unless you explain to me truthfully why you invited me, a strange man you had seen once for five minutes, to your apartment for the purpose of going to bed with me. That's an act that couldn't be included in any reference as an example of *good character*, unless it was accompanied by one hell of an explanation. And I don't want to hear any of the reasons you've already given me."

"That's blackmail, Lucas. How could you be so mean?"

"It isn't meanness, Susan. It's coming from my battle with what's going on inside of me. You thought only of what you wanted or needed; you didn't consider the effect that your scheme might have on me. I know you love Rudy, but if you don't tell me the truth, you won't get a reference from me."

She sat down, clutching her belly. He meant it. He wanted her to bare her soul to him, to expose her very guts.

"All right, Lucas. I'll tell you, and I hope you'll be satisfied. Last December, my doctor told me that dozens of fibroids were growing inside and outside of my uterus." He jerked forward, but she ignored him. "I would have no choice but to have a hysterectomy." She didn't look at him when she said that.

"I consulted experts in several other cities, renowned physicians. Each painted a picture more dismal than the previous one. I had no choice. I decided that before I submitted to the surgery that would rob me of what I wanted most in life, I was at least going to experience satisfying sex, to know what an orgasm was like at least once." She heard him suck in his breath, but she went on as if he weren't there.

"They said it wouldn't affect sex, but I didn't believe them. As you well know, I was not a virgin, but I didn't know how or what I was supposed to feel. And I wanted a chance at it while I still had a whole body. I chose you. When I met you, I had decided not to encourage intimate relationships, that it wouldn't be fair because I wouldn't be able to have children.

"However, after that diagnosis was confirmed repeatedly, I pulled myself out of the dumps and decided to have one solid fling. Who else but you? Everything about you says *man*. You're handsome, sophisticated, the epitome of masculinity. Virile. The works. Two weeks after we made love the first time, I had the operation. I'm sorry if you've been hurt by this. I knew you couldn't impregnate me, but if you had, I'd be a happy woman."

She put on his desk a paper on which she'd written the case worker's name and address. "Send the letter to her." She got up and started for the door.

"Don't go, Susan. Please. I'm . . . I can't . . . I don't have words to tell you how sorry I am. How—" He stood, but anticipating his next move, she rushed out of the office.

He'd pushed her to the limit. He closed and locked his office door, walked over to the park that faced his house and sat on a bench. She would never forgive him. He closed his eyes and let the sun burn his face. What if she did forgive him? If he followed his heart, he would never have the family for which he longed.

I love her, and she's finished with me.

He went home, dressed and drove to Hamilton Village, telling himself that the distractions there would force him to concentrate on his work.

"Has Susan been here today?" he asked Willis after searching the entire eighth floor for her.

"Haven't seen her. Say, why don't you, Aunt Noreen and I drive down to see Gramma this weekend. I can't go next weekend, because I promised my dad I'd visit him in Denver."

Lucas agreed with Willis's suggestion without giving it more than perfunctory thought. His mind was on Susan and the awful let down of not finding her there.

"Why don't you call Mama and see if she wants to go?" he asked Willis. "I don't care one way or the other."

Willis dropped the plane he'd been using to determine whether the floor was perfectly level and walked over to Lucas. "Man, what's wrong? I've never seen you like this."

"Long story, and I don't think you want to hear it."

"Susan, eh?" Willis pushed back his hard hat and scratched his head. "The more I see of this love crap, the more certain I am that I want no part of it. I thought Susan was different."

"She *is* different," he said, his tone adamant. "I'm the ass, not her."

Willis patted Lucas's shoulder. "Well, fix it, man."

Lucas dismissed that possibility with a shrug. "Fix it how?" Changing the subject, he said, "Maybe we can leave early Saturday morning and spend the night. Nana's got plenty of room."

"Works for me," Willis said.

Lucas went to the empty room that would eventually be the superintendent's office, sat on the floor, opened his briefcase and began to write.

> *To Whom It May Concern:*
>   *This is to confirm that Susan Pettiford, a local interior decorator, worked as an elementary school level tutor at Wade School during the past winter semester. Her work was admirable, and she deported herself impeccably.*
>   *I was particularly impressed with her love and affection for the children under her tutelage.*
> *Yours,*
> *Lucas Hamilton, M. Arch.*

He mailed the letter on the way home. For more than an hour, he sat on his deck, neither thinking nor feeling anything.

The squirrels that usually scampered up the steps and over to where he sat hoping for a handout stood watching him with curious expressions on their faces, for he seemed not to see them and didn't offer them any nuts. Drops of rain failed to shake him out of his lethargy, and not until lightning flashed around him and thunder roared over his head did he move. He folded the chairs, leaned them against the outer wall of the house and marveled that the sky had almost blackened and he hadn't noticed.

He went inside and, after considering his options, he telephoned Susan first at her office, then at her cellular number and finally at home, but at each location, it was her answering machine that responded. *Damn caller ID.*

Saturday morning arrived, and he still hadn't been able to contact her. He could have gone to her shop or to her home, but he didn't want to impose on her; he wanted a reconciliation. But if he could find no other way, he'd ambush her if necessary. He had to see her!

He arrived at his mother's house that Saturday morning with almost no interest in the trip to Athens, and he especially did not look forward to Willis's and his mother's enthusiasm. He wouldn't have thought that his mother would be so overjoyed at the prospect of meeting her son's paternal grandmother, but he supposed she may have longed to meet the woman who gave life to the man she loved. Feigning exhaustion, he let Willis drive his car, and while his friend and his mother spoke enthusiastically of the coming weekend, he stretched out in the backseat and went to sleep.

He awakened when the car came to a standstill. "I wonder whose town car this is," Willis said. "Custom built, too."

Lucas sat up. "Where? What car?" But his heartbeat had already begun to accelerate with excitement. He hadn't seen his father's car, but he could guess that the car belonged to him. He got out of his car to open the door for his mother and saw Nana standing on the porch rubbing her folded arms.

He rushed up the walk, greeted her with a hug and asked her, "Is that my dad's car?"

She nodded. "I didn't know he was coming. It's the first time he's been here since his operation. He'd said he'd be here next weekend. Otherwise I would have told Willis to let Noreen decide if she wanted to come while he's here."

"Don't worry about it, Nana. Sometimes Providence takes matters in its own hands. Where is he?"

"He's asleep. He got here around midnight. Exhausted. That's a long drive."

"Tell me about it."

Willis and Noreen walked up to them, and Alma Jackson opened her arms to Noreen. "I'm so glad to meet you, Noreen. My son talks about you so much that I feel I know you. Welcome." She opened her arms to Willis. "I fried you some green tomatoes and some real country-smoked bacon." Lucas looked from one to the other. "He told me he had that once and that he loves it," Alma said to Lucas. "Y'all come on in. Noreen, I have to tell you something."

He stood near the door in case his mother needed him, and couldn't help overhearing his grandmother's words.

"Noreen, honey, you're in for a shock. If I'd known Calvin was coming here today—"

Lucas stepped into the hall when Noreen gasped. "I would have told you and let you decide if you wanted to see him, Mama. He's asleep upstairs."

Noreen grasped Alma's arm and stared into her face. "Here? In this house? He's upstairs?"

Alma reached up and wrapped her arms around Noreen as best she could. "Sometimes, child, we learn that the Lord knows best. Go to the powder room down the hall and comb your hair. I didn't tell him you were coming, because I knew he wouldn't have slept a wink. Y'all make y'all selves at home while I fix some brunch."

Willis walked over to Lucas, shaking his head at the incredulity of it. *"Well, I'll be damned!"*

"Yeah," Lucas said. "I'm going to help Nana."

"I'd better go upstairs and prepare Dad for this," Lucas told Alma. "If he comes down here and sees her, he could have a heart attack."

"You're right, son. How's your work, and how're you and Calvin getting along?"

"Like any other father and son. We're learning about each other, but we get along fine, and I'm happy about that."

"Then what makes you sad? Is it because Calvin and your mother will meet here? You know that once they see each other, there'll be no keeping them apart."

"Yes, ma'am. I know it, and I don't intend to meddle. I love both of them and I'm not going to interfere with whatever little happiness they can find. Thirty-six years of suffering is penalty enough."

"Yes, that's true, but you didn't answer my question. How's your work?"

"Nana, if I hadn't fallen in love, my world would be as perfect as anyone could expect."

"Doesn't she love you?"

"Oh, she does, but—"

"Then you can fix it. When a woman loves a man, he's halfway to home plate—unless he's done something awful." She looked up at him with compassion in her eyes. "Did you?"

"I pushed her too hard, and she's hurting, but it may take more than love. I have to decide if I can forgo a cherished dream. Look, I'd better get up those stairs before Dad comes down here."

He looked down at his father asleep on his back with his hands locked behind his head. "Dad, you feel like getting up? It's almost noon."

Calvin opened his eyes and looked at Lucas. "I wasn't asleep. I was thinking of a dream I had." He sat up. "Lucas! I didn't know you'd be here this weekend. How nice!" Lucas sat on the side of the bed and looked at his father. "I didn't expect to see you here either. I told you about Willis, didn't I?"

"Yes. He's your friend and partner."

"Well, he and I thought this would be a good time to . . . uh . . . Nana said she wanted to meet Mama, so—"

Calvin threw back the bedding, bounded off the bed and grabbed Lucas by the shoulders in an excruciating grip. "Is Noreen Hamilton here with you?"

"Yes, Dad. She's downstairs. But you'd better get dressed first."

Calvin stared at Lucas. "Get dressed? Oh, yes. Did Mama tell you I'd be here this weekend?"

"No, sir. When I saw your car and guessed it was yours, I almost went into shock."

"Does Noreen know I'm here?"

"Nana told her. She reacted like a schoolgirl."

"Lucas, please, let me have this moment with Noreen. I know you don't approve, but it's . . . I think God has answered my prayers."

He put his arms around his father. "It's none of my business. I love both of you."

Calvin backed off and stared at Lucas. "You *love* me?"

How sweet it was! "Yeah. Hurry and get dressed. Nana's fixing brunch."

"You think I want *food*?"

He didn't try to suppress the grin that crawled over his face. "Maybe I'd better tell Mama to come up here. At least the two of you will be alone."

"Would you, please? Give me three minutes."

Lucas found Noreen in the living room staring into space, and Willis sat beside her with an arm tight around her, as if she needed a bodyguard. "Go upstairs, Mama."

"D-does he want to see me?"

"You couldn't be serious. He's as far out of his mind right now as you are out of yours. Up there, you'll be away from onlookers. Go on, now."

"You don't object?"

"Come with me." He led her to the bottom of the stairs, looked up and saw his father standing there. Waiting. He kissed her cheek and pointed toward the top of the stairs. She looked up, her right hand flew to her chest and she started up the stairs, slowly as if fearing that she would falter. Calvin widened his stance and opened his arms, and Noreen sprinted up the stairs and into Calvin Jackson's embrace.

Lucas turned around and bumped into Willis, who spoke for them both: "Well, I'll be damned, and after thirty-five years."

"Brunch is ready," Alma called.

"Put Mama's and Dad's in the oven or someplace," Lucas

said. "Food is not on their minds. Willis and I will do it justice, though."

Alma said the grace and passed the food. He wanted to ask her what she thought of his parents' reunion, for she seemed as calm as if the drama going on upstairs was an ordinary thing. However, with his usual candor, Willis led Alma to the topic.

"Gramma, how do you like Aunt Noreen? She's like a mother to me."

"She's a warm and loving woman, intelligent and very beautiful. I got more love from her in five minutes than I've had from Marcie in almost forty years. It breaks my heart to think of what she's been through. I'm praying that Calvin finds a way to make it right while I'm still alive to see it, and I'm going to tell him so right in front of her."

Lucas suppressed a sharp whistle as she looked at him. "And you, son, are going to do the same."

In order to do as his grandmother ordered, Lucas would need Susan's help and, to her mind, Lucas would not be included in her future. After he forced her to bare her soul to him, she drove home, lost her breakfast and, later, her lunch as well.

"What's going on here?" Betty Lou asked her after putting a cold towel on the back of Susan's neck and sitting beside her on the edge of Susan's bed. "If I didn't know it was impossible, I'd think you were pregnant. Now, I want you to start at the beginning and don't skip one thing, because if you do, I'll know it. You've always orchestrated your affairs without help from anyone, but you're not doing that now. Who is this man you love but won't commit to and who won't commit to you? What kind of nonsense is that? I want to hear this. Start with the day you arrived in Woodmore."

She did as her mother asked, omitting nothing, not even her seduction of Lucas, and ending with the drama in Lucas's office that morning. With tears cascading down her face and into her lap, she told her mother, "I love him, but I'm not going to forgive him for what he put me through this morning."

Betty Lou got up, walked to the window and gazed down at

the lake. "Really! I think he had a right to know why you did that, and he's certainly right in saying that you used him. You made the man fall in love with you, then you had him understand that you had nothing to offer him. Of course he's hurt, and he's bitter."

"But I tried to stay away from him, and he wouldn't let me."

"Nonsense! You didn't try very hard. And anyway, if you hadn't taken that drug the first time, you couldn't have become addicted to it. Blame yourself. The sad thing is that he's also addicted. I want to meet Rudy, so wash your face, change your clothes, and let's go over to Ann Price's house. Right now. Seeing the child will make you feel better."

"I'd planned to wait until I got the call from the agency."

"I see you trust him, because you believe he wrote that letter and mailed it immediately."

"I know he did. He's straight as the crow flies, as Papa used to say."

"That's good. Now let's go, and after that, I'd like to see how your work at Hamilton Village is coming along. You're a wonderful decorator, and I'm so proud of you."

"I'll take you to see Rudy and Nathan now, but we'll have to visit Hamilton Village another time. I don't feel like dealing with Lucas Hamilton again today, and I won't."

When they arrived, Rudy and Nathan were sitting on the floor in Ann's living room playing Chinese checkers. Ann opened the door, and Susan introduced Ann Price to her mother. When the children heard Susan's voice, they raced to greet her. Susan soaked up their hugs and affection, the unfettered love she needed after her breach with Lucas. She gathered them in her arms, hugged and kissed them. "Rudy and Nathan, this is my mother, Mrs. Pettiford."

"You're her mother?" Rudy asked as if in awe that Susan should have a mother. "Does she have a father, too?"

"Not anymore, because he died," Betty said and turned to Nathan. "Who was winning?"

He ignored the question. "Are you going to take Miss Pettiford away with you?"

"My goodness, no. I came to visit her for two weeks, then I'm leaving."

"Oh," he said, his face bright with a smile. "I was afraid you came to take her away. I always win when we play checkers."

Ann served them tea and homemade biscuits with jam, and it did not escape Susan that her mother scrutinized Ann carefully. She wondered what Betty Lou looked for and what she saw. After an hour, they left Ann's house and went to Susan's shop.

"Mom, why were you sizing up Ann?"

"I wasn't sizing her up. Her skin looks as if her blood is barely circulating. Have you forgotten that I'm a graduate, public-health nurse? Ann is definitely not well. She was almost too tired to lift that cup of tea."

"I know she's sick, and I help her as much as she'll let me."

"Don't you work every day?" Betty Lou asked Susan. "I mean, who's taking care of your shop?"

"I work every day and nights, too, Mom, and I would have been in my shop all day today if Lucas hadn't upset me."

"Listen, honey, don't let a man jerk your chain. I've taught you to keep your chin up no matter how badly you hurt. Of course, he did hand you a solid blow. I can't wait to meet the man who can make you cry."

"It wasn't Lucas, it was the fear of losing Rudy."

Her mother raised an eyebrow. "Don't fool yourself. You're not going to lose Rudy. Ann Price is ill, Rudy is crazy about you, and there aren't that many people willing to adopt a child who's almost seven years old. And what are you going to do about Nathan? He's going to need you, too, and soon."

The following Tuesday morning, Susan and her mother entered the shop shortly after eight o'clock, and the telephone rang immediately thereafter. Without thinking, Susan said to her mother, "Could you please answer that, Mom?"

"Pettiford Interiors. May I help you?"

"This is Lucas Hamilton. May I please speak with Ms. Pettiford?

"Just a second." She covered the receiver with her hand. "It's Lucas Hamilton."

"I won't speak with him, Mom. I'm not going to begin my day with a load of misery."

"I'm sorry, Mr. Hamilton, but she said she won't speak with you. I'm her mother, Betty Lou Pettiford, and I want to meet you. Do you have time to come by the shop?"

"Yes, I do. Thank you, Mrs. Pettiford. I'll be there in about twenty minutes."

"He'll be here in about twenty minutes, he said, and I want you to act like a woman and tell him whatever's on your mind. Hmmm. He's got an electrifying voice."

Susan glared at her. "Really, Mom? How could you do such a thing? Well, nothing's on my mind."

"Then it won't bother you if he and I have lunch together someplace, will it? At least you'll have a chance to tell him you met his father . . . before I tell him."

"Mama, why are you doing this? You never meddled in my private affairs before."

"I never saw you so far out of control that you lost two meals, either. I'm your mother. I've lived a long time, and I know that half your problem is guilt. You're so sure he wouldn't marry you, because he wants to be a father. Give him a chance to tell you that. If he loves you, he'll have a hard time doing it."

Susan stared at her mother. "You believe you know what you're talking about, and maybe you do, but I'm definitely not counting on it."

The door buzzer rang, and Betty Lou looked in that direction. "That's Lucas Hamilton, and what a specimen of a man! Answer the door, Susan. If I answer it, I'll bring him right on back here."

Susan got up and went to the door. She had forgotten her mother's habit of straight shooting and, as she always said, of keeping her closets airy and clean. "Hi, Lucas. Mom's in the office."

"Hello, Susan. I didn't come here to see your mother and she knows that, although I'll be glad to meet her. Has Social Services contacted you? I mailed the letter an hour after you left my office. It's been a week."

"Thanks for writing the letter."

"I've hardly slept since you ran out of my office without waiting to hear what I had to say."

"You said you were sorry, and that about covered it. Look, Lucas, I don't want to seem rude, but I've a lot of work to do, and you want to open Hamilton Village I on this Saturday. Come meet my mother. I . . . uh, met your father at Enid's reception."

"Yes, and it surprised him that you didn't mention to him that you knew me. I'd told him about you, although I didn't mention your name. He told me he'd met the woman who decorated Enid's house, and that she was an excellent decorator."

"Mom was with me, and she requires more explanation than I wanted to give just then."

Susan's mother stepped out of the office. "Mr. Hamilton, I'm Betty Lou Pettiford, and I am delighted to meet you. I met your father, and I don't have to tell you that seeing him is like looking at you." She grasped his hand in a strong handshake. "I've heard good things about you."

"Thank you. I'm glad for this opportunity to meet you, Mrs. Pettiford. If you have time, I'd like to show you Hamilton Village, a retirement complex that I've designed and the company I co-own is building. And if you could go over to Danville with me, I want to show you around some of my holdings in Jackson & Hamilton Enterprises."

Susan gasped. "When did you change it from Jackson Enterprises?"

"Dad changed it, the day he turned it over to me. What do you say, Mrs. Pettiford?"

"I'm ready when you are, Mr. Hamilton."

"I'd like you to call me Lucas." He looked at Susan. "I'll take good care of her."

"I know that, Lucas. I can't imagine you doing otherwise," she said, and could have bitten her tongue. In those few words, she had just told her mother and Lucas what she thought of him.

"Thanks so much for your confidence," he said without the semblance of a smile.

Betty Lou looked from one to the other. "If I didn't know better, I'd swear you two just met," she said, in the tone of one who is disgusted and not bothering to hide it.

Lucas held the door for her and spoke softly, "You'd be nowhere near the truth."

Susan closed the door and went back into her office. If Lucas wasn't interested in her, why would he go to such lengths in being gracious to her mother? The telephone rang, and she checked the caller ID display. Calvin Jackson. Why was he calling her?

Chapter Fourteen

Lucas drove Betty Lou first to Hamilton Village. He made no effort to hide his pride in what he had achieved there. "This is my friend and partner, Willis Carter. I'm the architect and he's the builder," he said, introducing her as Susan's mother.

"And Susan decorates our model apartments," Willis said. "They make a great team, Mrs. Pettiford, but something tells me right now that they're too stupid to accept that fact."

Betty Lou eyed Willis. "I know she's being stupid, but I'm surprised at your suggestion that he—she pointed to Lucas—caught the same virus."

Willis took Betty Lou's arm and walked down the hall, leaving Lucas alone. "Believe me, Mrs. Pettiford, Hamilton is a great guy. I've known him since he was eighteen, and this is the first time—"

Lucas caught up with them. "The first time I've considered murdering anyone, you were about to say, Willis?"

Willis winked at Betty Lou. "I'd better get back to work. See what you can do to straighten those two out, Mrs. Pettiford. It's been nice meeting you."

"I expect we'll meet again," she said, "and I'll look forward to it."

She's very smooth, Lucas thought. Smooth, direct and plain spoken. He liked that, and he liked her. He took her to the eighth floor.

"Our model apartments are on this floor. Susan has decorated about three-fourths of them. When she finishes these, she'll do the same in the two other buildings. What do you think?"

"I knew she was good at this, and after seeing how she decorated your sister's house, I was convinced that she's above average. I like what I've seen here."

"To say that Susan is an above average decorator is like saying that Mt. McKinley is a big hill."

Betty Lou leaned against the side of a breakfront, folded her arms and looked at him. "Lucas, I can see that you're proud of Susan. I know why she behaves toward you as she does, and I've told her that I think she's being foolish. Work out your feelings about this before both of you are deeply hurt."

He looked down at Betty Lou and failed in his attempt to smile. "What is behind all this? I know what she told me, and I believe her. Is there more?"

"She told you the facts; what she didn't do is explain her attitude. It's best you get that from her. I know you have mixed feelings, and you're entitled to have them, but if you don't come to terms with this one way or the other—"

"You don't have to tell me. Knowing how my parents suffered throughout my lifetime is lesson enough for me. How about lunch? A drive over to Danville takes about half an hour. After we eat, I can show you my set-up over there. Would you like that?"

"My day is in your hands, and I see that I'm going to enjoy every minute of it."

He didn't want to discuss his relationship with Susan with her mother, but he sensed in her an ally, and he had a feeling that he was going to need one. "I appreciate your interest in this," he said, "but I've learned that getting Susan to change her mind is almost like squeezing beet juice out of turnips."

Betty Lou placed a hand on his arm, stopping him as he opened the door of his car for her. "What I get from you so far, Lucas, is that you love Susan, that you're in a dilemma, and that you need to talk with her. Right?"

"Right on all counts."

"What do you think of her adopting Rudy?"

"She loves that little girl, and Rudy loves her. I wonder if having Rudy will be enough to make Susan happy."

Betty Lou looked hard at him, and he could almost read her thoughts. She asked him, "Are you sure that isn't a question you're asking yourself?" He had no intention of replying to that question, and she didn't pressure him, but grasped his hand and held it. "You'll have my respect no matter what you do. I consider myself blessed to have met a thirty-five-year-old man of your caliber, and especially to have been introduced to him through my daughter. Now. Enough about Susan. Tell me about your Danville business."

They ate lunch in what had become one of his favorite restaurants, and he told her about his work, his business and his life. Then, he took her to his Danville office. She stared up at that fifteen-story building that bore the name Jackson-Hamilton Building, in large letters. "Hmmm. Calvin Jackson definitely loves your mother and the child she bore him."

"You're right. He does, and I'm only just learning how deeply."

"Only those of us fortunate enough to love and to have been loved can truly understand it and its influences," she said in a manner and tone that led him to realize that she had experienced both and perhaps deeply.

He introduced her to Miriam, his secretary, took her into his office, and told her, "My architectural and building interests are separate from this." But he couldn't get Susan out of his thoughts. He walked over to the window and with his back to Betty Lou said, "If Susan separates Rudy and Nathan, she'll have a problem, because Rudy loves Nathan as much as she loves Susan. I hope she can see that."

"Don't worry. That may take care of itself." He turned and looked at her, hoping for an explanation, but she offered none. Instead she said, "I'd like to know the cost of that two-bedroom, den, dining room and living room apartment in Hamilton Village. I've been escaping reality with the Peace Corps in Africa ever since my husband died, and it's time I came home. I'm fifty-six."

"What are you doing for the Peace Corps?"

"Lucas, I'm a graduate public health nurse, and I do everything there from teaching people how to brush their teeth to delivering babies and caring for people with AIDS. I never stop working, but I'm needed, and I don't have time to think about my loss."

She had his undivided attention then. "Do you want to work here?"

"I have to work. I can't imagine sitting around doing nothing."

"Would you work for me?"

She stared at him. "For you? I've never done clerical work, but—"

"I mean as a public health nurse. Hamilton Village is a retirement complex, and I intend to have a health service, dining room, and recreational facilities including a swimming pool on the grounds. It will be a gated community to ensure safety and the freedom of the residents to enjoy the grounds at all times."

"Job or no job, I'm moving there. How do I get that apartment?"

"But I want you to run the health service, too. Willis said we have more than enough applications to fill the first building and most of the second one. I'll bring you the floor plans tomorrow. Take an apartment on a high floor, so that the trees won't eventually block your view. They grow fast, you know."

"I don't need the floor plans. I want the apartment that has the living room decorated in avocado green and brown, and I want it on the ninth floor."

"Good as done. Do I have a Public Health Nurse?"

"I'll have to give a couple of months notice." She stood and stretched out her arms, as if to express her joy. "What a day this is! After procrastinating all these years, in less than an hour, I sat here and made up my mind to come back home. My children will be so happy."

"And I got what I thought it would take me forever to find." He walked over to shake her hand, but she enveloped him in a hug, and said, "Let's go. I can't wait to tell Susan. Who'd have thought I'd commit to do all this?"

And who would have thought I'd find myself in such a dilemma that I would use any excuse to avoid facing it and dealing with it? I don't want to duplicate my father's folly. But I need—

"I'll take you home," he said to Betty Lou, "but I'm not sure I want to go in. I don't handle rejection very well."

"Nobody does, Lucas. But when you've lived as long as I have, you manage it."

Sitting alone in the office at the rear of her shop, Susan was about to face a dilemma of her own. She stared at the caller ID screen on the telephone and let the phone continue to ring. Finally it stopped, and the caller, Calvin Jackson, did not leave a message. That meant he wouldn't take a chance on her not returning his call. For the third time since Lucas walked out of her shop with her mother, she pricked her finger with a needle and had to trim away the expensive fabric that bore the red evidence of her inattention. The phone rang again. Calvin Jackson. She lifted the receiver.

"Good afternoon, Mr. Jackson. This is Susan Pettiford."

"Thank you for taking the call, Ms. Pettiford." Somehow, she suspected that he had tongue-in-cheek when he said that. "I'm thinking of having the executive suite in one of my office buildings redecorated, and I like your taste. Would you be willing to have a look at it and let me know whether you'd be willing to do it?"

"Why, uh . . . I'm honored, Mr. Jackson, but I've got a bit much on my plate right now. May I think about this overnight and call you back?"

"Of course you may, but I won't be satisfied unless you agree to do it. When may I expect to hear from you?" *A man who left nothing to chance and who would expect her to keep her word.* "Sometime tomorrow afternoon, sir."

"I appreciate your considering this, and I look forward to speaking with you tomorrow. You still have my number?"

"Yes, sir. I have it, and I will call you tomorrow."

She hung up and shook her head in wonder. A tidy sum that

would net her, but something didn't ring right. If Lucas was owner and CEO of Jackson-Hamilton, how did Calvin Jackson get the authority to redecorate the executive suite of one of the office buildings?

"I'm not getting into that," she told herself, but remembered immediately that she had promised to give the man an answer the next day. What would she tell him? She packed her briefcase, removed her smock, turned out the lights and was about to leave her office when the telephone rang.

"Susan, this is Mark. Can you get over to the Social Services agency in twenty minutes and bring some ID? Those people have no idea what they're doing, and if they louse up this time, I'm going to court."

"What's up?"

"Just please hurry and meet me over there, Susan. I have to make a run for it."

She reached the agency with five minutes to spare, and Mark rushed up to her. "Come with me, Susan. I don't want to give that woman an excuse to drag her feet another second."

"Sorry. She's left for the day," a secretary told them, "but you can go to the director's office three doors down. I imagine you're fed up with this, Ms. Pettiford. I know I would be."

"I'm Mrs. Moody," the director said. "Rudy's case worker has been assigned elsewhere in the system. I had no idea that this thing had dragged on so long. Do you want to change her last name?"

"That can be done later, if the child is willing," Mark said.

"Sign here, Ms. Pettiford," the director said, "and you may take Rudy home with you. I've sent someone to talk with her, and I'm told she's anxious to go with you but not happy to leave her friend, Nathan. I wish you luck. And thank you for making this child happy."

Susan sat down and tried to breathe. She could hardly believe that, at last, Rudy was hers. With unsteady fingers, she signed the certificates, then wiped her wet face. "I . . . I've never been so happy in my life." She shook hands with the woman and stood. For a minute, she thought the floor would come up to meet her, but Mark steadied her.

"Can I take her home now?"

"She's yours. Why not?"

She looked at Mark, certain that she seemed strange to him, because she didn't think she would recognize herself. "What will I do? I don't have any ice cream in my house, and Rudy loves ice cream."

Mark's laughter helped her settle down. "In that case, you buy some. Every supermarket in Woodmore is open."

"Okay. But I'd better get Rudy first. A bird in hand is worth two in the bush."

When she arrived at Ann Price's house, she found Rudy sitting on her suitcase with Nathan beside her, his eyes red from crying. "Maybe you can let him go with her just for tonight," Ann said. "I knew he'd be sad, but he's miserable."

"If you don't mind, he can stay with me for a few days, Ann. I'll bring him back with me when I bring your laundry."

Ann wiped her hands on the back of her pants, and she realized that her friend had also been crying. "You're still planning to do my laundry? With Rudy gone, I thought you wouldn't do that anymore. It's been such a great help."

"I'm not a sometime friend, Ann." What she didn't say was that she could afford to pay to have the laundry done. And that she would. "I'll bring my mom and the children to see you day after tomorrow."

She didn't want Rudy and Nathan to share a room, so she put a folding cot in her den/office for him, moved her computer and drafting table into her bedroom, and left her mother in the guest room. "You two get acquainted with my mother while I make a phone call," she said to the children.

Lucas answered on the second ring, and she knew that he wanted to hear from her. "Hello, Lucas, this is Susan."

"Yes, I know, how are you?"

"I'm very happy. I have Rudy at home with me, and she's legally my daughter. I brought Nathan for a few days, because he was so unhappy when he learned she was leaving them. Lucas, I—"

"I can't tell you how happy I am for you. We have to celebrate."

"Then, come over for supper. The children will be excited to see you. I'll figure out what I can scare up for us to eat."

"Better still, why don't I pile the bunch of you in my car and we go to a roadside restaurant I found and have a feast?" Lucas asked her.

"All right, if you still want to after I tell you this."

"What?"

"Your dad called and asked if I'd decorate the executive suite in one of his Danville office buildings, and I told him I'd let him know tomorrow afternoon. I figured if you were supposed to be head honcho these days—"

"Hmmm. Knowing that she cared about his interests gave him a good feeling. Don't let it bother you. Tell him you'll do it, and hike up the fee. I'll deal with him."

"But—"

"Don't worry. Nothing's going to impair my relationship with him. I'll just have to remind him of a couple of things. It's good pay, and you're a first class decorator."

"Well, if you don't mind."

"Oh, I mind his little slip, but I'm glad you'll be doing it. Let me know which building he wants you to work in. See you in a couple of hours, and give my regards to your mother."

"Am I going to stay with you all the time, Miss Pettiford?"

"Yes, darling, and I'm going to be your mother, so from now on, this is your home, and I want you to call me Mother or Mom or Mommy, whatever feels comfortable."

Rudy walked up to Susan and looked up at her with an expression of disbelief. "You're going to be my mommy? And I'm going to be your little girl? The social worker said that, but I don't ever believe anything she says." Rudy looked up at her for a long time, and then she wrapped her arms around Susan's thighs. Susan didn't realize the child was crying until she felt the moisture on her body. She hunkered before Rudy, put her arms around her daughter and rocked her until Rudy stopped crying.

"What's Nathan doing?" she asked Rudy.

"Your mother is teaching him how to make popsicles."

"Rudy, my mother is your grandmother, so you should call her Nana. All right?"

Rudy's face bloomed in a bright smile. "Yes, ma'am, and I'm going into the kitchen right now and call her Nana."

Lucas dressed, got into the town car and headed for Danville and his first confrontation with his father. Calvin opened the door. "This is a pleasant surprise."

"Hi, Dad. I can't stay long because I have a dinner date at seven in Woodmore, but I had to ask you this in person."

Calvin stepped aside. "Come in, and let's go in the den where we can talk." He sat down. "I won't ask if you'd care for a drink, since you're driving and you seem aggravated. Aggravation is enough to unsettle a driver without the added effect of alcohol. What's wrong, Son?"

With his right elbow on his right thigh, Lucas propped up his chin with his right thumb and forefinger, and stared at his father, the man to whom he was becoming increasingly attached. Suddenly, laughter poured out of him.

"You knew I'd take you to task for giving Susan that job, didn't you? What was your point? Either I'm owner and CEO of this company or I'm not. If there is anyone who understands and appreciates propriety in business matters, it's you. How'd you get off track? Or perhaps I should ask *why* did you?"

Calvin didn't bat an eyelash. "So she consulted with you before she gives me her answer. Interesting. I was not satisfied with the fact that she talked with me, knew I was your father and didn't tell me she knew you, not to speak of how well she knew you. So I figured you hadn't done your work there. It won't hurt to spiff up that suite upstairs above your office. Suppose you want to invite the governor or some politicians you'd like to impress? The only thing that makes a dent with those fellows is money or the appearance of it. I don't believe in bribes, but the appearance of money is just as good."

"So your aim is to get Susan into my hair. Well, you wasted your time, Dad, because she stays in my hair."

"Good. She's a beautiful and charming woman, and I liked her. She has a nice mother, too."

"Yeah. I like her mother. By the way, I haven't been able to get a peep out of *my* mother about what's going on between you two. She's not even telling Willis. She told him she doesn't want to jinx it."

"She's never going out of my life again, Son. After what we shared at Mama's house last Sunday, I can never be without her again. Nothing had changed, except perhaps we love each other more than we ever did. Marcie agreed to a divorce provided she could file the charges, and I told her she could accuse me of anything she wanted short of a crime. She filed this morning. In exchange, she gets this house and everything in it except my personal belongings. I told her to photograph everything in here, put it on eBay, and she can sell it for a couple of million. I couldn't care less. Luveen's good at that sort of thing, and I'm sure she'll take care of it for Marcie. I dislike ninety-five percent of the stuff Marcie put in here and don't give a hoot for the other five percent."

Calvin got up, walked to a picture of his father and stood beside it. "Marcie and I have not been in the same bed simultaneously in over twenty years. After my affair with Noreen, Marcie had several and she let me know it. Finally, I stopped pretending, and she welcomed my honesty.

"As soon as Noreen's passport arrives, we're headed for Italy. I've always wanted to see the works of those great architects and artists, those multi-talented geniuses, especially Michelangelo, Bernini, and Botticelli. Noreen wants to see the Vatican and Michelangelo's *The Last Judgment*. Most of all, we long to be alone together.

"The things we discussed and dreamed about all those years ago that seemed so mysterious and out of reach that we could speak of them as if we knew them will at last be real to us. We saw that movie, *Three Coins In A Fountain* together, and we want to go to the Trevi Fountain stand with our backs to it and toss coins over our shoulders.

"I want to show her the world, Son. Everything."

"Where will you settle, Dad?" He wanted his mother to see

the world, to enjoy life with the man she loved while she was still young enough, healthy and eager to embrace life, but he wasn't satisfied with what he'd heard.

"She doesn't want to leave the home you built for her and that she loves, and I don't want to leave *her*. That answer your question?"

"Look," Lucas said, biting the bullet, "Don't you have plans to get married?"

Calvin Jackson rolled his eyes toward the ceiling. "Of course. Hopefully, before we leave, but she told me not to sweat it, that I shouldn't count chicks before they hatch or some such foolishness as that. She said I shouldn't tell you because you'd be disappointed if it didn't come off."

"I'd be disappointed and probably mad as the devil if you two went traipsing around the world shacking up along the way. I'm not old-fashioned, but I place a value on propriety."

Calvin winked at him. "I'm straight. You get it right with Susan."

"Why shouldn't she get it right with me?"

"Because it seldom works that way," Calvin said. "Are you having supper with her?"

"With her, her newly adopted daughter, her daughter's friend and her mother."

Calvin gawked for a second only, straightened out his face and said, "Tomorrow, you'll call me and explain all that to me. Have a good evening." He enjoyed the warmth of his father's embrace and then headed for Woodmore. So his dad wanted to get him and Susan together. He wondered what his mother and grandmother would say, not that their opinions of Susan would figure into his thinking.

Betty Lou opened the door in response to his ring. "Come in, Lucas. Susan will be down in a minute."

"Who is it, Nana?"

"Mr. Hamilton!" Nathan squealed, and launched himself into Lucas's waiting arms.

"My, but you're growing." He knelt and hugged the boy. "I think you're going to be tall."

"Yes, sir. I hope I'm going to be just like you, sir. Rudy lives here now, Mr. Hamilton." He heard the wistfulness in the child's voice and a sadness that, he supposed, accompanied a feeling of having been excluded.

"Now, she has a real family just like you do," he said, hoping that his words would be balm for the boy's feeling of inadequacy.

"Hi, Mr. Hamilton." Rudy gazed up at him, waiting for him to recognize her. He scooped her up in his arms, hugged her and set her down beside Nathan. She raised her arms to him again and, when he leaned down, she kissed his cheek. "Miss Pettiford is my mommy now, Mr. Hamilton, and I have a nana, too. Mr. Hamilton, would you please ask my mommy if Nathan can be my brother?"

"I would, Rudy, but his grandmother may not let him go. He's her youngest grandchild, and she loves him a lot."

"Hello, Lucas." He whirled around and managed to suppress a whistle. If she wasn't interested in any kind of relationship with him, why had she dressed in that eye-popping, slithery red jersey dress that advertised her sweet breasts, hips that he itched to cradle, and striking legs. He swallowed heavily.

"Hello, Susan. I assume you're ready?" She nodded. Betty Lou walked past them, and he locked the door with Susan's key, took the children's hands as they walked on either side of him and stepped out into the twilight.

I'd be happy with this family. He nearly stumbled as he reflected upon the thought that flashed through his mind. It seemed so natural to have Susan and the children in his care. Betty Lou only made them seem that much more like a family.

Oddly enough, as he later reflected upon his evening, he couldn't remember a happier occasion, unless it was the moment when he saw his father embrace his mother for the first time. He stood in Susan's foyer looking down into the face he loved, wanting to make love with her until he went out of his mind and realizing that she wanted the same.

"Maybe we've needed some chaperons," she said.

"Speak for yourself. What I need right now is to be in your arms, buried so deeply in you that not even air can get between us. And don't tell me that you don't need the same. There're no chaperons at my house, and I'll always welcome you with open arms. By the way, I'm glad you have your daughter."

"Thank you for helping to make it possible."

She gazed up at him with such longing that he said, "Oh, hell, Susan," locked his arms around her and eased his tongue into her waiting mouth. With one hand at his nape and the other at his buttocks, she worked at him as if she thought she needed to imprint herself in his memory. He backed away from her.

"Do you want to go home with me?"

She looked past his shoulder. "I can't have everything I want, so I'm going to try and content myself with what I have." She cradled his face with her hands. "I love you, but you deserve so much more. Good night. Please slam the door locked." She turned away from him and ran up the stairs.

I love you, but you deserve so much more. So that was it. She thought she wasn't good enough because she couldn't have children. He closed the front door, tried the lock for security and ambled slowly down the walk. Shaken up by what he regarded as her confession, he walked down to the lake, sat on the bench she had placed there, and told himself to think with his heart and not with his head. Hours later, he got into his car and drove home.

Susan sat at her kitchen table eating breakfast facing Rudy and Nathan, and her heart went out to the little boy who seemed to put so much effort into being happy. He wasn't, and she didn't know what could be done about it.

"I've decided to take an apartment in Hamilton Village," Betty Lou said, "the one in which you decorated the living room in avocado green and brown. Lucas said he'll make certain that I get the one on the ninth floor."

Susan stopped eating. "Then you really are coming back here to live?"

"I'll try to give six weeks notice. I've promised Lucas that I'll manage his health service. It's a retirement complex, and he has to offer health care. I'm just what he needs, and that job is exactly what I want."

Susan took several sips of coffee as she pondered the news. "The best thing is that I'm getting my mother back. Mom, will you bring the children down to the shop around one. We'll have lunch, and then I want to take them shopping."

"Are you going to take Nathan shopping, too, Mommy?" Rudy asked.

"Of course, I am, darling." She looked at the boy. "You want to go with us, don't you?"

His face brightened. "Yes, ma'am."

"Good," she said, "and before we come back home, we'll stop by to see your grandmother for a few minutes."

She went to her shop knowing that her mother would take care of Rudy and Nathan, but what would she do when her mother went back to Africa and, later, when she was at work in Hamilton Village? She'd better begin looking for a nanny. Thoughts of her additional responsibilities did nothing to dampen her spirits. *She'd take Nathan, too, if it were possible.*

But at that moment, Lucas was taking steps that would remove the possibility of her adopting Nathan. He knocked on Ann Price's door. "Good morning, Mrs. Price. I hope you remember me, I'm—"

"Of course, I remember you, Mr. Hamilton. Come on in. Would you like a cup of coffee?"

"I'd love it, Mrs. Price. As a bachelor, I settle for instant in the mornings, and I'm not very fond of it."

She brought the coffee, sat down and exhaled a long—and he thought labored—breath. "What brought you here, Mr. Hamilton?"

"Last night, I took Susan, her mother, Rudy and Nathan out to supper at one of my favorite restaurants, and we had a wonderful time—"

She interrupted him. "When I'm gone, Nathan's not even going to have what I could offer him, much less the comforts Susan can give him. I'm so happy for Rudy, but Nathan is grieving his heart out. He's an orphan. My daughter got with a bad crowd after

Nathan's father went to Iraq. He was a good man, sent me money every month to help me take care of Nathan after Delia—my daughter—took off. He was killed over there and she took a hit in a drug bust. Until Nathan met Rudy, he stayed to himself, hardly talked to my other grandchildren, just sat in a corner and read or watched TV. He didn't even play. He loves Rudy more than anybody in the world, because she needed him, and he knew it."

"Let's go back to the beginning. What did you mean, when you're gone?"

"I'm terminally ill with leukemia. My sister is coming for my three older grandchildren, but she can't take Nathan, because he'll just be seven next month and needs close supervision. She works. I'm hoping that Susan will decide that he shouldn't be separated from Rudy. Mr. Hamilton, I'm so sick, but I put up a front for the children's sake."

"I didn't realize that you aren't well, and I'm terribly sorry about it. If I can help by arranging hospitalization or even home health care, I'll be glad to do it, and I have the means. So don't hesitate to let me know what you need."

"All I need is a home for Nathan and a place where I can sleep away in comfort. I don't want the children to know this, because they'll refuse to go with my sister."

"Do you have legal custody of Nathan?"

"Yes, and I have the papers."

"Would you allow me to adopt him?"

She stared at Lucas. "Allow you to . . . Are you serious?"

"That's why I came here this morning."

"The Lord answers prayers. I prayed all night for some guidance about what to do with that child. Yes. I'll sign the papers whenever you're ready. I don't want to wait, because . . . well, you never know. Just one thing. Will you make sure that he can see Rudy?"

"If I'm fortunate, they'll be living in the same house."

"You mean . . . you and Susan?"

"Yes."

"Well, I do declare. I think we'd better go to the courthouse right now. This is a blessing."

He dialed his friend Mark on his cell phone and told him

what he needed. "Wow! You don't have to tell me the rest; I can easily guess it. You're getting two for the price of one."

"Correction. I'm getting three." He drove Ann to the courthouse where they met Mark.

"This shouldn't take long, Mrs. Price," Mark said. "You have the authority to do this."

Lucas left the courthouse less than an hour later assuring himself that he was indeed a father. He took Ann home, and drove straight to his mother's house.

"It's so nice to see you, Son, but in the future, call before you come. Calvin's taking me to supper later, and I'd hate for you to come all the way out here for nothing."

"I hope you and Dad manage to marry before you leave the country."

She sat down, obviously surprised. "Has he been talking to you about our plans? I don't want to shock you, Son, but I'm only fifty-seven and . . . Oh, it was so wonderful being with him Sunday."

"Let's get back to the subject. I was happy for both of you. You belong together, and if I was ever in doubt, that uncertainty was erased at Nana's house Sunday. Still, get married before you leave."

"He wasn't supposed to talk about this."

"No? I'm his son, and he behaved like it by telling me what's going on, even if my mother didn't. I have something to tell you. You're a grandmother."

"*I'm a what?*"

"I've just adopted a six-year-old boy, and if I'm lucky, I'll soon have a six-year-old daughter."

"What's this? You can't have your own children?"

"I suppose I could, but I'm in love with a woman who can't, and this is the way we're solving it."

"I see. Am I going to like this woman?"

"I hope so. She's a loving and giving person. I decided that I don't want to spend the best part of my life pining for her as Dad did for you, so I'm going with my heart. As soon as I get her to agree to marry me, we'll bring the children to see you."

"As soon as you get her to—"

He hugged her. "I have to run. Willis called a meeting for this morning, and I'm about to miss it. I'll call you and remember: no shacking up with my father." He laughed all the way to Hamilton Village. For the first time in his life, he felt whole. He had parents who loved him and each other, a woman who loved him, and he would soon have two children who adored him and who had their own special place in his heart.

Susan was feeling less sanguine, and especially in her dilemma over what to do about Nathan. After lunch with her mother and the children, she took them to Woodmore Department Store.

"Nathan, you need some summer T-shirts, shorts and sneakers, and Rudy, I think you need the same, except that I want you to have a couple of skirts. Girls ought to wear dresses at least once in a while. Nathan, you need a jacket to match those navy blue pants."

"For goodness sake," Betty Lou said, "don't you realize that these children will quickly grow out of all this stuff you're buying? Four T-shirts and three dress shirts are all he needs for now. Next year, you'll give those things to the Goodwill Industries or another charity. The same goes for Rudy."

"You're right, Mom. I'm going to have to give her winter clothes away."

They finished shopping and, as promised, she drove by Ann Price's house. "We can't stay long, but we wanted to know how you're getting on," Susan told her.

"I'm just fine. Have you spoken with Mr. Hamilton?"

"No," Susan said. "I haven't seen him today."

"Oh. Well, give him my regards," she said.

That was strange. Ann hadn't mentioned Lucas to her since the tutoring session ended. "How do you feel, Mrs. Price?" Betty Lou asked.

"I'm not so good, but I'll rest after a while."

"I don't like it," Betty Lou said, after they left. "She needs care that she's not getting. I'm leaving day after tomorrow, so there isn't much I can do, but I'll do what I can."

The children rushed into the house with their parcels, laughing and teasing, and Susan could only think how sad Rudy would be when Nathan had to go home. "I'll find a way," she vowed. Lucas arrived immediately after Susan, her mother and the children returned home.

"Hi," was all she said when she opened the door and saw him standing there.

"I need to talk with you, Susan."

"Can it wait? I want to feed the children and establish some kind of routine for them. Can we talk after supper?"

He seemed to weigh the idea. "If I come for you at about nine, will you go home with me? It's important."

"All right."

After he left, she noted that the sun was still relatively high, went to the telephone in the breakfast room and phoned Cassie. Maybe she could encourage her friend to embrace the idea of motherhood. "We haven't seen much of each other lately," she said after their greeting. "I want you to meet my daughter and her little friend."

"Your daughter? You mean—"

"I've been trying for months to adopt her, and she's finally mine."

"Bring her over to see her aunt Cassie. I was just sitting here trying to design some wallpaper. It isn't too close to supper to give the children ice cream, is it? I've missed you, Susan, but I haven't seen your car, so I knew you were busy."

"We'll be over shortly, and you can give them one scoop. Okay?"

"I'll get supper started," Betty Lou said, as Susan left with Rudy and Nathan. To Susan's astonishment, Cassie hovered over the children like a mother hen. "I'll teach you how to make animals out of paper," she told them and quickly folded a single piece of paper into the shape of a giraffe. "It's called origami, and it was invented in Japan," she said.

"Can you make any other animals?" Nathan asked her. She said she could and that she'd show them another time.

"I want to learn how to make birds," Rudy said. "I love birds."

"That does it for now," Susan said. "Finish your ice cream, I want us to walk down to the lake." She thanked Cassie and enjoyed the woman's warm embrace. "How's it going?" she whispered.

"Nothing showed last month, so I'm hoping and praying."

"Go to the drugstore and get one of those tests. You'll know in a minute."

"I know, but I'm scared of being disappointed."

What a change! "I don't think you will be. Give Kix my regards. I hope I'll soon be congratulating him."

She walked down to the lake and sat on the bench with the children on either side of her. "Miss Pettiford, can I come visit Rudy and stay sometimes?"

"Of course you can, Nathan. This will be your second home. I love Rudy. She's my daughter. But I love you, too." She put an arm around him and hugged him. "We'd better go, Nana probably has supper ready."

"I think you wish you could have both of them," Betty Lou said as she and Susan cleaned the kitchen after supper.

"I do, and I have a mind to try. I don't want Nathan to go to a foster home. Well, we'll see." She put her hand on her mother's wrist, tugging at it as she'd done when a child. "Mama, Lucas is coming for me at nine, and I'm going home with him."

"Will you be back tonight?"

Susan frowned, taken aback at the question. "Of course."

Betty Lou rolled her eyes toward the ceiling and threw up her hands. "You're one for the books. If it was me, you can bet I wouldn't be so sure."

Chapter Fifteen

Lucas rang Susan's doorbell and waited. He didn't remember when his nerves had been in such disarray. The door opened, and she gazed up at him. "I'm ready," she said, closed the door and walked past him out to his car. He wondered what was behind that unusual behavior, but decided not to mention it.

"How was your first day of motherhood?"

"I'd be happy if I didn't have to worry about Nathan. Ann's not well, and Mama said she needs care that she isn't getting."

"I'm glad you told me. I'll take care of that tomorrow morning." He didn't want to begin their evening by discussing problems, so he turned the radio dial to a classical music station and said to her, "Lean back, relax and think about pleasant things." He parked in his garage, closed the garage door, took her hand and entered his home with her for the first time. It occurred to him that she'd been in his studio, which was adjacent to his home, but never inside his house, and he watched her closely for her reaction to his tastes.

"What a wonderful house, Lucas. It looks just like you."

"Thanks, I like it, but I'm going to have to sell it and build another one. Or at least, that's what I hope." He brought the wine and two stem glasses, took her hand and joined her on the sofa.

"Yesterday, you told me that you love me, and I believe it. I've loved you for a long while, Susan, and I can't see myself living without you." She sat forward, poised to accept whatever came. "I don't want to suffer over half a lifetime as my parents suffered," he went on. "By the way, they're planning to marry soon."

"What? You're joking. That's the best news I've heard since . . . How'd it happen?"

"I'll tell you some other time, that's just a little of my news. When you said you loved me, you also said I deserved better than you, and from that, I finally understood why you've said there can be nothing between us. I love you more than I would love my own child, and I would love my child with my whole heart. Do you understand what I'm saying?" He knelt before her. "I need you, Susan and I will love you and care for you and our children as long as I live. Will you marry me?"

"You think that now, but—"

He covered her mouth with his own and had the pleasure of knowing that his touch sent tremors through her. "Rudy needs a father, and Nathan needs a mother."

She stared at him. "Nathan? What do you mean?"

"He's my son now." She gasped and clutched his left arm. "Mark and I went with Ann to the judge this morning, and I've adopted Nathan. He was an orphan and Ann was his legal guardian. She signed the papers. Nathan doesn't know it yet, because he's been with you all day. Tomorrow, I'll talk with him and bring him home."

"Are you sure you won't be sorry?"

"I do nothing rashly. When the four of us were together two nights ago, I was so happy, and I knew it was the family that I could cherish forever. My love for Nathan is not contingent upon your marrying me. He's mine. He let his palms skim her thighs. Will you marry me, Susan?"

She slid to the floor and wrapped him in her arms. "I love you so much, and I never dreamed that I could have a life with you. Yes, I'll marry you."

"After two weeks with me, the judge wants to see Nathan, and he'll ask Nathan if he's happy in his new home. Then the judge will give me the boy's birth and health certificates."

"Nathan will be out of his mind with happiness. He'll be

delirious. The child has been so morose all day, that I had decided *I* would try to adopt him. Ann's so sick."

He put a finger to her lips. "Beginning tomorrow, she'll get
the best care there is. You know, we'll have to teach Nathan and
Rudy how to be brother and sister, otherwise, they may grow up
to be lovers, and we don't want that."

"No, we don't," she said in a voice filled with awe. "I suggest
you have breakfast with us at my house tomorrow morning and
we can tell our children then."

He knew that his face shone with his happiness, a joy so great
that he thought he would burst with it. "Right," he said. "And
after that, I'll round up my mom and dad, provided I can find
them, and the children can meet their other grandparents."

He stood, lifted her to her feet, poured each of them a glass of
champagne and whispered in a voice that shook with emotion,
"To the rest of our lives together."

She drank the wine down without moving the glass from her
lips. "Any more in that bottle? I feel so good that I could drink
every drop of it."

He laughed to express his happiness. "Would you care to see
my etchings, madam?"

"I presume these etchings are upstairs in your bedroom."

"That's the safest place for them," he said, enjoying the fun.

"I thought you'd never ask."

He took her hand and they raced up the stairs. An hour later,
she crawled on top of him, demanded more, and with the freedom to have him as she wanted him, she loved him until their
powerful releases exhausted them both.

"I know you didn't plan to spend the night," he said the next
morning when they awakened shortly after six o'clock, "but it
was wonderful that you did. Think we can get to your house in
an hour?"

She found her pocketbook, showed him her toothbrush and
winked. "I also leave nothing to chance," to quote you.

When Betty Lou wandered down into the kitchen at a quarter
of eight, he'd set the table and Susan had breakfast nearly ready.
"Who stayed where?" she asked, and since she looked at him, he

answered, "We stayed together. Where, doesn't matter. I'm glad you're down here before the children. We have a lot to tell you."

Betty Lou listened to their story and, at last, managed to close her mouth. "Well, I'll say. I didn't think I could be this happy again. Susan, I was hoping you would see Lucas for the man he is, and I'm so glad you came to your senses."

At the sound of Rudy and Nathan running down the stairs, Susan said, "You tell them, Lucas."

It didn't surprise her that he spoke to Nathan first. "Come around here, Son." Nathan walked around to him and rested his forearms on Lucas's thigh. "Mrs. Price is ill, but don't worry, I plan to see that she gets good care. Your cousins have gone to Boston to live with Mrs. Price's sister."

"What about me? Can I stay with Miss Pettiford?"

"No. You're going to stay with me. At my request, your grandmother signed the papers yesterday, and I am your father, just like Susan Pettiford is Rudy's mother. You are legally my son, and I will take care of you."

Nathan stared at him. "You adopted me? Aunt Betty Lou explained to Rudy and me about adoption. That means you're going to be my dad?"

"I *am* your dad, now, Nathan, and that's what I want you to call me."

Nathan climbed into Lucas's lap and put his head on Lucas's shoulder. "I didn't think anybody wanted me."

"Now, you know better. I want both of you. Something else. Susan and I have decided to get married, and all four of us will be living together, so you're both getting a mother and a father, because I will also adopt Rudy and Susan will adopt you, Nathan. It will all come together after I build us a bigger house."

Nathan jumped off Lucas's lap and ran to Rudy. "Now we can stay together." He turned toward Lucas. "When are you going to build our house, Dad, and how long will it take? Can I start calling Miss Pettiford Mother now? Can I, Dad?"

"Unfortunately, you have to wait till we're married. Now, excuse me, I have to call my own dad, and I must make arrangements for Mrs. Price."

It took him so long to come back to the breakfast room that she had begun to wonder if something had gone amiss.

"Betty Lou, I'd appreciate it if you'd go to Mrs. Price's home with me. She sounded as if she's practically out of it. I promised Dad, I'd take all of you to my Mother's house this evening around five. So Betty Lou, pack today, since we may be out rather late and you have an early flight."

Only despondency would describe him when he returned to Susan's house later that day. "The poor woman is almost gone," he told Susan. "I put her in a Woodmore General private room with private nurses. The rest is up to Providence."

"She didn't even know we were there," Betty Lou said. "But I've known some to snap back from that stage." She shook her head. "I'm hoping for the best."

That evening, Lucas packed his new family and his future mother-in-law into his town car and headed for his mother's house to introduce his new family to his parents.

"So I get what I wanted," Calvin Jackson said to Susan. "I'm delighted to have you as my daughter-in-law. He hunkered before Rudy and Nathan who faced him holding hands. "I'm your grandfather, and I want you to call me Granddaddy."

"Yes, sir," they said in unison.

"And you're to call me Nana," Noreen said.

"But I call her Nana," Rudy said, pointing to Betty Lou. "Can I have two nanas?"

"You certainly can," Betty Lou said.

"I have an idea," Calvin Jackson said, as he stood at the head of Noreen's supper table carving a roasted and stuffed fresh ham. "Let's have a double wedding complete with all the trimmings. "What do you say to that, Susan?"

"I think it would be wonderful. I can't believe I have two beautiful, healthy children and this wonderful man. Six weeks ago, I thought it would never come to pass."

Noreen got up, walked over to Calvin and nestled in his arms. "I had almost forty years of certainty that I could never walk the streets of Woodmore holding this man's hand. I didn't even pray for it. But today, we went into the ritziest store in town, and when we left, this diamond was on my finger." She buried her face in Calvin's chest and allowed herself to enjoy the luxury of being in his arms in the presence of anyone who cared to watch.

"What's a double wedding?" Rudy asked.

"You take that one, Dad," Lucas said. "My son just spilled something on his new jacket, and I have to clean it off. Come on, Son."

"If this isn't the happiest day of my life, it's pretty close to it," Betty Lou said. "I can't wait to get back here from Africa and enjoy my grandchildren."

Epilogue

Forty-six days later, on a balmy September Saturday at precisely six o'clock in the evening, Betty Lou patted Rudy and Nathan on their shoulders and sent them down the aisle to the altar of Woodmore's First Presbyterian Church, where Calvin Jackson and Lucas Hamilton awaited their brides. As she walked, Rudy strew pink rose petals and colorful African Orchids along the bridal path. Betty Lou adjusted Noreen's white lace veil and bridal train and, to the tune of "Here Comes The Bride," Noreen went to meet her groom who, as she approached, broke precedent and took a few steps to meet her.

"You're more beautiful than you've ever been," Betty Lou whispered to her daughter, "and you're blessed with the love of a fine man and two wonderful children. I couldn't want more for you." She wiped tears from her eyes, and Susan slipped her arm through the arm of her brother, Jack, and went to join her life with that of Lucas Hamilton. As she walked up the aisle, the long train of her ivory-silk bridal gown swept aside the petals, and when she reached Lucas, his brimming smile turned to tears and, for as long as she lived, she would remember his whispered, "I'm the luckiest man on earth."

GETTING SOME OF HER OWN

GWYNNE FORSTER

ABOUT THIS GUIDE

The suggested questions are intended to enhance
your group's reading of this book.

DISCUSSION QUESTIONS

1. Two issues germane to the happiness and well being of women and men in our culture propel this story. What are those issues?

2. What misconception is behind Susan's seduction scheme?

3. What steps does she take to appeal to Lucas's senses as she plans the seduction, and what folklore substantiates her choices?

4. What is the clue that Susan chose as her "victim" a man who will not be bamboozled even by a stunning woman and mind-blowing sex?

5. Why doesn't he believe her when she explains her behavior?

6. When we first meet Lucas Hamilton, what drives him?

7. What accounts for his love/resentment attitude toward his mother, and do you think his attitude is logical?

8. Do you think Susan's passion to have a child would be as great if she could bear children?

9. Some women fear the pains during the actual bearing of a child, but Cassie dreaded and feared the pregnancy. Considering her husband's affection for her, do you think her unwillingness to have children is rooted in vanity, low self-esteem, or what?

10. In this story, the three central female characters use questionable means to get what they want or to ensure that their decisions prevail. Did they have other options? What were these options?

11. Susan defies Lucas. In what context? Why, and what is his reaction? As a man who plays by the rules, why doesn't he apply the rules to Susan?

12. Can you explain Lucas's emotional reaction when he looks down at his father for the first time? When he hands his father a glass of water? When he touches his hand?

13. What happens to his long-held wish to give his father his comeuppance? How does his father deal with this?

14. Why is Lucas reluctant to tell his mother of his visit with his father? What is Noreen's reaction to the news that Lucas has visited his father?

15. Why does Lucas agree to his father's request that they run Jackson Enterprises? What is Noreen's reaction to that?

16. How does Lucas deal with his father's recalcitrant employees? What does this tell us about his personality?

17. The more Lucas sees of his father, the closer to him he becomes. He learns from his father that he has a grandmother. What is his reaction, and how does this affect his relationship with his father?

18. Calvin Jackson has a family conference that includes Lucas. What does Lucas learn at this conference, and how does it affect his perception of himself?

19. Susan is the one person with whom Lucas shares the changes in his life, yet she refuses to share with him the one thing that prevents him from being closer to her. Is he being too demanding, or does he have the right to know?

20. What are the circumstances that bring to a head a resolution of Susan and Rudy's mutual need of each other?

21. Is Lucas justified in blackmailing Susan?

22. What accounts for his decision to adopt Nathan?

23. Lucas hears Calvin Jackson tell his wife of his everlasting love for Lucas's mother and his love for the son she bore him. How does this affect Lucas? What is the impact on his relationship with Susan?

24. Why does Lucas finally tell his father Calvin of his mother's love for him?

25. Do you think that events in this story aptly led to the conclusions?